CARELESS

Storm

Contents

Author's Note	vii
Special Note	xi
Prologue	1
Chapter 1	9
Chapter 2	15
Chapter 3	23
Chapter 4	31
Chapter 5	37
Chapter 6	41
Chapter 7	51
Chapter 8	57
Chapter 9	65
Chapter 10	73
Chapter 11	77
Chapter 12	83
Chapter 13	89
Chapter 14	97
Chapter 15	105
Chapter 16	113
Chapter 17	121
Chapter 18	131
Chapter 19	137
Chapter 20	145
Chapter 21	153
Chapter 22	165
Chapter 23	173
Chapter 24	183
Chapter 25	187
Chapter 26	195
Chapter 27	203
Chapter 28	211
Chapter 29	217
Chapter 30	227
Chapter 31	233

Chapter 32   241
Chapter 33   251
Chapter 34   261
Chapter 35   269
Chapter 36   277
Chapter 37   285
Chapter 38   291
Chapter 39   299
Chapter 40   307
Chapter 41   313
Chapter 42   319
Chapter 43   327
Chapter 44   335
Chapter 45   341
Chapter 46   347
Chapter 47   355
Chapter 48   365
Chapter 49   373
Chapter 50   377
Chapter 51   383
Chapter 52   385
Chapter 53   393
Chapter 54   401
Chapter 55   407
Chapter 56   413
Chapter 57   417
Chapter 58   427
Chapter 59   433
Chapter 60   443
Chapter 61   449
Epilogue One   459
Epilogue Two   465
Also By Katherine Jay   473
Sneak Peek of Fierce Storm   475

About the Author   483

Author's Note

This book contains subject matter that some people may find triggering. A list of the main potential triggers can be found on Katherine's website:

http://www.katherinejayauthor.com

Please note, triggers are not listed here to avoid spoilers for the book.

CARELESS STORM'S SOUNDTRACK

One Thing Right - Marshmello, Kane Brown
I Ain't Saying - Jordan Davis
Careless Whisper - George Michael
Flame Trees - Cold Chisel
Happier - Marshmello, Bastille
Missing You - John Waite
Back For Good - Take That
Breakeven - The Script
Listen To Your Heart - Roxette
End Game - Taylor Swift, Ed Sheeran, Future
Night Changes - One Direction
She Will Be Loved - Maroon 5
20 Good Reasons - Thirsty Marc
Stronger - Britney Spears
Ghost - Justin Beiber
Loved You Better - Jonas Brothers, Dean Lewis
Gets Me - Antonio Cipriano
Tattoo - Loreen
Remember - Becky Hill, David Guerra
Dark On Me - STARSET
Headlights - Restless Road

Special Note

While Careless Storm can be read as a standalone, it takes place after the events of book three, Reckless Storm, and contains spoilers for the ending (including flashbacks)

If you haven't read Hayley and Reed's story, and don't like spoilers, then I recommend you begin with Reckless Storm, as a major storyline in Careless Storm focuses on Zane's part in their story.

Reckless Storm, and all of the San Francisco End Game books are available now on Kindle Unlimited.

To everyone looking for their person...
don't settle, they're out there, and they'll
never have you questioning your worth.

PROLOGUE

BLAIR – SPRING BREAK

BLAIR AGE 16 / ZANE ALMOST 18

Sierra's high-pitched squeal draws my attention and I force my eyes open, squinting as the bright sun burns through my retinas. I lift my head off my beach towel, focusing just in time to catch my brother, Cade, running through the sand, my friend Sierra dangling from his shoulders, slapping his ass as he beelines for the water.

I snort at the scene before Zane's vibrant chuckle drowns out the world around me, and like always, my attention shifts to his mouth, his infectious smile sucking me in.

"I can feel you watching me, B," he rasps, the edge of his lips lifting into a cocky grin while I study him closely. "And if I can feel it—"

"Ugh." My shoulders sag. Moment ruined. "Why don't we just tell him? It's not like we're doing anything wrong."

"He's my best friend, B. And *your* big brother."

"Barely. He's not some wise old man that knows what's best for me."

"You're still off-limits, Little B. No matter what."

Zane finally glances my way, hitting me with a burning gaze that heats me more than the sun does, but still, I roll my eyes. Despite our closeness in age, my "big" brother calls me Little B whenever he wants to annoy me. Which is pretty much daily. I'm not little. We're only a year apart in school.

Zane calling me Little B now is his way of saying we have to be mindful of Cade. We have to choose the right moment to tell him we've been seeing each other behind his back. Because while Cade's a good guy, he's also very opinionated when it comes to my dating life. Namely that no one is good enough for me. *No one.* And that includes our friends.

Lifting to my elbows, I bring myself closer to Zane, raising an eyebrow in challenge as our arms brush. "I could tell him, you know?" I joke. I'd never do that unless we both agreed.

"I do." Zane's breathy snicker brings about my smile. "And honestly, I've thought about that a lot. Wondering if I'm going to wake up one day with Cade holding a knife to my throat." Zane delivers his fear without humor, but the second I giggle, his laughter appears. "Okay, he's too soft for that. The worst he would do is call me an asshole and tell me to stay the fuck away from you. From both of you. Which I'd be willing to risk if I wasn't also concerned about him cutting you off."

"Aww, are you admitting you care?"

"Never." His lips quirk into a grin and my heart races.

"Zane!" Sierra calls out, interrupting us as she stomps out of the water, glaring with her hair plastered to her face and her hands on her hips. "What the hell was that? Why didn't you help me?"

"You went for his balls, Sierra. You told Cade he'd lost weight. You're on your own."

Sierra frowns, confusion clear in her creased brow. "Isn't that a compliment? I said he looked trim."

Oh, shit. I internally grimace on Cade's behalf.

"He's been working out for *months*, Sierra." Zane stifles his joy, obviously enjoying the mess his sister got herself into. A hole she keeps digging.

"He has?" Sierra tilts her head, raking her eyes over Cade's shirtless body, and we all break out into laughter, including Cade.

"Looks like you want another swim, Little S. You better run." He takes a step toward her and she squeals again, rushing toward Zane, soaking us both as she hides behind him.

"You better stop him, Zane. This was *your* idea."

And the plot thickens.

"What?" I giggle, my eyes flashing to Zane. "You told her to say that?"

"Guilty." He lifts his shoulder in a shrug and bites back a mischievous grin.

"Zane told her to say it," I call out to protect my friend, a sassy smile pulling at my lips.

Zane pins me with a glare of betrayal, his jaw dropping in mock horror. "Wow, *Little B.* You threw me under that bus without flinching." He shakes his head, struggling to hide his amusement. "Get ready for payback."

No sooner have the words left his mouth than my brother dives on top of him, tackling him to the sand, Sierra only just managing to get out of the way.

We both erupt in giggles while Zane hits me with a fake scowl.

But I don't mind. I'm here for the payback. He's leaving for college as soon as the school year is done. If he's exacting his revenge, at least I'll get to spend a little more time with him.

I plan to soak up every second I can.

ZANE – SPRING BREAK - ONE YEAR LATER

BLAIR 17 / ZANE ALMOST 19

Cade's gym bag digs into my ribs while Blair's featherlight touch brushes against my hand. I work hard to hide my smile, peering out the window, my gaze focused on the tree-lined streets passing us by. It's no accident I'm stuck in the middle seat with Blair pressed against me. She's trying to get me in trouble. But I refuse to let her succeed.

We haven't seen each other since Christmas and it's now spring break, but as desperate as I am to kiss her, I'm not about to maul her on my ride home from college. Especially with her brother in the front, yapping about some girl he met in the parking lot, while their dad, Tim—my former high school teacher and my father's best friend—drives us home after Cade's truck chose yesterday to break down.

"Zane," Tim interrupts Cade's rambling, his eyes meeting mine in the rearview mirror. "Tell me again why you don't have your truck on campus?" His nostrils flare with frustration. "I'm losing brain cells listening to Cade's love life."

Blair snorts out a laugh, while I stifle my own, seconds before becoming the object of Cade's glare.

"Mom thought my truck might be a distraction," I tell him. *And she's probably right.* "It's currently at home waiting for me, undoubtedly getting excited as we speak."

"You and your fucking truck." Cade shakes his head, hitting me with his obnoxious chuckle.

"Language, Cade," Tim scolds. "What's wrong with taking pride in something you love? Maybe if you cared about *your* truck, you'd be driving yourself home."

"You're right." Cade smirks and I wait for what's coming. "I'll try harder to be more like Zane." *There it is.*

"Woah. Hold up," Tim's quick to respond. "Let's not forget I taught Zane. I take it back; I'm happy for you to be you."

My smile breaks through, but I school my features as Tim shakes his head.

"I'll have you know that I've changed since my high school days, Mr. Stevens. I'm much more dedicated to learning now." I manage to maintain my straight face for all of ten seconds before I burst out laughing. "At least, I'm dedicated to football. And since I plan on playing in the pros, I'm heading in the right direction."

"True, but you'll need to keep your grades up if you want to hold on to your scholarship. It's—"

"Not a free pass," Blair, Cade, and I all repeat on cue. We've heard this spiel many times before.

"Yeah, okay." Tim laughs to himself. "Work hard, don't do drugs"—his eyes flash to mine when he says the word *drugs,* and I'd be offended if he hadn't busted me the one and only time I tried Molly—"*and,*" he continues, "avoid distractions. There. I've said my bit. Now you're on your own."

"What do you consider *distractions,* Daddy?" Blair leans across me and her left breast brushes against my arm, forcing me to bite back a groan. It hasn't escaped me that her tits are fuller since I last saw her, and it's taking everything in my power not to give them the attention they deserve.

"For you..." Tim's eyes lock on Blair's, giving her a fatherly grin before hitting her with his response. "*Boys*. Stay away from them. They're nothing but trouble." Shifting uncomfortably closer to Cade's bag, I wait for Tim's gaze to shift to mine, but thankfully, it doesn't. He's known me forever, and while I may not be the best example of a decent guy, I'd never hurt Blair, and I'd like to think that he gets that.

"Hear! Hear!" Cade beams and I can't help but chuckle, even though I'm fucked.

After Mr. Stevens drops me at home, I do my bit, playing the part of the dutiful son, and spend quality time with my family—catching up and promising I'll call more often the next time I'm gone. *Though we all know I won't.*

No more than an hour passes before I'm sliding into the front seat of my truck, breathing in the familiar scent as I relax. Freedom. No classes, no practice. It's just me, my friends, and the salty beach air. Fuck, I need this.

But I need something more.

I need *B*.

My chest tight with anticipation, I hightail it out of there, desperate to see Blair before the inevitable group chat lights up my phone, and we're summoned to meet up.

Despite the urgency I feel, I take in the familiar surroundings as I drive, counting the stoplights like I used to when I was a kid. *Three to reach Cade and Blair's house. Five to the beach.*

When I pull into the street behind the Stevens's house, I slow my truck as I approach, creeping along in the hope that it makes my obnoxiously loud engine a little less distinguishable.

I come to a stop as Blair steps into view, hitting me with her soft, innocent smile, and like always, I'm taken by her. She has this casual air about her that makes life seem a little less hectic, and when I'm with her, everything else becomes white noise. It's always been like that, but it took me a while to realize what it was. That it was *her*.

We've been playing this game for the past two years, sneaking around, stealing moments whenever we get the chance, and my obsession never wavers.

Blair has me hooked on her every word, her every movement, and it's not even the fact that she knows everything about me.

She's just *Blair*, my Blair, and I'm trying really hard not to fuck things up.

When she reaches the curb, I lean over to open her door, watching as she jumps in. Innocent smile gone, she rakes her lustful gaze over my body, and I force myself to look away, taking off before she's finished buckling her seat belt.

"Looking good, Fitzpatrick." Her hand curls around my bicep before she gives it a squeeze. "I noticed you've bulked up even more since Christmas."

I snort, rolling my eyes. "Is that why you couldn't stop touching me in the car?"

"Definitely. Why else would I do it?"

"Why else?" I huff. "I wonder... Anyway, back to me bulking up. It's impossible *not* to with the amount of training we do. I've doubled my gym time since high school."

"And it's working for you." She bites her bottom lip and I shake my head with a chuckle. I'm aware of what she's doing, and it's not going to work.

"Thank you." I ignore her attempt at making me weak and squeeze her leg. "You look..." I trail off and she leans in, waiting. "Exactly the same." I pretend I haven't noticed her tits and she pouts. "Don't be sad." I lightly pinch her chin. "I'm happy about that. Never change. Promise me you won't."

"I promise." Her cute little pout morphs into a smile, and she falls silent for a beat before twisting to face me. "Soo..."

"No, Blair. I have *not* been hooking up with random cheerleaders while you're stuck here finishing your senior year."

She snorts, hiding her mouth behind her hand. "Good to know, Fitzpatrick." She lets out a breathy laugh. "But I wasn't going to ask that."

"You weren't?" I glance her way, my eyebrow cocked in disbelief.

"I was going to ask if you'd hooked up with anyone on the *dance* team. They're usually more bendy."

"More bendy, you say?" I bounce my eyebrows and she laughs harder. "Thanks for the tip, B. I'll keep that in mind."

Blair punches me in the arm just as we come to a stop in a deserted parking lot, and I can't help but smile. Despite being months since we've seen each other, it's still easy between us, like it always was.

I turn to face her, but before I've had the chance to unbuckle my seat belt, she's leaping across the console, slamming her lips to mine. And God, does it feel good to have her back in my arms.

"It's been too long," she speaks against my mouth, her knees settling on either side of my hips as she straddles my waist.

I slide my seat back and groan. "It's been an hour," I mumble, trying hard not to smile. Teasing. Pretending I'm not as desperate as she is.

Blair pulls away, and if looks could kill... "An hour?" She huffs adorably. "We were in the car with my dad and brother. All I got was the occasional pinky touch."

"It was a meaningful pinky touch though, full of feelings. And let's not forget about the boob brush. Also meaningful." She opens her mouth to argue but I stop her. "I didn't realize you measured our quality time by how often your lips were attached to mine." I raise a brow in challenge and she rolls her eyes, biting her lip again, this time to suppress her grin.

"You're hilarious."

"I try." Grabbing her face between my hands, I pull her close again, biting her lip before sucking the flesh into my mouth. Blair rocks her hips as her impassioned moans vibrate against me, making my cock twitch beneath her. A grunt catches in the back of my throat, and I lose myself in the moment, savoring the kiss until Blair's hand moves between us and she tries to unbuckle my jeans.

"Blair," I warn, sinking my hands into her hair, deepening the kiss in the hope of distracting her.

Grabbing my shoulder with one hand, her fingers bite into my skin as she lifts off me, giving herself better access to my zipper.

"*Blair*," I repeat, my tone stern as my cock involuntarily grows to greet her.

"I want it all, Zane," she murmurs against my lips, ignoring me, rubbing her palm over the bulge in my jeans. "I want you to be my first. Tonight."

"Fuck, Blair." I break our kiss as my hips buck. "You're killing me."

"I'm killing you? *You're* killing *me*. You and your need to treat me like a princess."

"Come on. You're no princess, despite what your parents believe."

"But you're still making me wait?"

"I'm not fucking you in a parking lot."

"You're not fucking me anywhere." She holds my stare confidently, but her voice wavers ever so slightly, and if I wasn't paying close attention, I wouldn't have noticed.

"God, B." I swallow a lump in my throat and squirm uncomfortably. "What changed? I thought *you* wanted to wait? I'm just doing what you asked."

"I missed you and now that you're here, I can't remember why I was stalling." She sucks in a quivering breath and puts on a smile, twisting her hips until a guttural growl releases from within me, my cock begging for action.

What I wouldn't give to sink inside her, to be the first and *only* one to make her mine. But we agreed we'd wait, and despite what she's saying, I'm not convinced she wants more. Not like this.

She deserves better than a quick fuck in a parking lot, or while we're hiding in her yard, sneaking around behind everyone's backs.

No amount of teasing is going to change my mind, even if she claims to have changed hers. I know her better than that.

I agree with Cade when he says no one is good enough for her. But she has free will. And if she's choosing me, you better believe, I'm going to be deserving of that choice.

That's *my* promise.

That's what I'm doing now. Waiting until I'm sure that she's ready.

Even if it kills me.

CHAPTER ONE

BLAIR

PRESENT DAY – AGE 24

I'm lost in thought when my phone rings, snapping me out of my stupor. Four more days and I'm leaving the only home I've ever known. Ninety-six hours until I'm following my man halfway across the country. Just over five thousand minutes until I'm alone.

I'm kind of freaking out.

Even my usual pros and cons lists haven't eased my mind.

Taking a deep breath, I put on a smile and answer my phone with as much warmth as I can muster. "Hello."

"Hey Babe," my boyfriend, Nathan, answers, his voice light. "How are you feeling? Two shifts to go."

"I'm feeling good," I lie. "Excited even. How's the new apartment?"

"Lonely without you in it." He laughs to himself while I frown. "How long until you're here?"

"Four days."

"Four days? Nooo. I miss you, baby." *Baby?*

"Are you out with the boys?" I ask, confusion set in my features. It's midafternoon and he's usually incredibly strict with his schedule.

"I am." He laughs again and the sound of it makes my chest tight. "They're all being quiet for me. How did you know?"

"Lucky guess." *That and the fact that he usually only says "baby" when he's out drinking with friends.*

"We're looking after him for you," one of the guys calls out and I genuinely smile. I'm happy for Nathan. I am. I'm just having trouble being happy for myself. It's the nerves. I've finally found a job that I love, and now I'm moving. It's terrifying to think about starting over again.

"Please tell your teammates that I'm grateful, and that I'm looking forward to meeting them soon." Nathan's been in California since preseason training began months ago, and I've been hearing all about the guys on his new team.

After a phenomenal college football career, Nathan signed with Florida to stay close to home, but when his mom got sick, his game suffered, and last season, they traded him to Los Angeles. A move he only agreed to because his mom lost her battle with breast cancer last fall.

His new teammates have been incredibly supportive and I'm thankful for that. He needs them. And I don't think he realizes how much.

"I'll tell them," Nathan interrupts my thoughts. "But first, I can't wait to see you. I'm counting down the days."

"Me too." I force a smile and hope that he hears it in my voice. "I better go. My shift's about to start."

"Okay, baby. Love you."

"Love you too."

He hangs up and I sink back into my seat, my eyes flashing to the clock on my dashboard. I've got fifteen minutes to get my shit together. It's time for a pep talk.

I'm doing the right thing. Nathan loves me. I love him. I'm going to find work so fast that I'll regret it, wishing I'd given myself more time off. They say change is as good as a holiday, right? And in California, it'll feel like a vacation twenty-four seven. I'm ready. I'm *ready*. Let's go.

I bounce my shoulders and jump out of my car, giving her a pat before I walk away, glancing back at the hunk of junk longingly. Cars are surprisingly sentimental to me, particularly this one, and that little Honda has been with me through good times and bad. I hate the fact that I'm leaving her behind.

But I'll say it over and over if I have to...change is as good as a holiday.

Taking a deep breath, I turn back toward the hospital I currently work in and release it slowly, willing the tension to leave me along with the carbon dioxide.

Four days.

Less than a week and I'm jobless. Yay for me.

"You're here." My friend Kayla greets me with an overexaggerated sigh the second I push through the doors to my ward. "It's been a rough shift. I need to go home. But at the same time, I want to stay because I'm going to miss you."

"Are you okay?"

"Yes. No. I'll fill you in soon, but first... I'm desperate for some chocolate. Are you ready to begin or do you need a minute?" I glance down at my bag, then my watch and laugh.

I technically have ten minutes left before I'm due to start, but since I'm religiously early for every shift, they're accustomed to my presence ahead of time. "You go. I'll dump this quickly and see Billy at the desk."

"Thank you." She squeezes my arm, rushing off while I smile after her, only snapping into action when she disappears out of sight. *I'm going to miss her too.*

My boss, Billy, rubs his hands down his face as I approach before his weary eyes meet mine. With a wince, I rest my elbows on the high counter and flash him a tight-lipped grin. "I heard it's been a rough twelve hours?" *What am I walking in to?*

"It has. But you're here now. Are you starting or..."

"I'm starting."

"Great, can you check on bed ten? I trust you not to get awestruck."

"Awestruck?"

"You'll see." He bites back a soft smile while mine slips away. *Okay then.*

"Bed ten. I'm on it." I've just made it to the end of the service desk when he calls out, beckoning me back over.

"As a heads-up, he's under police guard."

"He's what?" My eyes widen as I panic. "Is he dangerous?"

"No, I assume it's just protocol after what happened."

"What happened?"

Billy schools his features before his eyes flash down the hall. "I'll fill you in when you get back."

God, what's with the delayed gratification today? Everyone's a tease.

Forcing a grin, I nod, walking away, and after rounding the corner, I find the door to bed ten and halt. They're messing with me. There are no officers here. It must be a prank for my last week of work. *Well, guys...you got me.*

With a laugh, I knock on the door and open it an inch, calling out hello before listening for a response.

"Hello?" I call again. But nothing.

Grabbing the chart as I enter, I flick through the pages and frown at the notes. Knife wound. In and out of consciousness on arrival but stable since. And, sure enough, in bright red letters stamped across the page...Police custody. Meaning, no one comes in or out unless they have clearance.

And I just waltzed through the door without question.

I'm confused as I glance up at my *dangerous* patient, and freeze at the sight of him. My heart jolts before picking up speed, racing as I take in his light brown hair, styled in a now messy mohawk, my eyes drifting to the intricate tattoos peeking out from beneath the sterile hospital gown. A panic takes over me when I see the gold ring on his pinky, knowing that if I were to move it an inch, I'd find a tiny burn scar hiding underneath. As though no time has passed.

Zane Fitzpatrick.

The one that got away.

Oh, God.

...

Red and blue lights flash in the distance, and a gut-wrenching pain rips through my middle, feeling like I've had the breath knocked out of me. I double over, my hands clenched at my stomach, but it doesn't help.

I couldn't stop the sting if I tried.

I knew.

Call it intuition, call it a sign from some divine order...but I knew. And I'm devastated to be right.

With a wheezing breath, I take off running again, reaching the crash site just as the jaws of life cut through the windshield.

An EMT climbs onto the hood, stomping over a truck I hold dear to my heart, and I choke back the tears.

"Noo." I sob uncontrollably as my legs give out, a pain shooting through me when my knees hit the dirt.

"Save him. Please. You have to save him."

...

The crash of a metal supply cart, somewhere in the hallway, drags me back to the present and a shiver runs down my spine. Shaking off my thoughts, my eyes dart to Zane's chart and I run through the checklist.

My heart lodged in my throat, I switch over to clinical mode and get on with my job, the job I've been doing for over a year now. A job that I love.

He's just like any other patient. *He's just like any other patient.*

In fact, staring at him now, while he's sleeping peacefully, it's easy to pretend he's a different guy. That I'm not standing beside the hospital bed of the boy I once knew.

A vivid image of Zane brushing hair away from my face seeps into my mind, and I fight not to let it break me. Not to let my cheeks heat, because I can still feel the welcoming burn of his touch, all these years later.

God, I've spent countless hours thinking about him. Wondering if he's okay.

On the inside anyway.

On the surface, he's fine. He's the NFL's bad boy. He's on TV. In magazines. The news.

I want to know about the feelings he keeps hidden, the secrets he holds deep within his soul.

Has he moved on? Or is he still a little bit broken like I am?

I'm desperate to find out, but at the same time, I shouldn't be here. I'm not ready to face him.

I *can't* face him.

Not now.

Maybe not ever.

Chapter Two

ZANE

Slamming my eyes shut, I bury my fists into the sockets and let out a silent scream. That fucker must have messed me up worse than I thought, because I am seeing things. No, not just seeing things—I'm goddamn delusional.

With a quiet groan, I remove my hands and open my eyes one at a time, slowly taking in the sterile room, and... "Fuck me." She's standing in front of me. Blair fucking Stevens is here. And she's shooting me well-deserved daggers.

I try to sit up but the cut on my side pulls, and I bite back a wince. Though it's significantly easier to focus on that than the hollow pit forming in my stomach. "Fuck me," I repeat, unable to form any other words as my chest burns.

"Nope." Blair pops the *p*, her hand on her hip, as she stares me down. "You missed your chance years ago."

I almost question what she means until her eyes widen and she covers her perfect little pout with her hand. *Oh, right...the* fucking me *part.* "Forget I said that." She shakes her head almost violently, causing her hair to loosen and a thick curl to fall to her cheek. "I'm glad to see you're okay." She tucks the stray strand behind her ear and I follow the movement. "I'll just check your vitals and be on my way."

She fusses with the monitors behind me before shoving the claw on my finger and securing the blood pressure torture trap around my bicep. I can handle a lot of pain, but fuck, those things cause me grief.

Grief. Jesus. Not the best word to think about right now.

I flinch as the machine tightens around my muscle, and when Blair notices, she frowns. "What's going on there?"

"You know..." I trail off as I shrug. "I hate hospitals." The word alone brings up memories I buried deep, and being here now is excruciating. Not to mention, it's as if they want you to suffer, with the stark white walls and bleak interior. It's what nightmares are made of. Particularly mine.

"So, nothing has changed," Blair muses and the smallest smile tugs at her lips, until I selfishly wipe it clean off her face.

"*Everything* has changed." She knows that as well as I do.

Blair nods, as if in response to my inner thoughts, and a melancholy expression darkens her beautiful features.

"Okay. Well, if you don't need anything..." She trails off, glancing behind her. "I'm going to continue my rounds."

"Thanks. I'm good."

Walking backward, she collides with the edge of the open door, snapping herself out of the daze she's been under.

Then she's gone.

As though I imagined the whole damn thing.

And fuck, maybe I did. I am in the hospital after all. And Blair's not a nurse. She wanted to be a writer. It's all she ever talked about. She was going to travel the world, setting her books in whatever exotic location she found herself in.

That can't be her.

Maybe I'm still sleeping. Or God, am I in a coma?

Confused as ever, I stare at the door long after Blair—or not Blair—has gone, a million unwanted thoughts running through my head. Blair fucking Stevens.

I knew coming back here was going to be hard, but it's so much worse than I ever could have imagined. There's a reason I haven't been home for years.

I want out.

I'm more convinced than ever that I conjured Blair, when for the next few hours, I have a different nurse taking care of me.

And this one has a strange, knowing smile on her face. As though the machines are telling her I'm crazy. That I'm seeing images of the girl I left behind. The girl I never got over.

Countless memories assault my mind, and I'm almost at my breaking point when the doctor stops by. I expect him to notice my impending madness, so when he clears me for discharge, it catches me off guard. And I almost beg him to let me stay.

For as desperate as I am to escape this hell, how the fuck is it fair that I'm fit enough to go home when Reed's still unconscious a few doors down? How the fuck do I face a waiting room full of my teammates when most of them hate me?

The questions run rampant while a familiar darkness threatens to seep out of the deep recess in my mind. But before I allow it to completely break me, the door to my room creaks, and I glance up to find San Francisco Storm's media liaison, Keeley, hovering in the entry, her expression sympathetic.

Just what I need.

"Can I come in?" She smiles awkwardly, her long auburn hair pulled into an uncharacteristically messy bun as though she hasn't slept since before the game on Sunday. "The nurse mentioned they're releasing you soon. She thought you might want some company."

"And you're the unlucky one they sent?" I bark out a lackluster laugh and as expected, Keeley frowns.

"Don't be a dick, Zane. I'm the one always asking them about you. The nurses have been keeping me up to date."

My brows furrow as I process what she's saying. "I thought they could only provide updates to family."

"I'm your *girlfriend*, Zane." Keeley walks closer, one of her manicured brows lifted in challenge. "Or have you forgotten? God, you must have hit your head *really* hard." She places her palm on my forehead and I shake her off.

"Ha. Ha. Very funny. I'd definitely remember that." Keeley is damn fine, and if she'd been into football players, I have no doubt we would have fucked already. But we definitely wouldn't be dating. "I'm surprised they believed you."

"They didn't. But I guess one of the nurses felt sorry for me. She's been nice enough to provide as much information as she can."

"Why?" I frown, glancing away as Keeley's look of concern makes me uncomfortable.

"God, I don't know." She throws her hands in the air, bringing my gaze back to hers. "The kindness of her heart."

"No. I mean, why do you care?" A hint of vulnerability comes out in my tone, and I clear my throat to cover it up, ensuring it doesn't happen again.

"We *all* care, Zane. Everyone in that waiting room." Keeley points out the door, presumably toward where my teammates are waiting. "They're here for you as much as they're here for Reed."

At that I scoff. "I highly doubt that. They all hate—"

"Cut the woe is me bullshit. If anyone out there hates you, it's because you made them feel that way."

"I didn't know—"

"Believe it or not, this has nothing to do with you fucking my brother's ex. It's your attitude. Lose it and you'll find yourself with more friends than you could ever imagine."

Jesus. She's a feisty one. But hang on... "Easton's your brother? When did that happen?"

"When he was born. Catch up. He's out there too. You might even have a friend in him."

"What if I don't want any friends?" *Fuck.* I grimace, cursing under my breath. I didn't mean to say that out loud. The last thing I want is for her to pity me, exactly like she's doing right now. "Please put those sad eyes away. I'm fine. I don't need friends. But—"

"I think—"

"*But,*" I repeat, louder this time, "I wouldn't mind having teammates I get along with. Though, I'd say I blew my shot with your brother."

When it comes to life's fuckups, I've got too many to count on one hand, but I refuse to feel guilty about sleeping with Easton's ex, despite the fact she wasn't his ex at the time. I didn't know who she was. I'm not responsible for that lapse in judgment.

And I will die on that hill. Though, I can admit that I was a dick about it.

Keeley's lips pull into a wide grin as she pats the side of my bed. "I knew there was a good guy hiding underneath that rough exterior. And you'd be surprised about East. What you did for Hayley and Reed..."

She trails off, and the sincerity in her eyes has my throat clogging, and as much as I'd love to change the subject, I can't.

"I did what anyone would do," I say instead, refusing to be painted as a hero in this. "A man is on life support because of what I did. It's nothing to be praised for."

"You can't blame yourself for that, Zane. If you hadn't come back to help them, I can't even imagine—" Keeley chokes back emotion, and I release a long, drawn-out sigh.

"Okay." I raise a hand between us to stop her from talking. "Thank you. For caring."

She stares at me for a beat before huffing out a laugh. "That's a start. I'll take it. Baby steps. But we're all here for you. Whether you want it or not."

Keeley hangs around until I get discharged, and then offers to walk me to the hotel our team owner booked, so everyone could stay close by. And by everyone, I mean all my teammates that opted to stay until they knew Reed was okay. Something we still don't know.

Refusing her offer, *politely*, I consider taking the next flight out of here, but think better of it. Because like my teammates, I can't leave without checking in on Reed, and on top of that, there's still the tiny issue of me being investigated by the police.

While they're not presently charging me with anything, I was advised not to leave Florida until they had Reed's and Hayley's statements.

And despite the fucked-up shit I often say and do, I'm not stupid.

After finding Reed and Hayley asleep, I tell Keeley I'll be back in the morning and grab my bag—reminding myself to check that I have everything since someone else must have packed up my original hotel room. Avoiding my teammates, I slip out, needing a clear head and a proper night's sleep before I throw myself into that situation.

I need to be free.

Only the second I make it outside and into the warm night air, my legs lock in place, my body heavy as the weight of the past twenty-four hours crushes my soul.

No, it's been longer than twenty-four hours. The tension hasn't left me since our flight first touched down on the Jacksonville runway.

It's been years since I was last here, and that's not by accident.

I left home a few weeks after my nineteenth birthday, and I never looked back. If I could have avoided it forever, I would have.

But here I am, and God, it's worse than I ever could have imagined. As if I needed more of a reason to hate the place where I grew up.

I swear it's cursed.

For me, anyway.

An image of her lifeless body scars my already fucked-up mind, and I slam my eyes shut—as if that will help—swallowing back the bile rising in my throat.

I want to escape, but with my lids closed, my thoughts drift into unwanted territory, and the events of last night torment me again, making me relive every heart-pounding moment.

Hayley's terrified call for help.

The adrenaline coursing through my veins.

A flailing body slamming into mine.

The anger.

The heartache.

Hayley crying in my arms.

But the one moment that hurts the most, the one I'll never get over, is the split-second decision that could cost a man his life. The moment I pushed Hayley aside, racing forward, tackling...

I jolt as something pulls me out of my thoughts, and it's not until the world around me comes back into focus that I hear it again.

"Zane?"

Huh? I glance up and immediately regret it.

"Fuck, it is you." My high school best friend steps into the bright hospital lights, his eyes wide as he takes me in. "Blair said you were here, but honestly, she's my sister, and I only believe half the shit that comes out of her mouth." He laughs to himself and I force a soft smile. At least I'm not delusional. Blair *was* here. And she decided she didn't want to see me again.

Not that I blame her. I probably would have run, given the chance.

"What the hell happened?" Cade reaches out to do God knows what but thinks better about it, letting his hand fall to his side. "You look pale."

"Thanks." I huff out a laugh. He's always been one to tell it like it is. "I got in a knife fight."

"And you lost?"

I wish. "Unfortunately, there were no winners in this fight."

"But you're alive." Cade smiles wide, ever the optimist. "You cheated death. Again. You better be careful, Fitzpatrick. I hear that the third time's a charm."

His smile fades while I shake my head.

I hate to say it but, "I've heard that too." Only I'm not sure I could handle a third. My body might survive it, but I'd lose my mind in the process.

We fall quiet for a beat until Cade slaps me on the back and turns to face the parking lot. "Are you ready to blow this joint?"

"What?"

"I'm busting you out. Hand me your bag. We're going home."

I stare down at the bag in my hand, before laughing under my breath. "I'm not going home, Cade. I can't."

"Why? Because you fucked up years ago, running away instead of facing your problems, leaving behind everyone that ever cared about you?"

"Yep," I say honestly, his words barely causing a sting. "That about sums it up."

"Fucker." He smirks like I'm joking. "Get in the truck. If you're lucky, I'll show you where my sister lives."

My eyes widen at the mention of Blair. "Why would—"

"Woah." Cade throws a hand up between us. "I'm going to stop you before you lie to my face. I've forgiven you for running away. I've forgiven you for not even bothering to pick up a phone to check in. But I will *not* forgive lying anymore. God knows you did it enough when we were kids."

Damn. Okay. I nod and opt for silence over lying again. But he doesn't let me off the hook.

"Anyway, Blair told me she went home sick after you woke up. I think the two of you should talk. You're both mourning the same loss; maybe you can heal each other."

"It's been years."

"Exactly. And it's safe to say that since you haven't been back, you're still not over it. Neither is Blair."

"I'm not going home." *And I'm not talking to you about your sister.*

"Yeah. You are. Get in my fucking truck before I make you."

I stare at him unmoving, taking in his slim build compared to my muscular form, a body that's been forged by hours in the gym, working myself to perfection. He can't make me.

Not anymore.

He may have been stronger when we were teens, but he gave up on football when he started college. He's no match for me now.

"I'm not going home," I repeat, louder this time, standing my ground. "This isn't even home anymore."

Cade's eyes widen before his expression turns cold. "It's not home anymore? So what? Is San Francisco home? Because from what I've been seeing in the media and on that TV show, that isn't home for you either. Seems to me like you're pushing your teammates away like you did with us. Which I guess means you're homeless."

Fuck. I don't think I've ever looked at it that way, but he's right. I don't have roots, just footprints. I exist wherever I happen to be. But I kind of like it that way. Never making a home means I never have anything to wreck. Anything to lose.

Cade stares at me in challenge, his gaze boring into mine until he seemingly finds what he's looking for. "Get in the damn truck, Zane." He shakes his head as he turns to walk away. "I'm not leaving here without you." *Conversation over.*

Fuck my life.

CHAPTER THREE

ZANE

"*H*elp!" *Hayley's distinct voice permeates the air, breaking through my internal darkness. It takes me a moment to get my bearings but when she calls out again, I register the panic.* "*Reed!*"

Taking off in a run, I round the corner toward our hotel and almost lose my footing on the curb, the adrenaline keeping me moving.

Hayley's fear plays on repeat in my mind, and I reach her and Reed just as he throws her out of harm's way, slamming her into my chest.

The urgency strikes me, but everything happens in slow motion.

A flash of silver draws my attention as Reed falls to the ground, and acting on instinct, I push Hayley aside, running toward their attacker, tackling him to the ground before he raises the knife again.

Hayley cries out, but I don't have time to process what she's saying as an excruciating pain radiates through my side.

Without thinking about the consequences, I fight back, grabbing the man beneath me, slamming his head into the ground when he tries to take control.

It's not until he stills that I realize what's happened, Hayley's cries jolting me out of my anger.

...

"Zane?" I'm pulled back to the present as Cade's annoying tone seeps into my memory and I shake off my thoughts.

"What?" I ask, not even bothering to hide my confusion.

He frowns for a beat before repeating himself. "I asked if you remember that girl that flew in for the summer each year. The one that wouldn't give us the time of day? Gabriella?"

"Nope," I lie in the hope that he'll stop playing this game. Of course I remember her. Cade was obsessed. Told us all he was going to marry her one day. But I'm not in the mood to take a drive down memory lane. The memory of last night is debilitating enough.

Although, the irony is that's exactly what I'm doing. I'm taking a drive toward the town I hoped would forever be a memory. A torturous memory that keeps me up at night, but a memory all the same.

And the closer we get, the more I'm regretting it.

Nothing good can come from being back here. I've got enough on my plate right now.

Cade scoffs beside me, pulling me out of my thoughts. *Again.* "Fuck off," he grates but there's a lightness to his tone. "You remember her. Everyone does."

"Sorry." I shrug. "I must have blocked her from my mind."

"Whatever, man. We're engaged."

"What?" My head darts in his direction so fast my neck hurts. "You're engaged? To Gabriella?"

"Yep."

"Well, fuck me."

"I didn't think you remembered her." He smirks triumphantly and I can't help but chuckle.

"I'm shocked you're engaged at all. I thought you wanted to stay single."

"People change. I thought you'd end up with my sister."

I open my mouth to argue, but that's what he wants. He wants me to admit I was fooling around with Blair behind his back. To admit I deserted her. But I refuse to open that dialogue. That was another life, and there's no point in dredging it up now. I've punished myself enough.

"That's her house, by the way. The white brick house with the perfect little picket fence." His voice turns bitter and I want to question him, but that involves me showing an interest in her life, and I can't. It's better if I move on and pretend I never saw her, pretend she never walked back into my life at the precise moment I needed someone.

When I ignore him a second time, Cade laughs to himself, and a few minutes later he's turning onto an all too familiar street, making my pulse spike as my childhood home comes into view.

"Why the fuck would you come this way?"

"It's the shortest way to the bar. If I'd gone around, it would have been another ten minutes."

Ten minutes? He'd put me through hell for ten fucking minutes. My skin crawls and I ignore the sweat collecting on my brow, staring straight ahead, refusing to look at the house I grew up in.

My parents left not long after I did but refused to sell, leaving the house to deteriorate, the flowers to die, and the weeds to take over, engulfing the tree swing we had out front. It's— *Dammit.* I wasn't going to look.

"You're an asshole," I snap, to which Cade shrugs nonchalantly.

"And you're not over it. Think of it as therapy."

Fuck. How did I forget he gave up football to be a goddamn social worker?

"Don't even think about using me as a case study or work experience, Cade. I'm not interested."

"I'm fully qualified, fucker. I don't need your issues for that." I breathe a sigh of relief until a smug grin forms on his face, "You were my topic junior year."

"Asshole," I repeat, wanting to punch him.

We're silent after that until he pulls into a parking lot and my jaw drops. "This is Halo's?"

"Yep. They came into some money a little while back and renovated the joint."

"Well, damn."

The old run-down biker bar we used to frequent—because they never carded us—is now a stylish venue with fancy signage and outdoor seating. I've got to admit this is more my vibe these days, but I did not expect it.

"You seem shocked. We've got class around here."

"Yeah, okay. But who's we? You said we'd be getting a quiet beer together."

"We are." He shrugs and I hiss under my breath.

"Who's *we*, Caden?"

"Don't Caden me. It's just us. But you might run into someone you recognize."

Closing my eyes, I let my head fall against the headrest and sigh. "I doubt others are as forgiving as you are."

"I'm going to save my money and not take that bet. I've gotta be honest...you don't have a lot of supporters around here. But you're back. And it's time we changed that."

I slowly open my eyes, hitting him with a death stare, and my stomach churns. "I'm not here to get my friends back. I'm fine with the way life panned out."

"Yeah, okay. Humor me then."

As if straight out of a movie, the door slams against the wall when we enter Halo's, and the goddamn bar goes quiet. Not the music, or the sound of the billiard balls crashing on the tables across the room. But the people closest to me freeze, their eyes wide as they stare.

I'd do anything to turn and walk away, but Cade's not having it, cupping my shoulder as he guides me inside.

"This is creepy," I whisper and he laughs.

"Did you forget you're famous?"

"Fuck no, but everyone fell silent at once."

"Don't let your head grow too big." He chuckles again. "It's the door. After the rebuild, it slammed shut on its own. And we all froze. Like there was some kind of ghost inhabiting the building. Now as a joke, people freeze whenever it slams. I may have orchestrated that moment to give you a rush."

I can't stop the incredulous laugh that bursts out of me, and while it doesn't give me a rush like he wanted, it certainly makes me a little less uncomfortable. "You're still the same fucker, I see."

"Some things change. Some things don't. Come on, there's a table over there." He points to a table in the middle of the room and I fake a smile. *Yay.*

"Take a seat and I'll grab drinks. You want a beer?"

I'd love a beer. Actually, I'd love something stronger since Cade dragged me here against my will when I'd rather bang my head against a brick wall. But since I'm currently on medication, I reluctantly decline. "I'll have a soft drink. You know what I like. That hasn't changed."

"A Sprite?"

"Yep."

"Oh-kay." He glances over his shoulder as he walks toward the bar, brows furrowed as if he expects me to run. *If only.*

For the next hour, I nurse the same drink, while Cade fills me in on all the guys I used to know. As though no time has passed and me being here is nothing out of the ordinary. Completely oblivious to how uncomfortable I am. Or maybe he's ignoring it. Pretending he hasn't noticed my forced smile, or my gaze locked on the table where I'm currently taking my frustrations out on a poor defenseless napkin, tearing it to shreds while I listen.

When the conversation shifts to our douchebag ex-teammate still trying his luck with the cheerleader from our high school, I actually laugh.

Cade grins triumphantly, nodding as though my reaction makes everything right in the world, and I roll my eyes.

"See." He leans forward, his smile widening. "I knew this was going to be good."

I return his smile, but what I really want to do is throw a dictionary at his head and tell him to check the definition of "good" because this is anything but that. Though I'll admit, it's not as bad as I thought.

"Zane Fitzpatrick?" A voice from my past has my body tensing and my palm clenching around my glass. *Fuck.* Thought too soon. "Is that really you?"

"Yep." I wave, barely giving him a second of eye contact.

"What has it been? Five years?"

"Close enough." I shrug, hoping my curt response is the hint he needs to walk away, but all it does is piss him off.

"Is that how it's going to be?" He stands tall and leans over the table, his nostrils flared, his angry gaze boring into mine. "Tell me, have you bothered visiting your parents while you're here? What do you think of the redecoration?"

"Hey now," Cade warns, his eyes narrow as he glares up at our old friend.

"Do you even know where they live?"

"You don't have to answer that, Zane. Ignore him."

"No, fucker. Why shouldn't he answer? He *left*. He left and never looked back, leaving us all to pick up the pieces. You weren't the only one hurting, you know?"

I open my mouth to speak despite having no idea what the hell I'm going to say. But it doesn't matter; he continues on without letting me get in a word. "Why are you back, Zane? Did you think we all missed your stupid TV show? That we didn't see your cocky face talking up your new life? Bragging about how settled you are now that you're living in San Francisco? You may have moved on. But this town hasn't. It wasn't as easy for us."

Fuck. Why am I back? Why am *I here?* Shoving my chair with a force that sends it crashing to the floor, I jump up and beeline to the exit, ignoring Cade as he calls out after me.

I don't need this.

I don't *want* this.

I hold my breath until I make it outside, but before I can release it, Cade rushes out after me. "Where are you going?"

"I can't be here anymore, Cade. I shouldn't have come back."

"I get it. I do. He was a fucker. I'm sorry. But let me help. Or at least let me drive you somewhere."

"You've been drinking."

"So?"

"So?" Throwing my hands in the air, I kick the dirt in frustration. "Are you fucking kidding me, Cade? I'm not letting you drive."

Cade's face falls and he sighs. "Okay. That was stupid. But where are you going to go?"

"I'll hitch a ride back to the hotel."

"It's nearly an hour."

"I'll call a fucking Uber then."

"Take my car." He rushes forward, his hand in his pocket as he undoubtedly grabs his key. "I'll get Blair to give me a lift tomorrow. Even if I do have to get up at the ass crack of dawn."

I pause, his generosity throwing me off guard, and yet he was always like that. I shouldn't be surprised.

"Thanks." I take the handout. "I'll leave it at the hospital. I'll be going in to visit my teammate early in the morning." The thought of Reed momentarily stills me, and I subtly pinch my leg, pulling myself out of it.

"Anytime, man." Cade tosses me the keys without a second thought, and their weight feels heavy in my hands.

"Thanks again. I'll see you tomorrow."

"And if not, let's not make it another seven years." He smiles warmly before waving and heading back inside, completely trusting me with his brand-new Chevy, despite the fact that I've been a dick all night.

With a huff, I make it to the truck unscathed, staring at the steering wheel once I'm inside. I hate trucks. They're big and bulky and should goddamn protect you, but they don't.

Cade doesn't even need one.

Taking a deep breath, I bounce my shoulders and turn over the ignition, taking off down the road without looking back. Just like I did all those years earlier.

I drive the long way, avoiding my childhood home, and I've just turned the corner when a perfect little picket fence comes into view.

And as if I need another opportunity to torture myself, I slam on the brakes.

Chapter Four

BLAIR

Aloud pounding wakes me from my restless sleep, and I fight against my twisted sheet, assuming it was a dream. Until it happens again. Louder this time.

"Open up, Blair," Zane's deep voice rings through the house, and I freeze, trepidation clenching my heart. "*Please.*"

His voice softens and my head screams at me to stay quiet, to do all that I can in the name of self-preservation. But my heart always wins out, and today is no different.

Throwing a hoodie over my pajamas, I tiptoe to the front door and peek through the window, catching Zane pacing on my porch, a hand raking through his hair as he mutters to himself. I watch with rapt attention, taking in his familiar moves. But when he shakes his head and turns to walk away, panic runs through me, and without giving it the thought it deserves, I throw the door open, calling out in a loud whisper. "Wait!"

Zane spins so fast he almost falls over. "Blair?" My name floats from his lips and the sweet sound makes me almost forget the past. *Almost.*

"What do you want, Zane? You shouldn't be here." He shouldn't even know where I live. *Fucking Cade.*

Zane snaps out of his stupor in time to run forward, his large foot jutting out to block the door in case I try to close it. "I just want a minute. That's all."

His pleading eyes suck me in, and before I can think better of it, my shoulders drop. "One minute."

"Thank you."

"Let's start with why you're here." I fold my arms over my chest as if it'll protect my heart, and like the observant guy he is, Zane notices, sighing before he speaks.

"For whatever reason, you walked back into my life today, and I couldn't leave without checking in on you."

"As you can see, I'm fine. Great even. No need to worry."

"*Blair*?"

"What?"

Zane tries to push the door wider, but I hold firm. This is about as far as I can handle. "I'm a nurse at the hospital you were taken to; there was a high probability of you being my patient."

"Are you hearing yourself? That hospital is *huge*. And you're not supposed to be a nurse. Yet, the first time I step foot in Jacksonville again, I'm hurt and sent to the exact hospital you work in. That's not a coincidence."

"I thought you didn't believe in that stuff."

"I don't. Usually. But—" A door slams somewhere down the street, and Zane pauses, glancing over his shoulder. "Can I come in?"

"No."

"Why?"

"Because I don't live alone."

"I'll be quiet. Your roommates will never know."

"I don't have roommates."

Zane furrows his brow, and my fingers itch to smooth the crease lines between his eyes. "Your parents?" he questions, but it's obvious from the shudder in his voice that he knows the answer.

"My boyfriend."

"Right." He nods, as if uncaring. But while his stoic expression might fool others, the hint of disappointment shines through, and I want to scream because of it.

"He let you answer the door?" Zane frowns with a scoff. "To me?" He's fishing and I'm unsure of the right course of action. But it doesn't matter because he answers for me. "He's not home, is he?"

"No."

"Then why can't I come in?"

"It's a small town, Zane. People talk. You know what that's like. It's why we were always so careful." I close my eyes, cursing myself for bringing "us" up.

"It's the middle of the night, B. I promise he won't find out. *Please*."

"It doesn't matter what time it is. I'm saying *no* and you have to respect that."

His face pales, and he steps away from the door, cupping the back of his neck. "I'm sorry. I just spent hours with your brother and he never mentioned a boyfriend."

"Typical."

"Typical? You were always so close." His frown deepens and he glances away, lost in thought. "What happened?"

"You haven't been back in *years*, Zane. So much has changed since then."

When he nods in understanding, I breathe a sigh of relief until his expression turns inquisitive again. "Why'd you stay?" His question throws me off guard, and I swallow a lump in my throat. "After you graduated from college, why'd you stay?"

"I'd already started building a life here."

"You stayed for a guy?" His face contorts, doing nothing to hide his disgust. "You always wanted to travel the world. Live in different cities. *Explore*."

"Don't pretend to know me," I snap, releasing the built-up rage I've held close to my chest. "It's been seven years. *Seven*. I know why you left; I'm not angry about that. But as I said, a lot has changed. You can't possibly have thought we'd all be the people we once were."

"Your brother is." He lifts his shoulders in a half shrug and I finally smile.

"Actually, he *has* changed. A little. But yes, he's the exception."

"And you're okay, staying here?" His intense gaze has my insides squirming, and I sigh in frustration. He's never been one to let me get away with anything. And while I used to find that attractive, now it's driving me insane.

"God, if you must know, I'm moving in a few days." *Dammit*.

"House?"

"State." I stare at him, watching as his eyes light up in excitement. For me.

"That's a start. Where are you moving?"

I hesitate before answering, not wanting to admit that while I'll be in LA and he's in San Francisco, we'll still be in the same state. Too close for comfort. "It doesn't matter. But I won't be here."

"How does your brother feel about that?"

"Why don't you ask him?"

"I don't plan on seeing him again," he mumbles under his breath and I gasp, though I shouldn't be surprised.

"Isn't that his truck?" I ask nonchalantly, refusing to show him how affected I am.

"Yep." He pops the *p*. "I'm going to leave it at the hospital. I was planning on dropping the keys at reception. You've saved me a phone call. You can tell him they're there."

"So that's it? You're going to disappear again?" My chest aches as a pit forms in my stomach, but I refuse to acknowledge what that means.

"Why would I stay?" His eyes bore into mine, begging me to say "me" but I can't do it.

"Your parents?" I say instead, despite knowing the answer. They've been calling me since he left, because he never answers their calls.

"My parents?" He scoffs. "I bet they'd *love* that."

"What does that mean?" I question, my brows drawing together. They would love that. I never considered that when he walked away from me, he'd walk away from them too. But that's what he did. He left and never looked back.

I wait for his anger, but his expression drops. "It doesn't matter. We haven't really spoken in a while."

Tightness fills my chest but I fight to ignore it. And before I can respond, a car drives past, and the headlights make me blink, the brightness working to clear my mind. "*Shit*," I whisper under my breath. The last thing I need is for one of Nathan's friends to see me out here and tell him about Zane, making it out to be worse than it is. "I gave you a minute and it's been a hell of a lot longer."

"Yeah, well, you've never been great at time management."

I smile, but it doesn't quite meet my eyes. "I better—"

"Wait. Before you make me leave, I need to know... Are you happy?"

Dammit. I blow out a slow breath, buying myself some time while I gather my thoughts. Am I happy? Yes. Mostly. I love Nathan, and things are good between us. But could I be happier in another life? Unfortunately, that's also a yes. Though I don't deserve it.

"I'm as happy as I can be." I pause as numbness pervades me. I used to strive for greatness and now I'm as *happy as I can be*? God. *How did it get to this?*

Zane's nostrils flare, but before he can respond, I throw the question back at him, trying hard not to think about the magazine articles, the photos, the TV show... "Are *you* happy, Zane?"

He huffs as his lips quirk into a forced smile, undoubtedly wanting me to believe that it's real. But I know him better than that. "I am," he lies through his teeth. "Other than this minor hiccup." He lifts his tee to show me his bandage. "I'm living the dream."

"That's great, Zane." I force a smile of my own. "I always hoped you'd be happy."

"Thanks. Right back at you, B. Always."

Our fake smiles outshine each other until we fall silent, and I swear my heart's going to pound right out of my chest.

Needing a reprieve, I blow out a breath and say my goodbyes. "I better go back in. But for what it's worth, it was good seeing you again."

"You too, B. You too."

For the briefest moment, Zane's smile turns genuine and I lose my breath. I almost tell him I'm sorry, until he turns around and jogs down the steps, only looking back when he's reached Cade's truck, giving me a wave that I fear may never leave me.

Less than a minute later, he's gone.

My expression blank, I shut the door and nod to myself. *I'm fine.* I'm... My throat tightens and I barely manage a step before emotion overwhelms me and I fall to the floor, choking back tears.

I'm fine. So, why is it still so hard?

CHAPTER FIVE

BLAIR

SEVEN YEARS AGO

Gathering my strength, I drag myself up off the ground and run toward the scene in front of me, screaming for Zane. I'm steps away from his truck when strong arms wrap around me, pulling me back.

"No. It's Zane. I've got to help him."

"You need to let the emergency services do their thing," a soft, unfamiliar voice whispers in my ear. "Your cries won't save them."

Them? Them?

"How many people are in there?" I glance over my shoulder to see a young officer frown sympathetically.

"Two."

"Two?" Oh God, did he bring Cade?

"Yep, two." His voice cracks. "And one in the other car."

"The other car?"

My body shatters as I allow myself to finally see past Zane's truck to the mess of a car on the road behind it. My legs give out again, and this time I'm thankful for the officer's hold. I'm not sure my knees could handle another blow.

"Are they going to be okay?" I ask, my voice shaky.

"I can't answer that yet, but I suggest you start praying. Come on, let's move you back. Give them some room to work."

"No, I can—"

He doesn't let me finish, lifting me slightly and walking away from the *scene, leaving my heart behind. When we reach the curb, he sits me down, settling beside me without letting go.*

Not that I can feel his touch.

Time slows, but I'm not sure how long I'm waiting before someone calls my name. "Blair?"

With blurry, tear-soaked eyes, I glance up to find the one guy who shouldn't be here, my brother's rival, Nathan, fighting his way through the crowd, and I break down, crying hysterically when he reaches me. He can't be here. He can't.

"What's going on? Are you okay? Is she okay?"

"I think she knows the people in the truck," the officer answers when I don't respond, and I fight to stay alert as darkness overwhelms me.

Nathan curses out loud, and without looking up, I guess he recognizes the truck, realizing it belongs to Zane. The guy he's spent years hating along with my brother. "Is that—"

Crackling cuts him off as the officer's radio blares to life. "We've got the first out, unconscious male, late teens to early twenties, we're bringing him over now. Be ready."

Bile rises in my throat and while my body shakes, I force myself to stand, needing to see who it is. Desperate to find out if it's my brother or Zane.

I can barely see through the crowd of EMTs, but I have my answer when Nathan's panicked voice seeps into my subconscious. "Fuck, it's Fitzpatrick."

Thrashing about, I try to break free, but the officer refuses to let go, even when Nathan says he'll hold on to me.

I beg, cry, try to go floppy. Anything I can to get away, but it's no use. "You need to stay here, miss. They're doing all they can to save him."

"What about the other guy?" Nathan asks, seemingly making the same assumption I did, knowing that Zane and my brother are never far apart. Unless Zane's with me.

The officer doesn't respond, but when his body shudders, I glance over my shoulder to see him shaking his head.

"What does that mean?"

He shakes his head again.

"What does that mean?" I cry out, trying to break free for the millionth time.

Another few torturous minutes pass before the officer's radio blares again, and I hold my breath, waiting for information.

"The driver is free. Young female. Unresponsive. Lacer—" It cuts off and I burst into tears, my gaze dropping to the officer's radio, seeing him turning a dial.

"What did you do?"

"You don't need to hear that."

"I do. What was he going to say?"

I'm so caught up in what I missed that it takes me a moment to register what was actually said, and my panic rises. Young female? "It was a young female?"

Who?

I relax into my captor's hold, convincing him I've given up, but the second he lets his guard down, I slam my elbow into his ribs and take off running. I've just reached the ambulance when different hands clamp around my arms, tugging me back. "I've got you," Nathan whispers over and over, trying to comfort me, his grip tight.

But it's all for nothing.

Sierra's lifeless body comes into view before they roll her into the ambulance.

And the fight leaves me, their lack of urgency telling me she's gone.

Zane's sister is gone.

I've lost my best friend.

CHAPTER SIX

ZANE

After pulling into the hospital parking lot, I switch off Cade's truck and stare out the window, my vision blurred as my mind runs wild with thoughts. I'm not sure how much time passes as I torture myself with memories, but when the sun rises, the glow reflecting off the yellowing exterior, I realize I'm fucked. I was under strict orders to get plenty of rest. I was also told to take it easy and avoid stress, but that's impossible to do when I keep getting hit in the face with constant reminders of everything I hate about myself.

Of what I did.

The sooner I get out of here the better. But I can't leave until Reed's okay.

After snapping myself out of my stupor, I drop Cade's keys at the reception desk and double check the visiting hours—normally eight a.m. but for me "any time," said with a wink and flirtatious smile. I thank the receptionist with a grin of my own and head up to the waiting area, hoping to get some sleep before the others arrive.

Only no sooner have my eyes drifted shut than a gruff throat clears, jolting me awake.

"Zane." Easton nods, and of all the fucking people, it had to be the teammate that hates me the most.

"I thought visiting hours started at eight?" I ask, raising a brow, my lips curling into a smile.

Easton smiles right back, and honestly, I'm floored. "Let me guess...any time for you?" His voice softens as he winks and I burst out laughing.

"*Damn*. I thought I was special."

"Nope. Not this time. Though I get the feeling you think that a lot."

He raises a brow and I snort as my laughter fades. "Not as often as you'd guess," I say honestly, though he's not entirely wrong.

"Good to know."

We're quiet for a beat and it's so goddamn uncomfortable that I have to fill the silence. "Did you get any news on Reed last night?" I ask, fidgeting with a fray in my jeans.

Easton's silence draws my attention and he frowns, tugging his cap lower on his brow. "No more than the usual. He's stable and will wake up when he's ready."

"That's good though. Right? His body is healing. I bet he wakes up today."

"Here's hoping. How are you doing?"

My eyes widen and I actually peer over my shoulder to check if he's talking to someone behind me, to which he chuckles. "Yes, I mean you."

"Wow."

"Don't push your luck. You saved Reed and Hayley. And since we're the only ones here, I'll admit, you might have saved me too."

"I what?" This time my jaw drops as I stare at him in shock. He has every right to hate me. I slept with his girlfriend. His now ex, but still...

"I'm going to say this once." He holds a finger up in case I need clarification for what "once" really means. "If you tell anyone what I'm about to say, I'll deny it. But if you hadn't fucked Macy, I may never have found Paige."

Wow. "So, I did you a favor?" I bite back a smirk as frustration crosses his face.

"I'll repeat... Don't. Push. Your. Luck."

"Noted." I raise my hands in the air, my cockiness lingering. "Does that mean you're going to be nicer to me?" I ask because I'm incapable of letting things go. It's a curse.

He glares my way and I smile. "After today? Nope. But you can have the next twenty-four hours. You're still too cocky for my liking."

I grin, accepting the reprieve, while inside I'm still reeling from everything that's going on. If only he knew it was all a front. If only any of them knew. But no one ever took the time to get to know me. I fucked up with Easton. I get that. But my teammates chose sides without bothering to ask me any questions. Except maybe Reed.

Easton's phone rings and I take the opportunity to close my eyes, hoping it will stop him from talking to me again. But when he says, "Yeah, I'm here. I'll see you in a minute," I groan.

Sitting up, I run a hand down my face and accept the inevitable. More of the guys are coming, and there's no chance they're going to let me rest.

A couple of hours pass with the guys trying hard to include me in conversations, and I'm almost at my limit of fake niceties, when Luke announces that Reed's finally awake.

The relief that escapes me is so freeing I'm genuinely shocked. I hadn't realized I was holding on to so much tension.

He's okay.

It wasn't all for nothing.

"Do you want to go in first?" Luke asks me and I shake my head. I'm not ready for that. I wanted to be here until he woke up, but seeing him and Hayley is an entirely different story. I'm not sure I can relive what happened without spiraling back to the events of my past, especially knowing that Blair's here, somewhere, and likely avoiding me.

"Give him some time with Hayley," Thomas is quick to say before Luke can comment, and I can't tell if he's trying to help me or genuinely thinks that's what's best. Either way I'll take it.

As do my teammates, and when they all settle back into their general chitchat, I jump up, suddenly in need of a walk.

Keeley calls out, undoubtedly checking if I'm okay, but I wave her off. The answer is way more complicated than she could possibly imagine, and I don't have the headspace to explain.

With an emptiness taking over me, I wander the halls, and though I'd prefer not to think about it, my conversation with Blair comes back to mind.

She moved on. She's living with someone else. And while I never expected her to stay loyal to me after everything we went through, I also never stopped to think about how I'd feel when faced with that reality.

Especially when I'm not convinced she's happy.

Sure, she said she was, but she's obviously forgotten how well I know her. It may have been years since I last saw her, but I've known her since she was born.

I remember every one of her tells.

Like the way she always looks down, brushing her hair behind her ear when she's shy.

Or the way her lips thin for the briefest of seconds when she's trying to hide her annoyance. Exactly like she did when she opened her door last night and found me on the other side.

I've even worked out that when she scratches her neck while staring you in the eye, she's most definitely *lying*.

She can't fool me.

And it's breaking my fucking heart.

I make it outside the hospital without running into her, and breathe a sigh of relief. Not for me, because I'd do anything to see her again, but for her. She doesn't need me hanging around her workplace, distracting her from her job. I have no doubt she's struggling enough.

But no sooner do I relax than I hear my name again. Though thankfully this time it's my present calling, not my past.

"Sal, hi." I wave as our team owner, Salvatore D'Angelo, strides toward me, his ever-present confident facade replaced with a sympathetic grin.

Aimed my way.

"You're back?" he questions, coming to a stop in front of me. "I tried to catch up with you last night, but Keeley said that you left."

"Yeah, I needed some sleep, in a proper bed." Not that I got any. *Or even tried.*

"Understandable." He smiles. "How are you feeling?"

"Just like I did when I was out on the field on Sunday. I'm as good as new. Nothing a little pain meds won't fix."

"Good to hear." Sal nods a few times before his expression turns sympathetic again. "Only I didn't mean physically."

Dammit. I was worried about that.

"Mentally, I'm good too. I'm ready to play again. I just need the doctors to clear me."

"I'm sure they will. In a few weeks."

"A few weeks?" I gape in disbelief. "It's a scratch."

"I heard you lost a lot of blood."

"I lost a lot of blood the last time I got a papercut too. But you still played me after that."

"Zane—"

"*Please*. I have to play, I—"

His shoulders drop and I pause, switching gears. That was the wrong thing to say. God fucking dammit. "Never mind. I'll take a few weeks. The rest will do me good, and—"

"You'll need to see a psychiatrist before you're cleared. You should see one anyway, Zane. You—"

"Yeah, yeah. I'll talk to Bec." Our team's psychologist.

"No, Zane. You need someone who can specifically deal with the kind of trauma you've been through."

"I'm *fine*."

"I'm sure you think that but—"

"Can you force me?" I argue, almost rubbing my chest where it's knotted from resistance. Just the thought of revisiting... Nope. I can't go there.

Sal releases a slow breath before his mouth sets in a hard line. "No, we can't." He sighs in frustration and it's a relief to my ears. "But—"

"I promise, I'm fine." I refuse to take more time off than I have to. "And...to make me feel even better, I'm going for a walk. I'll be back."

I turn to leave but he calls out again, stopping me in my tracks. "I had a chat with Rivers last night."

Fuck. He's talking about our offensive coordinator. The only guy on the team that knows anything about my past. He was the head coach at the college I transferred to. And while he was only there a year, I'm sure he had a hand in my recruitment with the Storm. In fact, I'm sure he's the reason I haven't had as many repercussions as I deserve after speaking to the media about Easton. If Rivers has spoken to Sal, he's worried.

"He mentioned a bit about your past," Sal continues before I've even turned to face him. "He wouldn't give me specifics, but he said you'd been through a lot and that I needed to keep an eye on you."

"I'm fine." I spin around. How many times do I have to say that? "My past has nothing to do with what happened here. I—"

"No one is suggesting otherwise, but he did say that this might bring up some dark memories for you."

"Well, he's wrong." I smile wide while inside I'm burning. It's harder to forget the past when people keep bringing it up. The last thing I need is for said past to become something that defines me. "I'm *all* good." My smile wavers and Sal catches it, frowning.

"I'm not saying this to worry you; I'm saying this because I care. And I want you to know I'm here if you need to talk."

"Even though I fucked with your son-in-law." Yep, to make my life more complicated, Easton is now dating Paige, D'Angelo's daughter. It's one big happy family here.

Sal chuckles, unaffected by my attempt to rattle him. "*Future* son-in-law. But yes, even so."

"I'll keep that in mind." I turn to walk away again and my body tenses, waiting for him to call out. But he doesn't. He lets me go. And I have to admit, it gains him a little respect.

Not that I didn't respect him before now. The guys may have all freaked out when he came on board and started making changes, but I'd never been a fan of the GM he fired, or the new one they hired after that. In my opinion, Sal's done everything he can to better the team, and he's the one taking hit after hit with the negativity surrounding his decisions. It can't be easy.

After scanning the hospital grounds for any more distractions, namely for a certain childhood best friend to pop up out of nowhere, I deduce that I'm safe and finally get some alone time.

But the second I do, I regret it. Because the first person to flash into my mind is the one person I've spent years trying not to think about. My sister.

And of course, the first memory I conjure is the last time I saw her smile. Minutes before she died.

Why the fuck am I back here again?

I've been walking aimlessly for an hour or so when my phone rings, the local area code taunting me on the screen. I hesitate before answering, my chest tight as I say hello.

"Mr. Fitzpatrick. This is Sergeant Holmes from the Jacksonville Sheriff's office."

Fuck. "Hello," I croak before clearing my throat. "Hi." Please don't let that fucker be dead.

"I'm calling to let you know that we spoke to Ms. Jackman and Mr. Coombs today, and at this stage you are free to go back to San Francisco." I breathe a sigh of relief as he continues talking. "But you're not clear of it yet. As I'm sure you're aware, Mr. McKenna is still on life support, and until we learn of his fate, nothing is certain. We'll be in touch if we need any further information."

"You have my story; it's the same whether he lives or dies." My throat clogs again but I clear it and carry on.

"We'll be in touch when we need you."

"Okay, thank you." *Dick.*

I hang up and find a text from Keeley, letting me know we're due to fly home soon, meaning it's time I grew some balls and went to see Reed.

Taking a deep breath, I pocket my phone and head back inside, not at all ready. But as ready as I'll ever be.

The waiting area is devoid of football players by the time I walk through, and I count that as a blessing. They're most likely packing their bags and checking out of their hotel rooms, while my belongings are still waiting for me at the hospital reception where I left them with Cade's keys, earning myself another "anything for you" wink.

When I reach Reed's room, I hesitate at the open door, giving myself a little pep talk before I go in.

"Knock, knock." I announce my arrival and push through the threshold. "Mind if I come in?"

"Of course." Reed tries to sit up, but when Hayley gently pushes him back down, I actually smile.

"How are you?" she asks, her gaze leaving Reed's to give me her full attention, though I wave off her concern.

"I'm fine. I don't know why they even kept me here overnight, to be honest. It was barely a scratch." I lift my tee to show them my not so tiny wound dressing, and Reed tries to sit up again, this time making me chuckle to avoid processing the concern on his face.

"I should be asking how *you* are," I counter, needing to move on.

"I'm fine." He answers the same way I did. "But I don't think Hayley was referring to the physical pain."

"Right. I knew that." *What's with everyone asking about my mental health?* I'm fine. "But..." I trail off, not really sure what to say, and Hayley gives me an out.

"I'm sorry, Zane." She walks forward and lightly grips my arm, her expression broken, while I internally wince. "I'm grateful but sorry."

"Don't be sorry." I awkwardly pat her hand before stepping out of her reach. "I did what anyone would have done in my situation."

"That may be true for some of it. But I don't think I would have coped if not for you."

"Nah, I don't believe that." My eyes flash to the wound below Reed's rib cage. "You would have stayed strong for Reed. You didn't even notice you'd been cut until the medic asked you about it." My gaze shifts and I point to her arm, smiling when she grimaces. "You only had eyes for Reed. Speaking of, it's good to see you awake, man. You had us all worried."

"Believe me, I would have woken sooner if I'd known. Thank you for waiting around. I appreciate it."

"Ah, no worries." I swallow as I nod. "I had to take a few days off practice anyway, so where else was I going to go?" I lie with a laugh. I'm still not sure how long it will be before they let me practice again, but I'll be fighting to make it sooner rather than later.

The conversation moves on to Reed's injury and then my hope of playing again next week, and when there's a natural lull in our discussion, I sneak a glance at the exit. Trying to be subtle, I take a step closer, ready to say my goodbyes, but I've barely opened my mouth when Reed stops me.

"Zane, wait." I grip the armchair beside me, forcing a smile as my breath shakes. We've managed to avoid specifically talking about the event that brought us here up until now, but I feel my luck has run dry. "I know you're going to brush me off, but I need to say this. You are *not* to blame for what happened. I'm not sure how much you've been told, but he was stalking Hayley, following her around and taking pictures. He knew where she lived, he..." He trails off before shaking his head. "He knew a lot about her."

"About us," Hayley adds.

Reed's eyes flash to hers before he continues. "I have no idea what he wanted that night, but he hurt Hayley and he had a knife. Please don't let his current situation weigh on your mind."

Fuck. He was stalking them? A memory of that night comes to my mind and I curse softly.

The "he" they're referring to is our teammate, Landon. Or Mr. Mckenna as everyone keeps calling him. The fucker that pulled a knife on his mentor. The asshole that stabbed me. The coward that's lying in a coma, holding the power to ruin my life.

"I swear I knew something was off when he walked past me. But I couldn't pick it. I'm sorry you went through all that. Don't worry about me. Just look after yourselves."

No matter how often people tell me it's not my fault, it doesn't stop the little voice that tells me they're lying. I was the one that tackled him to the ground. I was the one that smashed his head into the concrete when he tried to stab me a second time. But worse than that... If he dies, he won't be the first death on my conscience.

How can it not be my fault?

I 'm home three days later, pacing my hallway when my phone buzzes with a notification.

> EASTON ADDED YOU TO A GROUP

The fuck? I pause, watching in real time as two messages come through.

> EASTON: Welcome to the group, Zane

> EASTON: Or what I like to call it... Hell

I can't stop the laugh that bursts out of me, though I'm not sure if it's funny ha ha or funny because I'm so goddamn confused.

> ZANE: With that introduction, I'm not sure I want to be here

> LUKE: You're going to love it

Luke's on the chat? What is going on here?

ZANE: I thought you hated me

LUKE: People change. Feelings change

EASTON: That's funny coming from you, Luke

REED: It's great to have you in the group, Zane.
I always knew this day would come

ZANE: Thanks

Reed too? Easton's right. This feels like hell.

LUKE: You better get ready for Reed. You'll
never escape him now

ZANE: I don't think this group is for me. I'm out

LUKE: You know, Zane… If you hadn't slept with
his GF, you and East could have been great
friends. You're more alike than you realize

ZANE: Yeah, we both like brunettes

The tiniest twinge of guilt gnaws at my chest, and when Easton leaves the group, I feel worse.

LUKE ADDED EASTON TO THE GROUP

LUKE: You need to chill, East. It's called a joke

Jesus. I don't know what the hell I got myself into, but I have a feeling I'm not going to like it.

CHAPTER SEVEN

BLAIR

ONE MONTH LATER

"I understand. Thank you for the time." My stomach knots as I hang up my phone and fall into a heap on our new designer couch, immediately jumping up with a groan.

"For fuck's sake." *Why do I keep forgetting how uncomfortable it is?*

Sure, it's beautiful and fits the pre-furnished classic styling to perfection, but give me a plush cloud-like cushion any day of the week. I need my couch to be so soft I could sleep on it. Because I do. Often.

Just not on this one.

"Hey babe." Nathan walks in and habitually kisses my cheek, making himself comfortable on the couch I despise. He looks right at home in his designer polo shirt and perfectly tailored jeans, his short brown hair purposely tousled to give that *I just got out of bed* look. It's sexy. Everything about him is sexy. And yet as I cup my cheek where he kissed me, desperate to hold on to his warmth, I'm lost. It doesn't give me the comfort it once did. *He* doesn't give me the comfort he once did. And I have no idea what that means. "What do you think about pasta for dinner?" he asks, pulling my gaze to his face as he closes his eyes, tucking his hands behind his head. "I've been dreaming about it since you made that new sauce last week."

"Do you mind if we get takeout?" I say, shaking off my thoughts. "I'm not really in the mood to cook."

Nathan sits up instantly, his eyes flashing to the phone in my hand. "What happened? Who was that?" His shoulders stiffen and I guess he's thinking about Zane.

I probably shouldn't have told him that Zane came by our old house, but I'm not a deceitful person, and that definitely felt like deceit. I may not have done anything wrong, but Nathan knows about my past with Zane, and more than that... They hate each other. Even now when they haven't seen each other for years, I know Zane would feel the same.

And we're about to find out when Los Angeles plays San Francisco in a couple of weeks. Their first game against each other since Zane transferred in college.

"It wasn't Zane." I ease Nathan's mind. "I told you. We haven't spoken. I still have him blocked on my phone."

"I didn't ask." He stares at me blankly while the hint of a smile begs to shine through.

I raise an eyebrow, and he laughs. "Okay, yes, I was thinking about it. You know me too well."

"I do. But you have nothing to worry about. Me, on the other hand... that was another 'I'm sorry but you weren't right for the position' call."

"Oh, babe." Nathan stands and immediately wraps me in his hold. "I'm a dick."

"Nah, you're okay. Your jealousy distracted me for a moment."

"I wasn't jealous." He puffs out his chest, standing tall. And while I appreciate him trying to distract me again, it doesn't solve my problem. I'm not sure what will.

"Of course you weren't." I wink and step out of his grasp. "Anyway, takeout?"

"Wait. What happened? What crazy employer didn't want to work with you?" His expression holds all the concern he can muster, and yet, I'm not convinced that it's genuine.

"Another hospital." I sigh. "I thought the world was desperate for nurses. But apparently, they only want nurses with a minimum of five years' experience, and I'm short a few years."

"This could be good for your studies though. You could get your master's degree in psychology. You still want that, right?"

If only. I would love more than anything to get my master's but... "I can't afford to do that. I'd need money to live while I'm studying."

"That's what I'm here for." Nathan's so excited by that prospect that I bite back my groan.

"Nathan. We've had this conversation."

"We have. But I want to discuss it again. Don't think of it as a free ride. You'd be helping me by cooking and cleaning."

I shiver uncontrollably. I've been there and the thought of going back —to being that dependent again—makes my stomach churn. There's nothing wrong with being a housewife, and if I had kids, I'd probably want to be home with them. But the thought of being Nathan's stay-at-home girlfriend doesn't sit well with me. It was hard enough when he supported me during my final year at college.

I want to help provide for my family. Even if it's just the two of us. I have no problems with Nathan outearning me because I'm never going to make the kind of money he does. But I want to earn my keep.

"It's not a bad thing staying at home to support your partner." Nathan lifts my chin, forcing me to look at him. "Plenty of wives and girlfriends do it."

"It's not a bad thing, but it's not *my* thing."

"Think of the positives—you could come to all my games, travel with me. We'd see each other more. Sleep in the same bed, instead of you falling asleep on the couch."

His brows furrow and I wince. "I know. I *know*. But I enjoy working. Please let me have that." It's all I've got.

Nathan sighs and I pause, waiting for his reaction. "You're right. I'm sure something will come up. In the meantime, I'll keep thinking good thoughts."

"Thank you. I appreciate that."

"What about tacos for dinner?" He changes the subject without so much as a moment of silence. "I'll grab them from that place down the road?"

"Sounds perfect." I smile, looking forward to the reprieve as much as the food.

Nathan presses another kiss to my cheek, and I hold my smile until he walks out the door.

What a mess. This is supposed to be a new beginning for me, and yet, it feels like the end.

After another rejection call the following morning, I get dressed for a hike and leave Nathan a note, setting off toward a popular walking track, since I'm not familiar with the area yet.

When I pull into the dirt-laden parking lot, I take a deep breath as I jump out of the car, soaking up the warmth from the sun, letting the fresh air fill my lungs while I run through my mantra.

Let the earth heal me and the solace give me the peace I need to move forward.

My eyes drift shut and I'm taken back to the beaches of Florida and the walking trails surrounding them, to the sounds of the trees rustling in the breeze, the waves crashing in the distance.

And for the briefest of moments, my heart fills with joy.

My psychologist suggested this mantra after Sierra died, and to this day, it's the only thing that works.

Because of that, I've kept this part of my life to myself. Nathan knows I hike, but it's not something that interests him so I'm thankful he's never asked to come. This is my time to heal. To forget. To just *be*. I'm a mess without it.

Stretching out my calves and hips, I grab the physical map I bought so I don't have to rely on cell service and take off in the direction of the mountains, ready to work up a sweat.

With every step, the tightness in my chest eases, and by the time I'm at the summit, I can breathe again.

Only now that I'm able to focus on something other than the path in front of me, the past few months flash through my mind, the images firing like an old film projector seconds before it explodes into nothing, and the happiness burns away.

My move to California was in the works for months. I had plenty of time to leave and yet something always held me back. As though moving away from our home was a betrayal to Sierra. Something she'll never get the chance to do. But if I'd known I was going to run into Zane again, I would have changed course much sooner. I would have veered left to avoid a collision.

God. A collision? What is wrong with me? It's like I take great joy in misery. I should be focusing on the beauty of the world. The warmth of the late September sun. The sounds of the birds chirping high above the trees.

The feel of the leaves as I brush past them or the crunch beneath my shoes. The amazing smells. God, the smells.

And the view.

I should be focused on the view.

I have so much to be grateful for, and instead I focus on what I'm missing. My old life. My old friends. Sierra.

Zane.

Not a day goes by that I don't miss what I once had. And seeing Zane just about destroyed me again.

When I thought I was doing so well.

He has a way of reminding me of the girl I once was, and since she's long gone, it's a hard pill to swallow.

Taking another deep breath, I close my eyes as the breeze cools my cheeks, letting the rest of my senses help to clear my mind of the chaos.

Praying for a sign that it's all going to be okay.

When I finally feel a small sense of relief, I open my eyes and jump.

"Jesus." My hand flies to my chest as my heart races, my eyes locked on the smiling young woman standing before me. My brows pull together. Is *she* my sign? Or is the universe trying to mock me?

Blinking a few times, I shake off my thoughts and wave. "Hi?" I question as she grimaces.

"Sorry. I didn't mean to scare you. It's just...I've hiked these mountains so many times and you're the first I've seen come up this high. I kind of got excited."

A small smile tugs at my lips and I drop my hand, ever so slightly relaxing. "Sorry, I freaked out. I—" I cut myself off. I was about to tell her I'm new here, but isn't that the start of a horror movie? After all, she did just say nobody comes up here.

"Don't sweat it. It's all good." She brushes off my concern. "Do you come here often?" Light laughter fills the air as she shakes her head. "Wow, if that wasn't the worst pickup line."

Her smile has mine widening and I rush to reassure her. "I've been known to use that line before. *Not* to pick up."

"Oh, but... never mind. Have you hiked here before?"

"I haven't. This is my first time." *Shit.* "But I've hiked a lot of other places."

"Oh, yeah? What's your favorite?"

Goddammit. I blow out a breath. "Please tell me you're not a serial killer? I've been watching a lot of true crime lately, and this is exactly how an episode would begin."

The woman bursts out laughing this time and I'm not sure if that's a good or bad thing. "You're adorable," she says, scrunching her nose. "And no, I'm not a serial killer. I played one in a series once, but that's as close as it comes."

"You're an actress?"

"I am. I'm surprised you didn't guess."

"Oh, I'm sorry." My cheeks heat with embarrassment. "I didn't recognize you."

"I didn't mean that." She laughs again and it has a softness to it that calms me. "I meant that a lot of people in LA are somehow involved in the movie business."

"I'm not."

"I can tell. I'm Jenna." She holds out her hand for me to take, and I shake it with a comfortable grin.

"Hi, Jenna, I'm Blair."

"Nice to meet you, Blair. Are you walking back down?"

"I am."

"Mind if I join you? I promise not to attack you. Unless you ask me to."

"What?" My eyes widen and she smiles.

"It's a joke. Full disclosure. I think you're beautiful, and I probably would have kept walking if I hadn't found you attractive."

"Oh." *I didn't see that coming.* "I'm flattered. But..." I tuck my hair behind my ear as my gaze drops to my shoes, suddenly interested in pulling up my socks. "I have a boyfriend."

I wince and Jenna laughs. "Shame. But that's okay. I'm happy to settle for friends." She holds out her arm this time, waiting for me to curl mine through, and I hesitate for a beat, not used to people being this forward.

Jenna smiles again, and when the warmth of it fills my chest, a thought hits me. I could sure use a friend.

"Sounds great." I throw caution to the wind, linking my elbow with hers.

Thank you, universe. I'm going to be okay.

CHAPTER EIGHT

ZANE

Storm wide receiver Zane Fitzpatrick will be back on the field next week after his serious incident with a teammate. But we're all wondering.... Did management make the right call in keeping him on the roster? How does this fit with D'Angelo's claims of Storm being a family-oriented team?

I toss my phone across the room and it immediately vibrates. Several times in a row. Meaning one of two things. It's either Cade checking in on me, which he's been doing regularly since I left him at the bar, reminiscent of when I first took off all those years ago.

Or it's the damn Storm group chat. Easton warned me that it would probably drive me crazy and I should have listened. They are fucking relentless. Always texting. Always getting involved.

Since I was first added to the group, I've discovered it's made up of my teammates, Easton, Luke, and Reed, along with my ex-teammate, Dylan. He retired two seasons ago and I was lucky enough to take over his starting position. But we barely know each other. In fact, I'd say that other than at the hospital back in Florida, and when we're on the field, I've barely spoken to any of these guys. Group chat aside.

Turning toward my bedroom door, I fight the urge to check my phone the second I get a notification, but like the addict I am, I give in, instantly regretting it.

> LUKE: Those media fuckers

> REED: Came here to say something similar

> LUKE: But with nicer language, right? You'd probably say "Those awful, awful men"

I bark out a laugh and shake my head. I've got to admit, they're at least entertaining. But it'd be better if the discussion didn't revolve around me.

> REED: Are you sexist now, Luke? The writer was a female

> LUKE: Bullshit. I checked before I sent the text

> REED: Lucky. Anyway, you're right. They're fucking awful. You deserve to be playing, Zane

> ZANE: I never doubted that

I should have been playing sooner. It's a fucking scratch. Despite what the media are reporting, my absence had nothing to do with *Mr. McKenna* —fucking Landon—still being on life support. The reason I'm not playing until game three of the season is that my stupid wound reopened on my first day of practice, all because I pushed myself too far.

The team doctors then decided I needed more time to heal before they'd let me back on the field.

Fuckers.

But here I am, finally ready to play. Ready to prove that I'm still on my A game, regardless of how long I've been out of action. I've got two weeks to practice, and I have no doubt I'm going to kill it out there.

I need this.

My breath shakes as a shiver runs through me. But I close my eyes to refocus.

Football is my life. If I don't have this, God knows...actually, no. They can drag the football out of my cold, dead hands, because I'll be playing until then.

I have to. I refuse to contemplate the alternative. Because if I'm being honest with myself...it's bleak.

After grabbing my gear, I throw my phone in my bag and toss it over my shoulder, heading out to my car. Bouncing my shoulders, I smile. I'm so pumped to be back into full practice that nothing could ruin today. Nothing—

Motherfucker.

The second I exit the parking garage, I'm hit with a wall of reporters, and the smile drops from my face.

There's been no fucking news. He's still in a goddamn coma, and the police aren't pressing charges...yet. I don't know what more they want from me.

"Is it true that if your teammate dies, he'll be the third death you were involved in?" I pause, my knuckles white as I clench the steering wheel. "And is it true that you abandoned your family in their time of need?"

Fuuuck. Bile rises in my throat as my chest tightens uncomfortably. Who's been talking? Was it that asshole after I walked out on him in the bar with Cade? That was weeks ago. Flashes go off as more questions are thrown my way, but a ringing in my ears blocks them all out.

My vision blurs as my sister's screams echo through my mind. *"Zane, no!"*

"Zane?"

The brakes screech.

"Zane!"

Fuck.

Snapping back to the present, I shake off my thoughts, schooling my features. Fuck the media. And fuck this.

Fake smirk back in place, I sit tall. I've been through it all before. I can get through it again.

When I first transferred from my college in Florida to Washington State, thanks to my old high school coach, I was constantly hounded by the media. They wanted someone to blame for the loss of an innocent life, and the police never named my sister. Rightly so. She may have been driving, but the accident was not her fault.

I should have been in her place.

I shouldn't have survived her, and the world is constantly reminding me of that.

But not today. I refuse to be affected. Today is supposed to be a good day. And it will be.

Squaring my shoulders, I smile back at them, waving as I slowly roll forward. And as the sea parts, I lower my passenger window, giving them exactly what they want.

"You're fighting an old fight. This story's been done. Come on. Be better. You can do it."

With that, I plant my foot and drive away, waving out the window when I'd much rather be flipping them off.

It's been years since anyone asked me about the accident. Not since the spotlight on my football career took center stage.

When I was finally able to play in Washington, I played my fucking ass off. I flipped the narrative, forcing everyone to talk about my career instead of my past, and there was no going back.

Why the fuck did I go back?

I should have faked an appendicitis, or told Storm management that I had severe gastro—anything to convince them to leave me behind. It was a fucking preseason game. They wouldn't have cared. But no. My stupid cockiness got the best of me, and I had to prove that I could do it, that I wasn't trapped by the past. That no matter what, I was a force.

And I did prove it, way beyond what I could have imagined.

Until I stepped off the field and it all turned to shit.

Memories of my childhood came crashing back to me. Moments at that very stadium with my sister and dad, dreaming of a life that would never come to be.

My mom and dad forgave me for many of my faults. They turned a blind eye when I got my first tattoo, and they barely gave me a slap on the wrist the first time I stumbled home drunk at two in the morning, when I was only fourteen. Dad even forgave me for trying drugs after Blair's dad told him about it. And he never mentioned it to my mom.

But when they arrived at the hospital the day of the accident, one look was all it took to convince me that their forgiveness had gone. There was a void in their eyes where the love had once been, and a thickness in the air.

They kept up appearances, staying with me while I healed, accepting their parental duties. They even found me a therapist, and thanked God that they hadn't lost two children that day, praying for my good health.

They did everything you'd expect of them, making everyone believe we were going to be okay. And I stupidly believed it.

But when I asked to transfer colleges—when I told them I couldn't live in Florida anymore—they never once asked me to stay.

They practically packed my bags and shipped me out the door. If I'd turned back, I doubt they'd have stayed outside long enough to wave. They never even bothered calling.

The light ahead of me turns red and I come to a stop, closing my eyes, my nostrils flaring as I take in a breath. Images of our last goodbye threaten to haunt me, but I push the pain down, burying it deep, where it belongs.

A horn blares and I startle, my eyes flashing open as I make a move, throwing a quick wave in my rearview mirror.

My heart feels heavy in my chest, but I refuse to acknowledge it. Not today. Not ever.

Me being gone was easier for my parents, and it turns out it was easier for me too. They could move on. And so could I.

Although, based on what Cade and my old friend said, it doesn't seem like my parents succeeded.

But that's not my weight to carry.

I did feel for them. Back then. I always felt for them. Always wondered if I'd made the right choice. But when they stopped answering my birthday and Christmas calls, I stopped caring. In general. I had to or I was likely to fall apart.

Instead, football become my focus. It was there when my parents weren't, and I'm not about to let anything derail that. Nothing will ever get in the way of my game. No teammate trying to attack me after I accidentally fucked his girl, no media agencies trying to paint me as a killer, dragging my name through the mud. And definitely no one from my past.

We have a Super Bowl to win. It's time to move on.

I'm walking away with a ring this year if it's the last thing I do. I need it.

Thomas launches the ball and I race forward, knocking our linebacker, Heath, as I secure the ball in my grasp. Nailing it again.

Jogging back to position, I line up for the next drill when the whistle blows.

"Alright boys, time's up. Back to the locker room," our head coach, Pierce, calls out, pointing toward the tunnel. "I want you showered and dressed before Johnson and D'Angelo arrive to discuss the upcoming fundraiser for the D'Angelo Foundation."

A few of the newer guys groan, but when Easton glares their way, they're all smiles once more. And I almost chuckle. Easton's girl, Paige, runs the D'Angelo Foundation, and they'd be wise to learn you do not fuck with Easton's girl. He's not likely to handle that *twice* without violence. Especially when it comes to Paige. She's a whole different ball game from his ex.

When we're dismissed, I rush off the field, the adrenaline still coursing through my veins, a triumphant smirk plastered on my face.

Fuck, that felt good.

Like the first time you sink into a tight pussy, or your first sip of whiskey after a hard day.

Like coming home.

No one can take that away from me. But fuck, I'd like to see them try.

I'm ready for my first game back, and despite the fact that the team is gelling without me, I'm here to show them what they're missing.

That with me...we're unstoppable.

This season is ours.

Mine.

We're ready no matter who we play.

"Hell, Zane," Reed interrupts my internal celebration, his smile wide. "You absolutely dominated that practice. Seems like the media lit a fire in you."

I roll my eyes, biting back a smirk. "Why are you here, Reed? I didn't think you'd been cleared to play?"

"I haven't. Yet." He frowns and, of course, lets my comment slide, even though it was a dick thing to say. "Don't worry." His smile returns. "I'll be ready soon. I need to keep on top of things until then."

"So that's why you're here? It's got nothing to do with you wanting to look out for me? Wanting to be here for *my* first practice back?"

"Definitely not." He laughs to himself, waving me off as he wanders away.

And next comes Thomas. Quarterback. Team captain. And a genuinely nice guy. Meaning...it's hard to be a dick to him. Believe me, I've tried.

"I think he's really here because Hayley's filming a new role in LA, and he's lonely." He winks and I bark out a laugh.

"Poor Reed."

Thomas only lets his smile linger for a beat before his expression turns serious and my buzz leaves me. "What's up, Cap?"

"You played well out there, but I need you to take it easy for your first couple of days."

For fuck's sake. "I've been cleared. I'm good. The doctors made me wait longer than necessary so the fucking scratch didn't tear. Again."

"You're not fooling anyone with this scratch business. A scratch wouldn't have kept you from the game for a month. You need to accept the fact that we're looking out for you. We want you ready for your first game. *I* want you ready. I know you've been training. You're fit. But when it comes to head-on tackles and drills, I need you to ease into it. At least for this week."

I smile while the urge to tell Thomas to fuck right off is strong. "Thanks, Cap. I appreciate the concern. I'll take it easy."

"Good." He smiles back, somewhat relieved. "Los Angeles won't know what hit them when you get on that field."

"Hell, yeah." I nod as he walks away, but the second I turn to my locker, my face drops. *Los Angeles.* My first game is against L-fucking-A. In all the excitement of getting to play, I never bothered to check the schedule. My first game back, and I'm playing against Nathan-douchebag-Morgan. The reason my sister and I were out driving that goddamn night to begin with.

A rage simmers inside me. That asshole's been my biggest rival since high school and... My thoughts trail off as I picture his smug face and my anger clears.

I'm looking at this all wrong. I get to play against Nathan.

Looks like I finally caught a break. Thomas is right. LA...you better be fucking ready.

CHAPTER NINE

BLAIR

I'm curled up on the somewhat comfortable armchair in our unnecessary home office, when my phone vibrates across the desk.

I jump, startled, dropping my book as I stand.

> JENNA: Thank God you rejected me because look at this hunk of junk

A photo comes through of a gorgeous specimen of a man, and a laugh escapes me, a weightlessness taking over.

Yesterday she was on a date with a hot young businessman from New York, and the day before she met a beautiful redhead when we were out for a walk. I don't know how she keeps up. Some days I struggle to keep up with Nathan.

> JENNA: Should I take him home?

Smiling, I sit back on the chair, typing my response. She's trying to distract me after I told her about Nathan's game against Zane. She's been doing it all week

> BLAIR: I'm tired just thinking about your dating life...

> BLAIR: But if you're not... Go for it

> JENNA: Done. Thanks girl

BLAIR: Anytime

JENNA: Get ready for all the juicy details

I snort out a laugh and my mood lifts, once again owing it to Jenna. It's been two weeks since we first met, but I swear my life has changed color. She's bringing me out of my shell and forcing me to stand tall, when I really want to cower, providing support when I've been feeling so lost.

The best part—she has no connection to my life back in Jacksonville. And for the first time, I'm free.

"There's that smile again." Nathan brushes my arm as he walks in, his own smile wide. "I think someone likes California."

"It's growing on me, sure." I offer a nonchalant shrug and he laughs.

"Either way, it's good to see you happy again. It's been a while."

My smile drops as I frantically shake my head. "What? No. I'm happy. You make me happy."

"Oh, I know. But you've been down since you saw—"

"Nope." I throw my hand up between us. "Not talking about the past, remember?"

"Because that's healthy." Nathan raises an eyebrow and I can't help but laugh.

"I promise, I'm good. And it's nice having a friend."

"Ah yes, the elusive Jenna. When am I going to meet her?"

"This weekend? She said she'd come out after the game." My chest tightens at the thought of Nathan's game against San Francisco, but I don't mention it. We've had a big talk about the fact that he'll be playing against Zane, and decided it was best *not* to mention it again.

"Speaking of...I got you your usual seat in the front row. But if you'd prefer not to go..." He trails off and I have to wonder if for the first time, he'd prefer I wasn't there.

"I promised I'd come."

"I know, but—"

"No buts," I cut him off again. "I'll be there. Rain, hail, or shine."

"It's October in Los Angeles. I think you'll get the shine."

"If you jinx it..." I pause, reaching for his hand and giving it a tight squeeze. "I'm not going to be happy."

"I thought it didn't matter?" He stifles a laugh while I growl.

"I lied. My hair hates the rain and I want to look nice."

"You always look nice."

"Thanks." He squeezes my hand back, a lot more gently than I did his, walking away with a bounce in his step.

My brows draw together when he's gone, and an uncomfortable twinge has me rubbing my chest. *"You always look nice."*

He tells me that often, but this time it feels like he's talking about the weather instead of trying to make his girlfriend feel better about herself.

Nathan's a great guy and he looks after me. He always has. But he's not big on descriptive notions of love. Does he like my eyes? Does he think I smell nice?

I have no freaking idea.

Until Jenna told me I was beautiful, I hadn't realized I was missing out. Now I can't help wondering, if a stranger can tell me that, why can't he?

Ignoring the tension itching to send me spiraling again, I release a slow breath and focus on my book. Nathan and I have been together for years. He makes me happy. There's no reason to be questioning that now.

So why am I?

Despite Jenna's many successful distractions, I'm still a mess when Sunday come around, but I promised Nathan I'd support him. Just like I always do.

Faking a smile, in the hope that I can convince myself I'm okay, I reach for my new Los Angeles jersey, running my fingers over the letters printed on the back, the feeling making my skin prickle.

Coincidently or not, Nathan gave it to me last week. Before then, I was unnamed, and now, the weight of the jersey feels heavier in my palms.

"I'm leaving, babe," he calls from downstairs before the front door creaks open. "I got your black heels out of the closest; they're in the hall. I'll see you in the stands."

"Thanks. I'll be there," I call back, hearing his distant "love you" as the door slams shut.

My eyes drop to my outfit, taking in my designer black jeans and finest silk bra. The perfect attire to pair with my patent leather black heels.

Counting down from five, I pull myself out of the resistance toward his name and slip the jersey over my head, letting it mold to my body before I check myself out in the mirror.

There she is. Nathan Morgan's other half.

Putting on a smile, I pull my thick, curly hair high into a tight ponytail and touch up my makeup. Ensuring I'm picture-perfect with Nathan's name on full display.

And my insides squirm. *What the hell is that about?*

I know the drill. This has been my life since Nathan turned pro and yet today it feels wrong.

But why?

Ignoring my thoughts, I spin on my toes and head downstairs, making sure I'm ready for the weekly call with my brother and dad. We've had this standing catch-up since I moved away for college, and if I miss it, I'm likely to have one of them banging down my front door come morning.

My family lives and breathes football. Always have. My dad was an incredible college football player, destined for the pros until he snapped his Achilles his senior year. If he wasn't such a positive man, it would have destroyed him.

My grandfather, on the other hand, *was* an NFL great. He played through to his retirement and went on to coach at a D1 college, and he was still coaching when my dad played.

While I wasn't expected to play like Cade was in high school, I *was* expected to learn everything about the game, and I was expected to watch.

Because of that, I'm what you'd call a die-hard fan. Of the Florida Sting Rays. Nathan's previous team. The team I grew up supporting. The same team my family supports.

The only saving grace about Nathan moving to California is that at least the two teams are in different conferences, so I can tell myself I have a favorite for each.

I've just poured myself a glass of water when my phone rings, blaring the video tone I set for my brother. Staring at the screen, I watch it ring until it stops—because that always pisses Cade off—then I call him right back, a smile dancing on my lips.

"You're a little shit, you know that?" he says as soon as I answer, his lips cocked in a grin.

"And you need to watch your language," Dad calls out in the background, making me laugh.

"Hi, Dad." I wave even though Cade's not facing the phone his way. "And hi, Bro."

"How's Cali life treating you, Little B?" He uses my old nickname and I cringe. It's been years since he's used that name and I'll bet all my money— which is sweet fuck-all at the moment—that he's using it now because he's got Zane on the brain.

Ooh, that rhymes. I smile to myself and Cade raises a brow.

"I'm guessing life is good. I haven't seen you smile like that in a while."

"Actually, if you must know, I rhymed in my head and was a little pleased with myself."

"God, you're a nerd sometimes." He shakes his head, until the phone's ripped from his hand.

"I love it when that happens," Dad cuts in. "What did you rhyme?"

Dammit. "It doesn't matter. How are you, Dad? You're looking good. But that's about to change after a day with Cade. Please tell me you're not watching the game together?"

"You bet we are. Wouldn't miss it."

"The Florida game, right?"

I cross my fingers and hold my breath, only releasing it when Cade calls out, "The price is wrong, B," quoting his favorite movie without annoying my dad with his language.

"Of course, we're watching LA and San Francisco," Dad confirms. "I've kept up with Zane's career and it's his first game back after..." I close my eyes, my chest constricting at the mention of Zane's name, and it takes me a second to realize Dad stopped talking.

I open my eyes and wince. He noticed.

"Sorry."

"No, Blair. I'm sorry. It can't have been easy seeing Zane again."

The tightness in my chest thickens. It's odd hearing Dad talk about him again after spending so many years avoiding the topic.

"I promise, I'm good," I lie as convincingly as I can. "Let's talk football. What are we thinking?"

Dad barely hesitates before launching into his thoughts about the games this weekend, with Cade and me offering our opinions. And when we get to the game of the moment, Dad and Cade pause.

"How was Nathan feeling when he left and during the week?" Dad asks, his expression so serious that I laugh. "Come on, Blair. We need to know... Was he confident?"

"He's always confident; you should remember that from his Florida days."

"You're right. Okay, well, I think—"

"Wait," Cade interrupts. "What Dad really wants to ask is...did the dick mention Zane?"

"Cade!" both Dad and I yell at the same time.

"Sorry, I'll rephrase my question. Is Nathan freaking out about going up against Zane for the first time since his freshman year in college?"

My muscles tense but I fight hard not to appear affected.

"If he is, he didn't mention it."

"Hmmm. Okay." Cade brushes his chin with his fingers. "I'm going to say San Francisco for the win. 24 to 14. Zane to score the first touchdown."

"Wai—"

"That's close to what I was thinking," Dad speaks over me. "I'm calling it at 27 to 10 and I think it'll be Wilder that gets the first touchdown but Zane will dominate in the second half."

"Yes!" Cade snaps his fingers. "I like it. What are you thinking, sis?"

I groan, no longer able to hide my pain. It was so much easier when they supported the team my boyfriend played for. "Well, obviously I'm picking LA for the win."

"Really?" Cade frowns, his expression making me laugh.

"Why is that so hard to believe? They won their first game and—"

"They got their asses handed to them last week. I'll bet their confidence is down. Especially considering how well San Francisco has been playing."

"I'm supporting LA."

"We know. We can tell by your hideous jersey." Cade turns up his nose, and I roll my eyes. "That wasn't the question."

I glance at Dad, hoping he'll save me but he looks away. Four years of birthday celebrations, Thanksgiving lunches, and Christmases. Four years of Nathan proving that he's a good guy and that he loves me. And my parents still don't like him, because Cade and Zane got in their heads. It was a football rivalry that turned personal, but it was years ago. They all need to move the fuck on.

"I think LA will win. 17 to 14 But I think Cade's right that Zane will score the first touchdown." As much as it pains me to admit it out loud.

"Okay. I think you're lying about the LA win, but you do you."

"Cade," Dad warns. "She gave her answer and we have to respect that. Remember when you were convinced that New York was going to beat Philadelphia in the Super Bowl, and we all thought you were crazy, but chose never to tease you about it?"

"You're teasing me about it now."

"*After* the fact is fine. Feel free to call Blair tomorrow and gloat."

"Thanks, Dad. I appreciate the support."

"Any time, Princess. So, next is Washington versus Minnesota. What are you thinking?"

We move quickly through the rest of the games, but by the time they hang up, I'm running late. And I can't be late. Nathan hates that.

Skipping lunch, I book an Uber, my heart trapped in my throat until it finally arrives.

By some miracle, we're blessed by the traffic gods and I settle my ass in my seat just as the San Francisco players run out on the field, ready for their warmup.

And damn. I wish I'd been later.

It takes all of ten seconds for my eyes to lock on Zane, and my heart jolts. I've seen him play over the years, but seeing him this close...

He smirks to his teammate, and my mind drifts to the cocky smile he used to bestow when he'd wink at me in the stands, the memory so vivid it makes my pulse spike.

It's like nothing has changed, and yet as he said when I first saw him in the hospital, *everything has.*

Still, it's hard to look away.

Even in a warmup, he owns the ground he walks on. He was always like that. Always had a presence. Always destined for greatness.

Unlike my dad and brother, I've tried hard *not* to keep up with Zane's career since he left home. Unless I was being slapped in the face with news about him and his career, then I was none the wiser. And I was okay with that.

But when he was lying in that hospital bed, looking more innocent than I'd *ever* seen him, I admit I was worried. Especially when news broke of the possible charges against him.

It broke my heart to think this moment may never come. That he'd never have the chance to play again.

But he's back, and I can't help but be a little happy for him.

I'll never say this out loud, but I'm ninety-nine percent sure that Storm is going to win. And I hate to admit it, but I kind of hope that they do.

God, I'm a horrible person.

Chapter Ten

BLAIR

FLASHBACK BLAIR 17 / ZANE ALMOST 19

I shift on my towel as Zane finishes his drink and wipes below his lip, catching the last drop with his finger before licking it dry. My mind drifts, imagining what else he could do with that tongue, and my toes curl into the sand.

As I'm watching him, a sharp pain shoots through my lip and I silently gasp, releasing the flesh from where it's trapped between my teeth, glancing away before Zane notices.

They weren't kidding when they said absence makes the heart grow fonder. Or in my case, it's made the lust grow stronger because I have never wanted Zane more than I do right now. And my mind is drifting into dangerous territory.

Especially with my brother sitting a few feet away.

"Any idea where your teammate Bianci will go in the draft?" Cade asks Zane, and my eyes bounce between them.

Zane purses his lips before his mouth lifts into a smirk. "How much?"

"What?" Cade frowns.

"You made a bet with your dad, didn't you?"

"What? No. I..." Cade trails off, shaking his head with a laugh. "Okay, I bet him fifty bucks that Bianci goes to Philly."

"Philly?" Zane's eyes widen but he schools his features. "I mean, yeah. Good thinking." He bites back a grin and I burst out laughing.

"I think you just lost fifty bucks, Bro."

"What? Why? Where do you think he's going?" He bounces his question to me, a little cockiness to his tone.

"It's true that Philly needs fresh blood in their defense, but their tackles are strong. They're likely to pick Fisher as their number one. I'd have my money on Bianci going to Dallas. They haven't had a decent tackle since Rover retired two seasons ago."

Zane chuckles beside me. "I hate to say it, Caden, my man, but I think Little B's got you beat."

Cade eyes Zane suspiciously before his gaze snaps to mine. "You fuckers," he groans. *"You told her to say that, didn't you, Zane?"*

"Really, man? When? Your sister just got here. I've been with you the entire day."

Cade frowns but he can't argue with the truth. At least, he can't argue with what he believes *to be the truth.* Not that we were talking much during our moment in Zane's truck.

"Dad told you then." Cade continues to sulk, and I raise my hands in innocence.

"I had no idea about the bet, Cade. You're acting like I'm clueless about football."

"No," Zane cuts in before Cade can argue. "He's acting like a guy that hates losing. We all know you're a freak when it comes to stats and knowledge, B. It's one of the reasons we love you."

"Probably the only reason," Cade quips and the two of them laugh to themselves while my football-loving heart beats out of my chest.

Love.

Zane used the word "love" and while sure, it was said in a very platonic, sisterly like manner, it was still music to my ears.

Zane doesn't use that word lightly. Ever. It's not his thing.

But every moment we spend together brings me closer to feeling *it from him, even if he never voices the word.*

Cade moves the conversation on to other potential draft picks, and I give my two cents when I can, but the second his crush arrives, the conversation is over. She's not that interested in football and when she's around, neither is Cade.

"What about a swim?" he asks with renewed enthusiasm, his eyes bouncing between us, secretly hoping we'll say no.

"I'm enjoying the sun," I say with a shrug and Zane shakes his head.

"Not right now. I'm expecting a call," he lies, waving his phone for reinforcement. At least, I assume it's a lie because Cade shoots him a wink before setting off toward the ocean.

"And they were finally alone," Zane jokes when they're out of earshot, his gaze firmly locked on the beach in front of him.

"Unless you count the other forty or so people lazing around in the sand." I lie back as the words leave my mouth, shielding my eyes from the sun.

Zane chuckles quietly, and when the sound hits my ears, I uncover my eyes, anticipating his smile.

And he does not disappoint.

The way his lips curl, paired with the sparkle in his eyes, should be illegal. Bad boys aren't supposed to have alluring smiles like that—they're dangerous enough.

But they do. They all do.

Especially Zane.

It's that *exact* smile that sucked me in almost two years ago. Before that, I was only ever interested in good guys. The ones that finish their homework before taking you out. The ones that bring you flowers on a first date and fumble their words as they try to impress your parents.

Zane is none of those guys. He'd rather get drunk than do homework, he has more tattoos than one should have at almost nineteen years of age, and he even has his nipple pierced. Not that we've ever discussed that. He did it before Christmas, and I've been pretending not to notice. But my God, does it add to his appeal.

Zane's the type of guy that gets into fights easily. He doesn't care what anyone thinks about him and he doesn't conform.

To the outside world, he's a bad boy.

Hell, I even call him my *bad boy* because he's running around with his best friend's little sister. With me.

But he's not a bad boy at all. He's far from it.

If he was as bad as he believes himself to be, he'd be willing to risk a relationship. Without regret. Like I am. But he won't.

He's one of the most decent humans I know.

And one day, he's going to figure that out and his world will never be the same.

My chest tightens as I think about that notion.

God, I hope I'm around to witness it.

"You're making it really hard for me to keep my cool, Little B," Zane interrupts my thoughts, and I'm snapped from my stupor to find I'm staring at his abs, my lip once again trapped between my teeth.

I huff out a laugh. *"Well, maybe if you gave me some love, I wouldn't have to be daydreaming about it. This is on you, Fitzpatrick. The ball's in your court."*

"Little B," he warns while I laugh at the tension building in his gaze.

"I know." I fill in the space before he can. *"When we're in college together, we'll find it easier to be alone."*

Zane's getting his own dorm room next year so we won't have to sneak around anymore.

"Exactly." He snaps his fingers. *"But if you keep looking at me like that, your brother's going to kill me before we get the chance."*

"He's weak. You can take him." I wave off Zane's concern and he snorts in amusement.

"That may be true, but if it's a fight to the death, I'm gonna back down. I have a sister, remember? I know how I'd feel."

I do remember. As much as I love Sierra, sometimes I wish they weren't related. If Zane had a brother, he might be more willing to corrupt me.

"Okay, fine," I reluctantly concede. *"I'll stop openly staring at your gorgeous body. But you have to do something for me."*

"Anything."

"Put a damn shirt on or get out of my view."

"No can do, Little B." He winks. *"It's too hot for that."*

With a groan, I drag my T-shirt over my head and lie back down, throwing an arm over my eyes as I softly arch my back, putting my bikini-clad breasts on full display. Two can play at that game.

Zane's laughter cut off, and I bite back a victorious grin, struggling not to giggle.

Not so easy now, is it, Zane? *"How long is it until college?"*

CHAPTER ELEVEN

ZANE

The Los Angeles hype music assaults my ears, and as I jog across the cushioned turf, the pitch of the crowd changes.

The players are on the field.

Nathan is on the field.

And I couldn't be more excited.

My lips curl of their own accord, my smile vicious with thoughts of that pathetic excuse of a human, thinking he stands a chance.

I wasn't seeking motivation for my first game back. The fact that I was playing again was more than enough. But getting to wipe the smile off that fucker's smug face makes it all the more delicious.

I've waited years for this moment.

It's my time to shine.

A TV camera slides past in my peripheral vision, and I imagine Cade and his dad watching from their homes. We may not be close anymore, but I can say without a doubt that Cade's merciless smile would look a hell of a lot like mine.

Nathan is what you call a liar and a cheat. And what's worse is that he hides behind his puppy dog persona. His good guy vibes.

"He's so sweet, he couldn't possibly have stolen Jimmy's bike."

"If he started the fight, then why is he the one too banged up to go to school?"

"This is high school. Players don't fix games. Why would they?"

"Cut him some slack. His mom is sick. He didn't mean to scratch your truck."

Every time he fucked up, there was some asshole making excuses for him. And that's not including the stuff I'm convinced he got away with. I can't remember a time that he ever owned up to anything, while I just had to blink and they'd reprimand me.

Yes, his mom got sick when he was in his senior year, and yes, he was a fucking sweet little kid, always smiling and making people happy. But that doesn't give you permission to be a jerk, and it doesn't give you a free pass to mess with my friends. Or worse.

I take in a breath as my heart pounds against my rib cage.

All that aside... You don't manipulate my girl and get away with it.

If he hadn't invited Blair to that damn party all those years ago, her light would never have dulled. I wouldn't be thinking about her twenty-four-fucking-seven knowing it's better for her if I stay away.

All our lives would be different.

My sister would still be alive.

Sorrow clogs my throat, but I force myself to swallow it down, curling my toes in my cleats, grounding myself to the present.

That's not on him. He may be an asshole that throws blame around like it's free fucking candy, but I'm not that guy. I own up to my shit and that one's on me.

Doesn't mean I can't hate him for setting the wheels in motion.

Thomas calls my name, and like cold water's been splashed across my face, I jolt back to the present, flexing my jaw when I feel myself scowling.

I let Nathan distract me. I haven't even laid eyes on him yet and I let him pull me from the game.

Cursing myself, I run backward and scoop up the ball, launching it at Thomas. "I'm here, and I'm good," I reassure him before he can ask, hoping it'll ease his mind after catching me zoning out during practice. His concern is the last thing I need.

Standing tall, I jog to my next position, readying myself for the catch until my eyes lock on Nathan and my steps falter. He's waving toward the crowd, his smile wide as though he's the player single-handedly turning his team around, and I almost call out to put him in his place. At least until Easton runs past me, bringing my attention back where it's needed. Back to my team.

Focusing just in time, I see Thomas throw the ball in my direction, and I race forward, dodging my teammate before easily securing it in my grasp.

I keep my mind on target for the remainder of our warmup, but when it's time to vacate the field, I naturally seek out Nathan again. I can't help it; I'm excited for the moment our eyes first meet. To watch the *sweet* smile fall from his face.

When I finally find him, he's running toward the sidelines, removing his helmet as he clings to the fence. Leaning forward, he plants his lips on some poor woman in the crowd and I can't help but laugh. *Once a dick, always a dick.* We'll see who's smiling when the game ends.

I roll my eyes as I start to turn away, but when he steps back, the hint of familiarity stops me and I jolt, my pulse instantly picking up speed.

Nope. No. No way.

An irrational anger takes over me but I laugh it off.

It can't be Blair.

There is no way she's over there sucking face with that— *Motherfucker.* She lifts her gaze and there's no denying it. I'd recognize those lips from a mile away. It's her. But she's not happy about the public display of affection. The smile she's projecting is the one she brings out when she's trying to avoid attention.

Too bad it didn't work, because she sure caught mine.

How is this even possible?

Blair's boyfriend is Nathan?

She moved to California for him?

After pushing me away.

Fuck.

Turns out, the joke is on me. Because win or lose, that fucker gets the last laugh.

I was wrong to say I didn't need any extra motivation for this game. Because I have *never* played as hard as I'm playing right now.

Luke slaps me on the back as we line up for what could be our final play, and while his smile is wide, all I can do is quirk my lips in response.

"You are on fire, my man," he praises, his eyes full of respect. "Whatever you're doing, don't stop."

I widen my grin while inside I'm fuming. I can't even say who's summoned the most wrath. I refuse to think of that right now. But I'm pissed at them both.

The whistle blows, and our center snaps the ball back to Thomas. Thomas twists left as though he's going to throw my way, but in an epic move that he's mastered over the years, he pivots and throws right, sending the ball spiraling toward Easton who catches it easily.

Luke's there to block their defense as Easton flies toward the end zone, diving over the line in a touchdown that ends the game.

And the crowd roars. We won.

It may not be our home stadium, but it's not far to travel, and we have loyal fans that always make the trek.

We're loved. And it shows.

I'm as pumped as the rest of the team, celebrating on the field, but the second I'm off, I jog toward our locker room, ignoring my coach as I rush to shower. I'm dressed and ready in record time, but before I get the chance to leave, Thomas is there, intruding on my personal space.

"How are you feeling?" He cups my shoulder, his eyes full of concern.

"I'm good, Cap." I brush him off. "Better than ever, and I have to go."

"Go?"

"Yep. Can't explain now, but I'm leaving. I'll see you at the bar." I turn to grab my bag but Thomas ignores me.

"You've got media—"

"Yep." I nod, spinning to face him again. "Tell them I'm busy."

"Zane. I—"

"Let him go, Kelly," Luke joins the conversation out of nowhere. "I know that look. We've all been there."

"What look?" I ask, not bothering to hide my puzzled expression.

Thomas frowns until Luke raises an eyebrow, and he laughs, a silent conversation seemingly taking place before Thomas concedes. "Right. Okay. I'll see if I can cover for you. But I make no promises."

What? "I'm confused by what's happening, but thanks?" My voice rises but I ignore it. For all I know, this is a perk to being a part of that damn group chat. But if it is...am I going to have to repay the favor to Luke one day?

I question it for all of two seconds before deciding I don't care and throwing my bag over my shoulder to leave. After pushing the door open, I squeeze through the crowd hovering in the halls, refusing to make eye contact.

They know I'm an ass; my behavior won't come as a shock to them.

I have no idea what the hell I'm doing, but something deep inside me is screaming at me to find Blair.

Her being here feels like more than just a coincidence, and I've always been a "fuck it" kind of guy.

Up until a couple of months ago she lived in another state. Her boyfriend played in another conference. Yet today, my first game back, she's here, in the crowd, *watching me.*

She may not have been outwardly cheering me on, but on the few occasions I glanced her way, she was always staring back at me.

Throwing my cap on, I keep my head low and move through the supporters, ignoring my name when it's occasionally called, and it's not until I reach LA's locker rooms that I finally pause.

My pulse races as my gaze flits from brunette to brunette, searching. But no one even comes close to Blair's understated beauty until...

My breath catches.

There she is.

Alone.

With her back resting casually against the wall, a memory attacks me of the many times she waited around for Cade—for me—looking like the goddess she always was.

Only this time, she's waiting for someone else.

For *him.*

My stomach drops as my heart catches up with reality. She still looks the same, so it's easy to forget how much time has passed. At least until I focus on the unfortunate addition of that hideous jersey.

Talk about a knife to the gut. I've experienced the agony of a stab wound, and yet, *this* is more excruciating.

Thank God I can't see her back, because if I saw that dick's name printed there, I might be forced to rip it clear off her chest.

What is she thinking? *Morgan? Fucking* Nathan? *Really?* She had to choose *him.*

I let out a sigh as I watch her, drinking her in, getting my fill since this could be the last time I ever see her. Although, I thought the same thing when I left her standing on her porch back in Jacksonville.

A loose hair falls to her cheek and my palm flexes, itching to brush it behind her ear. I haven't been able to get her out of my head since I last saw her, and I'd take any excuse to touch her again.

A familiar pull tugs at my chest, and my mouth tingles at the memory of my lips first caressing hers. The first time I let myself consider her in a different light—as her own woman rather than my best friend's little sister. The girl I'd known since she was a kid.

She's as perfect now as she was back then.

And just like that, I'm sucked back into her orbit.

She's like an addiction I never knew I had, and it's only after I've taken a hit that I realize how dangerous it is.

My chest aches from the hole I thought time had well and truly mended, and when she smiles to herself, all rational thought exits my brain.

I should walk away.

God knows that a better man would.

But I've never been one for making wise decisions. And Blair knows that well.

She called me her bad boy, after all.

Maybe it's time I lived up to my name.

Chapter Twelve

BLAIR

Shaking off my thoughts of Zane, I check my phone for what feels like the millionth time and shift awkwardly, clenching my clammy hands around the device that's recently become my security blanket. I've never felt truly comfortable waiting for Nathan in front of his locker room, but here, I feel completely out of place.

A group of confidently beautiful girls chat animatedly beside me, and when I accidentally meet their eyes, I grin, trying to ignore the what-is-she-doing-here look on their faces.

It's a fair question.

Sure, I'm wearing Nathan's jersey along with my designer shoes and expensive jewelry. And I'm not shy in saying I'm beautiful in my own right. But I'm not acting the part. I don't hold the confidence of someone waiting for their man. I probably look more like a stalker.

This is the only part of attending Nathan's games that I hate.

Dating a football player was always in my sights, only growing up, those sights were set on a different guy. I wanted this life. I was prepared for it and all that it entails. But I never considered how isolating it would be. Back then, I pictured myself with the football girlfriends and wives, watching the games together, bonding. I never once imagined I'd be hovering around outside the locker room, alone, and not feeling excited about waiting for my man.

I've got to admit, I don't love it.

I check my phone again, bouncing in anticipation when a text comes through from Cade.

I've been waiting for this. His moment to gloat. A distraction. It couldn't have come at a better time.

> CADE: I missed the final minutes of the game.
> Do you happen to remember the score?

I bark out a laugh, covering my mouth as I glance up to check if anyone's watching me. *Only Cade.*

> BLAIR: Lucky for you, I do. LA won. 28 to 24. It was a close game but Los Angeles was too strong in the end

> CADE: God, you're full of it. I always thought he'd put a spell on you

> BLAIR: Cade...

> CADE: Don't Cade me. I'm joking. Sort of. Mostly. Anyway, condolences to your man but at least it was a good game

> BLAIR: It was a good game. Did you see Wilder's catch in the first half? It was right in front of me

> CADE: That was insane. And what about Leon's rundown? That had to be a record time. I can't believe he caught Bennett before he made it across the line

Cade starts typing again, and as I wait, a longing smile pulls at my lips. This is what I thought being a football girlfriend would be like. I thought I'd be having these conversations when the play happened, with the other partners. But maybe that was a deluded thought. Not everyone is as die-hard as we are.

> CADE: I'll even admit that Nathan's move to block Langham was genius. His skills improved during the offseason

Cade's not wrong. Nathan moved to LA as soon as he was traded and worked his ass off to prove he was the right choice. He got faster, stronger, more determined. It was truly admirable to witness. Not that I'm going to tell Cade that.

BLAIR: He was always good, Cade. You just didn't want to see it

CADE: (Laughing emoji) You have blinders on when it comes to him, little sis. He better be treating you like a fucking princess

I'm not a princess. Despite what my parents believe.

And the thing is, I don't want to be one. Nathan knows that. Zane always knew that. Cade is yet to figure it out.

I groan when Zane's cocky smile flits across my mind, but before I can focus on anything else, I glance up and suck in a strangled breath.

Jesus.

Locking eyes with Zane across the hallway, my brows draw together as the world around me fades into darkness.

Is he real? He should still be in his locker room and— *God, I'm imagining him now?*

Blinking a few times, I laugh before shaking my head.

BLAIR: He's treating me fi

"Blair?"

"Fuck. You're here?" I fumble my phone and accidentally press send as I step forward, cursing under my breath.

Barely a second passes before my phone vibrates in my hand, but I'm too caught up in the fact that my imagination is talking to me, that I completely ignore it.

"You shouldn't be here," I scold, my eyes bouncing around the stadium halls. "Won't you get a fine?"

"Yep." His shoulders lift in a nonchalant shrug and my eyes widen.

"Yep?"

"To both. I shouldn't be here and I'm going to get a fine."

"Then, wh—"

"Are you seriously dating that fucker?" He talks over me, stepping closer until I'm forced back into the wall. "Please tell me he's blackmailing you or something."

"Blackmailing me?" I scoff, standing tall as I stare at him.

"It would make more sense than the alternative. Or is this some dark, twisted fantasy? He was there when...when everything happened. Maybe you found solace in that. Maybe being with him is like a punishment you think you deserve."

"What the fuck, Zane? Why...why would you even say that?"

"I don't know." He throws his hands in the air and curses through clenched teeth. "I'm trying to make sense of it, B. Because I thought you hated him just as much as we did. But then you went to that party and—"

"And what?"

"You *know* what."

The fight leaves me and I let myself crumble, my back hitting the concrete wall behind me with more force than I expected, making me wince.

Unfortunately, I do know. All too well. I'm never going to forget it. But this isn't about that.

"I'm not punishing myself, Zane. I moved on."

"I noticed. It was hard *not* to notice, with him mauling you on the sidelines." Zane closes his eyes, letting out a sigh before straightening and shaking himself off. "Sorry. I didn't come here to argue. Or to bring up that damn kiss. I just wanted to check on you."

Ignoring the way his eyes soften and my heart pounds, I focus on his words. *"That damn kiss."* I'd almost forgotten about that, and yet, it was truly monumental. Nathan has *never* kissed me during a game. Not once. Warmup or otherwise. Now that Zane's mentioned it, I have to wonder if he was putting on a show. For Zane.

It wouldn't be the first time he'd done something in his life solely for the purpose of pissing Zane off. Or my brother for that matter. But I thought he left that behind years ago. And more so after we started dating.

Premeditated or not, Nathan's not going to be happy to find Zane here.

"You should go." A commotion behind me draws my attention, and I glance back to see a few of the guys heading out of the room. "Now, Zane. You need to go *now*."

Zane's eyes flash in the direction I was looking and he grins. "Aww, are you worried about me? I can take him."

Tension coils in my neck as I fight to keep my voice steady. "Think about it, Zane. It's going to look like you came around here, after a game, wanting to fight."

"Why would it look like that? We're two old friends enjoying a chance to catch up."

"I *meant* Nathan."

"So did I. I'm not stupid. I'm not going to jeopardize my career for that piece of—"

"I get it; you hate him. But he's my boyfriend and I don't have to listen to this. It was good seeing you again. But please. Go."

Panic rolls through me as the crowd gets more rowdy, and when I glance over my shoulder, I find Nathan as he exits the room.

"*Please.*" I spin to face Zane. "You have to—" My words cut off as I'm met with a sea of strangers, not even a hint of Zane anywhere in the distance.

As though he was never really here.

Someone touches my arm and I jump, spinning around as my panic deepens. "Nathan?" My pitch rises and he frowns.

"Are you okay?"

"Yeah, sorry." I smile through the fog in my head. "I was in another world."

"I bet. That took forever. I—"

"Morgan?" someone calls out, interrupting him. "Are you coming with us?"

I don't recognize the face, but Nathan waves in acknowledgment.

"Sure am. Give me five." He turns to face me again, his eyes raking over me from head to toe. "You look incredible. Where were we?"

"I—"

"That's right, you were in another world. I hope it was a good one." He winks and I fake another grin. It seems I'm doing that a lot lately. And like always, Nathan doesn't notice, moving on. "God, I'd love to take you out and show you off tonight, but the boys are heading out to drown their sorrows," he explains lightly. "Are you okay to get home?"

What? "We're supposed to be meeting Jenna, remember?"

"Oh, right, yeah." He glances behind him and I follow his gaze, finding a few of the guys waving to hurry him up. "It's just the guys wanted a boys' night. Apparently, the partners don't usually come out after a loss. It's a tradition."

"Oh, okay." *What the fuck?* "I have an easy solution. You go out with the boys and I'll meet Jenna."

"Are you sure?" He fakes a pout as he curls his arms around my waist, pretending I have a choice.

"I'm sure. You're new. You should go with the flow. Don't piss off your teammates in your first season. You'll have plenty of time for that."

Nathan laughs before pulling me into him, holding me until we're a breath apart. "Thank you, Blair. I won't be too late." He presses a chaste kiss to my lips before stepping back. "Damn, you're perfect. I love you, babe. I'll see you at home."

"You will." I meet his gaze and hold it. "Have a good night."

"You too."

He waves as he walks away, and when he reaches the guys, they cheer, giving him a shake as they mess up his hair.

My stomach knots, but when my phone rings, I'm pulled from my disappointment, remembering Cade. *God*, I was so preoccupied with Zane and Nathan that I didn't even notice his *fifteen missed calls.*

Shit!

I bet he's on his way to the airport.

If anyone treats me like a princess, it's him.

Chapter Thirteen

ZANE

The hum of the crowd surrounds us at the bar as the drinks flow and happiness consumes my teammates. Another win, another step closer to the Super Bowl.

I'm as happy as the rest of them, but every time Luke wanders over to talk to me, I hold my breath, waiting for him to question me about why I ran off. Or to tell me I owe him for stepping in with Thomas.

To my relief, he never once brings it up, opting to talk about the game or whatever's going on in his own life. Typical of Luke.

Though I don't miss the knowing smiles he shoots my way when my gaze flits to the door. Or my phone. As though Blair's about to walk in off the street, or miraculously unblock my number after our emotionally charged exchange.

"Even Wilder had a smile on his face," Luke continues on and I laugh, welcoming the distraction from my roving thoughts.

He's not wrong. Even *I've* noticed the grumpy asshole is significantly less grumpy since he hooked up with our team owner's daughter. Maybe I did do him a favor after all.

Luke's play by play retelling rolls on and on, and while I'd usually imagine myself banging my head against a brick wall, I smile.

I was at the game. I played. I know what happened. But Luke knows that, and I have a feeling he's trying to help.

My phone vibrates in my hand, and even though I know it's not her—it's likely to be Cade—I face the inevitable, excusing myself for a minute with the promise to return.

> CADE: Just tell me if you saw her, fucker. She said she's okay but something frazzled her enough to send a half-typed message

My shoulders drop as I let out a sigh. He's been texting me for the past few hours, concerned for Blair. But he doesn't need to be because his panic over her text is unwarranted. I watched her press send when I appeared. I'm the reason she did it. Not that I'm going to admit that.

> ZANE: I think you're reading too much into this

> CADE: Answer the question

> ZANE: No, I didn't see her. But while we're on the topic of your sister. Why the fuck didn't you tell me about Morgan?

My phone rings and I curse out loud, pushing through the crowd toward the exit. "A message would have sufficed, *Caden*." My jaw clenches as I reach the street, scanning the area for somewhere quiet to talk.

"I told you not to *Caden* me. And it wouldn't have *sufficed*, because I wanted to hear your voice when you responded to what I have to say."

"What the hell does that mean?" I duck into the doorway of a closed tech store and sink back against the glass.

"It means that I didn't tell you because I didn't want your jealous ass to go after her."

"The fuck? I thought you wanted us to talk? Why would I be jealous?"

"I wish I'd video called you so you could see my face right now. Want me to describe it?" I picture him staring at me with a "do you think I'm stupid" look and I laugh.

"Nope. I get it. But you're wrong. I'm not jealous. I'm worried. As should you be. Is she safe with him?" My thoughts flicker to one of the many fucked-up things Nathan did when we were younger, and my stomach knots as I wait for Cade's response.

He huffs and I hold my breath until he finally responds. "She's safe. I've been keeping an eye on things. He seems to have changed. They've been together for years. Four, I think."

"Four?" *That stings.* Four years is serious. And she moved states for him. I guess I should be happy she's happy. Only... "Is she happy?"

Cade's quiet for a beat and I'm about to repeat the question when he curses softly. "She says she is."

Fuck. "She says a lot of things she doesn't mean."

"I know."

Double fuck. I groan, letting out an audible sigh as I stand tall. "What do you want me to do?" I ask, a big part of me hoping he says "nothing" while a little part of me wants him to tell me to break them up. Because that's what I want to do. I'm just not sure I'd be doing it for the right reasons.

In fact, I *know* I wouldn't be.

But if she's not happy—

Cade beats me in the sigh department, letting out the mother of all sighs, and I'm about to tell him he's being dramatic when an angel walks into my line of sight. A drunk angel who's using her friend to support her weight. *Shit.*

"I've got to go."

"What? Why?"

"Because I'm out celebrating my win and my teammates are staring at me through the window," I lie. "They're wondering why I'm being such an antisocial asshole."

"I can appreciate that. Can we talk tomorrow?"

My head falls back and I clench my fist before I answer. Why? Why am I letting myself be pulled back into that world? I left for a reason and I should have stayed gone.

"Zane?" he asks, his tone pleading.

"Yep. Sure. Let's talk tomorrow. Bye."

I hang up before he can say anything else and take off across the road, not bothering to look for traffic until some fucker honks at me. "You're fine. You had plenty of room," I yell back, rolling my eyes as I reach the sidewalk, coming face-to-face with Blair.

Actually, face to foot is a better description—her face to my foot—as she vomits all over my shoes.

Jesus. She's blind drunk.

Blair groans without looking and my stomach knots. "Please tell me he's *not* hot," she asks her friend, and as her friend giggles, I allow myself to relax. A little.

"I hate to say it, babe, but he's fucking gorgeous." Her friend eyes me slowly as her grip on Blair loosens and I chuckle softly, securing my hands on Blair's waist, helping her straighten.

"You okay there, B?"

Blair's eyes snap to mine and her face scrunches. "Motherfucker."

"Told you." Her friend laughs, misunderstanding Blair's reaction.

Being the nice guy that I am, I bite back my amusement, hitting her with an innocent smile. "What would it matter if I was hot, B? You have a boyfriend."

"Wait." Her friend's eyes widen as she completely lets go of Blair, forcing me to tighten my hold. "You two know each other?"

I readjust my grip until I have Blair tucked into my side. "We do," I admit, surprised Blair's letting me hold her.

"How?"

Blair groans again and a little of my joy shines through.

"Want me to fill her in? Or..." I trail off, squeezing her waist as she huffs, stepping out of my grasp—or rather stumbling out of my grasp. I move to grab her again, but she waves me off, holding a light pole for support.

"This is Zane. The guy—"

"Noooo." Her friend's eyes flash to Blair before settling back on me. "Are you kidding me with this?" Her lips part, and she shakes her head. "We were just—"

"Leaving," Blair finishes for her. "We were just leaving."

That's not what her friend was about to say, but I let it slide. "Leaving so you could puke?"

"No," Blair denies at the same time her friend says, "Pretty much."

Holding back my amusement, I glance around the busy street and frown. "How are you planning to get home?" Fuck, *home*? The thought of her going back to a place she shares with Nathan makes a shiver run down my spine.

"Don't worry, we don't need your help. You don't have to look so disgusted."

"Disgusted? What—" Oh. *Yep, I'm disgusted, but not for the reason she thinks*. "I'm not *worried*, but I am going to help. Where is home? And speaking of home... Where's your goddamn *boyfriend*?"

"He's at the strippers." Her friend answers before Blair can speak, and Blair covers her mouth with her hand.

"He's not. I mean, I don't know. Jenna's making assumptions."

Ahh, she has a name. "Nice to meet you, Jenna."

Jenna's wide smile is visible behind Blair's hand, and I'm going to guess she pokes her tongue out because Blair recoils quickly, embarrassment tinging her expression. "Ew, Jen."

"Sorry." She giggles. "Nice to meet you too, Zane. I've heard"—Blair shoots her a glare and she nods—"nothing about you," she finishes. "Nothing at all. But tell me. If you were a football player. Hypothetically. And you were in your hypothetical hometown of say, San Francisco, and your girlfriend was watching your game—"

"Jenna. Stop. Please."

"What? It's just hypothetical."

"Nathan went out to drown his sorrows with the guys and Jenna thinks he's at a strip club."

"Would it matter if he was?" I ask with a frown, genuinely curious. "I'm assuming you trust him since you've been together for *four* years."

Jesus, did my voice just rise? I need to get my shit together.

Blair flinches. "*Ouch*. I see you've been talking to Cade. How long did you wait before you called him?"

"*He* called *me*." I point to my chest. "He was worried when you sent him half a text and then proceeded to ignore his calls. Tell me, why is that? Why would he be worried knowing you were likely to be with your man?"

I feel Jenna's gaze bouncing between us but I hold my stare, challenging Blair to answer.

"He doesn't trust Nathan," she snaps. "The same way I'm sure you don't. But I do." She points to her chest just like I did. "And you're right. If he's at a strip club, what does it matter? He's coming home to *me*."

I slam my eyes shut and suppress a shudder. I don't need that visual.

"Do you two *hate* or *love* each other?" Jenna questions and I stifle a snort, deciding on the spot that I like her.

"Neither," Blair responds for both of us. "We're neutral."

"Okay. Thanks. I just needed to get my head around it, because honestly... Tension, meet knife."

A laugh bursts out of me and this time Blair aims her glare my way. "Careful, B. You're not acting very neutral right now. You look like you want to kill me."

"Kill, no. Punch, maybe."

"She loves me," I say to Jenna and she laughs so loud it draws a bout of unwanted attention—namely, the chick with the phone aimed our way.

Blair opens her mouth to comment, but I get in first. "I think we should take this off the street. My hotel is only a block down the road and—"

"I am *not* going to your hotel room, Zane."

"I wasn't suggesting that. It has a lobby, with couches."

"Ooh, I love the sound of couches." Jenna moans blissfully. "And my apartment is so far away." Holding her palms together, she turns to Blair and begs, "Please, Blair. These boots were not made for walking...or standing around."

"Ugh. Fine. It would be nice to wash my mouth out."

"Can you clean my shoes while you're at it?" I raise a brow in humor.

"Nope. That's on you. Don't stand in front of a woman who's about to..." She waves her hand around.

"Puke?" I ask.

"Yes, but I was going to use a better term."

"Oh, babe." Jenna pats her arm. "For what you did, there isn't one."

Blair's the one to laugh loudly this time, and in the process, she stumbles until I steady her again.

"I'm fine." She shakes me off. "Where's your hotel?"

She's not fine. But I'm smart enough to know she's not going to let me help her. No matter how badly I want to. Instead, I resort to casual humor to hide my concern. "This way, ladies."

I hit them both with a cheesy grin and Blair fake gags. "How many times have you said that in reference to your hotel?"

"Said what?" I know exactly what she's referring to, but I want to see the jealousy in her eyes.

"This way, ladies," she mocks, attempting my voice as she rolls her eyes.

"Once or twice," I lie. "But never in LA."

Jenna's lips quirk into a grin while Blair's eyes flare with a jealous rage she disguises as disgust.

And a spark ignites inside me.

Does she still want me? Can I still elicit the soft little mewls I once could by running my finger along the nape of her neck?

Her lips part as though she's imagining the same thing and I've got my answer. *Yes.* Even with the fucker around. A stupid happiness takes over me, but I don't let it get too far. Not yet.

"Come on." I gesture in the direction of the hotel. "There are too many eyes here." I reach for Blair's hand, but she snaps it back before curling her arm through Jenna's.

"Let's go," she says and I snort out a laugh.

"Great. The blind leading the blind." *What have I gotten myself into?*

CHAPTER FOURTEEN

BLAIR

Zane's staying in a fancy hotel—of course—and while I don't feel out of place, I am definitely *underdressed*. I'd be more at home in a stylish silk dress and sky-high heels rather than my skintight jeans and off-the-shoulder blouse. After dropping my bag home, I opted for a more casual outfit than I'd normally wear out since I would no longer be on Nathan's arm, and I'm regretting it. Among other things.

Like following Zane into his hotel.

If I was thinking more clearly, I'd probably stay outside, but the second we push through the opulent floor-to-ceiling doors, there's no going back. The soft looking velvet couches are screaming my name, and I desperately need to sit down.

Walking slowly, I concentrate hard on placing one foot in front of the other, determined not to make a fool of myself, and I almost wish I'd let Zane take my hand. The journey with Jenna felt more like being dragged by a dog on a leash. We barely managed a few steps without one of us stumbling and the other tripping in the opposite direction, meaning the short two blocks seemed to take hours.

"We made it," Jenna cheers loudly and I audibly groan. Zane's going to have something to say about that, but at least he was there to catch me the few times I *did* fall. "Look how lavish those chairs are," she continues, awe in her expression. "Blair, do *not* puke. You'll get us kicked out."

I pause, focusing on my stomach for a beat, and when it doesn't rumble, I smile. "Honestly, I think the worst of it made it onto Zane's shoes. We're good now."

"Perfect." She beams.

"Yes, *perfect*." Zane rolls his eyes and laughter bubbles out of me.

"Ew. You stink, Zane. Can you please go and change?"

"What are you, twelve?" Zane stares at me deadpan, but the corners of his eyes crinkle, giving away his amusement.

"I was *way* more mature at twelve. You know that. This is me drunk. Something you *don't* know."

At that he raises an eyebrow, and his beautiful lips quirk into a smile. My gaze lingers on his mouth longer than it should before I register what his expression means.

Wait? I frown, my attention shifting to his knowing expression. *Has he seen me drunk*? I've only been this bad a handful of times and most of them were in college, except for Cade's eighteenth birthday when I found the alcohol he'd snuck into the house.

And...

The night of the accident.

Since I doubt he'd joke about that night, I'm guessing... "You saw me at Cade's birthday?"

"I did." His smile widens. "I'm the one that hid the alcohol in the closet. I was on my way to get a couple of bottles when you snuck out."

"But that was *before* I started drinking." My forehead creases as I try to recall anything I can remember of that night.

"Who do you think got you into bed?" Zane questions and my eyes widen of their own accord.

Jesus. "I could have sworn Sierra did that."

At the mention of his sister, Zane subtly winces before schooling his features. "Nope. It was me." His smile returns but it barely moves his cheeks let alone reaches his eyes.

A weight settles on my chest as I study his features. What I wouldn't give to find out what he's really thinking right now.

"Zane—"

"I'm going to clean my shoes." He abruptly changes the subject, jolting me. "Don't leave. I'll be back." He jogs away, and the second he's out of earshot, Jenna wolf whistles, clearly *not* reading the room.

"Damn, that man is fine. You didn't tell me he was *that* hot."

Unable to stand anymore, I fall back onto the couch and let my body sink into the cushions, closing my eyes with a sigh. "I figured you'd look him up."

"I was planning on it, but didn't get the chance."

My lips lift into a soft smile. Trust Jenna to pull me out of a mood. Her and this phenomenal couch. I could easily fall asleep here.

"So...Miss Stevens," Jenna continues on, but I'm only half listening as my mind drifts into patterns. "I'm curious..." She trails off.

"Mm-hmm?"

"How does it feel to have *two* football players in love with you?"

"What?" I blink a few times as I huff out a laugh. "Zane's not in love with me." Not anymore. There was a time I believed he was. Or that he'd get there. But that was a long time ago. A lifetime. I can barely remember what it felt like.

My heart wrenches as though trying to remind me, but before I can process it, Jenna laughs.

"Bullshit." She shakes her head, her smile incredulous. "I could see it in his eyes."

"You're drunk." I wave her off but my traitorous heart dances at the thought.

Jenna's laughter rises, keeping me from escaping into a memory. "You're right. I am *blind*. But I can still recognize a loved-up man—or *woman*—when I see one. It's a gift."

I pretend she's not insinuating something with the "*woman*" comment and say my piece. "If he's loved up,"—I straighten in my seat, curling my legs up in front of me—"it doesn't matter anymore. We had something years ago but it's long over."

"Mm-hmm." Jenna nods a few times, her lips pursed. "Keep telling yourself that."

"I *will*." Annoyance plagues me and I jump up, needing to distance myself from Jenna's drunken musings. "I'm going to rinse my mouth out and then... Do you have any gum?"

"I sure do." She hands over her purse. "This baby has everything you'll ever need."

"Thanks. I'll be back."

Jenna waves and before I've taken a step, she closes her eyes and snuggles herself into the couch opposite where I was sitting, resting her head on the arm.

"Don't be long," she calls out as I brush past her. "Lover boy will be back."

Ignoring the sting of her words, I search the foyer for a bathroom and beeline for the full-length mirror, thanking the universe that I managed to keep myself clean.

Taking my time, I thoroughly rinse my mouth out before running my fingers through my mussed-up hair. And when I'm done, I take a deep breath as my reflection attacks me. Her judging eyes stare back at me, her brows high on her forehead, questioning my life choices.

God, what am I doing? My insides squirm as a shiver runs through me.

Not only am I drinking to quiet the noise in my head, but now I'm here with Zane. One of only two people my boyfriend despises.

I need to get out of here.

Squaring my shoulders, I blow out a breath and open the door, striding confidently toward Zane and Jenna. But when she laughs at something he says, I falter, all my strength whittling away.

This can't be good.

"I actually haven't met him yet," I overhear as I get closer, tiptoeing so I can listen in. "I can only judge on what Blair's told me."

I internally groan. Zane's asking about Nathan.

"Okay. Then how long have you known Blair?" he asks, his body stiff as though he's running an inquisition.

"You mean B?" Jenna bites her lip, her expression exuding sass, and my muscles tense. "I think it's adorable that you call her that, by the way. I've known her for a few weeks."

"Fast friends?" Zane ignores her teasing, but I can't do the same, since I know what she's doing, and it doesn't sit well with me.

"Blair's awesome." Jenna smiles and it's full of so much warmth that it thaws my indignation. "But I don't need to tell you that. I'm sure you know."

"I do." Zane's shoulders bounce as he lightly chuckles, and while I wish I could take a moment and wallow in the familiar sound, I've heard enough.

Taking a step closer, I open my mouth to announce myself until Jenna continues. "She told me about the game," she says and I frown. *What game?*

"What about it?" Zane asks, his expression similar to mine.

"How Nathan kissed her to make you jealous." Her head tilts to the side and I curse under my breath. *Of all the things she could have said.*

"He what?" Zane snaps and... *Dammit. What is she doing?*

My stomach knots as I rush forward, curling my fingers around Zane's bicep as he clenches his fists, his gaze darting to my hand.

What's that saying? *"Loose lips sink ships."* I smile through my annoyance, trying to placate a pissed-off Zane. Jenna has a lot of explaining to do.

"Zane, Jenna is—"

"Is it true?" His deep accusatory tone inflicts a similar burn to whiskey, and I swear he gets taller, making me straighten beside him as I release my hold.

"You didn't know that?" Jenna asks and I quickly cut in.

"How would he know that, Jen?"

Her brows pull together before she glances away, seemingly lost in thought. "You're right. My bad. What's Nathan like?" she asks Zane and I groan.

"Jenna, what are you doing?" I release a slow breath, my voice dripping in resignation.

"I just want to know, that's all. I haven't met him, and of course you're going to say he's amazing. I needed a second opinion."

"He's my boyfriend."

"And yet, Zane here seems to be worried about that."

"What?" I glance up at Zane, my heart pounding as he folds his arms across his chest, his returning stare unwavering. *Guess he's not going to deny it.*

"You're drunk, B," he says pointedly. "And that's not like you."

"It's not?" I grate as my insides coil, the tension that's been lingering fast approaching breaking point. "How the hell do you know? You *left*." A rage simmers inside me as it all becomes too much. The pain. The uncertainty. The memories I've been trying to outrun since Zane first drove away. "Maybe I became a drinker," I lie. "Maybe this is an average Sunday night for me."

In my periphery, I see Jenna shake her head no and I stamp my foot like a child. "*Jenna?* Whose side are you on?"

"Right now? This guy." She points to Zane and her betrayal cuts me like a knife. "Until such a time as I meet Nathan. I'm good at reading people, and Zane gives off a good vibe."

"Thanks." He smiles and I want to slap it off his face.

"I'm going to go." I spin on my heel. I can't be here anymore.

"Wait." Zane rushes forward, grabbing my wrist, but when I shoot him a glare, he releases me. "Not yet, please," he begs. "Stay here until you sober up."

"Oh, I'm plenty sober *now*. I think it's best I leave. It'll give you two a better chance to talk about me when I'm gone." I wince at the venom in my voice, but right now, I'm too worked up to care. I need to sleep it off.

Jumping up from her seat, Jenna's eyes alight with panic. "I'm sorry. God, what am I—"

"Don't worry, Jen. I'll call you in the morning." I'm angry now but she's drunk. Zane, on the other hand...

"No, babe." She interrupts my spiral. "I'm coming. I'm sorry." My shoulders drop, some of my fight dissipating.

"It's okay, I promise. I just can't be here right now."

"I understand." She runs to catch up with me, her heels clacking on the polished floors. "It was nice meeting you, Zane," she calls over her shoulder, linking her arm through mine, and I think he mumbles "you too" but I refuse to look back.

I refuse to do *anything* until we're in a taxi on our way home. It's only then that I finally speak. After I've calmed down.

"I'm sorry I snapped," I say, releasing a slow breath. "It's just that was a lot and—"

"Why are you sorry? I said *way* more than I should have."

"Yeah, well... Zane's the kind of guy you want to talk to. He's alluring like that."

"He is, but it's no excuse. I'm sorry."

"Thanks. I appreciate that."

"At the risk of pissing you off again, I have to say, he doesn't seem like the asshole you described him to be."

I let my head fall back as I sigh dramatically. "That's because he's not. It's easier for me to think of him that way."

"He hurt you?"

"We hurt each other. But that was years ago. It's time to move on."

"He doesn't look like he's willing to do that."

"He will. He'll go back to San Francisco and all will be forgotten. It's only because he's here. You know...out of sight, out of mind." I shrug and when I open my eyes, Jenna frowns, wanting to challenge me or say more, but thankfully she doesn't.

"Want to stay at my place?" she asks instead, as we pull up in front of her building, the wrought iron lights giving the art deco building a fairytale glow.

I smile, considering it for a second before shaking my head. "Thank you, but I should go home. I don't want Nathan to worry."

"Of course. I really need to meet this man. ASAP."

"You do. How about you come over for dinner this week? He's around most nights."

"Sounds perfect. See you then." She presses a kiss to my cheek before thanking our driver. "Talk tomorrow." She waves as she gets out, closing the door behind her.

And then there was one.

After taking another deep breath, I focus on the scenery around me—the passing lights, the shadows cast from the buildings—desperate to keep my mind off Zane. But it's hopeless.

Why was he there? And why am I still so drawn to him? I thought I'd moved on. With Nathan. I honestly believed that seeing Zane again wouldn't have this much impact, but I was lying to myself. And that's messed up on so many levels.

I love Nathan. I do. And he's good to me. Yes, there's a chance he was out watching naked women dance, but he wasn't spending time with his ex. He'd never do that to me.

Out of respect for him—and myself—I should have said no. I should have walked away.

God, he's going to flip out when I tell him. Because I have to. I do. One thing about me is that I never hold back. At least not when it comes to things that I've done.

When it comes to my feelings, that's another story.

My chest fills with an anxious weight, and when the taxi pulls up to my complex, I can't bring myself to get out.

I let the meter tick over as I stare at the buildings, taking in the manicured lawns and perfectly shaped hedges. This building screams wealth, and I can barely afford this cab fare on my own. I don't belong here, and I don't think I truly realized how much that's affecting me until now.

My driver clears his throat and I rush to apologize.

After paying the fare, I make the short trek through the gardens, taking my time to reach my condo near the back.

It's dark when I get in, meaning Nathan's still out, and when I check the time, it's not as late as I thought.

After a long, hot shower, washing away the events of the night, I brush my teeth twice and slip into my comfortable pajamas before staring at our bed, imagining Nathan crawling in behind me, his heavy arm draped over my waist as he breathes loudly in my ear.

That's if he doesn't try to start something.

A shiver runs through me and I make a split-second decision to bypass the bed, opting to sleep on the armchair in the office.

The thought of being in our bed when he gets home makes my skin crawl, and while I can't even begin to process what that means, I don't want to get in a fight about it. Especially if he's drunk.

Curling myself into a ball, I tuck my hands under my head and will myself to sleep, praying the alcohol helps me drift off.

And it must work, because before I know it, I'm being shaken awake, my head spinning as my eyes flash open.

Nathan?

Chapter Fifteen

BLAIR

I rub my eyes a few times before prying open my lids, my hooded gaze locking with Nathan's look of concern. God, of course it was Nathan. Who else did I think it would be?

His body sags, and he releases a drawn-out sigh. "Thank God," he breathes out. "You had me worried."

"Why?" I frown, squinting when he accidentally shines his phone in my face, the light momentarily blinding me.

"Shit." He moves away but the bright spots linger. "I couldn't find you. I was worried you hadn't made it home."

What? "What time is it?" I search for my phone but when I can't immediately find it, I give up, glancing at Nathan in confusion.

Nathan checks his screen before cringing. "Just after five."

"Five?" I sit up and my head throbs so painfully that I actually grab it, hoping to ease the discomfort. "Are you sure?" I frown, my confusion thickening.

The Nathan I know says that anything after midnight is *way* past his bedtime.

"I'm sure." He cringes again and the guilt in his eyes snaps me out of my grogginess.

"Are you just getting home?"

"The guys wanted to stay out, and you told me to make an effort."

I did say that, but I don't like the way he's using my words as an excuse. "Plus," he continues on, "I've been home for about thirty minutes; I was looking for you."

My brows furrow. "I'm here. You found me."

"Why aren't you in bed?"

Shit. "I fell asleep reading."

"Where's your book?"

Dammit. I internally cringe as my eyes subtly bounce around the room, but when I see one of my favorite books peeking out from under the chair, I relax. "It's there. It must have fallen."

Nathan glances in the direction I'm pointing and visibly relaxes himself, making the guilt shift to me.

"I thought that maybe you were avoiding me."

And now I feel worse. "Why?"

"Because of what I did."

What? I straighten again but still don't stand. "What did you do?" A million thoughts race through my mind, and of course, Jenna's assumption screams at me the loudest. Was she right? Is he talking about the strip club?

"I kissed you to piss off Fitzpatrick," he admits, and disappointment crushes my chest. "I was hoping it would throw him off his game."

I knew. I *knew* and yet I didn't want to believe it.

I stare at him for a beat, my mind back in the Los Angeles stadium. I should feel sick about it, but in a moment of madness, a thought hits me, and I burst out laughing.

They're both insane. Nathan *and* Zane. It's like we're back in high school. And in this instance, Zane won.

When I calm down, I blow out a breath and smile sympathetically. "While I don't like it, I understand you wanting to piss him off. Only, I thought you knew better than that. For Zane, anger is like *fuel*. Of course, he was going to play his heart out after that. Just look—" I cut myself off. *No.* We're not talking about Zane and how well I know him. "The point is, I'm not avoiding you."

"You're not?"

"No." *Not for that reason anyway.*

Nathan sighs again before stumbling forward to grab my hand. "Come on. Let's go to bed."

"I... I'm kind of awake now. I might go for a hike."

"A hike? At five."

"Yeah. Sunrise is pretty magical."

Nathan stares at me, and when his eyes roll into the back of his head, my stomach lurches. *How did I not notice how drunk he was?* Now that I'm more awake, it's obvious.

"Okay." He nods as he sways. "Go for your hike."

"Thanks." I stand and—even though I wasn't seeking permission—feel relieved as I walk past. But I only make it a step before he grabs my arm and pulls me to a stop.

"God, you smell amazing." He steps closer, crowding me in. "Come to bed. Just for a minute and then you can hike." His breath warms my skin and I curse myself when I shiver uncomfortably. *What the hell is going on?*

"Not today, Nathan. I'll miss the sunrise."

"Come on."

"Not today," I repeat, pulling my arms from his grasp as his brows furrow.

"What's going on?"

"Nothing. I told you, I want to go for a hike."

"Nah." Nathan shakes his head, his gaze a mix between hurt and disgust. "This is more than that. This is about Z—"

"Where were you tonight?" I ask, cutting in before he mentions Zane. I can't think about him right now, even though I'm pretty sure he's the reason I'm acting so strange.

Nathan recoils as though I slapped him before his face falls. "You know?"

"Know what?"

"I promise nothing happened." His throat bobs. "I didn't touch any of them."

Oh, God. My heart jolts and I swallow a lump in my throat, thankful it isn't bile.

"Who?" I play dumb. "You didn't touch who?"

"The girls." His voice comes out as a whisper. "I didn't touch them."

I cringe, and while I don't particularly want to hear about the details, his reaction suggests there's more to the story, and I can't ignore the sinking feeling in my gut.

"Where were you? And why do you look so guilty?"

"The guys said I needed a lap dance. That they all do it. I couldn't say no. I couldn't." *Jesus.* Nausea finally takes over me and when he steps closer, I step back, needing to put some distance between us. "I didn't touch her," he rushes out, his voice panicked. "You know me, Blair. You *know* me. I didn't enjoy it. I love you."

My skin prickles. Jenna was right. About everything. But at the same time, he's not the only one that messed up tonight. And like Zane said... It doesn't matter because I trust Nathan and I *do* know him.

My head drops as I run a hand through my hair. "Nathan—"

"Please, Blair." His anguished tone makes me physically ache, but when he steps forward again, I still shake my head. "Fuck." His voice strains. "I promise, nothing happened." He drops to his knees. wrapping his arms around my legs.

"Stop."

"I'm so stupid." His voice shakes. "I—"

"I believe you." I sigh, running a hand down my face. "Please stand up."

"So, you're not repulsed by me?"

"No," I say honestly. If anything, his admission eases some of my own guilt.

"And you're coming to bed?" He smiles and I feel nauseous again.

"No. I'm going—"

"Why? If you believe me, why won't you come to bed?"

I pause, my mind whirling. He's never been this pushy. "What's going on?"

"What do you mean?"

"Why are you so desperate for me to come to bed?"

His eyes widen before his expression turns. "Do I need a reason to have sex with my girlfriend?"

"No, but this isn't like you."

He glances down at his phone and it's then that I panic. Did he see me with Zane? Does he think I went back to his hotel? Is this a test?

My heart races as I wait for him to respond, waiting for the anger in his eyes, but when he finally looks up, his expression breaks me. "I want her gone, Blair. I don't want the image of that woman bouncing around in my lap to be burned into my brain. I don't want the guilt."

Holy shit. "You want me to fuck someone else out of your head?"

"What the hell, Blair? That's not... Since when do you talk like that?"

"Since my boyfriend had a lap dance and proceeded to tell me he wanted to fuck so he could forget about it. Think about that, Nathan.

You're drunk, so I'm going to give you a pass. But I'm not coming to bed. I'm going for my hike, and I suggest you forget last night ever happened."

With that, I storm past him, holding my breath as I bypass our bedroom, emotion threatening to overcome me. My hands tremble as I collect my exercise gear from the clean hamper in the laundry room, and by the time I get outside, I'm wound so tightly, I could snap.

What a freaking day, night, whatever.

Like Nathan, I need to forget the last twenty-four hours ever existed. It's time to move on. Period.

I have to.

For the next few days, Nathan's more attentive than usual while never once mentioning what happened to elicit the change. At one point, he even asks me about my job hunting, despite telling me I don't need to work.

From the outside looking in, he's the perfect boyfriend, but I can see the subtle hints of embarrassment. He's ashamed of what happened, and because of that, I'm racked with guilt.

While he was out watching half-naked dancers, I was at a hotel with Zane. And despite the fact that, like me, I'm sure Nathan knows I'd never cheat on him, emotionally, Zane has me questioning my feelings. And in the end, that's worse.

Nathan knows my history with Zane. He knows how broken I was when he left. I can only imagine the pain it's inflicting, knowing he's back in my orbit.

God knows it's inflicting a deep enough wound on me.

When Thursday night arrives, so does Jenna to meet Nathan, and I'm instantly nervous. It's not that I think she won't like him, because everybody does—my family and Zane aside— but I'm worried about what she'll say. In the short time I've known her, I've learned that she speaks her mind, and no matter how many times I've asked her *not* to mention Zane, I have a feeling she'll slip up.

Especially if she doesn't get a good vibe from Nathan, like she did with Zane.

My panic deepens as I rush to open the door, but the second I see her smiling face, all the stress escapes me.

"Hi," I sigh. "Thank you for coming."

"This place is incredible, Blair. But it's not what I imagined for you." And that's exactly why seeing her relaxes me. We been friends for less than a month but I truly believe that she knows me, more than anyone does, except maybe Z— Nope. It's just her.

"Come in. I'll show you around. The condo came furnished, but I've added a few touches of my own. Let's see if you can guess what."

"You are on. I'm going to nail this."

"I have no doubt." I smile at her giddiness, leading the way.

"So where is the man of the house?" she asks after I've shown her the living room—to which she cringed—and the office, where she immediately lit up when she saw my bookshelf.

"He's in the shower. He should be down—"

"I'm here," Nathan calls out, his timing perfect as though he planned it. "You must be Jenna."

Jenna spins to face Nathan, and I don't miss the way her eyes sweep over him in a scrutinizing gaze. "That's me," she tells him, her smile warm despite the fact it's obvious she's yet to finish her appraisal. "It's nice to finally meet you," she continues. "Thank you for inviting me over."

Nathan's genuine happiness brings about my own and I relax a little more. "You're very welcome," he says, exuding charm. "I hope you like pasta."

At that, Jenna's eyes light up. "I love it. I'm all about the carbs. Do you cook?"

"Only pasta." He winks and she laughs out loud.

"He's funny." She grins my way, and I can't say I'm shocked that she likes him. He gives off those golden retriever vibes that everyone finds endearing.

"Funny? I'll take it." He pretends to wipe sweat from his brow. "But I'm not sure Blair's ever called me funny."

"You make me laugh *all* the time."

"Not the same thing." He winks again and my heart flutters. This is the guy I fell in love with. But it feels like I haven't seen him since he moved to

California. "Anyway." He claps his hands together and beams at Jenna. "Enough about my personality traits. Has Blair shown you around?"

"She has. Actually, we were in the process. I'm getting a vibe for who you are."

"So, we're staying on my personality traits then." Nathan chuckles, and I wish more than anything that I'd see this version of him more. The genuine soul who loves life. "Tell me..." he trails off, mischief in his eyes. "How am I doing so far?" he whispers with a grimace, as though it's some big secret, and Jenna's putty in his hands as she laughs again.

"So far so good. But it will all come down to the pasta."

"Speaking of... I'm going to go and find a better recipe. Excuse me for a moment." He presses a kiss to my cheek, straightening my dress before darting off to the kitchen, and the second he's gone, I feel Jenna's stare boring a hole in the side of my head.

I hesitantly turn to face her, cringing at her wide-eyed expression. "Say it."

"You are fucked," she whispers, confusing me.

"What does that mean?"

"Oh, Blair. They both give off good vibes. How are you going to choose?"

My eyes flash to the kitchen door as my heart lodges in my throat. "Jenna," I whisper-yell. "There is *no* choice." I lower my voice as I step closer. "I'm with Nathan. That's it."

"I get that; I do. But something tells me that whatever you had with"— she mouths *Zane* and my pulse spikes—"is not over. All I'm saying is that I can see why."

My shoulders drop as I sigh. "It's over, Jen. Way over. I'm sure he's got another woman in his bed as we speak."

Dammit. I sink my head into my hands, slamming my eyes shut, instantly regretting my words. And to make matters worse, when I slowly look up again, Jenna's grinning.

"What does it matter?" she asks as if proving a point.

"It doesn't." I shake my head. "That was a stupid thing to say. Come on, I'll show you the bedrooms."

Chapter Sixteen

ZANE

The high of winning my first game back has me walking around like a god for the next week. But it was seeing Blair that really got my blood pumping. And not necessarily in a good way. No matter how I look at it, I can't seem to get my head around the fact that she's been dating that asshole. For four goddamn years. It makes me want to shake some sense into her.

Only, I know Blair—at least, I used to know her—and she's never been one to just fall into something. If they're together, she made that decision for a reason. And her reason would have been well thought out. Most likely with a pros and cons list. Or a spreadsheet.

Doesn't mean I have to like it, or accept it for that matter. No one could convince me that he's the right guy for her. She's worthy of more. Of better.

And she *used* to believe that.

I still remember one of the last arguments we had, and there were many. But in this instance, she'd said... *"I don't want to be a princess, Zane. But I deserve the world. And if I'm not* your *world, then what are we doing here?"*

It was a valid question, and one I wished I'd answered at the time, instead of telling her she was being ridiculous.

But I can't think about that now. For now, I'm choosing to focus on the present.

Blair may have walked away from me the other night, but that's the longest time we've spent together since I was nineteen, and no one can take that away from me. I knew I missed her. I've never stopped. But I didn't realize how much until I felt her warmth again and got to witness her beautiful smile.

I thought I had it committed to memory, the way she curls her lips and the little dimple she gets on the left side of her face, but fuck, my mind did not do it justice.

It was nice to see her happy. I don't think I've ever admitted how much that's been weighing on my mind. But being happy with that fucker feels like torture. She said he's good to her and I have to believe that. But that guy lives in his head. At least he did back when I knew him, and I doubt that's changed.

So much keeps playing on my mind... Like, does he even know the real Blair, or did she settle? I wanted her to move on. I wanted her to have the life she deserved, without me there as a constant reminder of the accident. But she chose Nathan. And he was there too.

So, I have to wonder...has she moved on at all?

I torture myself with thoughts of Blair for my entire drive to the stadium, but once I arrive for our Saturday practice, I shake off my thoughts, purging all negativity from my mind.

Despite everything that's been haunting me, I'm still obnoxiously happy when I enter the locker room. I'm not sure why, but it doesn't feel like that was the last time I'll see Blair, and that's enough for me.

Reed's by the door when I walk in, and even his presence makes me smile. "Any closer to being able to play?" I ask, genuinely curious this time.

He frowns and I instantly regret my question until that frown turns sympathetic. "What's going on?" *And why do I get a feeling that look is for me?*

"I'm guessing you haven't seen the news?"

"What news?" I ask casually as my stomach sinks, and when he winces, I panic. "What news?" I repeat, my mind taking me back to the night of the accident and the days following. The flashing lights. The media surrounding us. The headlines. Dread spreads through me like wildfire, and yet my body chills.

Did something happen to Blair? No, it can't have. Reed doesn't know her.

He gestures for me to move away from the door and I follow as he speaks. "There's a story about—"

"*Zane!*" D'Angelo cuts in, calling out from across the room, beckoning me over when I turn his way.

"What story?" I ask, ignoring the guy that calls the shots, too anxious to wait.

But of course, Reed doesn't ignore him. "I'd say D'Angelo's about to fill you in. You better go."

Fuck. I throw my bag down and follow him into the hallway, my mood fading fast.

"What did I do this time?" I grate when we reach the end of the corridor, being a dick for no reason, and despite the fact that he could fire me on the spot, I don't take it back.

Standing tall, I wait for Sal to argue, but he shocks me when he curses under his breath, his voice pained. "You don't know?"

"No, what the hell is going on?"

"Why don't you come to my office?"

I still for a beat, shaking my head. "No, fuck that. Tell me now. Have I been dropped? Is that it?"

"Definitely not," Sal's quick to reassure me. "You have our support, one hundred percent. But a story has come out... It's about your past in Jacksonville and—"

"Goddammit. Blair."

"Who?"

"Just a friend who doesn't need *my* past coming back to haunt her. I thought we were done with this. What are they saying?"

With an agonizingly slow breath, Sal fills me in. "Old reports from a Florida news outlet are resurfacing about you being involved in an accident a few years back. A collision that killed two young women." His voice trails off as a ringing fills my ears, along with a deafening screech that makes my head ache. My heart pounds to unbearable levels until Sal grabs my arm, his touch snapping me back to the present. "There's more." He winces as though he hates breaking this news, but he needn't worry—it's not news if I've already heard it. "The reporter says that while you weren't driving, they believe *you* caused the crash." He pauses, his expression apologetic.

But it's true.

"Did they name the driver?" I stiffen, my muscles tight.

"No."

Thank God. The tension leaves my body as I sigh.

My sister was underage at the time of the accident, so her personal details and the specifics surrounding the accident were concealed from the general public. Only those that knew us know. I wasn't sure if they'd still honor that now, years later. But thankfully they have.

"Is it big?" I ask, wondering if Reed and Sal only heard about it because they have alerts for the team, or if the world knows and I'm the only sucker here playing catch-up.

Sal cringes again and I have my answer. It's big. Which means if Blair hasn't heard yet, she soon will.

Fuck. I need to talk to her. *No,* I need to talk to Cade. Blair never wanted to talk about it back then, and I don't think that's changed.

Sal says something else, and I tune in enough to get the gist of him asking if I'm okay, or if I need anything, but I wave him off on both counts.

I'm fine. I've been through this before. I can handle it. It's other people I'm worried about. Namely Blair. She doesn't need a refresher of the shitty things that happened in her past.

All because that *asshole* is lying unconscious in the hospital. Taunting me. Making me question if I'm about to add another death to my list. Another one I got away with.

Straightening my posture, I pat D'Angelo on the arm and jog back to the locker room, walking in on a few of the guys talking about the headlines, with Luke telling them to shut up.

"Yeah, yeah. But what I don't understand is how come this never came up when they were making the show?" one of the rookies asks. "They need season two."

"Are you fucking kidding me?" Luke seethes. "You're talking about your teammates' lives."

"So?" The rookie lifts his hands in the air. "I missed out. I want to be a part of it."

"Wow. The irony," Luke muses and I actually smile.

"What irony?" the rookie asks, cockiness gone, his brows pinched in confusion.

"He means that you're just like me," I cut in, answering for Luke. "Desperate for the spotlight. But to answer your question, they never found out what I did back then because I gave them enough to stop looking."

The guys fall silent until someone curses behind me, and I don't have to turn to guess who.

But I do, finding Easton with a scowl that could crush souls. "You little fucker," he seethes. "You dragged me into the spotlight... No, actually, you dragged *my son* into the spotlight to protect yourself?"

"Yep," I say confidently, only it's not quite true. I didn't do it for me. "I'm sorry about your son. But I'd do it all again if I had to."

When our previous owner decided to produce a TV show about the team, I knew they were going to start digging, and I needed the attention to go elsewhere. In the beginning, I managed to hold them off with just my cocky persona, because Amelia—Luke's now wife and the director of the show—was a decent human being. But after she left, the producers wanted more. They needed the drama surrounding her departure to disappear, and to do that, they started looking for something bigger.

And I had the story of a lifetime.

Only, I wasn't handing it over.

Instead, I took advantage of my situation with Easton.

I figured if I gave them all the juicy details about our fight, including me sleeping with his ex, they wouldn't go digging.

I was right.

In a TV series showcasing the lives of a football team, what's more dramatic than internal fighting? Juicier than teammates fucking each other's partners? More shocking than the fact that said teammate's partner knew who she was sleeping with, and did it to piss him off? Easton's ex, Macy, *chose* me to get back at him. On purpose.

It was the perfect story to tell.

I'm not proud of it, but it worked. And as I told Easton, I'd do it again in a heartbeat.

Easton huffs under his breath and I admit, I feel bad. But I couldn't risk the accident making headlines again. For my sister. My family. And Blair.

But now that it has, the least I can do is help.

Blair came back into my life for a reason. Maybe this is it.

I make it three quarters of the way home after practice before reluctantly calling Cade. I avoid talking to him at the best of times, but discussing his sister is even less appealing, so when he doesn't answer, I consider it a win. Until he calls right back.

"You had to go and hurt someone else, didn't you? You're lucky he's not dead."

"The fuck, Cade. What kind of person says that?"

"The kind that's just finished talking to his sister because her best friend's all over the news again. Sort of. You know what I mean."

"Yep." *Unfortunately, I do.*

"Is that why you called?" he asks, already knowing the answer.

"It is. I wanted to ask if she was okay, but I can't call her."

"Why? Her number's the same."

"She blocked me."

"No way." Cade bursts out laughing and I wince. He hit a nerve.

"Way," I respond, my voice dripping in sarcasm. *God, I wish I was there to punch him.*

Cade hums and I can picture his amused expression. "Good for her. Consider this a proud big brother moment. When did she do that?"

"Seven years ago."

"*What?*" He pauses for a beat, and while the truth stings, the break gives me time to preemptively roll my eyes, despite the fact he can't see me. "Wow," he overexaggerates. "Well, there you go. I always thought she was upset over you leaving."

Fuck. I wince again. "She *was*." But that's not the only reason she blocked me.

"I—" Cade starts to say more but I don't let him. That's not why I called.

"How's she doing?"

"Not great, but she had a feeling it was coming, after you—"

"Put a guy on life support? Yeah, I get it. You know it was an accident, right?"

"Yep. That doesn't make it any easier on Blair."

"Fuck. I know. I should go and see her."

"Nope."

"Nope?"

"You need to let her deal with this herself. If she wants to speak to you, she'll unblock you and make the call."

"Yeah, that's not going to happen."

"Then you've got your answer."

I sigh. Loudly. Not bothering to hide it. "You're a dick sometimes. You better be looking out for her."

"Always. But you know what? She wants me to look out for *you*. And here I was thinking the two of you were only friends because of me."

My chest tightens but I ignore it. "You've already admitted you didn't believe that. I'm hanging up."

"Wait. I love you, man. I'm worried about you too."

"Don't be. I'm fine."

"Yeah, yeah. I knew you'd say that."

"Then we're good. Take care of Blair." I hang up as he's saying something else, but it doesn't take a genius to figure out what. *He will.* Only he's lying. Because Blair won't let him. She proved that when she asked him to look after me.

Cade's right though. I need to let her handle this the way she wants to. But fuck, it's going to be hard.

Doing the right thing, I focus on football and not much else for the next couple of weeks. But when an opportunity presents itself, I struggle to be good.

"Zane?" Reed calls out on my way into practice and I laugh incredulously. He can't help himself.

"You're back?" I say excitedly, knowing that he's not. "Congrats, man." My lips pull into a smirk and he scoffs, jokingly rolling his eyes.

"You're hilarious. I'm not here to practice; I'm here for *you*."

"How many times do I have to tell you—"

"Hayley knows Jenna," he interrupts my joking and I freeze, racking my brain for who the hell that is. Jenna. Jenna. *Wait...* My eyes widen in recognition.

"From LA?"

"Yeah. She said you might want her number, but I wasn't..."

He trails off when I curse under my breath.

"Shit. Don't tell me she's fucking with us. Hayls said she was genuine and—"

"No, it's okay. I know her. I do. I want her number." *I shouldn't. I really fucking shouldn't.*

I promised myself I'd leave Blair alone. She has my number. All she has to do is unblock me and use it.

But now Jenna's reaching out and I have to wonder why.

And she knows Hayley?

Is that some kind of kismet? Is that even the right word? Either way, there's no way I can let this gift pass.

"Give it to me. I'll get in touch."

"Done. I'll get Hayley to send it."

"Thanks." I turn to walk away until curiosity gets the better of me. "How does Hayley know her?" I ask, trying to figure out just how coincidental it is.

Reed's genuine smile lights up his face. "They're working together on a miniseries in LA. Would you believe they only have one scene together and still managed to figure out the connection?"

"Doesn't surprise me. Girls can talk. They're much better sleuths than we are."

"You're not wrong. But now that's out of the way. How are you doing?" I inhale slowly, ready to tell him I'm fine until he continues on. "Have the media been hounding you?"

I pause, my breath caught in my throat. *They haven't.* And I haven't questioned it until now. "Surprisingly not," I tell him, my mind in a spin. "Lucky me." I force a smile and Reed laughs.

"Maybe they realized it was old news."

"Here's hoping." I smile again, my cheeks hurting from the unnatural movement, when what I really want to do is scream.

Because...I seriously doubt the story has vanished.

And if it's not me they're hounding...

Who the fuck is it?

Chapter Seventeen

BLAIR

My eyes glaze over as I stare down at the phone in my hand, guilt consuming me while I will it to stop ringing. Zane's parents have been calling all morning, and I don't know what to say to them. I don't know how to help. Especially after seeing Zane. It feels like a betrayal of sorts. They should be talking to each other.

The front door rattles and I breathe a sigh of relief. Nathan's home. He was a rock for me when the accident first hit the news, and I need him to be that for me now.

"Nathan?" I call out, hearing the thud of his bag dropping to the floor. "I—"

"Of course, I'm in," he says excitedly to someone that isn't me, his voice getting louder as he approaches. "Just let me shower and I'll be there."

He hangs up as he reaches me, pressing a kiss to my cheek. "Hey, babe. I'm glad you're home." Without registering my stunned expression, he moves around me to the fridge and rummages through the contents. "The guys are all heading to Reggie's place"—his captain—"for a bonding session. We've got our biggest rivals this weekend, so they want to talk strategy."

"Don't the coaches help with that?"

"Usually, yeah." His head pops out from behind the door and he smiles. "But Reg has been playing for twelve years; he knows his stuff."

"Are you going to be late? I wanted to ta—"

"Nah. I'll be home by nine thirty. I need my beauty sleep ahead of practice."

"Okay. Do you have a min—"

His phone blares in his hand, cutting me off as his laughter fills the air. "These guys are way more full on than the Florida boys, but they're a good bunch."

He grabs an apple and brushes past me again, answering his phone as he heads down the hall. "Let me guess," he says to whoever's on the line. "You need a ride."

There's a beat of silence before he chuckles. "Of course," he continues. "I'm always here if you need me."

I choke back a laugh as my stomach sinks. *Are you sure about that, Nathan?* Because right now, I don't think I've needed you more.

For the next couple of weeks, Zane's parents call every other day to talk to me about the press hounding them. They've had calls, people showing up at their house, their workplaces.

It's a lot, and I hate that I'm here when I should be there comforting them. I don't even know why I'm here. Nathan's spent more time away than at home lately and I'm more alone than I've ever felt in my life. I understand he has commitments and away games. But even when he's here, he's never really here.

I need him to be present. Absence is *not* making my heart grow fonder, and I don't think he realizes the damage he's doing.

I'm questioning everything and don't know what to do anymore. Or who to talk to.

When I find another missed call from Zane's mom, my heart breaks. Zane's shielded expression from when he told me they hadn't spoken in a while comes back to mind, and my sadness is crushing. They've all been through so much. I can't imagine walking in their shoes. Being an outsider is difficult enough.

I'm at a breaking point when my dad calls Thursday night, but like always, I keep the smile on my face as we talk, not wanting to worry him.

"You'd tell me if it was getting to be too much for you, right?" he asks, referring to the increased media attention surrounding the accident. I smile, genuinely this time. I may not be able to see Dad, but I can picture the concerned look he's undoubtedly giving me. "You know, I'll be on the first flight out of here."

"I do. Thanks, Dad. But I'm fine. I feel awful for everyone else involved."

"Is Nathan there? Is he helping you?"

"Of course," I lie, hoping the slight lift in my voice doesn't give me away, as longing works its way into my chest. "I'm lucky to have him." At least I was. Now I'm not so sure.

"Mm-hmm." Dad grumbles, his skepticism rivaling Cade's.

"*Dad*," I scold jokingly, but it's not lost on me that he's not far off base with his reaction this time.

"I know, Princess. You can look after yourself."

"I can and I will. I'll talk to you on Sunday, okay?"

"Wouldn't miss it. Love you."

He hangs up and the happiness instantly drops from my face. It's just one thing after another. I still don't have a job, Zane's parents are looking to me to solve all their problems, and Nathan's MIA.

I don't bother checking the time when I fall into bed on my own— once again left waiting for Nathan to get home—but I'm half asleep when he softly shakes me awake.

"Hey, baby," he whispers, wrapping his arm around my waist as he slides in behind me, his semi hard erection pressing into my ass. "I've missed you. I didn't expect tonight to run so late. I—"

"It's fine."

"No, it's not. I said I'd be home and I wasn't." There's genuine remorse in his tone as he pulls me against him and tightens his hold, breathing into my neck. "Forgive me, please?"

The sincerity in his voice hits me and for a moment, I lie still, letting myself breathe now that I'm wrapped in the protection of his arms.

But I should have known my peace couldn't last.

Nathan's erection grows while he gently caresses my stomach, snaking his hand under my silk camisole, his fingers dancing toward my breasts. I hiss back a sharp breath and he mistakes it for what it's not.

"You know I love your stomach, babe." He squeezes me beneath his palm. "But if you're worried, I'm sure there's something we could do. You don't have to suck in."

What? "That's not—"

"I'm never going to stop loving you, no matter what."

I squirm in his arms because... *What the hell does that mean?*

His hand drifts back down my body until he brushes the waistband of my shorts, and when his fingers glide beneath the elastic, my heart jolts violently, my insides knotting uncomfortably. This isn't right.

"Nathan, stop." I grab his hand to still him, wriggling out of his hold. "I've had an awful day and I'm not in the mood."

"You're never in the mood anymore. We haven't had sex in *weeks*."

"I—"

"Before you blame me, I know it's my fault. Believe me, I do. I've been busy. But I promise, you're still my number one, even if it doesn't feel that way."

A moment of guilt settles in my chest until I realize it shouldn't. He can acknowledge his faults as much as he wants, but he completely ignored the fact that I'd had a bad day. "I need you home more, Nathan. I've had a lot going on and—"

"You're right. I'll try harder. I promise."

"That—"

"Come here." He pulls me into him and I involuntarily stiffen. "I promise. I'll keep it PG," he adds in reaction to my obvious rejection. "I just want to hug you. I love you."

Tears prick my eyes, but I let him hold me, praying he doesn't notice. And it's in that moment, when I'm overcome with resignation, that panic takes over me.

He doesn't feel like my Nathan anymore. Not since moving here.

But the scariest part is, I don't think he's the one that's actually changed.

I don't think I'm the same Blair.

With a constant fog clouding my brain, I go through the motions over the next week. But while internally, I'm a mess, I must play my part well, because Nathan's none the wiser. And I'm not sure if that's a good or bad thing.

I've even got a smile plastered on my face as I hang up from speaking to Zane's dad, and for the briefest of seconds, I let myself believe that it's real.

"They're going to be okay," I mumble to myself, sighing in relief. "They're going to be okay." I fall back onto our rock-hard couch, immediately jumping up again. "Why is this couch so damn uncomfortable?" My fists clench in frustration. "Why is it *all* so damn uncomfortable?" I throw my hands in the air as Nathan appears out of nowhere, offering me a sympathetic grin that makes bitterness fill my mouth.

"Come here." He opens his arms wide but I shake my head.

"A hug won't fix this."

"The couch?" He raises a brow with a knowing smile.

"Nothing will fix that *stupid* couch. This isn't about that."

It's about Zane's parents, it's about the stupid media frenzy, and it's about Sierra. How is it that for years no one has mentioned the accident, but Zane appears in my life and now it's all coming out? I can't handle this again. I barely survived it the first time.

"Of course this isn't about the couch." Nathan steps forward until I shake my head again, making him pause. "You've been a little off for days, but I can't help if you won't tell me what's going on."

Days? Is he kidding me?

"I've *tried* to talk to you." I let the days comment slide. "Several times. But you're always too busy. You're out with the guys, or taking on extra practice and training. While I'm stuck here. Alone. Dealing with the fallout of the accident again. I'd moved on. And now the past is back to mess with me."

"No, you hadn't."

"What?"

"You hadn't moved on." He stabs me with a metaphorical knife and I gape. "I'm surprised you're even telling yourself that. Yes, I've been busy. But I'm not blind. Things have changed since you saw Zane again. That's not the reaction of someone that's moved on."

My heart jolts, and for the first time in way too long, I allow myself to feel. To encompass every emotion I've been avoiding, letting it all come to the surface, and it's thick. "You think everything I'm feeling is because of

Zane?" I scoff, my expression reflecting the disbelief that I feel. *Is it hot in here?* I inhale sharply. The air around me is stifling.

"Am I wrong?" he challenges, and I open my mouth to refute but he keeps talking. "You miss him. And while I've never liked it, I've always understood it. He was your first love. He's going to leave a mark. But he left and you promised me that door had been permanently closed. But it's not. It's wide open again. You haven't moved on from that part of your life at all, but you should. For your own sake, not mine."

My brows furrow and a hysterical laugh bursts out of me. "That's not why I'm hurting. Yes, it was hard seeing Zane again. And confusing. But I'm struggling because none of this feels right. I moved for you, and now I see you less than I ever did. I'm upset because the accident that changed my life is back in the spotlight and you're not here to help me through it. I'm breaking because Zane's parents are getting harassed by the media again, and I'm not there when they need me. I'm here."

"They shouldn't be your problem, Blair. Zane should be there. He should never have left them to pick up the pieces alone."

I freeze and my heart sinks as realization hits me. He doesn't get it. And maybe he *never* did. But he was there for me, and I let myself fall for him.

He was amazing back then. But now... "Of everything I just confessed, the one thing you're arguing about is the one thing that doesn't concern you. You're right, Zane should be there for them. But they've always been family to me, and they called *me* asking for support. You know me—I'd never say no to someone asking for help. It's one of the reasons you fell in love with me, right?"

"It is. But it's hard to hear about your ex's parents. It's—"

"Stop," I cut him off. *Dammit.* He still has no clue. "This isn't about that. Not entirely. I understand that's hard for you; I do. But that should be the least of your worries because the problem is closer to home. Can't you feel it?"

"I—"

"Wait. Before you say anything, this has nothing to do with Zane. I've been lost since moving here, and I've tried talking to you about it, but you brush it off...telling me it takes time. The thing is, I've had time. I've got nothing but time. I have *nothing* else. And instead of being here for me, helping me through it, you've been spending your time away."

"Come on, Blair. You know I've been doing that for *you*." He reaches for my hand and for some stupid reason, I let him take it. "It's going to take time for us both to get settled. That's all this is. We can't just pack up and leave. We're better than that. Change is hard." He squeezes my hand and smiles sympathetically. "Just you wait... By Christmas you're going to be wondering why you were so worried in the first place."

What? "You're not listening," I whisper, my chest aching as I finally pull back my hand. What am I still doing here? "This isn't working."

"Maybe not now, but it will."

"No." I shake my head. "This is bigger than you're thinking. I need to figure out how I feel."

"About what?" For the first time, a moment of panic mars Nathan's features. "About us?"

"About *everything*."

"Including Zane."

"No, Nathan. I told you; this isn't about him. We haven't spoken since he was in LA weeks ago. I'm not sitting here questioning my feelings for him; I'm questioning my feelings for *you*. I'm questioning *us*. Our relationship."

"Blair," Nathan voice breaks and his crestfallen expression makes me want to take it all back. I want to pull him into my arms and tell him it's all going to be okay. But I can't. The tension surrounding us is so thick it's screaming at me to walk away because staying wouldn't be fair to either of us.

"I'm scared, Nathan," I admit, emotion clogging my throat. "I don't want to lose you. But..." I trail off as my heart tears in two.

"But?"

"Too much has changed between us and I don't—"

"Fuck." He shakes his head over and over before looking me in the eyes. Really looking at me. And it makes me wonder if he's ever truly looked at me before. He must see something in my expression because he steps forward and palms my face, his eyes wide with concern. "I'll be better," he promises, staring down at me. "I'll make sure I'm home more. I'll help out around the condo. Hell, I'll buy a new couch. I'll buy you anything you want. Just please don't give up on us. *Please*. You haven't even given me a chance. This is all coming out of nowhere."

I'm shaking my head before he's finished talking. "It's not. I've been feeling this way since we moved."

"Why didn't you tell me?"

"I tried."

"No." Nathan states firmly, rearing back. "That's not something I'd forget. You've never once said that." His nostrils flare before he curses under his breath. "What can I do to fix this?" His voice is rushed. Panicked. Unsteady. And I feel bad. *I* feel bad.

"It's not that easy. There isn't a quick fix."

"There *has* to be. I can't lose you. You said you were happy to move to LA. You said it would be good to get away. I wouldn't have come—"

"Yes, you would have. Football is your dream, Nathan. It always has been and I wanted this for you. I've dreamed of being a football wife. Of being there when you rise to your full potential. To fame. But something changed in me. And now, every time you walk out that door, I'm torn between resentment and guilt. Resentment because you're leaving me behind, and guilt because I'm happy to see you go."

"Jesus Christ." He rakes a hand though his hair and his expression almost breaks me. "Is there anything I can do to change your mind?" His eyes plead with me to say yes, but I can't shake the feeling that if I stay, we're both going to crumble.

"You can give me time."

"Fuck. You don't need time. You need to stay so we can work this out."

"I can't."

"Let me fix this? I'll do anything. I need you by my side."

My already broken heart shatters as tears coat my eyes. Nathan's not a bad guy, and I hate doing this to him, but he's not good for me.

He may be willing to do something now that he knows there's a problem, but I need someone who puts me first before things fall apart.

Or maybe...I need to be alone. To find myself again.

Nausea consumes me as I lose my breath, the air around me so thick it feels like a knife slicing my throat. And for once, Nathan notices.

"Blair." He rushes forward, pulling me against him. "Breathe with me. Please." I take in a few quick breaths but it doesn't help. "Slowly, Blair. Deep breaths."

Doing as asked, I breathe in through my nose until my belly fills and release it slowly, feeling my body relax. It only takes a few breaths and my head clears.

"Thank you."

"Anytime. I always want to be here for you."

"I know. It kills me to be at this point."

"I don't think you want this. You just had a panic attack over it."

"No. That's not what that was. I'm scared of starting over. But I still think it's the right thing to do."

"Blair, please."

"I need air. No, I need *space*."

"What kind of space?"

"I'm going to ask Jenna if I can stay with her for a few days. I'll see how I feel after that."

"Please don't do that. I need you, Blair. I—"

"No, you don't." I cup his cheek, a soft smile tugging at my lips. "You've never needed me. You've got your teammates, and you've got football. You'll be okay."

"Blair."

"It's just a few days." I wave him off and turn to leave until his next question stops me in my tracks.

"Is it?" he asks, his voice breaking. "Is it really *just* a few days?"

I pause, his words making me falter. The truth is... "I don't know. But I can't figure it out until I'm gone."

CHAPTER EIGHTEEN

BLAIR

Jenna pouts, her expression pinched as she squeezes my arm. "I'm sorry I have to go, but I'm only filming for a few hours today." Her mood lifts, and she smiles expectantly.

"Jenna, I told you. I don't want to get in the way."

"You're not." She rolls her eyes and I appreciate the jokingly flippant response. She's keeping it light because God knows, I've got enough heavy in my life. "I love having you around."

"Thanks, Jenna." A sigh escapes me, and a little of that weight lifts from my shoulders. It's been five days since I walked out on Nathan and I haven't gone back.

I thought I'd miss him like crazy, but instead, I'm discovering things about the person I've become that I didn't realize. Things I never would have considered normal before.

Like the fact that I seek approval from Jenna whenever I want to put on the TV or listen to music. After cooking us a meal, I asked if there's anything she wanted me to change the next time I made it. Or if it tasted okay. While I was eating it, knowing full well it tasted fine. Great even.

I'd never noticed the things I did for Nathan, and being here made me understand why I've been so desperate to find a new job. My work was the only part of my life he didn't have a say on. He couldn't. It had nothing to do with him. Except when he wanted me to stay home.

As scary as it is to process what's changed in me, or why, the feelings I thought I had aren't there anymore. The love I once had has shifted and is fading. Fast. I don't know what to do anymore.

"Hey." Jenna snaps her fingers in front of my face, shaking her head. "No moping, remember?"

"Yes." I force a smile, a rushed laugh escaping me. "I won't mope." At least I'll try.

"Promise?"

"I promise." *To try*. "In fact, I think I might go for a hike. I want to visit the national forest. Get some fresh air into my lungs."

"Oh, yeah? Where? Which part?" Jenna's excitement has my smile widening for real, and for the first time since I left Nathan, I feel a spark of something new.

"I want to walk up to the Mount Wilson Observatory."

"Ooh, yes. You'll love that trail. It's difficult but beautiful."

"Sounds perfect. If I can get out of my head for long enough to enjoy it."

"I know you usually like to be at one with nature, but why don't you listen to music? It could help." She scrunches her nose and I laugh.

"Good idea. I might do that. Now enough worrying." I spin her toward the door, walking her forward. "You have to go."

"What time do you think you'll be back?" she asks over her shoulder as I continue guiding her toward the exit.

"I'll leave in the next hour, so maybe four?"

"Great, I'll make sure I'm home by then."

"Thank you for this, Jenna." I pause, letting her go so she can turn around. "I honestly don't know what I would have done without you." My eyes bounce around her space, and my chest warms.

"I'd like to think you would have kicked him out." She smiles comically and my smile falls.

"This isn't because of him. It's me."

"No, babe." She grabs my arm, giving it a squeeze. "It's not you at all. You moved here for him, and I'm glad you did, but you've been a little bit miserable and he's done nothing to fix that."

"But—"

"If you say it's not his job, I'm going to have to slap some sense into you. He's your boyfriend. Even if it's not his job, he should still *want* you to be happy. No matter how much I like him as a person, I don't like that. He's barely even tried."

"He says he is."

"So you said. But he should be trying harder. Why isn't he banging down my door to see you?"

"He's called."

"Called?" She waves her hands in a wild gesture. "Big deal. You deserve someone who will fight for you until their dying breath." Her nose scrunches again and I laugh.

"That's a little fairytale-esque. You don't believe in that stuff."

"I don't believe in it for *me*. But for you, I can see it. Would you prefer your life was a villain origin story?"

"No, I'd prefer my life wasn't dramatic at all."

Jenna releases a slow breath as she nods. "You're right. You deserve a boring life. A cookie-cutter husband. And two point five kids."

"Thank you. That's the nicest thing you've ever said to me." I fake a smile and she bursts out laughing.

"Shut up. You don't want that. But you don't want this either. You'll find your thing."

My body deflates as her words relieve some of the built-up tension. "I hope so."

"I *know* so." She squeezes my arm again. "Now I better go or they'll kill off my character. Another one of my characters."

"I thought they were doing that anyway?"

"They are. But not for another few episodes."

"Oh, yes. Go. Go. Go."

With a smile, she kisses me on the cheek and rushes off, waving one last time before the door shuts behind her.

The instant she's gone, a frown replaces my smile.

I may not know what I want, or how I'm supposed to move forward, but one thing's for sure... I don't like where I'm at. And something has to change.

Taking Jenna's advice, I adjust my earbuds and set off on my trek, a 90s pop playlist keeping me company. But as I trudge through the thick of the forest, smiling at the passersby, I couldn't tell you a single song that played. I may be physically present, but my mind is back in my condo, staring at my side of the bed, half made, wondering where it all went wrong.

Was it me? Should I have tried harder to settle in?

Or is Nathan right, and Zane had something to do with my change of heart?

Yes, I was worried about moving and work before I left Florida, before Zane came back into my life, but I wasn't questioning things like I am now. Maybe I would have worked harder if he'd never walked back into my life.

The weight of my issues slows me down for the first couple of miles, but as the elevation peaks and I hit my stride, the solace finally takes over, a calmness settling in my chest.

Like it always does.

"Stronger" by Britney Spears comes on, and a lightness fills me. There's even a bounce in my step.

I can get through this.

I deserve to be happy. If I want a cookie-cutter husband and two point five kids then that's what I'll have. I don't want that. But the point is…it's time to figure out what I *do* want and refuse to settle for anything less.

With or without Nathan.

My stomach tenses at the thought, but I put on a smile and shake it all off.

I've got this. I've—

"Are you kidding me right now?" I jolt as Zane steps into my line of sight, and the tension comes rushing back. *Goddammit.*

"Blair?" Zane's gaze widens in fake confusion and I roll my eyes. "What are you—"

"Cut the crap, Zane. What do you want?"

He raises his hands in surrender, but I see through the lie before he gets the chance to voice it. He's here for me. And I'll bet anything Jenna sent him.

"I'm enjoying the sights," he muses, his gaze traveling slowly from my face to my legs, his smirk making me squirm. "What about you?" he asks, his eyes meeting mine when he completes his inspection.

"I'm leaving." Spinning on my heels, I head back the way I came, but throw him one last comment over my shoulder, annoyed that he ruined my calm. "Don't follow me."

I can't believe they set me up.

I take a few more steps, determined not to let him get to me, but at the last second, pettiness takes over, and I spin back around. "And if you want sights..." I call out, holding my arms wide to gesture to our beautiful surroundings, "enjoy this," I snap, flipping him off.

I'm smiling when I turn around, but as soon as I'm facing away from him, my breath hitches and the fight leaves me.

Why can't my life be easy?

Why does this have to be so hard?

CHAPTER NINETEEN

ZANE

Can't say I didn't see that reaction coming. I was prepared for it. It's why I dressed for the occasion, knowing I was going to be chasing after her one way or another. You'd think I'd love the thrill of the chase being a competitive man, but Blair and I are way past that, and I'm thankful she chose down. I'd rather chase her toward her car than wander around for hours with no idea how far she's willing to go.

She picks up speed and I huff out a laugh. This isn't going to be fun. But I'm committed now.

"Blair, wait." I jog to catch up to her, chuckling again when she huffs adorably. "Jenna's worried about you and—"

She stops abruptly, whipping around to face me, and I almost run into her. "You admit it then? You admit this is a setup."

I wince, a hint of regret plaguing me. But again...I'm committed. "Do you think I'm here for a casual stroll?"

"I don't know. A little part of me was hoping the whole team was here for a bonding session. Any reason but the truth."

"Sorry." I raise my hands in a "what are you going to do" motion, further pissing her off. "I've only got the truth."

"Sometimes I wish people would lie more."

"No, you don't."

"There you go again, acting as if you know me. Why are you here?" With her arms folded over her chest, she stares at me deadpan, and I pause, waiting for her to start tapping her foot, because I feel like it's coming.

"Well?" She taps her foot twice and I hold back a laugh because now is clearly not the time.

"I told you. I'm here for you. Jenna's worried about you. She used the word 'moping' multiple times."

"I'm not moping." She forces a smile but it's obviously fake, and I believe Jenna more than I had previously.

"Blair—"

"No." She shakes her head, backing away. "God, this makes me so mad." She rakes a hand through her wild curls, and I follow the movement until she groans under her breath. "How did I miss it? So what? You decided to exchange numbers while I was in the bathroom at your hotel?"

"No."

"Was it really about me? Or did you want to fuc— Wait." Her brows furrow as her gaze shifts to mine. "No?"

"No." I smirk, not at all annoyed about the jealousy in her tone. "We didn't exchange numbers back then."

"Jesus. Did she steal your number from my phone?" Blair turns away, lost in thought while my smile widens. "That's so unlike her. I think. I mean, I don't really know her that well and—"

"She didn't steal my number, B. But that leads to something much more interesting... You still have my number?" I bounce my eyebrows, and the cutest little groan escapes her.

"Don't get ahead of yourself. It's only because I forgot to delete it. I've blocked you, you know?"

"I do. You can't get anything past me."

"God, you are so infuriating. Why are you here? And how are you and Jenna in contact if you didn't exchange numbers?"

"Carrier pigeon," I deadpan and the second the words leave my mouth, I lean back, putting some space between us, prepared to dodge a strike. That wasn't the best thing to say. But if she's mad at me, at least she's *feeling* something. And from what Jenna told me, she's been out of it for days, walking around like a zombie.

"Fuck you, Zane," Blair snaps, racing forward to poke me in the chest. "If you can't take this seriously, I'm leaving."

She turns again, but she's slow to walk away. She doesn't want to go. And while I could use that to my advantage, instead, I do as she asked.

"I'm sorry, B. I'm only here because Jenna thought you might need a friend." *And I missed you.*

"*She's* my friend." She turns back to face me.

"Someone you've known for longer than five minutes."

"Ugh." She sighs. "Why would she possibly think that someone should be you? You don't know me anymore than she does. I'm not the girl I was back then. I'm not even sure you'd call us friends."

Jesus. That stings. Though she's not wrong. If someone had asked me a few months back if I was still friends with Blair, I would have said no. But that was for my own sanity more than anything else.

"How did Jenna get your number?"

"She didn't. I got hers."

"How?" She stares at me in confusion before seemingly shaking off her thoughts. "Why?"

"She's working with the girlfriend of my teammate. They're on a TV show together."

"She's working with Hayley?"

"You know Hayley?" My brows furrow.

"No, but I remember her from the hospital."

"Of course. Well, yeah. They're starring together and somehow figured out they both knew me."

"And the why?"

"I don't know, B. I haven't been able to stop thinking about you since —" I cut myself off when two guys stop within earshot, both of them staring my way as they hover.

Blair frowns until she follows my gaze, releasing a huff. "Yes, he's *that* football player." She shoots them a glare. "And no, you can't take a photo with him."

"Woah, B." My eyes widen, impressed, as the guys walk away, mumbling not so quietly under their breaths. I mostly ignore them until their words register.

"The fuck did you say?" I step forward, ready to go after them until something, or more specifically some*one*, stops me.

The guys laugh, elbowing each other. "I said you need to control your mutt."

That's what I thought. *Little fucker.* "Who the hell do you think you are?" Blair tightens her hold on my tee but it's not enough to stop me, and when I break free, I feel her behind me as she wraps her arms around my waist.

"Oh, sorry, man, looks like *she's* controlling *you*."

"Motherfucker." I grab Blair's hands to break free but she locks her fingers together, holding on for dear life.

"Leave it, Zane. Please." She tries to keep her tone even but her pitch rises at the end.

"Fine." I give in, deflating in her hold. "You can let go now."

"Nope. Not until they leave."

Standing her ground, she waits, her hold on me locked tight while the guys laugh.

If I cared at all about the world's perception of me, I'd probably feel emasculated, but instead, I smile along with them. This isn't a bad place to be.

However, I know how to get her to stop.

"Feel free to lower your hands a little, B," I taunt, desperate to get another little rise out of her. "If we're going to be stuck like this, why not be productive?"

"Zane!" she squeals and, just as expected, jumps back, releasing me so fast you'd think she'd been burned. "You can't say that."

"I meant you could scratch an itch for me. What were you thinking?"

"That you're an asshole."

"An asshole that you care about."

"I don't."

"You don't? Then why not let me go after those fuckers?"

"Because it's my fault they got annoyed." Her expression drops, along with her shoulders. "I'm sorry I did that. I shouldn't have said anything. You've got your reputation to uphold and—"

"What the fuck? You have nothing to be sorry about. Something like that isn't going to ruin my reputation. I've done way worse, and even if I hadn't, it's not on you to hold back because of me."

"Still, I—"

"No, those guys were assholes. And what they said..."

"It's just words. And those words affect me less than you going after them affects you."

"Not true. At all. Has Nathan made you—"

"No. It's not that." She stares at me confidently, but I don't miss the way her voice softens. She's lying.

"You deserve better," I tell her, instead of specifically accusing that asshole of being a dick. And then, to save myself an angry retort, I move on. "Question, though... What does '*that* football player' mean?"

"Huh?"

"You said 'yes, he's *that* football player.'"

"Oh, ah. I meant nothing by it."

I bite back a smirk, letting her off the hook, happy in the knowledge that she's been keeping track of me. "Whatever you say, Little B. But now that's out of the way, are we going up or down?"

"Up." She smiles, pointing toward the peak of the mountain while I groan. Not the response I was hoping for.

"Up it is." Grabbing a stick, I take a few steps before realizing I'm alone, a laugh bursting out of me.

I spin around to find her on her way down, flipping me off in a move she seems to have mastered. And honestly, it makes my cock twitch. "You wound me, B," I call out, jogging once again to catch up with her. "I thought we were getting along." I chuckle to myself until she stops, hitting me with a pleading gaze.

Her eyes close as she sucks in a breath, and when they open again, there's an emptiness there that breaks me.

"I get that this is some big joke to you. But seeing you again is tearing me apart."

"Blair—"

"No, wait." She raises a hand between us, and I pause, my stomach in knots. *This isn't a joke to me.* At all. But I can't seem to stay the fuck away from her now that I've seen her again. She's like my old Blair but different, and just like back then, I want to get to know every part of her. She's always had a power over me, and time hasn't taken that away from her. "Before you say anything, before you act like we didn't go our separate ways for a reason, I need you to listen to me."

"I can do that."

"Good." She pauses, smiling at a family that walks past, her expression friendly until they're gone. "I know why you left. I'm not disputing that and I don't blame you for it. But I've spent *years* picking up the pieces of not only my own shattered life but your parents' too."

What?

"They needed someone to make sense of it all." She answers my unspoken question. "And I was the one they chose."

Fuck, my chest burns as I almost want to rub away the pain. "That's... I... They shouldn't have done that. That wasn't your burden to bear."

"What was I supposed to do? Ignore them, like you did?"

Her words cut me like a razor blade but I don't let her see it. This isn't about me. This is about what she went through. Though I'm shocked she thinks that way. I thought she knew me better than that.

"I'm sorry, you're right," I say instead of telling her how often I called them. How much I cared. She doesn't want to hear that right now. She wants to hear that I was wrong. That her efforts were just. "I should have been there for them. That responsibility shouldn't have fallen to you."

"It's too late for that now. But I appreciate the apology."

"Must be a rarity for you."

"What?"

Dammit, Zane. Why can't I ever keep my mouth shut? "Nothing." I smile. "Again, I'm sorry."

"It wasn't nothing."

"Fine, don't hate me, but I was referring to the fact that your golden boy never does anything wrong. In his eyes anyway. I can't imagine he apologizes much."

Blair shakes her head, but instead of snapping back at me like I expect, she laughs. She laughs so hysterically that people start to stare. "God, this is so *fucked up*." She almost yells the last part and groans out loud, burying her face in her hands. "I—"

"B," I whisper-yell, my eyes shooting to another family walking past. "I'm sorry. It's been a tough month for her and—"

"Oh, God." Blair drops her hands, and her face pales. "Oh, God. Oh, God."

"Not making it better," I say under my breath.

"I'm sorry," she blurts as the family moves on. "So sorry," she calls after them, sincerely worried, but before she can say any more, I cover her mouth with my hand.

"The damage is done, B. *Relax*."

Blair's eyes narrow and I instantly regret my choice of words. Of all the things I've said today, this is the one I'll be killed for.

Covering my hand with her own, she bites down on my flesh before shoving me away. "Relax?" She repeats my word back to me and I cringe.

"B—"

"No." She deflates, the fight gone. "I want to go home."

"Let me walk you—"

"*No*. You shouldn't have come back here. We said our goodbyes years ago. That was supposed to be our ending."

"But it wasn't. I kept my promise. I let you live your life. But then you were there and—"

"It's not fate, Zane. Don't try and pretend you believe that."

"I'm not. I just refuse to let you go again." My own honesty shocks me, but the second I say it, a weight lifts. It almost killed me leaving her seven years ago. I'm not sure I can go through that again. But also...I don't want to.

"That's the thing though..." Blair's gaze softens and she trails off, releasing a slow breath. "You don't have me, Zane. There's nothing to let go of."

I hiss, her words piercing my chest as my own fight leaves me.

Why does that hurt so much?

Chapter Twenty

BLAIR

Zane stills, and I find myself doing the same, a breath caught in my throat. For the first time, I think I got through to him. Only now that I have, I feel sick about it.

Throughout this entire conversation there's been an air of cockiness surrounding him. Actually, it's always been there. He wears it like armor. Now that it's gone, I want to take everything back.

"Zane, I—"

"No, I get it. I do, but you can't deny that it's weird we ran into each other again, after all these years. I realize what I'm saying sounds crazy. I've never believed in that shit, and I still don't. But you're *here*, standing in front of me. That has to mean something. I think."

His face contorts and I can't help but smile at his confusion. This whole exchange is not very Zane-like and he knows it.

"You're smiling?" He bounces his eyebrows, his own smile forming.

"I am. But you've got it all wrong."

"How so?"

"For one... Technically *you're here*. And that's not by fate. You knew where I was. It's basically stalking."

Zane's smile morphs into a smirk and a little of his cockiness returns. "It's completely stalkerish, but I wasn't referring to this. I was talking about *you* being a nurse at the hospital I was taken to and *you* being at my first game back. Both odd occurrences. Not to mention the fact that you live in California now."

Letting my head fall back, I look at the sky and count down from three to relax myself. *Fucking fate.* "If everything happens for a reason then why do I feel like moving here was a mistake? Why can't I find a job? Why are Nathan and I—" *Jesus.* Slamming my eyes shut, I wince, cursing under my breath. *Why the hell would I say that out loud?*

With a sigh, I open my eyes to find Zane staring back at me, concern in his gaze. "Ignore that. I'm going." I wave over my shoulder as I spin to leave.

"No, wait." Zane's calloused fingers curl around my wrist, and a shiver runs through me. "What do you mean you can't find a job? I thought there was a nurse shortage."

"Way to rub it in." I force a grin as he spins me to face him. "Thanks for that."

"Fuck. No. That's not what I meant."

"I know." I blow out a breath, my cheeks puffing in the process, hoping it will distract me from the pit forming in my stomach. "I've been asking myself the same question. But I don't have enough experience. I have *no* experience in California. It's like they believe nursing differs between states. I went through the right channels. I filled out all the right paperwork. But no one is hiring." My cheeks heat with embarrassment and I avert my gaze. "Or maybe they're not hiring *me.*"

"Shit." Zane releases my wrist and I instantly miss the warmth. "I'm sorry. God, you must be hating that." He runs a hand through his hair, visibly upset on my behalf. "Staying home was never your thing. Is there something else you can do in the meantime? To get that feeling back?" He glances away, lost in thought, and my lips part in awe at his assessment. His correct assessment. "What about your writing? I imagine that would keep you busy and—"

"What?"

"Your writing?" He frowns, clearly confused by my question. "I know you're a nurse now. But you were always writing when we were younger."

"I haven't written for a long time. It was a silly dream and—"

"What's silly about it?"

"Okay, maybe not *silly* because plenty of people write. But it was selfish. I was doing it for me. Because I liked to escape. Nursing helps others."

"The fuck." Zane frowns, shaking his head. "I seem to remember a big spiel you gave Cade when he questioned why you wanted to be a writer more than anything else. Do you need me to remind you of that?" This time when my eyes widen, he notices and smirks. "Yeah, I remember a lot about you, B."

"That was then. This is now."

"So, people these days *don't* need an escape from their stressful lives. They *don't* need books to make them smile, characters to help them believe in love, stories to give them strength. Hope."

Jesus. His memory is almost word-perfect. I can still picture that moment. Me putting Cade in his place, Zane giving me a slow clap at the end.

"I still believe in all of that. But being a writer doesn't save lives. It wouldn't have saved—"

"Agree to disagree on that one." Zane abruptly cuts me off and I stumble over Sierra's name. "If it's not what you want, I'll drop it."

"Okay, thanks." That's oddly respectful for Zane and I'm not entirely buying it. He'd usually push me on something like that. It's what I love— loved about him. Although, I can't help but notice it's the second time he's changed the subject when the topic has moved to his sister. Or close to her. This time I couldn't get her name out. Is this his way of avoiding the tension that initially tore us apart?

"We don't need to get into this," I say, letting him off the hook so we don't end up in unwanted territory again.

"I want to." He motions for me to start walking and settles beside me. "I'm just trying to get my head around the change. So, you're looking for a nursing job?"

"I am." I nod, giving in since we're at least moving in the right direction. To my car.

"Okay. What's Nathan doing to help you? Has he asked around? Spoken to the medical team at the Suns?"

"What? No. He's new to the team. He needs to focus on himself for now and—"

"Bullshit."

I scoff at his remark. "It's not bullshit, Zane. Stop trying to paint him as the bad guy. He was around. He *stayed*."

Zane freezes, his hands balling into fists. "He was *around*? Do you really want me to respond to that? If he hadn't been *around*, maybe none of this would have happened."

My breath hitches as grief overwhelms me. "*Zane.*"

"No, Blair. I get it, you love him and you hate me, but don't pretend he didn't play a part in all of this. He's not Mr. Innocent."

He stands tall, ready for a fight, but I'm not prepared to give him one. It hurts too much.

"I don't hate you, Zane." My shoulders drop as I sigh.

"What?"

"I don't hate you. I never hated you. How could I when I'm the reason you left?"

"B—"

"No, please. Maybe we need this to move on. Maybe that's the reason you're here. The reason Jenna's working with Hayley. The reason I'm in California and attended your first game after your injury. We could get closure. We never really had that."

"Is that what you want?"

"It's what's right." I start walking again and Zane strides to catch up, grabbing my arm to stop me.

"That's not what I asked."

"I know," I sigh, hitting him with a soft smile. "But that's all I've got."

"Then what do you want from me? To move on."

"I want you to tell me that we did the right thing. That you leaving was the right decision."

He thinks on that for a moment and I nervously worry my lip. "Are you happy with Nathan?" he finally asks, pinning me with his gaze. "I know you're not happy living here and not having a job, but does he make you happy? Because if that's a yes...we did the right thing."

Zane holds my stare, the pain obvious in the depth of his eyes, and when I hesitate for less than a second, he notices.

"I lost my best friend." I pause, wanting to tell him I lost him too, but I don't. I hold that truth close to my heart. "It took a while to be happy again. But I got there. I did." I'm not exactly answering his question, but it's close enough. "What about you?" I ask, shifting the focus. "You said so yourself—you couldn't stay because you'd constantly be reminded of Sierra. Did leaving work? Or did you take her memory with you?"

"That's not what this is about, B. That's all in the past. I want to know how you feel *now*. In the present." He once again changes the topic, and I can't move on.

"Zane, I think..." I trail off as a thought hits me. "Can you say her name?" I whisper, my breath catching as the question leaves my mouth.

"What?" Zane releases a breathy laugh.

"Sierra. Can you say her name?"

"Of course I can. But like I said, this isn't about that. It's—"

"Say it," I cut him off and he sighs, running a hand down his tortured face.

"Why?"

"Because I need to hear it from your lips."

"*Why*?" he repeats, his voice straining, his fingers curling into the fabric of his pants.

"Because you are the *only* one in this entire world that knows what she meant to me, the only person who understands. She was like a sister to me. Hell, I thought we'd be in-laws one day. I think about her all the time, and I hate the thought of you pushing her from your mind."

Zane's expression falls, and I swear I see water in his eyes before he turns away, schooling his features. And when he glances back, his expression is stoic.

"I will never forget her, B. But *please* don't make me say her name." His voice cracks, and he pauses for a beat, before whispering two words that break me. "I can't."

"Zane—"

"No, B. *Please*. I'm okay. I promise." He glances down at his watch, shaking his head. "I should let you walk. I know you, and I bet my life savings that you probably came here to think. I shouldn't have interrupted."

God-freaking-dammit. My chest aches and I desperately try not to compare him to Nathan but... "How the hell do you know me so well? Did Jenna tell you that too?" Even as I say that, I know that I'm wrong. Jenna wouldn't have said that. He just *knows*. "I never hiked back when you knew me," I say under my breath, struggling to process the feeling of comfort welling up inside me.

Zane smiles warmly and it takes me back to his smiles from the past. "Lucky guess." He shrugs, but I don't think that's true. He always paid attention. Always listened. Because it was what I deserved. His words, not mine.

"Thank you, Zane. For always being there for me back then. I won't say I wish things had worked out differently because that's not what this is." *And it's not fair to Nathan.* "But I will always wish you well."

"Right back at you, B. Only I *do* wish things were different. For all of us."

After Zane's gone, I wander aimlessly for twenty minutes before heading to my car, willing myself not to glance around the parking lot in case he's still there.

What a fucking mess.

I bark out a hysterical laugh as the vision of that mother's horrified expression comes to mind. That's not me. I'm not the girl who cusses loudly in public, or argues with teenagers seeking a moment with a football star.

Being around Zane makes me crazy, and at some point, I have to admit that's my fault, not his. I thought Nathan was wrong, that none of my doubts stem from Zane, because I was questioning my life before I ran into him. Now, I'm not so sure. Zane brings up feelings from my past that I'd buried deep long ago, and as confusing as that might be, I can't help wondering—like he said—if maybe it *means* something that he's back. Not that I'll ever admit that to him.

Guilt plagues me as I think about Nathan. He may not be an innocent party in all this, but if I was trying harder, it's possible there'd only be cracks between us, instead of a break beyond repair.

My head aches and I massage my temples as a text comes through.

Nathan, right on time.

Nathan: Thinking of you. I miss you so much

My guilt thickens and the tightness in my chest intensifies. I never gave him a chance. Maybe if he knew everything I was feeling, he'd step up. He has been messaging and calling every few hours since I walked out our door. I have to give him credit for that.

He deserves it.

> Blair: Want to meet me for a drink tonight? Paisley's at eight?

> Nathan: Yes! Thank you. I'll be there. I love you

I smile, picturing the excitement in his eyes, until a new feeling overwhelms me, a distant pit forming in my stomach.

What if I see him and the feelings aren't there anymore?

What if the love hasn't just faded... What if it's gone?

What if it's too late?

Chapter Twenty-One

ZANE

I'm not sure how long I sit in my rental on the side of the road, but I can't move, my conversation with Blair running on repeat through my mind.

What the fuck is going on with me? I'm in LA? With Blair? No, not with her. *For* her. And I no longer recognize myself.

All Jenna said was that Blair was struggling, and I dropped everything to be here. I missed practice. I lied to my coaches, telling them I was sick. For what? To confirm what I've been denying for the last seven years. That I'm never going to move on from that night. I'm never going to move on from Blair. No matter what I tell myself.

Did I hit my head in the game last weekend? Is that what this is? I'm crazy if I think this is a good idea. It's insane. But I can't stop. I'm not done.

I may have promised myself—and Blair—that I'd leave her alone. But that's not an option anymore.

I'm sorry, B.

Movement from the tree line draws my attention, and despite there being loads of people coming and going, I don't have to glance up to know that it's her.

And fuck, she's beautiful.

Sad but so goddamn beautiful.

That asshole better be treating her better than I think he is, and protecting her from dicks like himself. Because I want nothing more than to find where he lives and beat the shit out of him. God knows it'd be a long time coming.

The only thing stopping me is that Blair's still got her spark. He has to be doing something right. *In theory.*

Blair gets in her car and unknowingly follows my lead, staring into space as though lost in thought. While I watch her like she's prey.

A darkness washes over me and my chest tightens. She always planned to leave Florida. Seven years ago, moving to California would have been a dream for her. But something has changed, and it's clearly not what she thought it would be.

Fucking Nathan.

He should be helping her settle in, helping her to find a job and make new friends. Although she's got that covered—if she doesn't tell Jenna to fuck off for conspiring with me.

Nathan should be doing all that he can. Like I would.

Like I should...

An idea comes to mind and I grab my phone, taking a deep breath as I pull up my messages. I must be crazy if I'm about to do this, but Blair needs someone. And maybe I'm it.

With sheer reluctance and the vision of a gun to my head, I open the group chat, cursing myself before asking for help. If it's not about me, it doesn't count, right?

> ZANE: I have a good friend looking for a job in nursing, do any of you have contacts?

I expect Reed to offer to help, even if he doesn't know anyone—and when the three little dots pop up, I chuckle preemptively—but what I don't expect is for Dylan to respond.

> DYLAN: Your timing is perfect, man. My sister is a physical therapist at Heartwood U and they're looking for a doctor and nurse. They've been looking for a while. They're struggling to find someone that understands football

Football? Excitement takes over me as I realize how perfect this is.

> ZANE: Thanks, man. My friend knows everything one can know about football. Is your sister the PT for the team?

> DYLAN: Yep. The team Wes came from. I'm sure he could help you out too. Does she live in San Francisco? It's just under an hour drive from here

Dammit. I should have specified that she lives in LA. But it's better than nothing.

> ZANE: She doesn't but she might be willing to move. Thank you. I think she'd be perfect for the role

> LUKE: She? 😉

Of course, Luke chooses now to join the conversation. Ignoring him, I wait for Dylan to reply, my excitement building.

> DYLAN: If you send me your friend's details, I can pass them on

> ZANE: That would be great. Thanks, man

> REED: That saves me from helping. I don't have contacts but I was willing to track someone down

I chuckle again. *Of course you were, Reed.*

> ZANE: Thanks everyone. While I have you, any recommendations for a good place to eat in LA?

> DYLAN: Bo-Bo's Eatery

> REED: Bo-Bo's Eatery

> LUKE: Bo-Bo's all the way

Bo-Bo's it is. It saves me from having to think about it. My brain's a little fried right now.

Another message comes through and I groan.

LUKE: I thought you were sick? 😊

Dammit, Luke.

ZANE: Cough. Cough

LUKE CHANGED THE GROUP NAME TO "ZANE'S
SUPPORT GROUP"

Fuck. What the hell does that mean?

LUKE: I thought it was time

EASTON: I'll repeat my much earlier statement,
Zane. Welcome to Hell. It's your turn now

Zane: Fuck

A few hours later, I'm sitting in Bo-Bo's and trying not to moan like a horny teenager touching a woman for the first time. It turns out, those assholes aren't so bad. Dylan helped me with Blair, and this food might actually give me an orgasm. It's that good.

"Another beer?" my server asks seconds after I've finished my first one, and while I'm grateful for the attention, I shake my head.

"No, thanks." *One is my limit.*

"Can I get you anything else? You look like you're enjoying the food."

"'Enjoying' is an understatement. I'm only here for the night or else I'd be back tomorrow. For now, I'm full. Can I get the check when you're ready?"

"Of course." Her mouth curls into a flirtatious grin before she bites her bottom lip. "Do you come to LA often?" Her voice lowers and she runs a finger across the placemat near my hand. "I finish in thirty minutes. I'd be happy to show you around."

I quirk my lips and open my mouth to respond until my stomach knots. *Motherfucker.* I bet she'd be happy to fuck me too, and yet...

Jesus. Am I about to turn her down?

My phone buzzes across the rustic wood of the table, and silence falls as I glance down. I don't register who texted but I shrug apologetically. "I've gotta—"

"Yes. Of course. I'll get your check." She rushes off and I internally groan. I am. *I fucking am*. I'm turning down a sure thing. A smoking-hot sure thing who doesn't seem to know who I am.

For a ghost.

Well, not exactly a ghost because Blair's still very much alive. But she made it clear that what we had was dead, and I'm probably supposed to accept that.

Too bad I don't. And my dick sure as hell doesn't. *Unfortunately.*

Just to be sure, I check out my server's ass in her sculpted leggings, marveling at the way her cheeks bounce when she moves. But what do you know, not even a twitch.

Like the damn thing's broken.

What a fucked-up predicament to be in.

Grabbing my phone, I check my message and chuckle incredulously.

At least I have an ally.

> JENNA: You failed on the mountain, but I'm giving you another chance. Blair's going to the Paisley Hotel tonight. She wants to drown her sorrows. I offered to go but she shut me down. Maybe you should be there

I scratch my head as I smile. This girl's crazier than I am.

> ZANE: Not a good idea

> JENNA: Giving up already?

> ZANE: Nope. I'm just smarter than that

> JENNA: How so?

> ZANE: You may not know this about Blair, but she can be ridiculously headstrong when she wants to be. And God, can she hold a grudge. I wouldn't push her too far

> JENNA: So...don't tell her I sent you. Easy

I bark out a laugh, picturing Jenna's nonchalant shrug. But it's not easy at all.

> ZANE: I'd have to. I'm not going to lie

> JENNA: Good answer, Z-man. I will fall on my sword for you

Wow, this girl. She's really something.

> ZANE: Okay, Shakespeare. You do you

> JENNA: Thank you, I will. Blair needs you. Be there

I'm smiling to myself as my server comes back, my check secured tightly in her palm, but when I reach out to grab it, she shakes her head. "Uh-uh. You got an answer for me yet?"

"I *do*." I speak slowly, ready to deliver the blow. To her and myself.

"So?"

"I'm gonna go it alone."

The woman frowns for a beat before hitting me with a knowing smile. "That was your girl, wasn't it?" She points to my phone and I laugh.

"Definitely not. But it's still a no."

"Your loss." She tosses her blonde hair over her shoulder and I chuckle again.

"You're probably right." I'll undoubtedly regret it when I'm fucking my hand later tonight, but that damn ghost has me in a fucking chokehold. She doesn't even know it.

And let's face it, *I've always preferred brunettes.*

After paying the check and taking in the delicious smell one last time, I jump in my rental, setting the GPS for LAX.

I stupidly booked a late flight thinking I'd be spending more time with Blair, but if I'm lucky, I'll be able to sweet-talk my way onto an earlier one.

Because I am *not* going to the Paisley hotel. Whatever that is.

I'll give Blair the space she needs now, but I am not giving up. And if I find out that Nathan steps even an inch out of line, I'll be banging down his door and putting him in his place.

If I show up right now, Blair's likely to dick punch me, and I value my cock more than anything else.

Airport it is.

No diversions.

I'm *not* driving to the Paisley hotel. I'm *not* driving to the Paisley hotel. I'm *not*— Look at that...a huge fucking sign for the Paisley hotel.

It's on my goddamn route.

Universe, I told you, I don't believe in this shit.

Continuing on my way, I pass the front of the hotel, a cocky smile in place. But at the last second, I cut across traffic, skidding into the nearest side street as some douchebag blows his horn.

"Fuck off." Flipping him off, I pull into a no stopping zone and shove the gear into park. I'm not staying. I'm just having a moment. A day. A blip on the fucking radar.

I'm not fucking staying.

Taking a deep breath, I tap my hands on the steering wheel, huffing out a laugh. What am I doing? I'm leaving, is what. She needs space. It's time to go.

After another illegal turn, I head back onto the main road and pause, my gaze darting to the hotel one last time. I'm about to slap some sense into myself when the main door opens and all my good intentions fly out the window.

Blair walks outside, her expression pinched as she waves her hands around, Nathan running after her.

I should keep going—I don't think Jenna expected Nathan to be here —but I can't will myself to leave. I don't want to.

And when there's a parking space directly out front, I know what I have to do.

Darting across traffic once more, I pull into the space and come to a stop before they're down the front steps, calling out as I exit the car. "Blair."

They both turn, and while neither are happy to see me, it's the venom in Blair's expression that really stings.

"Are you kidding me?" she snaps, shaking her head. "I'm going to kill her."

"Who?" Nathan asks, confused.

"Jenna."

"Why?" I challenge, ignoring her glare. "Because she cares?"

"Go away, Zane."

Not possible. I slam my door shut and chase after her, standing tall when Nathan steps in front of me. "Move out of the way, asshole."

"Not a chance. She told you to leave."

"And if I'm not mistaken, she just walked out on you."

"That's not what happened." Nathan clenches his fists, but a moment of doubt crosses his face.

Blair jumps between us, the fire in her eyes making me smile.

"Lose the smirk, Zane. This isn't the time."

"You don't even know what I'm smiling about."

"It doesn't matter, but I can guess."

"Is this fucker bothering you?" I ask, waving to Nathan.

"He's my bo—" She stops abruptly and Nathan winces. "You're bothering me, Zane. I want you to leave."

"No."

"No?"

"I tried. I did. But fate had other ideas."

Blair groans, the frustration clear in the way she holds her entire body. "You and this stupid fate idea. Nathan, can you go inside? I'll be there in a minute."

Nathan's eyes light up and I actually pity the fucker. "Are you sure?" he asks, giving away the fact that things aren't all rosy between them. Though I didn't need this interaction to know that.

"I'm sure." Blair forces a smile. "Zane's leaving. Aren't you, Zane?"

"Nope." I continue to stand my ground.

"*Zane.*"

"I can't believe you ever liked this asshole," Nathan interjects and my lips curl. *Keep talking. Give me a reason to deck you.*

"Please, Nathan, go."

"Not until he does," he grates and my hands ball into fists.

"Do as she asked, before I make you."

He turns to Blair as though waiting for her to scold me.

"Please, Nathan," she asks again, her tone soft, her eyes boring into his until he gives in and walks away with a huff.

"I can't believe you like that asshole," I mock, imitating Nathan as I wait for him to disappear out of sight. "What a soft cock," I mumble, borrowing the term from Luke because it seems quite fitting.

"A soft cock?" Blair scoffs. "That's a new one."

"I think it's Aussie." I shrug.

"Okay. So what? He's a soft cock because he did something I asked him to do?"

"Nope. He's a soft cock in general."

The hint of a smile graces Blair's lips before she wipes it clear off her face. "Why are you following me?"

"I'm not. I was driving past on my way to the airport." With her hands folded over her chest, Blair hits me with a look that screams bullshit, and I laugh out loud. "I'm surprisingly *not* lying. I was at Bo-Bo's. It's just around the corner. Great food, by the way. We should go there."

"What? I'm not going anywhere with you."

"Yeah, you are. One day."

"God, you're insufferable." Her nose flares and I'd feel bad if I wasn't so desperate to spend time with her. "I have to go."

She turns to leave but I grab her arm, spinning her to face me. "What did he do? You were pissed off when you were leaving."

"It's none of your concern, Zane. Please go home. Stop forcing fate."

"That's not what this is. And you know it."

She sighs, running a hand through her curls. "I have to go. Please don't follow me again."

"I can't promise that. Trust me, I've tried."

"Why? Why is it so hard for you to let me live my life the way I want to?"

"Because you're not happy, B. You may think that you're hiding it, but you're not."

"Then don't look."

"What?"

"Don't look. If you leave me alone, you'll be none the wiser."

I huff incredulously. "Do you have any idea what you're asking?" *If it was that simple, I wouldn't be in LA now, would I?*

"Of course I do." Blair shakes her head, her frustration growing. "You disappeared from my life once; you can do it again."

"B—"

"No. You shouldn't be here."

"Why? Because he's here?" My eyes flash to the door, and I swear I see movement behind the semi-frosted glass.

"I don't mean *here* here. I mean LA. You shouldn't have come back. My happiness is not your concern."

"Your happiness is the *only* happiness I have *ever* been concerned about. I'd choose your happiness over my own. Any day. You know that."

Blair sucks in a breath but recovers quickly. "I knew that once, but it's different now."

"Not to me."

"Prove it." The door opens and a group of guys walk out, instantly recognizing me. One of them pauses, but he must see something in my expression, because he whispers to the others, and they move on without comment.

"Sorry, what did you say?"

"Prove it," she repeats, her hands on her hips, her expression unwavering. "Walk away, Zane. Walk away now and don't look back."

"I've done it before. I can do it again. If it's truly what you want." I call her bluff but I'm lying. "The thing is...I don't think you do."

Blair stares at me deadpan, her eyes void of emotion, hoping I'll believe the lie about to pass through her lips. "It's what I want."

"Fine. But I need you to promise me something."

"What?" Her gaze flits to the building, and she knows what I'm about to ask.

"Promise me you'll listen to your gut. If it doesn't feel right, don't stay with him. You deserve better."

"You don't know anything about our relationship."

"Maybe not. But I know *you*. And I can see the doubt reflected in your eyes."

"You're wrong."

"Okay. Well, if that's not reason enough, how about this? No one will *ever* be good enough for you. Least of all him."

Blair's throat bobs but her expression remains stoic. "And I suppose you are?" she challenges, thinning her lips, clearly expecting me to say yes.

"No. Not even close."

Her lips part but before she can say anything else, Nathan opens the door, waving for her attention.

"You better go before he explodes." I roll my eyes, a sinking feeling settling in my gut. "Please remember what I said. I'll be seeing you."

Turning to leave, I've only taken a step when she calls out after me. "No, you won't, Zane. You won't be seeing me. This is goodbye."

I grin to myself, waving over my shoulder without looking back, my lips curling into a soft grin. "We'll see. Night, B."

Chapter Twenty-Two

BLAIR

Damn him. Damn him, damn him. *"We'll see?"* We'll fucking see? That's not giving me the closure I need. The closure I *want*.

A sharp pang twinges in my gut but I ignore it. I've got too much on my plate to process it right now. Namely, Nathan hovering in the doorway, waiting for me with an uncertain smile.

If I could, I'd turn around and beeline to my car like I was originally planning to do. But that's not an option anymore. We need to talk.

"Are you okay?" he calls out, and on seeing me step forward, he breathes a sigh of relief.

He rushes forward, and my throat tightens as I hold up a hand to stop him. "Inside, Nathan."

I glance over my shoulder, catching Zane's intense eyes boring into mine, and my skin heats.

Walking slowly, I put off the conversation for as long as I can, but once we're in the lobby, it's time to face the music.

"Can we sit?" I point to the couches in the quieter lounge area and Nathan nods, his eyes flashing back toward the door.

"What's Zane doing here?" He follows me, failing to hide the venom in his tone. He should be thanking him. If it wasn't for Zane confronting us outside, I would have jumped in my car and driven home.

"Have you been seeing him?" he asks, his voice somewhat softer this time, more broken.

I wince, perching on the arm of a couch, my eyes wide in disbelief. "You think now is a good time to mention Zane?" My shoulders drop when he sighs, and for a moment, I feel guilty. Until I remember why we were arguing. "This has *nothing* to do with him. I gave you a chance. It's Monday, Nathan. You always have the evening off and you were *late*." My voice rises and I slam my eyes shut, letting out a breath before glancing around the room, thankful that no one is staring. "God, we should have gone somewhere more private." Or maybe I should have gone home when he walked in twenty minutes later than we agreed to meet.

"I booked a room," Nathan says and I balk.

"You what?"

"I booked a room upstairs. In case." He shrugs as an anxious feeling wells up inside me.

"In case what, Nathan? In case I wanted make-up sex?"

"Make-up sex?" He scoffs. "Why would I think that when we haven't had sex since Jacksonville. I booked it in case this happened." He gestures between the two of us.

Ignoring his sex comment, I shake my head. "So you were prepared for a fight?"

"I was prepared for you to highlight my wrongdoings, yes." He's so calm that it momentarily stuns me.

"And yet, you were still late."

"I told you; I couldn't help that."

I open my mouth to ask where he was, but Zane's deep voice echoes through my mind. *"No one will ever be good enough for you. Least of all him."*

Zane may be way off base with that comment, but something in his concern gives me pause.

"I deserve better than this, Nathan."

"I had a meeting. They wanted to talk to me about joining the leadership team. It's a big deal and—"

"That's great." I smile, genuinely happy for him. "But..." I bite my lip, hating that it's come to this. "I don't just mean today. I deserve better in general. You've been an amazing support to me over the years. I'm not negating that. But I've been flailing since I moved here, and I needed you. I—"

"Wait." Nathan glances over his shoulder. "Can we please go to my room?"

My eyes flash to the crowded space not too far away, and I reluctantly agree. I owe him that much for what I'm about to do.

"Lead the way." I gesture toward the elevators.

"Thank you." Nathan settles his palm on my lower back, guiding me forward, and for his sake, I keep up appearances until we're settled inside, reminding myself...

I deserve better.

We're quiet as we traipse through the lamplit halls, but when we reach his suite, I don't get time to admire the styling before Nathan rushes to defend himself. "I agree you deserve everything, Blair, but I'm really fucking confused because I've been giving you everything. I supported you during your final year of college. I've bought you anything you've ever needed. Now, I'm asking you to support me. Here. And you're angry because you deserve better?"

I open my mouth to speak, but when no words come out, Nathan continues on.

"You're right. I've been blind. I've been so caught up in making sure I succeed that I never stopped to realize you were hurting. But I was doing it for you too, trying to prove that we made the right choice. That moving to California was the right move. Looks like I failed. So tell me, how do I fix this?"

My heart drums against my ribs as I process his words. He's right to a degree. I'm supposed to be supporting him here like I said I would and... No. I've been doing *everything* for him too. *Dammit.* Why do I always question myself with him? I don't feel the same way anymore. I don't have to stay just because he wants me to, especially when he doesn't seem to think he's done anything wrong.

It doesn't escape me that Zane was right about Nathan's lack of apologizing. Now would be a great time for him to say sorry.

"I don't think you can fix it," I whisper, my words catching in my throat. "I don't think it's fixable."

"Blair, babe. No."

"I'm—"

"Wait." Nathan pats his pants, fumbling around in his pocket before producing a velvet blue box, holding it out in front of him. My eyes bulge as I fight to hide my panic.

"What are you doing? Please tell me you're not about to propose."

"I'm not."

"Oh, thank God."

He opens the box to reveal a princess-cut engagement ring, and my heart stops. "What the hell, Nathan?"

"I want to show you how committed I am. To *us*. Not just my career like you seem to think. I love you, Blair. I want to spend the rest of my life with you. I'm not proposing now because I'm not an idiot, but I want you to know of my future plans. That you're in my future plans. And always will be."

You've got to be kidding me. "No."

"No, what? I didn't ask anything. I brought this here to show you how much you mean to me. I'm doing it all for you. I—"

"My answer is no. I don't want to marry you. Not now and not in the future." My voice cracks as tears prick my eyes, and I silently thank Nathan for suggesting we come up here.

"Blair?"

"No, Nathan." I sigh, my heart heavy as I glance away. "Everything is so different here, and I feel like I've lost myself. Actually, no, that's not true. I can't blame California. I've been losing myself since the accident, only I couldn't see it until now. This may seem out of the blue for you, but I can't be with you anymore."

Nathan freezes before his face pales. "What?"

"I can't be with you anymore."

"For now?"

"Forever."

I turn to leave, refusing to let him see me break, but Nathan rushes forward.

"Wait." He grabs my hand, his calloused skin cold against my own. "Blair. Please. Give me another chance. I'll meet you tomorrow. Prove to you that I can be on time."

"It's not about that."

"Come home. Please. Don't make a big decision in the heat of the moment. You're upset."

"Actually, I'm not upset about that. Not anymore."

Nathan frowns, confused, while I see clearly for the first time in years.

This relationship isn't good for me. I *loved* Nathan. I may *still* love him but I'm not *in love* with him. I deserve more.

"It's over, Nathan. You've had so many chances. I'm sor—" I cut myself off, a soft smile pulling at my lips. If Jenna was here, she'd undoubtedly call me out for apologizing when I'm not in the wrong. "I'm not sorry," I say instead. "But I wish things had turned out differently. I wish this didn't have to end."

"Blair?" Nathan's eyes well with tears, and I bite my lip to stave off my own.

"No. I can't. Please let me go." My eyes drop to his hand in mine and he releases me, stepping back to wipe his eyes.

"Please think about this. Okay?"

"Nathan."

"Please."

I can't handle the devastation in his gaze, so I reluctantly nod, knowing it's wrong to give him hope. Then I walk toward the entry, my insides crumbling as a hollow feeling takes over me.

"I love you, Blair. So much."

"I know."

After pushing through the door, I walk slowly, focusing on my breath as my heavy feet move me. But when the door clicks shut behind me, I run, needing to get away. Reaching the elevator, I press the button in quick succession, praying for it to come.

My chest heaves as I fight back the tears. But while I'm emotionally lost and maybe a little bit broken, I'm lighter than I've been in a very long time, and that has to mean something.

Holding my breath, I wait until I'm inside before releasing it slowly and letting myself sink back into the paneling on the walls, my eyes drifting shut.

I did it! I did something for myself. And it's been a lifetime since I've done that.

My phone rings as I step into the lobby, and I stiffen until I see that it's an unknown number, and I relax. I'm not sure I could speak to anyone I know right now. But a stranger...

"Hello?" I answer to distract myself, my voice cracking. "This is Blair."

"Hi, Blair. Sorry to call so late. My name is Lucy and I work for the Heartwood University Lions. Is this a bad time?"

What? "Who?" I ask without thinking and instantly regret it. "God, I'm sorry. It's been a day."

"No, I'm sorry. I shouldn't have called after hours, but I couldn't contain my excitement."

My brows furrow and I frantically shake my head, even though she can't see me. "I'm okay to talk now. But excuse my ignorance...what are you excited about?"

"You don't know? Oh, *men*. My brother called to tell me you were looking for a job. We're looking for a nurse."

"Your brother?"

"Yes, Dylan. You are looking for a job, right?"

"I am." My pitch rises and I allow myself a small amount of excitement, but I don't let it get too big. "Did you say Heartwood University?" I've heard of it, but I can't recall where it is.

"Yes, we're only an hour from the heart of San Francisco, but I promise it's an easy drive."

"San Francisco?"

"Yes."

"Oh."

"Oh? You don't live there?"

"I'm in LA." I cringe as Lucy groans.

"Dammit, Dylan. He never said that."

"I'm sorry. I don't know Dy—"

"No, that's okay. You don't know any nurses in San Francisco, do you? Dylan mentioned you knew football, and we'd love to have someone that does."

"I'm sorry, I don't. But I—"

"Wait. You live in LA?"

I pause, trying to catch up. "I do."

"My friend is going to love me. Are you an LA Suns fan? Because they're looking for nurses as well. I think they need two. Would you be okay with me passing on your details?"

"The Suns?" *Nathan's team.* My stomach sinks as my gaze drifts back toward the elevator.

"The one and only." Her voice lifts and I can only assume she's excited to be helping me. But there's no way I can work for Nathan's team. Not now.

"Actually, Lucy. I'm not sure how long I'll be staying in LA. My life is a little up in the air at the moment. But I'd love to chat about Heartwood. I just don't know my plans yet."

"Oh my God. Yes! I'd love to set up a time to talk properly. We need someone to start next month. If you want, I can send you a bit about the role and give you a couple of weeks to think it over. We can chat after that? Maybe you'll have a better idea by then?"

"Really? I don't want to hold you up."

"If given the chance, I know the team would much rather hire someone that comes recommended."

Recommended?

I hesitate for a beat, not sure if I should ask my next question, my face pinched as I do. "Did Dylan happen to mention how he knows me?"

Lucy bursts out laughing and my cheeks heat. "He said he doesn't know you, actually. But he mentioned one of the guys on the team."

"What team?"

"The Storm."

The Storm? Zane? *Jesus.* My throat clogs with emotion as fresh tears coat my eyes.

"Thank you, Lucy. I really appreciate the call. And for everything. I'll definitely give it some thought."

I sniff softly, hiding it behind a fake cough, but she notices. "Are you okay?" she asks and I shake my head.

"I will be."

"Are you sure?"

"Yes, thank you."

"Okay, I'll text you a link to the job description and an info sheet. If you have any questions, please don't hesitate to call me."

"Thank you again."

"No, thank *you*."

She hangs up and a wail rips from my chest. Los Angeles has been looking for a nurse? Actually, two nurses. *Nathan's team.* And he couldn't help me.

Yet, after one conversation Zane practically gets me a job.

Zane. I still, my body trembling. *Zane helped me.*

My hands shake as I fumble with my phone, bringing up his contact, hovering over his name.

ZANE FITZPATRICK (BLOCKED)

I changed his contact after blocking him seven years ago. I wanted to stop myself from calling him while also reminding myself that there was a valid reason he hadn't called me. In case I ever felt sorry for myself.

Now, after all this time, I want to reverse it.

The elevator dings and my gaze snaps to the doors, praying it's not Nathan that steps out. And thank God, it's not.

My phone burns a hole in my hand. And when I can't take it any longer, I make a split-second decision, sending a text I might later regret.

> BLAIR: Are you still here? Nearby?

The three little dots dance across my screen and my heart stops.

> ZANE: I'm still out front

Oh, God. I sniff back more tears when another message comes through.

> ZANE: Thanks for unblocking me

A laugh bursts out of me and my lightness returns.

> BLAIR: Don't push it. Can you meet me somewhere?

> ZANE: Name it. I'll be there

Weightlessness takes over me, and I have no idea whether or not I'm making a mistake. But when I send him the address for a local lookout, it doesn't feel wrong.

In fact, the giddiness inside me feels *right*.

Chapter Twenty-Three

BLAIR

My strength wavers as I pull into the parking lot, and when I see Zane's car, I quietly curse myself.

What am I doing?

My heart gallops inside my chest, and it takes everything in my power not to throw my car into reverse and hightail it out of there.

I left Nathan.

Less than an hour ago, I was in a relationship with my boyfriend of four years, and now I'm meeting Zane. The guy I once thought was forever.

What kind of person does that?

The second I come to a stop, Zane steps out of his car, and when his steely gaze meets mine, the negativity drifts away. I'm here because after all these years, he's still the same boy I fell in love with. The same bad boy with a good heart. Only he's not a boy anymore, and I'm definitely not the same girl.

With a shaky breath, I curl my fingers around the handle and open my door, watching as Zane stalks toward me, his intense gaze boring into mine.

"What did he do?" His deep voice rumbles through the air, and it's like a breath warming my skin. But it's not the protective Zane I need right now.

Jumping up, I throw my arms around his neck, balancing on my toes to lock my fingers at the nape. "Thank you," I say, my gaze locked on his, hoping he can see the emotion reflected in my eyes. "Thank you."

What he did means the world to me, but it's more than that. In a few short hours, he reminded me I deserve better, and it's been years since I've believed anything close to that.

Since him.

"Why are you thanking me?" Zane's curious eyes sparkle, and his entire face lights up, sucking me in like he always did.

"I had a call from Lucy."

"Lucy?" He frowns, confusing me until his eyes widen and he laughs. "Well, fuck me, those guys work quickly."

"Those guys?" Releasing my hold, I step back, quirking a brow.

His face scrunches as he scratches his head, seemingly embarrassed. "There's a few guys on the team that all love helping each other out."

Well, if that's not the cutest thing ever. "You don't sound thrilled by that. I'm guessing you don't help in return?"

"I only found out about it when they added me to a group chat. After I helped Reed and Hayley."

"Oh." My hand flies to my mouth so he can't see my lips when they pull into a grin. "That's nice of them."

"Yeah, yeah. Enough about that. What happened? Did you, ah...like the job?" His hesitation makes me smile and I can't help but mock.

"Did you, ah...know it was near San Francisco?" With an arched brow that I hope is full of sass, I wait for his response, and when he cringes, I have my answer. "I thought as much. But I'm still grateful."

"So you're moving?" Wild anticipation flits across his face, but he doesn't let it linger and my heart picks up speed. He wants me there. Close to him. And I'm not sure how I feel about that.

"I'm not moving to San Francisco." *Not yet, anyway.* "The job sounds great, *amazing*, but I'm not sure it's the right time for me. You know?"

"Because of Nathan?" he asks, his tone curt as his eyes fill with disappointment.

"No. It has nothing to do with Nathan. But as I said, I'm still grateful for the help."

"Is that why I'm here?" His lips pull into a smile, but he holds a little of it back, not quite letting it reach his eyes.

"Yes, *sort of.* Do you want to walk?"

Without a word, he motions for me to lead the way, and my heart jolts. I'd almost rather we were arguing because I have no idea what I'm doing right now.

The breeze kisses my face as we walk quietly toward the lookout, the sound of our footsteps deafening in the night time silence. The higher we get, the faster my pulse races until my head spins.

What is going on with me tonight?

Since Zane's distracted by the rugged path in front of us, I smile to myself in the hope that it calms me. But all it does is make me deranged, and I can't take the silence anymore.

"Zane, I— *Woah.*" My ankle rolls as I trip and stumble forward, my stomach in knots while I fall toward the gully running beside us. Reaching for a branch, I catch myself, but a searing pain shoots through my hand. "Jesus Christ." I falter, keeling over, nausea swirling through me.

"Blair?" Zane rushes to my side, tucking himself under my arm as he lifts me to standing. And with his height, that can't be comfortable. He hovers low while I stand tall, only then taking a peek at my hand.

"Oh, fuck." Blood pools in my palm and I dry retch when it drips down to the dirt, my body trembling. "Dammit."

"Jesus." Zane flies into action, curling his arm under my legs, effortlessly lifting me into his hold.

"What are you doing?" I shriek, but it comes out a little stuttered.

"I'm taking you back. We need to check out your hand, and to do that, we're gonna need more than the light of your phone."

"It's just a scratch. I'll be fine."

Zane chuckles but otherwise ignores my protest. "I've heard that before."

"When? I've never said that."

"It wasn't from you. Now stop wriggling. I need to dodge the trees."

"Yes, sir." Giving in, I reluctantly curl my arm around his neck and let him carry me back, my heart racing as I study his features, focusing on the rigid line of his jaw, fighting not to touch the light dusting of stubble. It's darker than when we were younger.

Zane laughs at my appraisal, tightening his hold, his huge palm dangerously close to my heaving breasts.

We reach the parking lot in record time with me bouncing around as Zane jogs to the car. Without letting go of me, he opens his door and positions me under the light, squatting down to perch me on the seat. "Fuck, that's deep." He curses, his calloused fingers brushing across my palm. "You might need stitches."

"I know."

"You *know*?"

"I can feel it, Zane. I'm a nurse, remember? Do you have anything in your car that I can use to wrap it?" I glance into the back seat, finding it empty.

"I didn't bring anything with me. It was an impromptu visit."

"Why?"

"For you."

"I get that but—"

"We are *not* talking about that now, Blair." His panicked voice makes me laugh, and for a moment, I forget the sting of my hand and the pain in my heart.

"Okay. Can you reach into my pocket and grab my key? I think I have a sweatshirt somewhere in the trunk."

"Somewhere? We don't have time for that." Standing tall, Zane reaches behind his neck and drags his tee over his head—doing it in that way only men seem to do—and I watch with amusement. But when he squats down, my laughter cuts off, shocked to find his bare chest.

A stupid thought because...*what else did I expect him to be wearing?*

I inhale deeply, and with his shirt off, the smell of his skin assaults my nostrils, making me dizzy. He smells of sweat, masculinity, and nature, and the combination brings back memories I'd long forgotten. Stolen moments in his truck. His chest flush with mine, our hands roaming, mouths molded together while we fought not to go further than we should.

My lips part as my breath quickens, and it's not until Zane announces he's done that I'm pulled out of the past.

Freaking pheromones.

"There. That should help until we can get you to the hospital." He glances up with a lopsided grin, seemingly unaware of my lust-filled reminiscing.

"Thank you," I rush out, my wide eyes directed at his face while I work hard not to focus on his features.

"I didn't do much." He stands and reaches for my good hand, pulling me up to meet him. "Let's get you to the ER and..." He says more but with my line of sight trapped on the metal bar pierced through his nipple, I'm momentarily stunned. Another memory flashes through my mind—this one of the two of us flirting at the beach—and my breath hitches. God, it's beautiful. His entire body is beautiful. Like a work of art. Chiseled from stone. Strong and—

"Blair?"

"Huh?"

I lift my gaze, cringing when I find Zane's lips pulled into a smirk. "You always were fascinated by this thing. Even if it did take you *months* to ask about it." He bounces his pecs, drawing my attention like a moth to a flame. His muscles tense, making the bar move, and I can't stop the rushed breath that escapes me. "Fuck, Blair." Zane's pained groan penetrates the silence and I smile, knowing he's as affected as I am.

"We should go before you lose more blood." He turns away until I reach out to stop him, the pain in my hand gone.

"It's not hurting anymore. Let me have a look before we race over there. ERs are busy enough without people going in for a scratch."

"It's worse than a scratch."

"Let me be the judge of that. Here." I hold my hand out for him to remove his tee, my eyes locked on the wound instead of the chiseled abs begging to be touched.

His T-shirt could pass as evidence of a horrific crime scene, but when he peels it back, I'm pleased to find that I'm right.

"See, it's stopped. I've got some magic glue at home." *At the home that I share with Nathan, but that's not the point.* "I'll seal it up and it'll be back to normal in a few days."

"Magic glue?" Zane asks, his expression oozing with skepticism.

"Sorry, skin glue. I worked in pediatrics on one of my rotations and I changed the name. It's the same thing. Either way, I'll be fine."

"Are you sure?"

"Yep. I'm a nurse."

"So you keep reminding me. And yet you almost vomited at the sight of the blood."

"Because it was *my* blood. That makes *all* the difference."

"Of course, my mistake. I remember that being the case when we were younger. A certain surfing incident comes to mind." Zane smirks and my eyes zero in on the curl of his lips, my throat thick with emotions.

"Enough talk of my misfortunes. Please change the subject." *The last thing I need is to be reminiscing about the first time things changed between us. A moment I will never forget.*

"Don't like talking about your blood?"

"Something like that." I smile while my heart runs wild inside me.

"Okay. Consider the subject changed."

"Thank you."

"I'm guessing that *lover boy* doesn't have a piercing." Zane changes the subject as asked and I choke on thin air, faking a cough to hide it.

"He doesn't."

"Shame," he snickers as my gaze snaps to his, confusion in my eyes. "Piercings can be a lot of fun," he explains, trailing off before lowering his voice. "It increases the pleasure."

Oh, God. Heat flows through my body but I ignore it, focusing on his words. Are we really talking about my sex life? "For those that have the piercing, right? How could *your* nipple piercing increase *my* pleasure?" I regret the question as soon as I've voiced it, but it's better than where my mind really wants to go.

"I thought we were talking about Nathan." Zane raises a brow, making me internally groan. "But I wasn't talking about *this* piercing."

His gravelly voice has me clenching my legs, and I don't know why but my gaze drops to the bulge in his sweats, a lump stuck in my throat.

"Bingo," Zane gloats, snapping his fingers. "Not as innocent as you used to be."

His words sting, but I take in a breath and stand tall, rolling my eyes. "It was the obvious choice. What else could it have been?"

"My tongue." He's quick to answer and I cringe. *God, why do I have his dick on the brain?* Of course it's... Wait. No. He doesn't have his tongue pierced. I would have noticed that. It must be...

Zane grins and I curse myself internally. He never said he had another piercing, just that they're fun. *Dammit.*

"You're messing with me."

"Am I? Want to find out?" He grabs the waistband of his sweats and I leap forward, slamming my uninjured palm on top of his hand. There's barely a breath between us, both of us holding his pants, and I realize too late that this is *exactly* what he wanted.

"This works too." He bites his bottom lip, his teeth bright in the darkness. "All you have to do is lower your fingers and you'll have your answer." He slips his hand out from under mine and cups his junk, bouncing it a few times.

"Zane," I try to warn but since my throat's dry, his name catches, coming out raspy. I cough and try again. "Zane. What are you doing?"

He drops both hands and laughs it off, his light chuckle echoing through my head while it clouds with desire. I can't remember the last time I was this turned on, even when I had a boyfriend. And that's a problem.

Shaking my head, I step back, creating some much-needed distance between us, only to slam into the open door. "Dammit." I wince as I stumble, my cheeks heating with embarrassment until Zane catches me again and the world around me stills.

"Are you okay?" he asks, no hint of humor in his tone, while I fight not to giggle. I was never that good at hiding the effect he has on me. It's probably why my brother claims to have known we were seeing each other the entire time we were together.

"I'm okay. Just trying to get away."

"Why?" The question is breathy, and that breath warms my skin right through to the bone, making me mute. I can't answer because I don't know what to say, but I'm thinking clearly enough to know whatever I might come up with would have been a lie.

"Blair?" Zane questions, but I'm distracted by the way his throat bobs as he speaks, drawing my attention to the little spot below his ear that I always liked to nibble on.

"*Zane?*" His name floats around my head, and it's only when he releases a pained groan that I realize I said it out loud.

"I can't..." He trails off, shaking his head.

"Can't what?"

"*Blair.*" His voice strains.

"What?"

"Fuck it." Before I have the chance to process what's happening, he has one hand in my hair as he lightly curls the other around my waist, the pad of his thumb dipping beneath my top to brush my bare skin.

My breath hitches, but I don't protest as his mouth descends and his lips mold to mine, caressing, nibbling on the flesh. I flatten my palms against his chest, the sting of my cut *nothing* compared to the pain radiating through me from kissing Zane and knowing I shouldn't.

Hating that it feels so right.

His hold turns possessive, and I whimper as he grips my neck, his thumb skimming under the waistband of my jeans.

God, what I wouldn't give to let him... *Shit.*

I pull away, but an anguished curse rips from his throat and he seals our mouths again, slipping his tongue between my parted lips.

The world around me stills, the silence overwhelming, until Zane's desperate groan pulses against my lips, his tongue swirling with mine, and desire takes over me.

I want this. I've *always* wanted this, but it doesn't stop my insides from igniting in a tortured blaze. This kiss is like nothing I've felt before and yet it's so damn familiar that my chest burns in anticipation, knowing what comes next.

The last time we kissed, he broke me.

The thought makes me stiffen and I catch myself, pulling away again, my chest heaving as I struggle to take in air. "I...we...you kissed me," I say breathlessly, accusation in my tone.

"I know, fuck."

"Why?" My lips tremble as I whisper.

"It felt right."

"It wasn't right, Zane. It was wrong. *Very* wrong." I'm shaking my head, but my mouth waters for more.

A moment of guilt flashes across his face. "Because of Nathan?"

"Because of *me*." My voice cracks as my pulse races.

"Good, because I don't give a fuck about Nathan."

"You never have, so that's nothing new. But—"

"It's cheating. I know. And while I don't care about him, I care about *you*. I just couldn't stop myself. And that douchebag doesn't deserve you."

I bark out a laugh before covering my mouth with my hand. Zane smiles sheepishly, giving my waist a squeeze. I hadn't noticed he was still holding me, but now that I have, my skin is on fire. "Either way. It doesn't work like that. It's still cheating." *At least it would be, if we were together.*

"I know. But you *did* leave him and message me."

"I what?" *How the hell does he know that?*

"You left him at the hotel and messaged me. You can't blame me for taking advantage." He's keeping things light but I internally deflate, a slow breath passing through my lips.

"It's complicated."

"Hasn't it always been complicated between us, since that very first moment on the beach? We've always worked it out."

His tone lacks its usual cockiness and I stare at him for a beat, letting his words roll around my head. I think about our moment on the beach and the last time we kissed, but rather than the happy memories he's seeking, my stomach sinks. Yeah... *We always worked it out.* "Until we didn't."

Chapter Twenty-Four

ZANE

AGE 17

Blair squirms as I hold her in the shallows, my concerned gaze locked on her cheek while I gently stroke her palm. "Are you sure you're alright?"

"Is there blood?" she asks, the panic in her voice rising.

"Nope. No blood. But it is going to bruise."

"That's fine." With her free hand, she lightly pats the graze below her eye, making no move to break free from my grasp. "I'm good."

Her eyes meet mine, and her pulse races under the pad of my thumb, my traitorous heart pounding.

"Do you want to go home?" I ask as she shivers in my arms.

She just crashed off her surfboard and was under the water for longer than anyone should be. I can't imagine she's ready to head back out there. But this is Blair, so who knows. She can be stubborn at times.

Her brows furrow as I stare at her, and something about it sends a warmth right through me.

"Do you?" she counters, making me grin as her adorable expression morphs with confusion. "God, I'm sorry. I don't know why I said that."

"Maybe you hit your head?"

"I didn't. Just my face. But God, I'm so embarrassed." Her cheeks heat and I find myself following the pink hue down to her chest until her breasts heave, snapping me out of it.

"Why?" I rush out. "It's just me."

"True. Better you than Cade, but still." She glances away and I grab her chin, forcing her to look at me.

"Are you going to tell me what happened?"

"Nope."

"You've been surfing since we were kids, B, and I've never seen you fall that hard."

"Waves are unpredictable; people fall all the time."

Not like that. But... "Okay, I'll continue to picture the story in my head."

Blair gasps. "What story?"

"That you saw me jogging, shirtless, and lost all concentration."

"You wish." She lowers her gaze, her eyes now locked on my bare chest, and my pulse spikes.

"That may not have distracted you then," I rasp, "but it's distracting you now." Her eyes lift to mine and I chuckle, trying to ignore the way my muscles tense from her lust-filled appraisal.

"I'm not going to lie, Fitzpatrick. Your body is fine."

"Are you sure you didn't hit your head?" Grinning, I brush the wet strands away from her forehead, checking for myself.

"Maybe? But it doesn't make it any less true." Blair's eyes flutter and she stares up at me through her impossibly long lashes.

"You're not too bad yourself, Little B."

"Gee, thanks." She barks out a laugh and wriggles out of my hold, standing to full height. My gaze gets caught on the apex of her thighs and my throat bobs. No, nope, nuh-uh. This is Blair.

This. Is. Blair.

The girl I've known forever, my best friend's little sister.

A tightness works its way into my chest and I quickly look away. What am I doing? It's Blair.

"Zane?" Blair's breathy voice cuts into my mind and I glance up, making things worse when I notice her nipples pebbling through her bikini. A bikini that leaves nothing *to the imagination.*

Goddammit.

An irrational anger takes over me as I scan the beach for other surfers. "Why aren't you wearing a rash guard?" I snap, jumping up to stand next to her, shielding her from view.

"It's a hundred degrees out here." She rolls her eyes and gestures to my abs. "Why aren't you wearing a shirt?"

It's a valid point and yet the two questions are vastly different. I don't care who stares at my chest, but I care about hers. "Let's get you to the sand. I think I saw your towel."

"I'm fine."

"You're shivering, B. Humor me."

"Yes, sir." She salutes and my fucking cock twitches. What the hell? "Let's go."

She stalks toward the sand, throwing me a wave over her shoulder, and I can't stop myself from admiring her ass when it wriggles in front of me.

By the time I realize what I'm doing, it's too late. I'm already fucked.

I think I want my best friend's little sister.

Actually, no. I don't think that—I know it.

I want Blair. And she's completely off-limits.

CHAPTER TWENTY-FIVE

ZANE

PRESENT DAY

"*Until we didn't.*" *Until we fucking didn't.*

Blair's quietly delivered statement stabs me in the gut and I visibly cringe. *How can three little words pack so much emotion?*

She's right, though. We always worked things out, always made time for each other and found ways to sneak around, *until* the night of my birthday, when one little act sent both our lives spiraling out of control.

"Blair, I—"

"Nope. We're not talking about that now. This was a mistake. I shouldn't have messaged you, it's just..." She trails off but I don't need her to answer. I saw it in her eyes when she first hugged me. She finally understood what I've been drilling into her since the first time we kissed. Hell, maybe even before that. She deserves the world, and any man—including her boyfriend—that doesn't see that and doesn't help her achieve her dreams shouldn't be part of her life. It's the reason I couldn't completely commit to her. She knew that. I was always honest. *With her.*

But when S— my sister died, Blair seemingly lost that strength, and I'm determined to get it back. Anything to get her away from that *soft cock*.

A smile involuntarily tugs at my lips and Blair frowns.

"Sorry." I chuckle at her annoyance. "I was just thinking about the phrase 'soft cock' again. I must thank my teammate for introducing me to it."

Blair tries to hide her smile, but at the last second, it shines through.

"Despite the fact that you're referring to Nathan when you say it, I have to admit, I kind of like it. I'll probably steal it in the future."

"No doubt. Just don't say it to his face. That's not a very nice thing to do." I wink and Blair gasps.

"Zane!" She bites back her laughter, lightly shoving at my chest.

Catching her hand, I hold it in place and stare down at her, not bothering to hide the way my heart thunders in my chest. For her.

I love physical touch. Specifically, the kind that ends in a release. But it's always been different with Blair. When Blair touches me, she sets me on fire, leaving a scorch mark in her wake. A mark, that if visible, I'd proudly display like one of my tattoos, showing the world that she's mine.

That she'll always be mine. No matter the time or distance between us.

The last seven years have proven that.

"Blair?"

"I should go," she tells me, but the way her breathy voice lifts, you'd think she was asking permission.

"Do you want to?"

"No. I mean, yes. I want to. It's late and I have a lot to do tomorrow."

"Like finding a job." I raise a brow but keep the annoyance from my tone, feeling guilty when Blair sighs.

"Yeah, something like that."

"You should at least consider the job in San Francisco. It's only a half-day drive back to Na-than." I choke on his name but smile through it. "You could see him on your days off."

Blair's gaze shifts uncomfortably but she recovers, offering me a sassy grin. "That simple, huh?"

"Yep."

"So... if I was *your* girl..." She trails off, stepping closer as she walks her fingers up my chest, her eyes lingering on the wave tattoo that wraps around my rib cage. I draw in a breath as I watch her, my muscles twitching with her every touch. "If I was yours," she repeats, her voice light and flirty, making me picture what her being mine would look like, "you'd be okay with me living in another city?"

What? "Hell, no. I'd want you in my bed every night."

"That's what I thought. So why should Nathan agree?"

I cringe at her rationale. She's got me there and that notion pains me. "Fine. Don't take the job. But please, *please* tell Nathan about it. Make sure he knows what you're giving up for him. Maybe he'll work harder to look after you." Blair opens her mouth to speak, but I stop her, holding a finger to her lips. "Don't sass me with your 'I can take care of myself' bullshit. He *should* be looking after you."

"I wasn't going to," she mumbles against my fingers, sending a spark to my cock.

Down, boy, now is not the time.

"If you'd let me speak, I was going to thank you. That's oddly nice considering you hate the guy."

"Come now. I don't *hate* him." I wave her off and she scoffs in disbelief. "I *despise* that asshole. And nothing in this world will ever convince me that you're right for each other."

"I don't—"

"I'll respect your wishes," I cut her off. "You want me to accept your relationship, so I will. But I can't stay away anymore. Not now that I've seen you again." *Not now that I've tasted your lips.*

"That's not fair and you know it."

"For who? We're friends. Are you not allowed to have friends?"

"I am." She rolls her eyes. "But you and I have never been friends. That kiss was anything but friendly."

"I'll tell you what... I won't kiss you again, if you promise this isn't goodbye." The words taste bitter in my mouth, but I mean them. I may not care about Nathan, but I'm against cheating in general. Usually. Despite what my past with Easton's ex might suggest.

"*Zane.*" Blair folds her arms over her chest like I'm being unreasonable, but it does nothing to change my mind.

"The ball's in your court, Little B."

"Fine," she huffs, brushing her hair behind her ears when the cool night breeze blows it across her face. "This isn't goodbye." She gives me a shove, and while I could easily stand my ground and block her in, I allow her to move me, watching as she stalks toward the driver's side of her car. Holding back.

I've already pushed her too far tonight. *Baby steps.*

"This isn't goodbye," she repeats. "It's *see you later*. Much, much later. Think...another life."

Jesus. I flinch, the finality of her words stabbing me in the chest. And she's none the wiser.

Without a backward glance, Blair jumps into her car and slams the door closed. From the light of the streetlamp, I catch her cringe when her injured hand hits the steering wheel, but she doesn't give in. And before I know it, she's driving away. All while I'm left with a blood-soaked T-shirt and her whispered whimper playing through my mind.

The wind tickles my naked skin and I laugh at myself, jamming the heels of my hands into my eyes, groaning. Loudly.

Maybe time apart isn't such a bad thing. I'm so fucking gone for her that it's embarrassing.

But fuck if I can stop it.

After another quick detour, this time to find a new shirt, the buzz of chaos is almost comforting when I finally arrive at the airport. The more people, the easier it is to blend in.

I'm too late for an earlier flight, so I'm stuck waiting around for my original late one, regretting how I'll feel come morning. We may not have a scheduled practice on Tuesdays, but I've never missed an early morning workout, and I refuse to let tomorrow be the exception.

When the shrill tone of my alarm blares at 4 a.m., I slam my palm down on the clock beside my bed, groaning into my pillow. That is, until the image of Blair's wide eyes and heaving chest flits through my mind and I can't help myself.

It was worth it.

Kissing the perfect curve of her mouth was like coming home after a rough day. *God, I can still feel her lips. Still taste her.* She was sweeter than I remember, and I can't decide if it's because she's forbidden fruit or I just *really* like the taste of her.

Either way, I want more. *Too bad I promised I wouldn't kiss her again. Me and my damn morals.*

Accepting the inevitable, I drag my tired ass out of bed and throw on my workout gear. Ignoring the sting of my eyes, I force myself to scarf down a banana before jumping in my car and slapping my cheeks a few times. Anything to wake the fuck up.

When I arrive at the stadium, I wave to Jim, our regular security guard, and swipe my card to let me inside, pausing after I've stepped through the threshold. Like always, it's eerily quiet at this time of morning, and as I walk through the halls, the motion-sensor lights buzz, coming to life as I pass under them, bathing the space in a soft glow.

Setting my playlist to rock anthems, I go through the motions, running to warm up before working my way through my regular sets.

I'm nearing the end when the door slams behind me and I curse under my breath, sending out a silent prayer that it's not one of my coaches, or worse, one of the guys from the group chat.

"Zane, my man," Luke greets the back of my head and I visibly wince.

Of course it's him. I've been working out alone at this time on a Tuesday for three fucking years and he chooses today to show up.

"Luke, how are you?" I glance over my shoulder, giving him a nod then resuming my position below the bar, launching into my final set of pull-ups.

If I think Luke's going to tell me he's good and leave me alone, I'm sorely mistaken.

"I'm much better than you, I hear." He chuckles to himself. "How's the cough?"

I snort out a laugh and my arms quiver. "I'm on the mend," I croak out, forcing myself to complete one more rep before dropping my feet to the ground. "It's amazing what a little hot lemon and honey will do." I smile and grab my towel, wiping the sweat from my brow, throwing it back on my bag.

"Is that what you're calling her? I like it." Luke grins, his lips tight as though he's giving me props for the creative nickname.

"It's not a name, douchebag." Though I internally smile at the fact that he's not far off, honey to my Queen B.

"Okay. What do you call her then? And when are you getting married?"

"The fuck?"

"You missed practice for a woman, right? That usually means she's special."

"How... You know what? Never mind." When it comes to Luke, I've learned he's like a dog with a bone. May as well be honest, because he's not giving up any time soon. "She *is* special," I tell him, gesturing for him to spot me as I lie down on the bench. If he's going to be chatty, the least he can do is assist in my workout. "She's a friend," I offer, hoping he'll drop it.

"A friend?" He laughs, walking behind the bench press, standing in position as I begin my first rep, the weight slightly higher than I'm used to since I've got someone to spot me. "Why don't you ask Reed how *that* story plays out?"

My muscles tense. "What story?" I grunt, playing dumb, and immediately regret engaging.

"The 'we're just friends' bullshit. I give it a month."

"A month?" A strained laugh bursts out of me. "I wouldn't place that bet. It could be that long before I see her again." If she has any say in the matter. If it's left up to me, I'll be seeing her before the week is out. I might even stop in LA on my way home from our game against Phoenix this weekend.

My thoughts drift to Blair's mouth and I lose concentration, my strength wavering through my next press up, needing Luke's help to get the bar into position as my muscles give out.

"What happened then?" he asks, concern marring his expression.

"Like I said. I'm sick." I fake a cough and Luke blows out a raspberry.

"Lovesick, maybe. You need to get your head out of your ass or you'll hurt yourself."

"Thanks for the advice, *Dad*." I sit up and shake out my arms, turning around, armed with an over-the-top smile. "I'll keep that in mind."

"You do that." He scoffs, as though I'm some careless child, and I can't help but snicker. I care about things; my well-being just isn't high on that list right now. I'm too caught up in Blair.

Waving him off, I shift my attention to the row of treadmills across the hall, mentally planning out my cooldown.

But Luke's not letting it go. Even after I've walked away.

"Zane," he calls out from the other side of our gym, still in the same place I left him, frowning when I turn around. "Bring a friend next time. You're lucky I was here."

"You're right. Thanks. Same time next week?" I wink and he barks out an incredulous laugh.

While I may have been joking, I have a feeling these workouts will no longer be done alone.

CHAPTER TWENTY-SIX

BLAIR

I'm woken by my phone ringing a couple of days later, and when I see Cade's name, I groan.

"I'm sleeping," I croak groggily, my voice catching on my dry throat. If he doesn't get to the point fast, I'm hanging up.

"What's going on, Little B? Are you okay?"

"What?" I sit up, pulling the covers up over my chest as though it'll shield me from whatever's going on. "Why are you asking me that?"

"I'm worried about you."

"Did Zane call you?" I blurt out way too quickly, instantly regretting it. *Dammit.* I bury my hands in my eyes, shaking myself awake. Why am I talking about Zane to my brother?

"Why would Zane call me? Have you seen him again?"

"No."

"Bullshit."

"Why are you calling?" I change the subject, hoping he'll drop it, despite the fact I know he won't.

"Is Zane there?"

"At my home? That I share with my boyfriend? No. He's not." Not that *I'm* there at the moment, but that's beside the point.

"So, you're meeting up with him somewhere else then?" Cade scoffs and I groan.

"No, Cade. God. What is your obsession with Zane?"

"You are right; he called me."

"Goddammit." I wince. "I'm going to kill him. What did he say? I'm *fine*. It's just a scratch. We didn't even go to the ER in the end and—"

'What the fuck, Blair? I was joking. He never called. But you better believe you're going to tell me what's going on."

"Cade—"

"I think I need to visit. It sounds like you need your big bro."

"What?" I cringe as my head spins. "No. You don't need to come here. I'm fine. I ran into Zane and I tripped while we were talking. I cut my hand but I'm fine. F.I.N.E."

"Believe it or not, I know what fine means." I picture him rolling his eyes and roll mine right back.

"Fuck off."

"Maybe you are fine. God knows you've still got your snark."

"Only for you, Cade. Only for you."

"And Zane now too, I'll bet."

"If he didn't call you, then he didn't do anything wrong."

"What did the two of you talk about?" He circles back to my conversation, but I'm not giving him any more than I have to.

"I don't know. Life, the weather, what we had for breakfast."

"Okay. Cause I'm going to believe that. Did he kiss you?"

"What?" I choke on air and my lips tingle at the memory of the kiss. "Of course he didn't. He thinks I have a boyfriend."

"Thinks?"

"*Knows.*" *What is wrong with me today?* "He knows."

"You're a little skittish this morning, sis. Not at all like yourself."

"I'm fine."

"So you said."

"Why...did...you...call?"

"Oh, yeah. I'm on my way to your place. Thought I'd stop by for a visit."

"You're hilarious. Why are you really—"

"It's true."

"Cade! No. Turn around. I'm fine."

"Call it brotherly intuition but I think you're lying. And so does Dad. So...I'm on my way to find out."

"Go home, Cade," I rush out, my voice panicked. "Please. I'm thinking about heading back for a visit soon anyway. You're wasting your time."

"I'm already in LA, Little B. And now I'm more convinced than ever that I made the right call. I'll be there in an hour."

"Cade. No."

"Too late. Love ya. Bye."

"*Goddammit*," I scream into the phone when my lock screen appears and curse again under my breath. Cade's in LA. L-fucking-A. And he's coming here in an hour? *Universe, what did I do to you?*

Tossing my phone onto the bed, I get up and freeze, my foot hovering above the carpet. The carpet at Jenna's. *Shit.* Cade's not coming here. He's going to *my* place. So, in short, I'm screwed.

After rushing around like I'm late for the night shift, I stub my toe on the edge of the couch and still make it out the door in record time. Though my record time was thirty minutes, meaning I'll be lucky if I make it home five minutes before Cade.

I'd usually spend the drive listening to music or an audiobook, but I'm so anxious I suffer in silence, my mind too chaotic to concentrate.

Because every hour is rush hour in LA, the drive takes longer than expected, and I'm drenched in a cold sweat by the time I pull up, running through the garden to the condo the second I've parked my car.

After loudly jogging up the steps, I open the door quietly, tiptoeing into the house as though I broke in. Nathan should have left for practice by now, but that doesn't eliminate my guilt.

I've just dropped my bag behind the couch when Cade waltzes in, not even bothering to knock. "I'm here!"

"I can see that." I force a smile as I greet him, subtly kicking Nathan's shoes out of the walkway.

Cade's eyes drop to my feet but he smiles, rushing forward to pull me into a hug. "How are you?"

"Great," I say with as much sarcasm as I can muster. "My big bro's here for a surprise visit."

"You love it. Come on. Show me around." He playfully nudges me, and I roll my eyes before giving him a tour, finishing in the kitchen in case he leads me to drink.

"So…" Cade raises an eyebrow, his lips pulling into a self-satisfied smirk. "When did you and Nathan break up?"

"What?" I choke out. "We…uh…"

"Come on. You spent that entire tour tidying up after him. You're a clean freak. Your house in Jacksonville was always perfect. You're not living here."

"What the fuck, Cade?" I shake my head in protest but when he stares me down, giving me a tell-me-I'm-wrong look, my resolve slips. "Ugh, fine. We broke up."

"Yes! When? I mean, oh no, are you okay?"

"God, you're an asshole. Officially? Monday."

"Three days ago? Why didn't you tell me?"

"I'm telling you now."

"Only because I guessed."

"Either way, you know."

"What happened? Where are you living? Did he fuck up? No, wait. Is this about Zane?"

"God." I throw my hands up in frustration. "Why does everyone keep saying that? This is about me and Nathan. No one else."

"But you saw Zane on…" he trails off so I'll answer, and I confidently hit him with a lie.

"Tuesday."

"After you broke up."

"Yes."

"I bet Zane was thrilled."

"He doesn't know."

"What?" Cade smirks and it makes me want to punch him. "Why wouldn't you tell him, Little B?"

"Because it's none of his business. Or yours for that matter."

"I knew something was wrong. I knew it. What did he do?"

"He didn't *do* anything."

"Yeah, well, sometimes that's the problem."

"What?" I freeze and for a moment I wonder if Jenna called Cade too. I wouldn't put anything past her anymore, and while I forgave her for calling Zane, *this* is crossing a line.

"Seems like we're single together."

"What? Nooo." I shake my head, my gaze appraising my brother, looking for clues as to how he's feeling. "What happened?"

"I wasn't giving her what she needs."

"What was that?" I ask and then wince. God, it better not be sexual.

Cade's oblivious to my reaction as he sighs. "A baby."

"A baby? She wants a baby?" *He's only just turned twenty-six.* They've got plenty of time for that.

"Yeah. She's a couple of years older than I am and wants to get pregnant early so that her body bounces back."

"Okay. Wow. So, you're here for *you*. Not me. That makes things easier. And yet, I opened my big mouth and confessed everything."

"Yeah, you did." He smirks, and I have to admit that I'm happy to see him smiling. He loved Gabriella a lot, and this must be killing him.

"I'm sorry, Cade. I wish I knew what to do to make it better."

"You already did it. It's going to be nice not having to tiptoe around your boyfriend anymore."

Hysterical laughter bubbles out of me and Cade's smile fades. "That was tiptoeing? Cade, it was so obvious you hated him that no one would have flinched at a billboard in Times Square. *Tiptoeing around.* God, you're a dick."

"Okay, fine. I hated the guy. But with good reason. I'm hoping you can see it now that you've broken up."

My phone vibrates again, and a rush of panic passes through me, wondering if it's Zane. We haven't spoken since I drove away from the lookout the other night, and yet, every time my phone goes off, I'm desperate to check.

"Do you need to get that?" Cade asks, a little distractedly, and when our eyes lock, a moment of guilt takes over me. He's here because he needs me. Because he just broke up with his fiancée, and I'm thinking about Zane. *Goddammit.*

"Nothing is more important than my big brother right now. Come on, sit down. I want to know everything."

"What about Nathan?"

"*I* broke up with *him*. It's different."

"Doesn't mean you're not hurting."

"You're right, it doesn't. But I promise, I'm good. Now tell me, from the beginning. What happened? And how can I help?"

For the next hour, Cade fills me in on everything that's been going on in his life, and I welcome the distraction. It kind of puts things into perspective a little. Cade and Gabriella were engaged. They were planning a wedding while I wasn't even sure I wanted to marry Nathan. It's not something I dreamed of. I don't have a pros and cons list or journals full of my name with his last name like I did with Zane.

Blair Fitzpatrick. Blair Jasmine Fitzpatrick. Mrs. Fitzpatrick.

God, I spent hours writing my name over and over, never once questioning if it would ever come to be.

Ours wasn't a relationship that stemmed from a crush. When I said Zane was a friend, I meant it. I'd never given it another thought.

But the moment our lips touched, the moment his palms first cupped my face and his gaze bore into mine, I was a goner. There was no going back.

Until it all turned to shit.

And I moved on with Nathan. I moved on.

Or so I thought.

After talking through Cade's predicament for the better part of the morning, he eagerly helps me pack more of my clothes and we check into his hotel before I take him to meet Jenna.

It's not until he disappears to take his bag to his room that I finally get a chance to look at my phone. My pulse spikes when I see that it's *him*.

> ZANE: Just wanted to check up on you. To make sure you were alive after seeing all that blood

A soft smile pulls at my lips, but I don't let it shine until I read his next text and burst out laughing.

> ZANE: Don't make me fly back there to see for myself

> ZANE: Too late. My flight is booked, see you in a few hours

I scoff, calling his bluff as I lazily type out a response, ignoring the way my heart thumps against my rib cage. I don't want to see him, but I also do. I'm so confused.

> BLAIR: I'll be waiting. Did Jenna tell you where I live?

The three little dots instantly start moving, and my confidence wavers. It was a stupid thing to write; it will probably encourage him.

Rushing to stop him, I quickly follow it with another message, before he's had a chance to click send.

> BLAIR: Joking 😄

The dots disappear before I get his one-word response.

ZANE: Tease

Dammit. That's not what he was going to send, and now I'm desperate to know what it was.

ZANE: What would you do if I did turn up now?

Wrap my arms around you and never let go. *Jesus Christ. Where did that come from?*

> BLAIR: I'd send you to bunk with Cade

ZANE: Cade?

> BLAIR: He's visiting. You two are so alike it's scary. He also thinks it's appropriate to turn up out of the blue

ZANE: You can't see me but I'm laughing. I bet Nathan loved that

I may not be able to see him, but I can certainly picture the way his lips are undoubtedly curling, while his eyes sparkle with glee. And I both love and hate that it doesn't take much to conjure his image to my mind.

Snapping myself out of it, I take a deep breath and reply.

BLAIR: He's at practice. But he'll be fine

At some point I'll probably have to tell Zane we've broken up. But for now, it's easier to keep him in the dark. For both our sakes.

CHAPTER TWENTY-SEVEN

ZANE

Sinking back into my plush lounge chair, I smile reading Blair's response. I bet Nathan *won't* be fine, and I wish I was a fly on the wall when he finds out. My belly shakes from chuckling, and while I probably shouldn't be happy about someone else's misfortune, in Nathan's case, I don't mind. Maybe Cade's presence will be the kick in the ass he needs to be a better boyfriend.

But then again...maybe it won't. Once a douche, always a douche.

Still smiling, I begin typing a response to Blair, thinking about *poor* Nathan. But before I can finish responding, a message comes through from Cade, drawing my attention, and when I read the text, I freeze.

> CADE: Blair and the dickwad broke up. I just helped her move out

The fuck? I flick back to Blair's message exchange and re-read her last text slowly.

> B: He's at practice. But he'll be fine

No hint of a breakup there.
What are you playing at, B?
Ignoring Cade, I delete my half-typed message and change my response, my fingers pressing the letters much harder than I need to.

> ZANE: Maybe I will pay you another visit

Pressing send, I curse and toss my phone across the room, watching it bounce against the cushions of my armchair, falling to the floor with a thud.

They broke up? Blair's single. And she's moved out of the douche's house. I should be happy about that. But now...it's going to be so much harder to stay away, and I'm not sure she wants me around. In fact, I *know* she doesn't.

For the next couple of days, I force myself to focus on football. We have a tough game against Phoenix this weekend, and I'm already on thin ice for missing practice, despite being sick.

Cough.

When game day arrives, I give it my all, and it's safe to say I play one of the best games of my career. I'm a force. Unstoppable. And for the first time, it feels like I'm truly connecting with my teammates. Like we're in sync.

Maybe there's some truth to the whole "your teammates should be like family" bullshit. Not that I'm taking it that far, but I have to admit, they're growing on me.

Luke's all smiles when we get back to the locker room, so I take the opportunity to ask him for a favor. *Another favor.* I'm really taking advantage of this group chat shit.

"I've got to go back to LA," I tell him when he stops by to congratulate me on my killer touchdown. "My friend needs me, and I need *you* to cover for me."

His lips curl into a grin, and I almost take it back. Especially when he wraps an arm around my shoulder and gives me a brotherly squeeze. "Tell me the truth about you and this *friend*." He uses quote fingers to punctuate his request. "After that, I'll help."

I shove him off me. He's still sweaty from our game, and even if he wasn't, it's weird. "Not going to happen, Bennett. You're going to help me because you love that shit."

"Really?" He raises a brow, his expression unwavering, and it eats away at my confidence.

"Fuck. Why do you want to know so badly?"

"Call it bonding." He shrugs and I can't help but snort.

"Bonding or insurance?"

"Both. And you're going to oblige. Unless you want to ask Easton to cover for you?"

We both glance over at Easton, his don't-fuck-with-me gaze more prominent than usual as he throws his phone into his bag. "Okay, that's worse." I sigh, relenting. "She's a friend from back in Jacksonville, and she just broke up with her asshole boyfriend. She only moved to LA because of him, so she doesn't really have anyone else."

"*Fuck.*" Luke's face scrunches and he looks genuinely concerned for Blair. "What about her friend that knows Hayley?"

"*Jesus*, did Reed tell everyone about that?"

"Nope." Luke chuckles. "Reed's a vault when he has to be. That was Amelia. She's Hayley's best friend, remember?"

"Vaguely." I frown. "Unlike you, I don't feel the need to know everyone else's business. Are you going to help or not?"

"I am." He grins and it's a little unnerving. "I'm going to help because you asked. Not enough guys do that these days."

My frown deepens because *what the hell does that mean?* Though as curious as I might be, I don't dare ask. This conversation is over.

"Thanks, man. Just tell Coach I had to fly home early but that I'll be at practice tomorrow."

"Will you?" he asks, stopping me as I turn away.

"Honestly, I don't know. But I have plenty of cash. I'll pay the fine."

"I don't think it's about the fine."

"Would you go for Amelia?" I challenge him, already knowing the answer but needing to give him perspective.

"Fuck, yeah, I would. I'd go anywhere for her."

"Well, there you go."

He nods and falls silent for a beat, giving me the chance to casually sneak away, but before I've taken a step, his laughter fills the air. "Friend, my ass. Go get her, Fitzpatrick."

I roll my eyes but I can't hide the small smirk that tugs on my lips. She's not going to like it, but that's exactly what I plan on doing.

My flight from Phoenix to LA is longer than the advertised hour and thirty minutes, and despite our four p.m. game, it's getting late in the evening, making me jittery. Turning up to see Blair unannounced is one thing, but doing it when she's likely getting ready for bed is another thing entirely.

But I'm ready for her anger, frustration, pain, whatever she wants to throw at me. She's single now, and there has to be a reason for that. Here's hoping she doesn't kick me out the second she sees me at the door.

As soon as the wheels of the Boeing 737 touch down on the tarmac, I have my phone in my hand, instantly texting Jenna. She helped me once; I'm praying she'll do it again.

> ZANE: I'm in LA. Do you know where I can find Blair?

> Jenna: She's at my apartment. I'll send you the address. But Zane. If you hurt her, you better sleep with one eye open and a hand over your balls

Her quick response makes me smile but... *Jesus.* My hand drops to my crotch, and I break out in a full-body shiver. I'd be less concerned if she told me to protect my face. I happen to care a lot about my junk. It's still got so much to give.

> Zane: You have nothing to worry about

> Jenna: Good. She needs you

I highly doubt that but I'm going anyway. Pocketing my phone, I rush off the plane and beeline for the rental company, picking up a car as Jenna's message comes through.

Brentwood. Nice. I should be there by eleven p.m. That's not too late for a visit, right?

Ignoring the gut feeling telling me it is, I drive straight to Jenna's apartment, parking in a space someone just vacated.

It's been four hours since my game in Phoenix ended, and now that I'm standing in front of Blair's apartment—her current apartment—I'm not sure I'm ready.

We haven't spoken in three days. She didn't respond to my "I'm going to visit" text, so I'm probably about to be slapped. Or at the very least yelled at.

What the fuck am I doing?

"Are you going to come in, or hang around out front?" a voice calls out from somewhere above me, and when I glance up, I find Jenna hanging out of her window.

I lift my hand to wave, but a second later, Cade is beside her, and I audibly groan.

"Hey there." Cade smirks and I throw my head back with a sigh. "Nice of you to respond to my messages."

He's been texting since he told me about Blair, but I had more important things to worry about. Like getting my ass to LA.

"I've been busy. Can we talk about that later? It's not important right now."

"Well, ring the doorbell and we'll buzz you up."

"Does she know I'm coming?"

"Shut up!" someone else yells from a lower level, and I duck my head to hide my face.

"Just ring the doorbell, jackass. She doesn't know."

I sigh in relief, although maybe it's better if she knew. At least then it wouldn't be a shock when I walked in.

Cade wolf whistles while I jog to the door, and I flip him off seconds before disappearing under the protection of the arched entry. This would be so much easier if he wasn't here.

As promised, Jenna—or I guess Cade—buzzes me in, and I bounce on the balls of my feet, waiting patiently for the elevator to take its sweet-ass time traveling the short distance to Jenna's floor.

The doors open and I jump, coming face-to-face with both Cade and Jenna, hands on their hips, trying hard to be threatening. *I think.* It's not really working for either of them.

"Motherfucker." I shake my head while Cade smirks.

"Sister fucker."

"Nope," I'm quick to respond. "That never happened." I move to step around Cade, but his hand juts out to stop me.

"What are you doing?"

"Enough with the lies. You're here for her. Just admit it."

"Admit what?"

"Look me in the eye and tell me you never slept with Blair."

"I don't have time for this, asshole."

"Say it."

"Jesus Christ." I stare at him deadpan, my gaze never once wavering as I repeat his words back to him, enunciating each word clearly. "I never slept with Blair." *But God, I wanted to.*

"*Fuck.*" Cade's curse comes out as a groan, and I'm thoroughly confused.

"You're pissed off about that?"

"No. I'm sick of all the lying."

"What lying? I... Actually, it doesn't matter. I need to see Blair."

Cade's lips thin, and he folds his arms over his chest, trying to appear intimidating. "Why?" he asks, stepping closer to what I assume is Jenna's door.

"What are your intentions?" Jenna steps forward, her expression much more relaxed than Cade's, but it still gets on my nerves.

I internally groan. I don't have time for this. "I plan to fuck Blair's brains out and then ghost her, leaving you both to pick up the pieces." I stare at them blankly, waiting for them to smile at my obvious joke. But they keep their cool. "What is this? I'm here because my friend just broke up with her boyfriend, and I want to offer support."

"So, *she's* still your friend?"

"Jealousy does *not* look good on you, Caden."

Jenna finally breaks character, snorting out a laugh as she pulls me into a hug. "Nice to see you again, Zane. Blair's in her room. It's the second door on the left. Please knock. She's going to hate me enough for giving you my address. But it'll be worse if you walk in while she's flicking her bean or something."

"What?" I cough, choking on my words, but that's nothing compared to Cade's reaction. I swear he's going to vomit.

"The fuck, Jenna?" He turns a weird shade of green. "That's my sister."

"So what? Does that mean she's not allowed to masturbate?"

At that I laugh—a little for Cade's reaction and a little for Jenna's brazenness. I knew I liked her.

"She can do whatever she wants, but I shouldn't have to hear about it. Or worse—"

"I'm going to go in," I interrupt their back and forth, gesturing to the door. "I'll leave you two to argue this out."

I spin toward Jenna's apartment but someone stops me, a hand curling around the collar of my suit jacket, almost choking me. "Wait."

I reluctantly turn, my face stoic as I anticipate whatever warning Cade's going to give me.

But when the sincerity in his eyes hits me, my defense drops as the fight in me dissolves. "Don't hurt her, okay?" he whispers, his voice thick with emotion. "She's been through enough."

While I could easily tell him that I won't, just like I told Jenna, for some reason I can't form the words. "I..." *Fuck*. "I..."

Cade's gaze softens and he nods slowly. "I get it. You never set out to hurt her and you still did."

A sigh escapes me, and an uncomfortable energy settles between us. I wish he was wrong, but he hit the nail on the head with extreme precision, and all I can say is, "I'll try."

CHAPTER TWENTY-EIGHT

ZANE

I stride through the apartment, my smile wide, my swagger confident. But the second I reach what I assume is Blair's door, I falter. *What the fuck am I doing here?*

The last time I was this hung up on a woman I was a teenager, and it was the *same fucking girl*.

Only Blair could make me act this crazy.

Sucking in a deep breath, I stare at the painted wooden door and imagine how this little reunion might go.

Blair opens the door and immediately slaps me. Hard.

Blair opens the door, gasps, spins on her heels and slams the door in my face, telling me to fuck off.

Blair opens the door and gasps. We lock eyes and it's like no time has passed between us. She runs forward and leaps into my arms, slamming her lips to mine.

What the fuck? I chuckle silently. God, I'm delusional. And yet, I allow my mind to drift again.

Before I can knock, the door creaks open and her soft moans filter through the air. I quietly step forward, peeking through the gap to find her face down, her naked ass wriggling in the air as she pleasures herself. And a panic takes over.

My pulse quickens and I curse quietly under my breath. *Dammit, Jenna.* I shift uncomfortably, the visual making this impending interaction so much more awkward.

"Fuck." Thinking of kittens dressed as babies and the Storm losing a championship game, I adjust the bulge in my pants and man up, readying myself to knock. But before I get the chance, laughter filters from behind me.

Or more specifically, Blair's honey-like giggle.

"What are you doing?" she asks as I turn, her arms folded over her chest, her breasts filling out her skimpy silk pajama top.

She bites her lip as she smirks, and I lose control of my emotions—and my cock, as it twitches for attention. Everything about her pulls me in.

"I'm here to see you," I rasp before clearing my throat. "Is this not your room?"

"Nope." She giggles again. "You walked right past me with that determined look in your eyes. The one you get when you're focused on the end zone."

My mood lifts, along with my brows, and I smile as my heart races. *She remembers.* But since she's talking to me and it doesn't appear as though she's going to slap me anytime soon, it's best not to tease her for the moment.

"I'll admit, I was laser focused, though it seems I was misguided. Is this not the second door on the left?"

"I guess that depends on which direction you're looking."

"From the door, Blair. At least that's what most people would assume. Are you drunk?"

"Drunk? No." I eye her curiously and she giggles again, her amusement clear as day. I'm about to question her further, when it hits me.

"You *knew.*"

"Before you even left the airport."

"*Fuck.*" She rocks back on her heels, looking smug, and I've got to say, it's adorable. "So..." I hedge. "You're okay that I'm here, then? You're smiling." *That's gotta be good, right?*

"I am smiling. But the jury's still out on whether or not it's a good thing. I guess it depends on why you're here."

Well, that's easy. "Because you broke—" Blair shakes her head, silently telling me that's the wrong answer. I clear my throat and finish my sentence. "My heart," I say, taking my response in a *very* different direction. "You broke my heart, and I missed you."

"God, when did you get so corny?"

"Somewhere between then and now." I shrug jokingly until Blair's eyes sadden. I might have just killed her good mood. "Not the right thing to say, huh?"

"No." She shakes her head. "But honestly, I don't know what the right thing is anymore."

"Are you pissed that I'm here?"

"No. Confused but not pissed."

"I'll take confused. I'm here because I can't for the life of me push you out of my mind." I scratch the back of my neck. "Believe me, I've tried," I continue, somewhat under my breath.

There's a flicker of something in her expression that I can't read before Blair's brows shoot up to her hairline. "I think I need a drink for this conversation."

"Why?" *Oh.* Once again, I said the wrong thing. "I didn't mean that I've physically tried getting over you. Not the way you're thinking."

"It wouldn't matter if you did."

"It would matter to *me.*" It would matter a great deal. "I'm not saying I've been celibate since I left because that would be a huge fucking lie. But since seeing you again, my cock hasn't so much as risen for another woman. It may as well be broken. I feel like I'm back in my freshman year of college. You know, when I had all those girls throwing themselves at me, and yet, all I wanted was you."

With softly parted lips that I often imagine brushing against my skin, Blair squints as though trying to see through a smudged pane of glass. Like she's not quite understanding what I'm trying to convey.

"Sorry if that was the wrong thing to say, but I felt like it needed to be said... In case you were wondering." I shrug.

"How is it possible?" Blair asks, her eyes wide.

"How is *what* possible?"

"After everything we've been through, everything *you've* been through, you're still the same guy."

I huff out a bitter laugh. "Trust me, I'm not. I'm far from the guy I used to be, unless you're referring to my cocky football persona—that hasn't changed. But the good guy—the guy only you used to see—he's stuck back in Jacksonville, haunted by the memory of what could have been. Though I have to admit, with you in my life again, I wish I could be the man you remember."

Blair's gaze softens and recognition fills her eyes. She gets it and I wouldn't be surprised if she felt the same way. She's quiet for a beat, until another sweet giggle escapes her.

"You know...that might just be the nicest thing anyone's ever said to me."

"Really?" I bite back an incredulous smirk. "Even nicer than when I told you your writing moved me in ways I never thought possible?"

"You remember that?"

"I remember *everything*. And that's not always a good thing."

"Me too." Blair nods, her eyes glazing over as though lost in reflection. "Maybe Cade's right," she says wistfully. "Maybe we should have tried to get through Sierra's death together, instead of doing it alone."

I pause, a ringing in my ears. Like always, at the mention of my sister's name, my heart wrenches, and a weight settles on my shoulders, grounding me in place. "Maybe," I choke out, clearing my throat and smiling. "But Cade's not usually right about anything," I joke to hide my pain, and Blair sees right through it.

"I just realized the real reason you're here."

"I tried to tell you but you shook your head."

"Oh, no." She shakes her head again, but this one comes with the suppressed grin, as though she's mocking me. "You're here so we can finally talk. We didn't do it properly back then; we're doing it now."

"Yeah, that's not going to happen." I force a grin of my own, while inside my heart is pounding so fucking hard that it's actually hurting my chest. I know what she's doing. She wants me to say my sister's name. But I can't. "I'm more of a *live in the present* kind of guy," I lie. If that were true, I would have kissed her to silence her when I first discovered her giggling behind me. But I couldn't, because I remember the past.

Blair laughs and if I were to analyze it closely, I'd say it was a little manic and a hell of a lot sad. "You came here," she says, pointing to the floor. "You came to LA. Unannounced. Even though I basically told you I never wanted to see you again. I—"

"Technically, I announced it. I sent you a message."

She folds her arms over her chest, her brows pinching in sudden annoyance. "That's your rebuttal? You're going with, 'I sent you a text so it's all okay.'"

"Do you want me to go?"

Now that she wants me to talk, I want her to say yes, but I know what her answer will be, and I'm breaking out in a sweat because of it.

"No." She shakes her head. "I want you to stay and talk to me about your sister. I want to know how you feel."

Fuck. "I think I'm going to go." I spin on my heel, but Blair's tiny fists curl into my jacket, holding me in place. At least she thinks that's what's happening, but I don't care much for this jacket.

"Keep it," I say, shrugging it off my shoulders as I stride toward the front door. I've just reached for the handle—my breath frantic as I wrap my fingers around the steel—when Blair calls out.

"I need you, Zane." Her pleading voice freezes me in place, and my shoulders drop in resignation. I have *never* been able to deny her when she begs, and she knows that.

I inhale deeply but don't turn around. I'm not sure she realizes what she's asking. That bringing up S— I flinch, my head aching at the thought of her name. Bringing up my *sister* is likely to break me, and I'm not sure either of us is equipped for that.

"You said you had alcohol, right?" I ask, still unable to face her.

"I did."

"Fine." I turn to find her sympathetic gaze locked on mine and it makes me feel worse. "Where do you want to do this?"

"My bedroom?" Her voice shakes. "You know, in case Cade and Jenna come back?"

"Good idea. Lead the way."

I swallow the lump in my throat and gesture for her to go first, since I have no fucking clue which room is hers, and Blair hesitates for a beat before pointing in the opposite direction.

"The kitchen is through there. Why don't you get a bottle of something out of the cabinet above the fridge. I'm going to get changed."

"No."

"No?"

"Keep the pajamas on."

"Why?"

"Because if you're getting something out of me, I deserve something in return."

"And that's me in my pajamas?"

"Skimpy, silk pajamas. And yes." Honestly, her being naked and vulnerable would actually put us on a more even playing field, but I'm not that harsh, so I'll take the pajamas.

A little crease forms between Blair's brows as she contemplates my request, and after a beat, she smiles knowingly. "Okay." She brushes past me, seemingly on the way to the kitchen while my mind runs wild. *What the fuck does she know?*

She's barely gone a minute, and when she returns, balancing the alcohol, sprite and glasses in hand, I'm still in the same spot she left me, lost and confused. Which is apparently fucking hilarious because Blair bursts out laughing. "Oh, Zane. I promise I won't go too hard on you." She brushes her thumb across my cheek, but that's not where I feel her touch. I feel it *everywhere*.

My cock twitches at her proximity, and I run her words back through my mind. I would love for her to go hard on me. But down, boy... that's not what she meant. Far from it. But once again, my brain is trying to protect me.

"Lead the way," I say again, and when she does this time, I regret it. Her silk shorts are so tiny the curve of her ass pokes out from the bottom, teasing me.

And if I didn't know it already, I know it now...

This talk is going to be hell.

CHAPTER TWENTY-NINE

BLAIR

My arm shakes, a nervous energy coursing through me, as I hold the door open for Zane. I smile through it, pretending I'm okay, and gesture for him to enter. "You can sit wherever you like; make yourself comfortable."

There's really only two options—the bed or the leather armchair by the window—and no matter which he chooses, I'm taking the other one. I need to put some distance between us.

Zane takes the bottles from my hand as he walks past me, his expression telling me he sees through my veil, and my shaky arm turns into a full-body shiver. We've been this close since reconnecting, but having him in my space —albeit my temporary space—feels much more intimate.

When Cade first told me that Zane was on his way, a sea of emotions raged through me. First came the anger. *"Tell him to fuck off, Cade. He can't just show up whenever he feels like it."* Next came the denial. *"I don't want to see him. He's the last person I need right now."* Followed by the reasoning and begging. *"Can't you see this is a bad idea? Please convince him not to come."* And finally, the resolve. *"Maybe seeing him won't be such a bad thing. Maybe seeing him one last time will help me come to terms with everything that happened."*

In the short space of a few minutes, I'd convinced myself that it was going to be *that* easy to move on from my past. That I'd be able to start fresh again. Whether I took the job near San Francisco or went back to Jacksonville. Hell, I could move somewhere completely different. I've always dreamt of an apartment in New York City.

I deserve the chance to be who I want to be, and having closure is the best place to start.

At least that's what I was telling myself, until the moment Zane stepped into my aura. It's like my soul is drawn to his. I may be nervous as hell having him in my space, but I've also never felt calmer. Which might have something to do with the couple of shots I had before he arrived. But it also might not, because there's something about him that always made me feel that way. Even when I was pushing him away and he was telling me he was leaving, I felt a sense of peace that I'd never felt before—a mix between knowing we were making the right decision and that nothing is forever. Except when people die...which leads us back to now.

Why the hell would I tell Zane we needed to talk about Sierra? Sure, it's not healthy for him to hold back like he is, refusing to say her name, but that's none of my goddamn business. And it's likely to lead to other topics that I'd rather avoid.

After placing the bottles of vodka and Sprite on the nightstand, Zane settles in the armchair while I close the door and slowly walk toward the bed, lining the glasses up next to the drinks.

Not wanting to get too comfortable, I perch on the edge of Jenna's four-poster guest bed, shifting the lace curtain out of the way.

Zane watches my movements, then studies the room, a frown gracing his lips. "Is this yours?"

I laugh. "No."

Before it was relegated to the spare room, this had been Jenna's bed. She thought it would make her feel luxurious, but quickly discovered it wasn't for her. She's a light sleeper and said that she stuck her foot out of bed once and felt the lace brush against her skin, giving her a heart attack. After that, she was done with it.

I had no problem sleeping here until Cade arrived and told me it was fitting for a princess, knowing how much I despise that descriptor.

"The furniture is all Jenna's," I explain, keeping my tone light. "I don't have my own furniture in LA."

"What?" Zane frowns again, this time in confusion.

"It doesn't matter, but our condo came furnished, so I only had to bring my clothes."

I wait for Zane's smart-ass response, and he doesn't disappoint, only I wasn't expecting the words that come out of his mouth.

"I guess that makes the breakup much easier." He shrugs, hiding a smile.

It's not at all funny, and way too soon to be joking about that, but still, for some reason I laugh without restraint, filling the room with my hysteria. "You're right. My entire life fits in those four suitcases." I point to the forest-green cases on the floor. "I'm free."

The thought of that stills me, and my eyes flash to the bottle of vodka, immediately reaching for a glass. "Want a drink?" I ask, filling half the glass with alcohol before topping it off with Sprite.

"Easy there," Zane warns, but I wave him off.

"It's needed. I'm not a drinker, but this entire situation has led me to drink."

"I think that means you're not coping."

"You think? Did my hysterical laughter not give that away?"

Zane winces like my pain physically hurt him. "In that case, let me join you. I'm the one that asked for it. But you're going to have to let me crash on your couch. I don't drink and drive. For obvious reasons."

My heart jolts, and I lower my glass before I've taken my first sip. "What am I doing?" My voice cracks as moisture fills the back of my eyes. "This isn't me. I don't even know who I am anymore. But I know it's been a long time since I've recognized myself, and if I'm being honest, since seeing you again...it's like tiny fragments are coming back to me. Like I'm finding my way out of the darkness, and I don't know what to do with that."

My eyes widen over saying too much, and it's not lost on me that Zane mentioned feeling the same.

"Blair, I—"

"No. Please don't respond to that." I knock back a huge gulp of my vodka and shudder when it burns my throat. Despite knowing I shouldn't be using alcohol to solve all my problems, it feels good to numb the pain for a while.

Zane gets up and pours himself a glass, his vodka to Sprite ratio similar to mine, as though he's going down in solidarity. "To baring one's soul and living through it." He raises his glass to toast, and I can't help but giggle again.

"To baring one's soul and *hopefully* living through it," I repeat, a little less convinced.

"So..." Zane trails off as he sits back down, resting his ankle over his knee. "How should we do this?"

"Let's go back to the reason you're here."

"Okay." He nods, slowly lifting his glass to his lips, drinking the contents in one go. "Wow. That was strong." He half speaks, half chokes. "I don't think you should drink that."

Doing the opposite, I follow his lead, finishing the rest of my glass in a few gulps, smiling defiantly. "Go on," I say, my throat burning as I rasp.

"Fine." Zane scratches his head, and my eyes zero in on the tattoos peeking out from his sleeve and the ring adorning his pinky. Without permission, my head fills with memories from our past, and my heart picks up speed.

...

"There, that's better." Zane spins the ring around his finger and smiles. "No one will ever know I got burned. They'll never know we were together."

"God, this is always so hard. Maybe we should tell them. It's not like this is new. We've been..." I trail off, not wanting to call 'us' something we're not.

"Exclusively seeing each other," Zane fills in the blanks. "And I know. But I'm not ready for our bubble to burst. Both your dad and brother are likely to kill me. Especially after that." He points to the almost identical burn on my wrist and his lips thin. "Let's not forget how hysterical you got when I saved you just now, thinking we were going to get busted because of our matching scars."

"You didn't save me." I roll my eyes. "You make me sound like a damsel in distress. You reacted without thinking."

Zane raises his hands in the air. "I would never call you a damsel. Princess is much more fitting." He winks, teasing, and I dive across the blanket, tackling him to the ground.

"I am not a princess."

"I know. You're more like a queen."

...

"Blair?" Zane questions, bringing me back to the present. "Are you okay?"

"Fine." I wave him off, my heart racing as I pretend I *wasn't* thinking about the time I stupidly reached for my bag on the other side of an open fireplace and burned my wrist on the scorching metal. Only to have Zane rush to save me, burning his finger in the process.

"No more alcohol for you." Zane chuckles while I frown.

"What does that mean?"

"We haven't even started the conversation and you're already in your head."

"Wouldn't you prefer me to drink then? So you don't have to speak?"

"Good point. Yes. Drink away. Here." He gets up and reaches for my glass. "I'll even pour it for you."

I roll my eyes, shaking my head as I tell him to sit. "I'm fine. Come on. It's time to talk. And you're going first. Why are you here?"

"Fuck." He groans, this time raking a hand through his already mussed hair. "I was planning on giving you space for a little while, so you could make up your own mind about the job without me influencing your decision...either way."

"Either way?" I bite back a smile, having a feeling I know what he means.

"Well, knowing you, having me around was more likely to discourage you from wanting to move closer to me. You can be stubborn like that."

I bite back my smile. "Guess we'll find out. Since you're here."

"Figures." He laughs and I get lost in the light of his eyes, my mind drifting to the last time I saw him truly smile.

"Anyway," he continues, once again bringing me back to the present, making me blink a few times as my mind whirls. "I *was* planning on staying away, until Cade shared the news of your breakup."

"Wow." I shake my head, trying to focus. "You're really just throwing him under the bus these days."

Zane shrugs. "He told you I was coming, so we're even."

"Fair point. So, you heard I was hurting and rushed to my side. Like I'm a dam—"

Zane dives onto the bed and slams his hand over my mouth, making me squeal. "Let me make one thing clear." His deep voice seeps into my mind, and my body goes weak. "I have *never* and *will never* think of you as a damsel in distress, but that doesn't mean I don't want to protect you. There's a difference and you know it."

I swallow a thick lump in my throat as emotion wells in my chest, my head pounding like nobody's business.

Zane's brows rise, seeking a response, so I nod, unable to give him anything else.

"Thank you." He pulls his hand away, and I miss the feel of him against me. "I came when I heard you'd broken up with the *dickwad* because I thought you might need a friend, and because...like I said, I can't seem to stay the fuck away. I left my team in Phoenix and came straight here."

"You left your team?" I balk, confused, and Zane starts laughing.

"Are you really going to pretend you don't have the complete schedule memorized? I bet you knew exactly where my team was today, even if you never gave me a second thought."

My cheeks heat because he's right. I know that the Storm was playing Phoenix and I know they won. Easily I might add. But I didn't make the connection until just now. My mind's moving slower than usual. Maybe because from the moment Cade told me he was coming, I kind of lost it.

"Okay." I nod, buying myself some time to gather my thoughts. "That makes sense. And I *did* need a friend, but I have Jenna."

"Nope." Zane shakes his head, still perched on the bed beside me. "It's not the same. You need a friend that knows you."

"You knew the old me, Zane. Jenna knows the me I am today."

"Ouch. That hurts. But while it may be true, does she know how you deal with breakups?"

My eyes widen as a smile graces his lips. He nods his head slowly, clearly impressed with himself, and it makes me want to take him down a peg or two.

"I've only had *two* relationships, Zane. And one 'exclusively seeing each other.'" I put on a voice as I use quote fingers, since he used to refer to us that way.

"Yeah, and—"

"You were barely around for the first guy. I was fifteen."

"Barely around, huh? I seem to remember you said you'd never move on unless you had enough chocolate to numb the pain and a moment of madness."

"God, I'm starting to hate this 'I remember everything' bullshit."

"I'll bet." Zane's delicious chuckle makes my insides warm.

"Fine. Replace chocolate with alcohol," I say, making a show of getting another drink, this one without the Sprite, knocking it back faster than I should. It burns worse than before, and my head spins as though the shots I did before he arrived are finally catching up with me. I smile, ignoring the dizzy feeling taking over me. "I've grown out of the moment of madness stuff."

"Really?"

"Well, I didn't do anything *crazy* when you left...so I must have."

"Are you sure about that?" He raises an eyebrow and stares at me pointedly. But I don't get it. "You dated Jerkface for *four* years. That seems pretty damn crazy to me."

"Ugh." I fold my arms over my chest. "That's different. The first time I did something crazy, I went surfing in waves I couldn't handle."

"And I saved you then too. I mean...protected you in a non-damsel-like manner."

As much as I try to fight it, a stupid giddiness bubbles in my chest, and my lips pull into a smile of their own accord. "I thought this was going to be a serious conversation. Should I get Cade in here to provide a therapy session for us?"

"Hell, no. If he walks in, I walk out. Plus, I definitely prefer this more intimate setting."

He leans in a little closer and my heart jolts, making me sit back, creating some space between us. "Sorry. You make me incredibly uncomfortable," I say honestly, blinking a few times to clear my head. "And I think the alcohol is getting to me."

Zane frowns, the humor in his expression gone. "You only just started drinking."

"Actually, I started before you came over." I shrug and Zane's eyes widen in alarm.

"You said you weren't drunk?"

"I wasn't then. You never asked if I'd been *drinking*, only if I was drunk."

Zane's frown deepens and I bury my face in my hands, groaning when random images swirl through my mind. "Wow. That last drink really sent me over the edge." I fall back onto the pillows as my eyes drift shut. "The room's moving."

I groan again until the faint sound of a growl draws my attention and my eyes flash open.

"Did you just growl at me?" I sit up, my head spinning until I grab Zane's leg to steady myself.

Zane doesn't respond, but a gruff sound rumbles in the back of his throat. "Oh my God. You did! God, it's hot. So hot. Don't do it again. It's confusing."

"How the hell are you drunk right now, Blair? We were just talking."

"I'm not drunk. I can't be."

"Fuck. Are you on medication?"

"What? No." I shake my head until I'm dizzy again and pause. "Like I said... I'm not usually a drinker."

"When was the last time you drank this much?"

"The night you took me to your hotel."

"Shit. And before that?"

"It's been years." I smile innocently, biting my lip as I stare at him.

"Dammit, Blair." Zane runs a hand down his face, his torn expression confusing me.

"What?"

"Nothing."

"Tell me, please," I beg, pleading with my eyes, knowing he can't usually resist that look.

"You're killing me. You know that. We're supposed to be having a serious conversation, but you keep looking at me like you want me and I fucking want you too. I wish we could play pretend and forget life for a while."

"And do what?"

"What do you think?" His lips pull into a sly smile before he shakes his head and laughs. "Oh, B, what am I going to do with you?" His eyes bore into mine and it renders me speechless.

I'm not even sure he realizes the intensity of his gaze right now, but the way he's staring at me is only making me more nervous, and I itch to reach for the vodka again.

He's always made me feel wanted, and today is no exception. But do I want him too? Am I really giving him that look?

My body heats and I break out in goose bumps, my mind conjuring images of what it would be like to have Zane inside me. It's something I thought about many times when I was younger, and too many times since.

But I shouldn't be thinking about it now. I shouldn't be thinking about him leaning forward and—

"Christ, Blair. Stop." Zane slams his eyes shut, cursing under his breath.

I shake off my thoughts, groaning softly. "I think I've lost my mind."

I move to stand up when Zane opens his eyes, pulling me into him, curling an arm around me before softly raking a hand through my hair. "You're not the only one, B. We're in this together."

Chapter Thirty

ZANE

My heart stops as Blair stares up at me, her cheeks flushed, her usually neat curls messed up from my fingers. Her beauty never ceases to amaze me.

It takes all the strength I have to let her go. But I do. Because while she may not be drunk, she's definitely on her way there.

Her lips part, and my hands curl into fists as I watch the pink hue from her cheeks guiding a path down her neck and her chest, disappearing under the sexy pajamas I now regret insisting she wear.

She bites her lip again, and her chest rises as she inhales a deep breath. "You smell so good," she whispers, and I can't help but smile.

"How about you lie down while I go and get you some water"—I pause —"and Tylenol. Your head is going to ache come morning."

"No, I'm okay. We're supposed to be talking."

"I don't think now's the best time."

"Trying to get out of it?"

"No, I—"

"I know. You're just doing that thing where you get all protective again."

I scoff but gently lift her into my arms, repositioning her on the bed, her head on the pillow, her chaotic curls billowing out beside her face. My chest aches but I ignore it.

"It's strange, you know," she whispers, stretching her arms out wide as she twists her body into various positions. She pauses for a beat, and I don't ask what's strange because I'm not sure I want the answer. But she gives it anyway. "I probably should have known, but I never let myself think about it."

"Known what?" *Dammit.* I wasn't going to ask.

"About you. After all this time, you still care."

"Of course I do," I tell her honestly, the pain in my chest spreading. "I never stopped." I whisper the last part, and when she doesn't acknowledge it, I assume she didn't hear me. Chuckling to myself, I get up to leave the room, but I've barely made it to the foot of the bed when she stops me.

"Are you still attracted to me?" she asks out of nowhere, her voice lifting at the end. "You've always made me feel wanted, but do you *really* still want me? All of me. After all this time?"

I should ignore her and keep moving, but the vulnerability in her voice gets me and instead, I peek around the lace hanging from the bed frame, losing my breath, my body answering for her.

Our eyes meet and her lips open in a gasp, her breath frantic. As she stares at me, her emotions on full display, I can't fathom a time or place where I would ever not be attracted to her.

When I don't immediately respond, she lifts to her elbows, blinking a few times before turning away, her pink cheeks darkening. "I know I'm not as slim as I once was..."

Is she kidding me? "*Blair*, my cock is at half-mast when I'm just talking to you. I'm *more* than attracted to you. In my eyes, you've always been the most beautiful girl...woman to ever exist, and time hasn't changed that." I'm more honest than I'd usually be because it seems like she needs this win right now. And when she smiles, I relax.

"Okay, good to know."

"Good." I chuckle under my breath. "I hope that helps you sleep a little better."

I turn to leave but she stops me again. "Who needs sleep? I think we should fuck."

"You... what?" I half choke, half stumble as I spin back around, trying to see her face. Our eyes lock again, and she licks her lips while my cock throbs uncomfortably.

"*Blair*," I warn and she laughs softly.

"I'm sorry. I couldn't help myself. I needed to lighten the mood, and you know I've always loved teasing you."

"It's true. You always were a gorgeous pain in my ass."

Blair's expression turns serious and she takes a deep breath. "Jokes aside, thank you. It's been a while since I've felt as desired as I do with you."

I open my mouth to argue but slam my eyes shut. Now is not the time to bring up her dumbass of an ex. They only just broke up. How the fuck did he not make her feel desired every single day?

"Don't ever let anyone make you feel like you're not the most beautiful woman on this planet. Ever. Okay?"

"Okay," she whispers, her voice shaking as she nods, the emotion clear in her expression.

My chest tightens, thinking about all that we've been through together and apart.

"Your ring," she says suddenly, drawing my attention to the way I'm subconsciously spinning the ring on my pinky. I should have taken it off years ago, but I couldn't. The only time it leaves my finger is when I'm on the field. And while I don't plan on admitting it right now, I only wear it for her.

"This old thing," I joke, dropping my hand. "Another piece of jewelry to add to my collection."

Blair's eyes widen when I gesture to the bulge in my pants. "I still can't tell if you're messing with me or not," she muses, her eyes lowering to my groin. "Can I see it?" She sits forward, clearly more brazen with some alcohol in her system.

"You want to see my cock?" I balk. "You want to see if I've got a piercing?"

"I do. Very much so."

Fuck. If I didn't know how tipsy she was, and that she was likely using this as a deflection, it would be a major turn-on. But even my cock realizes it's not going to happen. It doesn't so much as twitch when she nibbles her lip in anticipation.

"Maybe another time. For now, you need to sleep."

"Ugh. I don't need sleep." She yawns, making me chuckle. "If we'd have slept together back then, I'd know the truth, so why can't I know now?"

I bite back another laugh and sit down on the end of the bed, reaching forward to pat her leg. My poor, beautiful, mixed-up Little B. "I didn't have it back then, so you wouldn't have known if I had it now."

"What you're saying is no? You're not going to show me." She pouts and I bite my lip to stop myself from laughing again.

"Not tonight." I stand up and bop her on the nose. "I'll be back."

Without waiting for a response, I jog out of the room and tiptoe through the apartment, grabbing a glass of water and rummaging around until I've located a Tylenol. I half expect Blair to be asleep when I return, but she's sitting up, her expression unreadable.

"Here." I give her the water and place the Tylenol on the nightstand. "Drink up and then it's time to lie down."

Surprisingly doing as asked, Blair quietly gulps back the water, handing me the empty glass. But before I can move, she grabs my wrist.

"Don't go. Please."

"I won't. I'll just be down the hall."

"No, I mean, don't leave me. Not yet."

I nod and Blair falls silent for a beat, running her hands down her face as the energy between us completely changes. "There's something I have to tell you." She pauses as tears coat her eyes. "But I'm terrified you'll leave."

My body tenses, the muscles straining as I visually appraise her. She forces a smile and I immediately sit beside her, putting her water glass down before grabbing her hand. "Why would I leave?" My voice cracks from the emotion pouring out of her, and when she lets go of my hand, I panic.

"It was all my fault."

"What was?"

My heart aches for her, but when the first tear glides down her cheek, dread shreds me from the inside.

"The night of the accident, I'd been drinking like this." She pauses and I freeze. I knew she wanted to talk, but now that it's happening, I feel nauseous. "I was broken and numb and I wasn't thinking clearly. I did some things... It doesn't matter, but I shouldn't have called you." She frantically wipes her eyes, her breathing rapid as she sniffs.

I rush to comfort her, the pain in my chest unbearable as I watch her break. "Blair, there is no situation, no universe, where I wouldn't want you to call me. No matter what."

"But it's my fault. If I hadn't called you, you never would have gotten in your truck. You never would have been on that road. That's why Sierra *died*. Because of *me*."

Fuck. My heart cracks as a wave of guilt makes it difficult to breathe. "No, Blair. It's not—"

"Wait, there's more... I'm the reason she was drinking, Zane. After you... No... Because we ended things, I started drinking at the first party. And I made Sierra come and drink with me. Told her I needed to drown my sorrows because of her stupid brother. She knew, you know? She knew the whole time. I couldn't hide it."

"I know," I rasp, unable to say much more as my beautiful girl shatters in front of me.

The last time Blair and I spoke, before I left Jacksonville, before I ran away, I'd reluctantly agreed that we were both to blame, that we'd both played a part in the events of that night. I knew it was wrong, but I was so fucked up over what had happened that I couldn't make much sense of anything. All I knew was that Blair was begging me. And I couldn't say no to her.

I knew my sister had one drink, but I never knew it was Blair that gave it to her. Either way, that's not what caused the accident. I took the blame for the alcohol in her system, and never mentioned it to Blair. Now it appears Blair omitted some of the details herself. She *never* told me she thought my sister had been drunk.

Not once.

"All this time, you thought it was you? I thought you were taking responsibility because you'd called me. If I'd known you were carrying that much—"

"If she wasn't drinking, the accident never would have happened..."

"She *wasn't* drinking," I say, my body numb, the last seven years of pain suffocating me from the inside.

"She'd still be alive..."

"She *wasn't drinking*!" I repeat, louder this time, my voice ragged as I draw in a breath. *I did this.* I always knew Blair's pain was my fault, but I never knew the severity of it all. How badly I'd fucked up. "She *wasn't drinking*, Blair!"

"It's my fault you left and— What?" Blair's eyes dart to mine, my words finally sinking in. "No, I saw her."

"If you saw her, then you saw her have *one* drink. That's all she had. She told me on the way that she'd only had one. I never would have let her drive otherwise."

"She lied to you, Zane." Blair scoffs incredulously. "Of course she lied, she—"

"There was barely any alcohol in her system."

"What?"

"The coroner confirmed her blood alcohol level was low. Not that I needed him to. I knew. She was of sound mind." *Not that my parents saw it that way.*

"But then why?" Blair squints before jamming her palms into her eyes. "No, no, no, no. I did it. It was my fault. My fault she died, my fault you left. It was *me*."

A deep ache burns in my chest. If I wasn't fighting so hard to hold my shit together, I'd undoubtedly have tears in my eyes. For her. Because *I* did this. I broke her.

"It was never you, Blair. *Never*."

Blair continues to shake her head but removes her hands, setting her shattered gaze on mine. "I thought you knew," I whisper as everything I remember of that night plays through my mind.

Having her staring at me makes my next words that much harder to say, but I swallow the emotion in my throat and push on through.

"*I* was the drunk one, B. It was all *me*."

CHAPTER THIRTY-ONE

ZANE

AGE NINETEEN

"*Hap-py Birth-day toooo yooouuu.*"

I roll my eyes as the cheers ring out. I told them under no circumstances were they allowed to sing, but my so-called friends just finished not one, but two drunken renditions of the happy birthday song. And there's a fucking cake.

Kill me now.

"*Come on, Zane.*" *Cade slaps my back before wrapping his arm around my shoulder.* "*Cheer up. It's your birthday.*"

"*I thought it was, and yet, I asked for none of these theatrics and here we are.*"

"*It's tradition. Don't be so sour. Your friends want to celebrate and shower you with attention.*"

"*No, they don't. Like you, they want to piss me off.*"

"*True. And it worked.*" *He turns to our friends, all staring my way.* "*He hated every second. We did it.*" *The cheers get louder, and I groan until my eyes lock with Blair's, her sympathetic smile bringing about my own.*

The cake's placed in front of me as she gestures toward the yard, biting her lip. And while this could very much be another twisted ploy from her brother, I quickly blow out my candles, following after her while my friends are distracted with food.

"*Please tell me you weren't a part of that?*" *I ask when I find her outside, a suspicious smile gracing her lips.*

"*I'll never tell.*"

"*Come here.*"

I launch off the back deck, grabbing her around the waist as she lets out a squeal. "*You owe me a blow job for that.*"

"*What? No way.*"

"*Zane?*" *my sister calls out, and Blair and I spring apart.* "*Are you out here?*"

Blair ducks down behind a garbage can seconds before Sierra steps out. "*I knew it.*" *She laughs.* "*You can't hide forever.*"

"*I can and I will.*"

"*They just want to celebrate with you.*"

"*God, you sound like Cade. You're not allowed to hang out with him anymore.*" *She flips me off and I chuckle.* "*Go back inside, Sierra. I'll be in soon. I promise.*"

"*Ooh, I see. You have one of your chicks out here.*"

"*One of my what?*"

She bursts out laughing as Cade appears behind her.

"*Told you that would get him riled. He's always so secretive about the woman he fucks.*"

I stiffen and cough to hide Blair's gasp from behind me. "*Fuck off, both of you. It's my party, and I'll cry if I want to.*"

"*Pussy. You've got five minutes and I'm dragging you inside.*"

"*Noted.*"

They disappear and I cringe as Blair lifts to her feet. "*It's not what you think.*" *I raise my hands in surrender.* "*I'm secretive because* there are no women.*"

Her frown has my stomach sinking and my fist clenching at my side, ready to beat the shit out of Cade. If she doesn't believe me, I'm going fuck him up. "*B, I—*"

She bursts out laughing as she leaps into my arms, slamming her lips to mine.

I stiffen momentarily, until I'm lost in her kiss. Fuck, she feels good pressed against me.

With one hand supporting her weight, I sink the other into her hair and tug on the strands, slipping my tongue into her mouth when she lets out a whimper.

"*I know that you're faithful,*" *she whispers, pulling away too soon, lightly brushing her nose against mine. "But it would be so much easier if we told everyone the truth."*

"Soon," I promise her, my chest tight with emotion.

"I'll take 'soon.' But for now, our time is up." She shrugs, gesturing toward the door. "I'll see you inside?"

"You will."

She runs off toward the side gate so she can enter the rented party space through the front door, and like every time she leaves, she takes a little piece of me with her. I need to man up and talk to Cade. But I can't do that while we're here. Especially when he's in spring break party mode. He once told me I'd never be good enough for B, and that was after I joked about it. He's going to be beyond pissed, and I can't have Blair caught in the crossfire.

But the second we're back at college, I'll tell him the truth, even if he doesn't want to hear it. Even if he's ready to fight.

*"*A*nother shot," one of the guys calls out and I hold out my hand, despite barely being able to stand.*

The alcohol warms me as it travels down my throat, and I smile lazily. "To my birthday," I say, rocking slightly as I head over to an empty table, dropping down onto the bench seat with a thud.

"How are you doing there, big bro?" Sierra asks, laughing at my expense as she walks past, bottles of water in hand.

"I'm in fine form as always, little sis. How are you?"

"Never been better. I think Jaxon likes me."

"Jaxon?" I jump up but she's quick to push me back down.

"Don't be an asshole, Zane. You know he's a good guy."

I smile, giving her a loving shove. "You're right. As far as guys go, he's decent."

"Better than you."

"Fuck off. You worship me."

"Ugh. I know. It's a curse. Always have, always will."

"Feeling is mutual, S. Go get him."

"What? How?"

"It's simple... You walk up and you say, 'Want to make out?' He'll probably blow his load on the spot."

"And that's why it's a curse. Right now, I want to hate you."

"But you can't." I smile wide and she pokes out her tongue.

"God, I wish I could tell you what I know right now. But instead, I'm going to let you stew on it."

"What?" I stare at her confused. "What are you talking about?"

"Nothing." She smirks before spinning on her stiletto heel and prancing away. Prancing. While I'm struggling to figure out what the fuck is going on. Sisters.

The night goes on with me unable to move from my seat, chatting to anyone that stops by, my gaze seeking Blair whenever I can.

After I've been staring at her for a good five minutes this time, she catches me watching and raises a brow, her eyes bouncing around the room before she makes her way over.

"I've barely seen you tonight," she says above the music, perching on my lap and wriggling to get comfortable.

I'd be worried if we didn't do this often, never attracting a second glance. The whole town knows we're friends. Most of them think she's like a little sister to me. If only they knew the things I wanted to do to her.

This time when she sits down, however, her short dress lifts dangerously high on her thighs, giving me a view of her black lace panties when my gaze travels down.

With an internal growl, I search the room for voyeurs, sighing in relief when I realize our legs are hidden from view.

Only I can see her, and fuck, that feels good.

"So..." Blair continues when I don't respond. "Where have you been?"

"I've been here." I lean in, letting my lips brush against her skin, loving when she shivers. "You seem to be having fun."

"You've been watching me?"

"I have."

"Then you'd know that while I am having fun, my night could be better."

"Oh, yeah?"

She swivels in my lap, repositioning herself until she can whisper in my ear, the movement drawing her dress even higher.

I close my eyes to stop myself from looking, imagining the smile on her lips.

"I want you, Zane. I wish you could touch me."

"Christ." I hold her away from me, checking her face for any signs of humor. But there's none. "You know we can't."

"So, I'm expected to just watch you flirt and be fine with it?"

"I wasn't flirting." I stiffen, trying to remember a moment where I had, but nothing comes to mind.

"I'm kidding. But I've thought about what it would feel like if you did. How it would make me want you more. Knowing you're mine." Her lust-filled gaze bores into mine, and she squirms in my lap.

"You're killing me, B."

"It's killing me too. Why can't we be together?"

I open my mouth to argue, but pause, throwing her question around in my mind. Why can't we be together?

Right now.

No one is watching.

Leaning back, I roll up my sleeve and glance down at the glimpse of her panties, trying to gauge how wet she is beneath the skimpy black material. It's dark, and in her new position, people wouldn't be able to see my hands.

But they would see her expression, unless...

"Can you keep a straight face?" I ask, the idea now firmly planted in my mind.

"What?" The question leaves her mouth on a breath, and her legs clench as she blinks rapidly.

"Can you keep a straight face?"

Her gaze drops to my hand hovering near her thigh, and her breath hitches. "Yes," she whispers. "But you have to keep talking."

"Talking?"

"Yes."

"Do you want me to tell you about my day while I finger fuck you, B?"

"God." She shakes her head no, but then whispers, "Yes, please."

"Anything for you."

Cupping her leg, I gently skim my fingers across the inside of her thigh, gliding my hand toward her core. She sucks in a breath but otherwise holds up her end of the deal, the picture of stoic perfection.

"*Did you like your cake?*" she asks, her voice strained, making me chuckle.

"*You know I didn't.*" I reach her panties, dragging a finger across the soaked material, biting back a groan. My cock twitches and Blair squirms on top of me, making it worse.

Her lips part and I squeeze her waist, drawing her gaze. "*Ask me what my favorite present was.*"

"*O-kay*" she rushes out, a fake smile locked in place. "*What was your favorite present?*"

"*Finding your pussy soaked for me, imagining you chatting with your friends, your arousal pooling at your entrance all night. Waiting for this.*"

"*Jesus.*" Her body sags and for the briefest of seconds she closes her eyes. "*You can't say that.*"

"*Sorry, would you prefer I told you that I like the new sneakers from your parents?*"

"*God, don't mention my—*"

My fingers dip under the lace of her thong, brushing against her bare pussy, and Blair hisses at my touch. "*I happened to think the cake was delicious,*" she says as I insert a finger inside her, her hips bucking ever so slightly.

"*You know what's delicious?*"

"*You better say food or so help me God.*"

I chuckle, inserting a second finger before scissoring them inside her. And fuck, she feels amazing. Warm. Tight. We've done this before, but there's something about doing it in public that makes it all the more sweeter. More dangerous.

I groan against her hair and her walls tighten, her pussy sucking me in.

"*Fuck. I'm definitely not thinking about food. Though I would like nothing more than to eat your pus—*"

"*You're not playing fair.*"

"*Do you want me to stop?*"

"*God, no. Don't stop.*"

At her desperate plea, I buck my aching cock into her ass and drag my thumb over her clit, feeling the bud harden. She moans then bites her lip, though she needn't worry. It was barely audible over the party noise.

"*I'm going to get you back for this,*" she rasps, wriggling as I increase the pressure, curling my fingers to rub her walls.

"I can't wait."

She clenches around me, and I'm just about to tell her to come when Cade sits opposite us, groaning as he slams down his drink. "She didn't come. Bianca promised she'd be here and she didn't come."

Another day. Another girl. But while his choice of words are laughable in this present situation, I freeze in panic, my fingers still inside Blair, my thumb on her clit while her brother whines about his love life.

"Maybe she's running late," Blair says, comforting him, now fully playing her part. Acting the innocent girl and caring sister that he believes her to be.

It takes me longer than it should to register what's happening, and I quickly remove my fingers, subtly wiping them on my jeans. Blair jolts at my abrupt withdrawal but continues talking as though nothing's going on.

We sit like that for a second, until she spins to face Cade and leans forward, rocking her soaked pussy against the bulge in my jeans. My balls tighten, and a bolt of electricity travels the length of my cock.

I'd say this is my payback right now.

"Blair," I warn, my whisper barely loud enough to be audible, but when she rolls her hips again, I know she heard me.

I bite back a groan and when she reaches between us and squeezes my length, I lose it.

"I've gotta go." Grabbing her waist, I lift her just enough to shift her to the bench seat beside me, then hightail it out of there, pissed off with myself just as much as her.

I slam through the back door, beelining for the shed near the fence, needing a moment to compose myself. Maybe a release if I'm being honest. But I deserve the blue balls.

What was she playing at?

God. I shouldn't be questioning what the hell Blair was doing... What about me?

What did I think was going to happen when she came? Feeling her arousal coating my fingers was likely to set me off and—

"What the hell was that?" Blair appears out of nowhere, her anger clear in the darkness.

"Me? You were talking to Cade while rubbing your pussy against my cock. And you think I'm the one in the wrong?"

"You dumped me on the chair and stormed off. Talk about suspicious."

"Your brother's drunk. He won't remember that."

"Then why did he comment? His exact words were, 'What's his problem? You sit on him all the time.'"

Fuck. *"Did you tell him my problem?"*

"No." She shakes her head and relief fills me, until she adds more. *"I can't keep doing this, Zane. You gave me whiplash in there. Pushing me away and then fingering me in public. I may not want to be a princess, but I deserve the world. And if I'm not your world, then what are we doing here?"*

What? *"You know you're my world, B."*

"Do I?"

"Yes, you're being ridiculous."

"Oh, okay. Let's go and tell Cade then." She holds out her hand for me to take, but all I can do is stare down at it, unable to tell her yes or no. I can't say yes, *because I don't want to tell him, but I can't say* no *either. Because the second I do she's going to walk away.*

And I'm not sure she's coming back.

"Well?" She drops her hand and crosses her arms over her chest.

I've fucked up. I know. But I can't...

I stay silent and she scoffs, shaking her head. "Find me when you grow up, and stay away from me for the rest of the night."

My heart jolts as she storms off in a huff, and I bang my head against the shed, kicking the empty boxes lining the yard. Fucking Cade and his closeted asshole ways. If she really knew how he was going to react, she'd never once question me.

But maybe she's right. Maybe it's time for me to grow up and choose—my best friend or my world.

Not a hard decision really.

Chapter Thirty-Two

BLAIR

AGE SEVENTEEN

My hair falls in my face when I flop back onto my bed, and rather than pushing it out of the way like one normally would, I spend the next ten minutes trying to blow it off my face. My arms aren't working.

I can't believe I listened to my dad about "working out my frustrations." I'm dying. I'm not even sure I'll be able to function at all today.

"You okay in there, kiddo?" my dad calls out, his knuckles rapping against the half-open door.

"No. I'm dead. Your workout killed me."

"But are you still pissed off?" He chuckles, smart enough to stay on his side of the threshold, because if I could, I'd throw something at his face.

"I'm more pissed off now than I was yesterday. I'm pissed off with the world this time."

"That's good. At least you're not laser focused on one thing...or person?" His voice lifts in question and it actually makes me laugh.

"I'm still not going to tell you, Dad."

"Fine. What about your mom?"

"Nope. This is between me and the thing or person I'm annoyed with."

"Yeah. Okay. Well, if the workout didn't help, what about a walk? When I was younger, I used to find hiking helped to clear my head."

"Hiking?" I mull over that idea, picturing the trail near the beach not too far from our house, the one that's usually shaded, and this time I smile. "That definitely sounds better than your workout torture. I'll try it tomorrow. If I can use my legs."

"You'll be fine. A good workout never killed anyone."

"How do you know? If they're dead they can't tell anyone it was the exercise that killed them."

"Yeah, yeah." He chuckles. "Do you need anything before your mom and I head out?"

"No. I'm sure I'll still be here when you get back."

"And you say you're not a princess?" Cade calls out from the hallway, obviously eavesdropping on our conversation.

"Go away, Cade. You gave up football because you couldn't handle the workouts."

"That wasn't the reason and you know it." He slams open my door and glares my way, while I burst out laughing.

"Thanks for cheering me up, Bro. Now leave me alone."

"Come on, Cade. Give her some space to deal with whatever she has going on."

"I know what it is," he gloats, his brows raised in cockiness.

"Bullshit," I snap back but my heart races in panic.

"I heard you tell Sierra that you missed out on submitting your story for that grant thingy because you got the dates wrong."

"Ugh. Dammit." Relief fills me as I fake annoyance. "Don't tell Mom, please."

"You owe me."

"Don't be a dick." Dad appears again and slaps Cade across the back of his head. "Your secret is safe with us, Princess. But your mom would understand."

"Thanks, Dad."

Dad drags Cade away before coming back to shut my door, and I throw my arms over my face, my pulse finally settling down.

I lie still for a beat until I realize what I'm doing and laugh to myself. Looks like my arms work after all. *I try to sit up, but it's no use. The rest of my body is still in recovery mode.*

Accepting the inevitable, I pull out my book, opting to spend the rest of the day reading.

Because what I really need is an escape.

I'm not sure how long I've been lost in another world when there's a soft knock on my bedroom door. I twist my head to check the time, but wince when my neck aches. Stupid hardcore workouts. My dad may be in his forties now, but he still pushes himself like he did in his football heyday.

Speaking of Dad, since he and my mom have only been gone for an hour, and Cade never knocks, I'm certain it's not them. My pulse spikes as I draw in a breath, secretly hoping it's Sierra, but inherently knowing that it's not.

"Come in," I call out, my voice wavering.

As suspected, Zane opens the door, his expression somber until he sees me in bed. "Are you okay?" He stiffens, making me laugh incredulously. He cares so much, and yet, it's not enough to be honest with my brother.

"It was daddy/daughter day at the gym today." I force a smile when Zane cringes.

"God, even I struggle to keep up with him sometimes."

"No you don't. But thanks for trying to make me feel better. How are you?"

"Awful, and that's without a Tim Stevens special."

"Good," I deadpan and he laughs.

"I'm sorry, B. I was a dick last night, but in my defense, I was pretty wasted."

"I know. And if I'm being honest, I'm not upset about last night."

Zane sighs in relief and my stomach sinks. I don't want to hurt him. But I can't keep up this charade.

"I'm not upset about last night, but that doesn't change what I said. I think we should take a break until a point in time when we both feel like we can be open about our relationship."

"B?" Zane's face pales and my chest tightens, but I stand firm. At least, I sit firm because I'm still struggling to move.

"I'm going to tell Cade. I promise. It just has to be the right time."

"I get it, I do. And I know you've got a lot riding on this. I'm Cade's sister, so he can only hate me for so long, but he could hate you forever. That man can hold a grudge."

"That shouldn't matter. When you walked away last night, I realized I'd choose you. If it was a choice, it's a no-brainer."

"But how would that work? Life would be awkward with my family. Think about Christmas and birthdays?"

"He'll get over it. I thought you wanted to tell him?"

"I do, but you were right. It needs to be done the correct way. In the meantime, we need a clean break. No more sneaking around. No more lies."

"B." Zane visibly swallows and my emotions get caught in my throat.

I'm actually surprised by how calm I am considering what's happening, but I'm also aware that I could just be numb. For all I know, the second Zane walks out my door, I might break and beg him to take me back.

"Is this really what you want?" Zane asks, his voice barely above a whisper.

"Yes," I whisper back. "Don't you think it's the right thing to do? I love spending time with you, and sneaking around was fun in the beginning, but it's taking a toll on us both. I said I deserved better last night. But the truth is, we both do."

Zane sighs, running his huge palm through his hair, the light brown strands falling in his face. "I see your logic. But I don't like it."

A smile tugs on my lips. "I didn't think you would."

"How long will this break last?"

"It's not a break, Zane. It's a breakup." Zane visibly recoils and I internally wince, working hard to keep going. "We can revisit 'us' when I'm in college. Discuss how we feel after Cade stops seeing me as his baby sister."

"That's never going to happen."

"I know. But when we're both there, it'll at least be a little more even."

"Fuuck." He shakes his head, and just when I think he's about to argue, the front door slams.

"Zane!" Cade calls out. "Are you here, asshole? Your truck's out front."

Zane stiffens before taking a few steps toward my door. "I'm up here," he calls out, his voice even, the picture of calm. "Just giving your sister hell for being so weak."

Cade's obnoxious laugh travels up the stairs before loud footsteps tell us he's on his way.

"Okay." Zane turns toward me, his expression weary, his intense gaze boring into mine. "But this isn't over." He half whispers, half mouths the last part and I nod.

"I know." I smile, letting it morph into a pout as Cade appears.

"She's so weak." He laughs. "Do you know she's been in that position since I left over an hour ago?"

"I do now. And where were you?" Zane's expression turns as he glowers at

Cade. *"We were supposed to meet at the beach." Zane points in the direction of the beach closest to our house.*

"I was there. You said Atlantic *beach. I've been waiting this whole time."*

"Why would I say Atlantic beach? That's almost twenty minutes from here."

"I don't know. Who knows why you do half the shit you do. Come on, let's go."

Cade huffs as he walks away, and Zane turns back toward me, shooting me a sad wink before he disappears after him.

And it all makes sense. He sent Cade away so he could talk to me.

But I bet he never considered it would end in goodbye.

Although, technically we never actually said that.

Maybe it'll all be okay.

I t's not okay. I'm *not okay. It turns out that not being with Zane is ten times worse than being his dirty little secret, and I almost wish I could take it all back.*

Almost.

The part of me that knows I'm doing the right thing is thankfully stronger than my heart but God, it hurts.

The movie I'm watching ends, and I mindlessly flick through the options on the TV trying to find another one. Not that I need it; I have no clue what the last one was about.

I've pretty much been sulking on the couch since I was able to get out of bed, and I'm content to stay here until school goes back in a few days.

After another ten minutes of scrolling, I settle on a comedy and find myself actually paying attention until Sierra appears in front of me, blocking my view.

"Come on." She grabs my hand, attempting to pull me to my feet. "We're going out."

"Where?" I groan and even I can hear how whiny I sound.

"We're party hopping. It's the last weekend of spring break, and we deserve some fun."

"I'm not in the mood for fun."

"I know. But I can't take you moping over my brother anymore."

"Shhh. Someone might hear you." Sierra is the only person I've talked to about Zane. I knew early on that it would be impossible to keep it from her. But I never told Zane that she knew. And I'm glad that I didn't. He'd hate his sister sympathizing with him.

"No one else is here." Sierra rolls her eyes. "Come on. Get up and get dressed into something you wouldn't be embarrassed to leave the house in." Her eyes drop to my ripped sweatpants and stained band T-shirt. "I'll do your hair and makeup while you snap out of this funk. It's gone on too long." She waves her hand in front of my face. "We're going out."

"Do I have to?"

"Yep. Look at me. I'm already styled to perfection. I refuse to let it go to waste."

"Okay. Sure." I fake a bout of enthusiasm. "Let's do this."

Just like Sierra suggested, we party hop around Ponte Vedra—where all the wealthy kids fight to throw the best spring break parties—and I'm significantly buzzed by the time we get to the third.

Not that it takes much alcohol to get me drunk. I'm not usually a drinker. But today, I am letting loose and trying to enjoy myself. Trying being the operative word.

"Who's here that we know?" I ask Sierra as I stumble up the steps, giggling at my clumsiness.

"I think Lily and Bryce are here"—a couple we know from school— "as well as the guys from the lacrosse team."

"Which means that Jaxon is here?" I smile knowingly. Sierra and Jaxon were flirting for the majority of Zane's party. "I wholeheartedly believe you'd make an adorable couple."

"Shh. Jesus. We haven't even kissed."

"What?"

"You don't even realize you said that out loud, do you?"

I wince, shaking my head no.

"God, that brother of mine really messed you up."

"I'll have you know that I ended it," I say somewhat proudly until reality sets in and my stomach sinks. "Moving on."

As though proving my point about the two of them, Jaxon seeks out Sierra the second she walks in, and other than mixing her a drink, I stay away, giving them time to themselves.

But it doesn't take long for me to regret it.

I'd be fine by myself if I wasn't forced to stare at couple after couple mauling each other on the dance floor, reminding me of how easy it is to be free to kiss whoever the hell you want without stressing about the consequences.

That should be us. That should—

"Blair Stevens, is that you?" I turn to find Nathan Morgan, the only guy both my brother and Zane truly hate.

"Hi, Nathan. I didn't expect to see you here."

"I wouldn't usually be caught dead at this party. But my cousin's hooking up with the woman of the house, so here we are."

"And you wonder why my brother hates you. You know this is a party with most of my school, right? My brother's old school. Your rival team."

"I do. And that's why I don't want to be here."

"I get that, but..." I lean in closer to whisper in his ear. "Shouldn't you at least pretend that you do, so the guys don't beat the shit out of you?"

"Let them try." He pulls back and winks, making me laugh uncontrollably. "I'm not here for long anyway," he tells me. "There's a party at my house. I'm just waiting for my cousin, then we're..." he continues speaking but I don't register anything coming out of his mouth on the account of Zane entering my line of sight. He laughs at something some girl is saying, shaking his head with a smirk.

My stomach knots, and I struggle to fight back tears, but I pinch my leg and smile, turning my attention back to Nathan.

"Sorry, I got distracted. What did you say?"

"I asked if you wanted to come with me?"

"Where?"

"To my party. You look a little sad here. Maybe a change of scenery will help."

I've never had a problem with Nathan. He's an ass to my brother and Zane, but they're both assholes back to him. I've always played it off as a *football rivalry and never anything more. He's always been nice enough to me.*

But...while I may be drunk, I'm sober enough to know that's a bad idea. "Thank you, but I'm going to have to pass."

"Because of your brother?"

"No," I say honestly, because if I was thinking about Cade, I'd go just to annoy him. I'm saying no for Zane. And because of that, my traitorous gaze flits back to where he's standing, and when I see him, it feels like someone knocked the wind out of me.

I clutch my chest as the girl he's with grabs his shirt, leaning in, and I have to stop myself from screaming when she presses her lips to his.

Bile rises in my throat and I feel nauseous. I'm not sure what's pounding harder, my head or my heart. Either way, I need out.

"What time are you leaving?" I turn back to Nathan, trying to control my composure.

"Ten minutes?" He seals the deal with the quick escape and I nod with relief.

"I'll meet you out front. I just have to say goodbye to a friend."

I don't listen to his response—I'm not even sure if he gave one—my mind already set on finding Sierra and hightailing it out of here.

When I turn, my steps falter, my chest burning with betrayal. We only called it quits three days ago and Zane's kissing someone else.

My head spins as I race to find Sierra, but before I can reach her, someone grabs my wrist, pulling me into a hard chest.

Zane.

"What are you doing?"

"What are you doing?" he counters. "You look frantic. What's going on?"

I try to wriggle out of his grasp but he holds strong, making me angry. "Let go of me, Zane." I rock as I'm yelling and his eyes narrow.

"Are you drunk?" It takes me a second to register his words because there's something off about them. He's slurring.

"Are you?" I snap back, which somehow convinces him to let me go.

"I'm not really in the mood to party, you know," he stares at me pointedly. "The alcohol helps."

"Seems to have helped a great deal. You looked like you were having lots of fun on the dance floor."

Zane's eyes widen before he curses under his breath.

"That wasn't... it's not... B, it's not what you think."

"Did you or did you not have your tongue down someone else's throat?"

"You know I fucking didn't. If you were really watching you would have seen that she kissed me and I shoved her away."

"After a good thirty seconds." I may have been talking to Nathan, but I was watching Zane from the corner of my eye.

"Blair."

"No, don't 'Blair' me. If our friends knew about us, no one would be trying to kiss you."

"Fuuck." Zane winces, running a hand through his hair, his shoulders dropping at the knowledge that I'm right.

"How many times has that happened?"

"What?"

"You know what? Never mind. I'd rather not know."

I turn to walk away but his fingers curl around my wrist this time. "Blair."

"Stop, we can't do this here. I'm leaving anyway."

"Where?" He drops his hold and steps back.

"To another party."

"Whose party?" As though expecting to get the answer somewhere in the room, he scans our surroundings, his expression confused.

"I don't see how that's any of your business."

"Fuuuck." He runs a hand down his face this time, groaning again. "Don't go. Please. I promise I didn't—"

"Let's talk about this tomorrow, when we're both sober. Rest assured, you didn't do anything wrong. We're not together."

"Thanks." He rolls his eyes sarcastically. "Whether we're together or not, I'm still not interested in anyone else."

I'm momentarily stunned, but I still can't stay here. "I..."

Zane's shoulders drop and he sighs in resignation. "If you really have to go, can you at least call me when you get there, and when you get home?"

"Zane." My heart skips, taking in the protectiveness in his eyes.

"Just do it, B. Please."

"Fine."

"Thank you." His eyes light up with relief. "Look after yourself, yeah?"

"I will."

I think he whispers 'thanks,' but I'm already on my way to find Sierra, grabbing another red cup of beer when I pass by the drinks.

I'm determined not to look at Zane, but at the last second, I glance back, finding another girl already in my place, her arms draped over his shoulder, her body pressed against him.

And instead of hating him for it, like I should, my chest aches for him.

Because I really wish that could be me.

And maybe, someday it will be. God knows, we both deserve to be happy.

Chapter Thirty-Three

BLAIR

PRESENT DAY

"It wasn't you, B. It was all fucking me." Zane's voice breaks and all I can do is stare at him while my head plays catch-up with our conversation. A tightness fills my chest, and I struggle to take in air. After seven years, I finally admitted to the guilt I'm carrying, and now he's spinning me a different story.

I shift uncomfortably, our conversation wreaking havoc on my heart, while at the same time, a weight has been lifted at finally getting my feelings off my chest.

But I'm so confused.

"Zane, I—"

"I wish I'd known how bad it was for you. Or how much you were carrying. Hell, I wish I'd taken a moment to pull my head out of my ass before walking away."

"That's hardly what happened, Zane. You were broken. We both were. You'd just lost your sister and—"

"I should have protected you!"

"From what?"

"Yourself. I know you. I used to think I knew you better than anyone else. I should have realized you were going to take this on. That you were going to carry some of the burden."

"I should have taken it all. There's no point in both of us carrying it around."

"B." Zane cocks his head, his expression pointed. "You know it's not that easy."

"Make it easy. It was an accident, but if I hadn't begged you to come and get me..."

"Stop. Please. Nothing you can say will make me blame you. Ever."

The intensity of his gaze makes me squirm as I fight back my tears. I've been holding my truth so close to my chest that it's hard to let go of. But with Zane's reassurance, I want to. He's always had that effect on me. Always been able to make me see the best in myself.

Zane glances away, lost in thought, and when he looks back, his expression breaks me. "Fuuck." He shakes his head, schooling his features. "It's amazing how much I can remember of that night considering how drunk I was. I hate it."

"Same." I force a smile at the irony. "It's like a movie got stuck on repeat in my mind. One I can't forget."

"I hate those movies; they're always the bad ones."

"The horrors." I huff out a laugh though it's anything but funny.

"Oh, it's a horror all right. I've spent so much time thinking. Regretting. Wondering what I would change if I could. I'm sure you know the drill."

"I do." I tuck my knees up to my chest, wrapping my arms around myself. "What do you think about the most? Apart from, you know." I wince. "The accident."

Zane blows out a breath, his cheeks puffing as his eyes close. "I think about the days leading up to the night. The point where you told me you deserved the world. And I didn't listen."

"Ahh." I giggle while my stomach clenches. "While I hate that part, I delivered a good blow."

"You did." He snorts. "And I wholeheartedly agreed with you. I was an ass. You were right to walk away. What do you think about most? Apart from, you know, the accident."

Pain grips my chest and I can't tell him the moment I think about the most because it would absolutely shatter him. But I can tell him one of my biggest regrets, where it all started falling apart. "I'm stuck on the moment I confronted you about the kiss."

"Fuck." Zane's face contorts as though that memory physically tortures him. "I never let myself think about that. The guilt is too much."

"Why? You never kissed her back. I overreacted."

"No, you didn't. None of that is on you. That's all me. If you hadn't seen that, maybe you wouldn't have left the party."

"So many maybes."

"I know," he rasps, looking away. "It's the maybes that keep me up at night." His voice lowers, and if I wasn't paying full attention, I might have missed the way the fight leaves him. As though he's resigned to the fact that he'll never move on. Never get over the guilt.

"I'm sorry," I whisper, reaching out to grab his hand. He's trying hard to hold his composure, and it's breaking my heart. "I'm sorry you—"

Zane frowns. "Why are you sorry? I get why you left, and I still remember what you said. If people knew about us, she'd never have kissed me. No matter how you look at it, I fucked up. I'd been fucking up for a while. But if I was to rank my fuckups and pick the worst, it would be letting you leave that night. I'm the one that should be sorry. You shouldn't have been at Nathan's, but you were, because of *me*—" His voice breaks this time and he doesn't know the worst of it. He stayed away because I asked him to, and he never even knew the full story. He still doesn't. But if I tell him—if I tell anyone—we're all transported back to the night. No one will ever move on.

Lifting to my knees again, I pull him into me and cup his face, lightly brushing my thumb across his cheek, needing to change the energy in the room. "We can't change the past, Zane. You're here now. Even when I pushed you away, you wouldn't stay gone."

"Like I said, once I saw you again, there was no going back. You've always been it for me, B."

My breath hitches, and in the silence of the night, it's deafening to my ears.

"Does that really shock you?" Zane asks, a sad smile gracing his lips.

"It shouldn't, but it does."

After he left home, I told myself that he kept us a secret because he never wanted the commitment. It was a coping mechanism, and after a while I started to believe it. I knew he was faithful. I never once questioned that. But since he always joked about not having time for multiple girls, it was easy to let myself believe that meant something more. Maybe he didn't have time for me either.

"God, I'm such an idiot." Zane abruptly jumps up, running his hands down his face, pacing the room. "You're the only one I've ever wanted, and yet... I refused to tell your brother. I kissed someone else. I let you walk away. I forced... my sister to drive me to find you. And I..." he trails off, closing his eyes, and when he opens them again, my chest heaves as I fight back the tears. I have never seen his expression so defeated. The devastation in his gaze has me breathless.

"You didn't—"

"We were fighting," he cuts in, refusing to look at me. "S... She wasn't going fast enough and I was yelling at her to move. She tried to pull over, telling me to get out of the truck. That she'd find you on her own. But I wouldn't let her. I needed to see you. I needed to make things right."

"Zane—"

"No, wait. Please. I need to get this out." He takes a deep breath, his eyes lifting to mine, while his gaze see through me, his mind somewhere else. Back in his truck, maybe. "I turned the steering wheel, B. I was so fucked up that I didn't see someone coming in the opposite direction. I just couldn't let her stop. To make things worse, the police said there were no signs of the car slowing down or moving off the road. She was never pulling over. She told me that to piss me off, to make me admit how much I loved you. Such a typical thing for her to do."

I freeze, letting his words sink in, until my protectiveness takes over. "Oh, God." I jump up and pull him into my arms, my gaze lifting as the first tear slides down his cheek. "Zane..." I trail off because nothing I say will ever ease that confession. I can't imagine how much that's eaten away at him.

Pulling him closer, I silently comfort him until he shakes me off. "You should hate me. You want to know why I let you push me away so easily? Why I left? It's because *I* couldn't look at *you*, *I* couldn't look at *anyone* without the weight of the guilt crushing my soul. But if you'd have called, if you'd ever reached out, I would have moved heaven and earth to be here. In a heartbeat. No matter how broken I was."

Sorrow and regret crush me, but I fight to stay strong. For Zane. "I always knew that," I whisper, trying hard not to let my voice crack. "And I never hated you. I couldn't."

"Yet you didn't call."

"I didn't." Shame creeps up my chest until I feel it on my cheeks. If I'd have known he blamed himself, I might have picked up the phone. But then again, maybe I wouldn't have. "You're here now," I say with a smile, as though that erases the past.

"I am." He finally smiles back at me, but there's no joy in his expression, no warmth. "I'm not sure I'll ever be whole, Blair, and I know I'll never be worthy of you, but I'm not leaving you again. Even if the best I'll get is your friendship. That accident has already taken too much from me. My sister... my sanity. If I'd done just one thing differently, none of it would have happened."

"You can't think like that. It'll kill you."

"I know. It's come close. The only reason I survived was football. On the field I'm a different guy. I have a different life. But it was always missing something. Fuck, if I'd just told Cade about us..."

"No." I shake my head. "I'm thankful you didn't because when he found out, he reacted exactly how you thought he would."

"What?" Zane raises a brow, his expression a mix of hurt and confusion.

"He flew off the handle. Starting yelling about me being too good for you and what a fool I had been. He told me you'd been sleeping around at college and that you'd never be a 'one woman kind of man.' Then he said he hoped you'd never come back."

"Wow." Zane huffs incredulously. "I knew he'd say I wasn't good enough, but that—"

"I know."

"He didn't seem to hate me when I saw him at the hospital, though. Or in the foyer earlier tonight."

I bite back my smirk, the memory of Cade coming back—tail between his legs—always bringing me joy. "That's because he apologized. Told me he overreacted because he was jealous. He didn't want to lose his best friend. To me. But it turns out, he lost you anyway."

"Because I kept my word and never came back."

"Exactly. I think he assumed you were still going to talk to him. That he was exempt from your goodbye."

"No one was."

I pause, thinking of his parents, lost without him. "It didn't take long for us to realize that. But thank you, by the way."

"For abandoning you?" He scoffs and I roll my eyes. We've already established that's not what happened.

"I'm thanking you for staying away when I asked you to. It was the best thing for both of us."

"But if I'd come back sooner, we could have had this conversation years ago. Maybe you'd never have hooked up with the douchebag."

"No." I shake my head with a laugh. "Everything happens for a reason. If you'd have come back sooner, I don't think I would have been ready to see you. Hell, I wasn't ready to see you when I did. It took me a long time to stop hating myself after what happened. I thought seeing you again would bring back the pain." Only that's not what happened. His presence made me stronger. It's making me stronger. Every day. I never would have survived this conversation with anyone else. "If you'd come back sooner and I'd found out how broken you were, it would have derailed me again."

"I'm not broken." Zane stands tall and smiles, while I stare at him deadpan.

"You're not? What's your sister's name?" A sharp pang hits me. I don't like hurting him, but it's not healthy to avoid it.

Zane groans low in his throat, proving my point. "*B...*"

"Exactly."

"But we lost so much time."

"Did we?" I bite back a smile. "Are you expecting us to pick up from where we left off? Now that we've talked." I'm trying to joke but as the words leave my mouth, my heart pounds in my chest. I never stopped caring for Zane. It just got mixed up with my feelings after the accident. And I've got to admit, he's making it hard to walk away again.

Whether he thinks I'm kidding or not, Zane laughs. "Fuck, yes, I am. You've been mine since the day I saved you from your surfboarding accident, and no amount of time or distance has changed that."

If only it was that easy. "Zane—"

"But," he cuts me off. "I'm not going to push you. I've waited years; what's a little more?"

"Always the gentleman." I laugh, knowing that's not a descriptor anyone else would ever use for Zane. And as if reading my mind, he adds...

"Only for you."

With my heart still thrashing around in my chest, I hold my smile, unsure what to do next until a yawn escapes me, snapping us out of the moment.

Zane's eyes flash to his watch and he groans. "Shit. I should let you sleep. The couch was in the front room, right?"

He moves to stand, and an irrational fear runs through me. "No,"—I reach out to stop him—"I don't want you to go. I'm not sure I could handle it if you did."

"Thank fuck." He sighs, making me giggle. "That's the last thing I want to do. I just wasn't sure if you still wanted me here after our talk."

My stomach knots. I knew he was carrying some heavy baggage, but for him to think he caused the accident... "I can't believe you've been harboring that guilt. All this time."

"Likewise."

"Maybe we deserve each other."

"Blair, if I'd known you blamed yourself, I would have come back sooner. I would have fought for you. But I thought you blamed *me*. You told me your life would be better without me."

"Because I hated myself, Zane. I thought your life would be better without *me*. Not the other way around. Only I should have known you'd never accept that."

"You're damn right I—"

A loud crash echoes through the apartment and we both freeze, our eyes on the door.

"Only me," Jenna yells out. "Just getting home."

Zane releases a breath, his gaze weary. "God, this is so fucked-up." He crawls onto the bed, resting his back against the headboard as he pulls me into his arms, curling me into him.

"Should we make a promise to be more honest with each other from here on out?"

I scrunch my face because I'm still holding back. "I'm sorry."

"You have nothing to be sorry about," he tells me again.

"You're wrong. I—"

"Blair, I shut down completely that day. When we first spoke in the hospital, I was completely numb. I can barely remember what you said. But I can remember your broken expression. I can remember your tears. And I can remember our agreement. But I wasn't exactly open to a deep and meaningful conversation."

"Me either, and honestly, I was scared of adding more to your stress. A little part of me didn't think you'd stay away."

"Really?"

"Yes. But then I let myself believe that you staying away proved that I'd been right. That you blamed me for what happened."

"It never occurred to you that I was staying away because I cared? Because you'd asked me to?"

"No. I was self-deprecating. I wasn't exactly thinking positively about anything. Including myself for that matter."

"Ahh." He squeezes me tighter. "It all makes sense now."

"What does?" I frown, glancing up at him confused.

"Nathan was a punishment of sorts. Because you hated yourself."

"No." I laugh out loud. "Wishful thinking on your part."

"Are you sure?" He raises a brow and I giggle when he smiles in anticipation.

"Yes, I'm sure. I loved him."

"Loved? Past tense?"

"Yes and no." I sigh quietly. "I don't feel the same way I once did, but it's not that easy to stop loving someone after that long." *Nathan's not the only example I have for that statement.*

Zane subtly winces before cupping my cheek, the sincerity and care in his eyes melting my heart. "Do you miss him?"

"I miss parts," I say honestly, and he nods, listening to my every word, even if it hurts him. "It took me longer than it should have to realize our relationship had been mostly about him. And as reluctant as I was to admit it, seeing you again helped me see that. It made me remember the woman I used to be."

"My queen?"

I roll my eyes, and he chuckles.

"You wouldn't have had to wait for me to come back if you'd listened when Cade told you how selfish Nathan was. Over and over."

"I never listen to Cade, and before you say anything, I wouldn't have listened to *you* either. I had to figure it out for myself. Your presence gave me that strength. If you'd just told me, it would have been obvious you were jealous, with the way you're fawning over me."

"Ooh, she's making jokes now."

"Who's joking? You just admitted it. Plus, you should see your loved-up doe eyes."

"I don't have doe eyes. I'm a fucking man." As if to prove his point, he flexes his muscles and growls. "See... man."

"Hmmm. Didn't I tell you you're not allowed to growl anymore?"

"Why? Does it get you all hot and bothered?"

"No." I nervously scratch the back of my neck.

"No?" he questions, and I see the moment he decides he's going to do something to test that theory.

With a soft rebuttal, I try to wriggle out of his arms, but it's no use. He grabs my shoulders, flipping me onto my back. "How about now?" He leans in close, his mouth brushing against my neck before he growls in my ear.

My entire body shivers as goose bumps coat my skin.

"You're right." He stops. "That doesn't get you hot and bothered at all." He sits up and I instantly miss the weight of him on top of me. But before I can say anything, *he* yawns this time.

"So...I guess I'm sleeping on the armchair?" He moves to stand again until I curl my fingers around his wrist, holding him in place.

"Stay here. Please. I want you to stay here." My heart races as he freezes, the playfulness gone as he stares down at me, his gaze shifting to the bed, clearly conflicted.

I almost tell him the armchair is fine. But it's not fine. I want him here.

Taking a deep breath, I let my fingers drop to his hand and nervously give it a squeeze. "Please. I want you to sleep next to me."

Chapter Thirty-Four

ZANE

I can't decide whether sleeping next to Blair is a dream or a nightmare, or a little of both, but there is no way in hell I'm walking away if she's asking me not to. Especially after she whispered, "*please*," peering up at me through thick lashes, her gaze begging me not to leave her.

As if she doesn't know how much it kills me every time we say goodbye.

When I don't immediately respond, Blair's shoulders drop and she uses her adorable pout to make me feel guilty, reminding me of the playful spark I used to see, instead of the reserved woman she's become.

I stare at her for a beat, mesmerized by the moment, and vow then and there that if it takes a lifetime, she *will* find herself again. I'll make sure of it. Because at the very least, she deserves that.

"Well?" she asks, scrunching her nose.

"You know I can't say no to you, B," I tell her honestly, my response accompanied by a half laugh. "So yes, I'll torture myself by sleeping next to you. All night long."

"Torture yourself?"

Is she kidding me with that question? "Blair, we have *never* slept next to each other, and here you are in skimpy silk pajamas, having trusted me enough to bare your soul, and I'm expected to just *sleep* next to you."

"Do you want more?" She swallows nervously and I can't help but smile. She's got the wrong idea entirely.

"I just want to hold you."

"Oh." Her eyes widen and a spark of heat ignites within her deep brown irises. "I'll allow it."

"Good." Lifting her up, I shift the sheet and comforter away, laying her back down, tucking her in.

Then, as she watches me with intrigue, I strip out of my shirt and dress pants, switching off the light before climbing in beside her, wearing nothing but briefs.

"Who's torturing who in this situation?" she asks with an adorable little huff.

"I evened the playing field." I wriggle around until I'm spooning her, and in the process, she settles her ass against my cock, making me bite back a groan. "Have a good sleep, B," I grate through clenched teeth. "I'll see you in the morning."

"Goodnight, Zane." She yawns again before sleepily adding a "Thank you."

"You're welcome." I smile as she gets comfortable, the floral scent of her hair calming me as I breathe her in.

Whether it's the effects of the alcohol or our emotional confessions, Blair falls asleep easily, while I lie awake, listening to the soft whistle of her breathing, my palm rising and falling where it rests across her stomach.

This shouldn't be the first time we're sleeping next to each other. We should have had years of this.

If life had turned out differently.

My stomach clenches, and I ache to go back to when everything was simpler, when we thought the worst thing that could happen to us was Cade throwing a tantrum. I would have taken him beating the shit out of me and never speaking to me again over the way life panned out.

Leaning in to Blair, I snuggle against her, my face in her messy brown curls, my body flush with hers, and let myself relax and be in the moment, falling asleep to the sound of her snores.

It feels like no time has passed when my internal alarm wakes me before the sun. And while I'm acutely aware that I should be going home, I can't bring myself to move with Blair still curled up against me. My shoulder aches from being in the same position all night, but I wouldn't change it for the world.

I'm not embarrassed to say I've dreamed of this moment, of waking up with Blair in my arms. It's how life was supposed to be. Before I ruined it all. If I could spend the rest of my days waking like this, I'd be a happy man.

Blair shivers, and I instinctively curl my arm farther around her, guiding my palm along her stomach, blanketing her in my warmth.

I've always run hot to her cold, yet another reason I believed we belonged together.

Feeling content for the first time in God knows how long, I stretch my fingers and sigh when they brush against her skin. Her top must have risen during the night, and try as I might to resist her pull, my hand slips under the silk, as though moving of its own accord, burning to feel her.

She doesn't move at first, but after a few minutes of my gentle caressing, her breath hitches, and she squirms. I pause my movements, pulling my hand away, but she grabs my wrist and repositions my palm against her skin, closer to her breasts.

I take in a sharp breath of my own and continue, running the pads of my fingers from her breasts to her stomach, circling her belly button before making my way back up.

She barely reacts at first, her breathing even, but on my third run, I snake my hand lower, dipping a finger beneath the waistband of her shorts, and a soft moan escapes her.

I stiffen at the sound—the tension between us wound so tightly, it could snap at any moment. Blair must notice because she stills, her chest heaving, her breasts rising as she turns back to look at me, her eyes bouncing between mine, waiting for me to go on.

Holding my breath, I slide my hand under her shorts, feeling her squirm as I stop just above her pubic bone. She jolts, looking away, and I expect her to stop me, but her palm covers my hand, her fingers lining up with mine as she guides our hands lower, silently consenting to what I desperately want to do to her.

My heart pounds as we move toward her heat, the beat so loud, I'd be surprised if she can't hear it.

I have never wanted another woman as much as I've always wanted Blair, and this moment is no exception.

When our hands find the edge of her pussy, she lets go, leaving me free to run my finger through her folds, hissing at the feel of her.

She stiffens when I pause, an anguished sigh escaping her lips, and I bite back a smile.

Patience, Little B.

Taking my time, I slip a finger inside her, inching in slowly as she tightens around me, her pussy sucking me in.

My patience gone this time, I add a second finger, and she squirms, melting against me, her head dropping back to rest on my chest.

I curl my fingers, fighting not to grunt when her pussy clenches.

She's so wet for me that my cock grows hard against her ass, her breathless gasp making me desperate to rock into her. To elicit more of her glorious sounds. But I'm moving too fast, too soon.

Slowing my moves, I open my mouth to apologize when she reaches between us, her light grip curling around the bulge in my briefs.

And fuck me...

I thrust forward as I stifle a groan, my cock nudging the perfect curve of her ass, making her whimper softly.

Precum soaks my briefs as Blair rolls her thumb over my tip, working me torturously slowly as I continue my thrusts, my fingers in sync with her moves.

She twists her head to face me again, and I finally release a groan, the intensity of her gaze eliciting the sound, the way her lust-filled eyes bore into mine. Unable to resist her gleaming pout, I lean forward and kiss the edge of her mouth, capturing her lip between my teeth as I slip another finger inside her.

"Oh, God," Blair mewls, breaking our kiss as she speaks, her voice so soft, it doesn't break through whatever trance she's under. And thank fucking God. I don't think I could stop this train if my life depended on it.

I'll be lucky if I can stop after giving her only one orgasm. What I wouldn't give to run my throbbing cock through her soaked slit, to feel her pussy coating my tip.

But not today. Today is about this moment. About finally coming together again.

We continue our slow rhythm for a while, our ragged breaths filling the air, until something shifts between us. I couldn't tell you what changed, but as if a button was pushed, the intensity kicks up a notch, and Blair rides my fingers, her hips rocking as I grind hard against her hand, the cotton of my briefs creating a friction I don't need right now. Unless I want to come like a teenager.

I grunt as I try to hold back but can't stop my hips from thrusting as Blair jolts back against me.

If anyone walked in right now, I'm certain they'd think I was fucking her from behind, the way we're moving in sync, breathless and hot.

I'd never usually settle for a hand job, but it's different with Blair. Everything's always been different with Blair, and she knows exactly what I need to make me come... The speed, the tightness. She's so good I can almost imagine it's her soaked pussy strangling my length instead of her delicate fingers. Only I've never been inside her to know that for sure.

And that's a goddamn tragedy on its own.

Blair changes her grip, and the heel of her palm nudges my piercing, making my balls tighten.

She inhales sharply and I smile, knowing she felt it too.

She doesn't comment, but her fingers explore, and before I can ask her what she's doing, she twists in my arms, making me remove my fingers as she brings her body flush with mine.

Her eyes widen with intrigue and my heart slams in my chest, awed by having her in my arms.

"Can I try something?" she whispers, and I just about come from the desperate sound of her voice.

"Fuuck. Anything."

I try to touch her again but she shakes her head, and I almost pout until she lowers my briefs, letting my cock spring free between us. She hesitates a beat before curling her fingers around my girth, rubbing her palm against my piercing.

"Jesus Christ," my voice strains as I fight not to blow my load.

"You weren't lying."

"I wasn't. Fuck, that feels good. I need to touch you again." *I am not opposed to begging.*

Blair nods and I sigh in relief, shifting my focus back to her pleasure, pressing my fingers inside her as she experiments with my dick.

She sucks me in, her pussy so wet that I easily slide two fingers back inside her, pumping them in and out, my muscles tight with restraint.

I start slowly, but when her breathing picks up, I curl my fingers against her wall, hitting her G spot at the same time I roll my thumb over her clit.

"Oh, God. Zane."

Blair squeezes my length as she comes hard, whispering my name, her body jolting, her arousal soaking my hand.

My stomach tightens as my release builds, and when I can't hold back anymore, I roll her onto her back, letting her watch as I explode onto her, my cum coating her stomach and breasts.

She cries out, her body bucking off the bed as she stares at my pulsing cock, her lips parted in ecstasy.

The sated sight of her makes me feral, and an unrestrained groan rips from my throat.

It takes a minute for me to calm down and then I pump my cock one last time, biting back a smirk when Blair whimpers at the sight.

Nothing has changed. She always loved getting me off. Watching me fall apart. So much so that I bet I could pull another release from her now. With barely any effort.

Testing the theory, I wriggle down the bed until my mouth lines up with her pussy, and fuck me, it's more beautiful than I remember—bare and soaked, glistening for more.

"Zane, what—"

Without letting her finish her question, I run a finger slowly through the arousal soaking her, moving toward her throbbing clit. I want to clean her with my tongue, but the second I press down on the sweet little bud, she cries out again, biting down on her hand as she thrashes against me.

I grin proudly, and maybe a little cocky too. But the real pleasure comes from knowing how much I still get her, how much I still understand.

My breathing returns to normal as I wait for hers to slow, moving up the bed, dropping down beside her as her warmth comforts me.

A beam of sunlight shines across her flushed skin, and a tightness works its way into my chest. "You are so fucking beautiful when you come apart like that. Thank you for letting me watch."

Blair's already pink cheeks brighten, and she shies away from me, until I grab her chin and force her to look. "I mean it, B. Everything about you is beautiful."

"Even this?" she whispers, pointing to the sticky mess I made on her skin, a giggle escaping her.

"Especially that." I chuckle, loving the way the heat returns to her gaze. *Yeah, I may be a little possessive.* But only for her.

Despite the intense desire to keep her branded with my cum, I grab a handful of tissues and clean her up as she watches me, her eyes wide, her lip trapped between her teeth.

When I'm done, she drags me back to bed, snuggling against me, her head on my chest.

Her eyes drift shut as I gently stroke her hair, and all too soon, my alarm goes off, the sound making me jump.

Slipping out of Blair's hold, I rush to silence my phone, an apology on the tip of my tongue.

Only she doesn't wake.

She's so peaceful, I can't bring myself to rouse her, but I have to go. I've already missed one practice this month. I can only imagine the consequences if I skip another.

Especially considering I left early last night.

As though doing a walk of shame, I quietly get dressed and sneak out of her room, tiptoeing down the hall.

My jacket's not where I slipped out of it last night, but when I reach the entry, I find it on a coat rack and silently thank Jenna. There's no way Cade was that thoughtful.

The door creaks as I open it, and I rush to leave when Cade's angry groan stops me in my tracks. I freeze and then turn slowly, my heart pounding, my hands lifted in surrender. But he's passed out on the couch, sleeping restlessly in true Cade fashion.

Thank fuck.

I chuckle to myself, and with one last glance toward Blair's closed door, I slip away, a smile on my face, feeling lighter than I've felt in a very long time.

Chapter Thirty-Five

BLAIR

The sun's peeking through the break in my curtains the next time I wake, and I smile as I stretch, my body aching for all the right reasons. I don't think I've come that hard since I was last with Zane. Just my hand on his pierced cock did things to my body that I've never experienced before. I may have had Zane's fingers working me into a frenzy, but I could imagine the way his cock would tear me apart, and if I'd been allowed to scream, the whole building would have heard me.

"It turns out piercings *do* increase the pleasure." I roll over to find Zane's side of the bed empty and cold. But instead of the hurt I'd expect to feel, I can't help but laugh.

Cade is going to blow a gasket over this, and I can't wait.

After stretching my body again, I rest my hand between my legs, smiling at the memory of Zane's fingers inside me. Just like when we were younger, that man has the ability to blow my mind and make me swoon all in one go, but I didn't expect the emotion to come flowing back so quickly, like we never even parted ways.

Movement around the apartment pulls me from my Zane bubble, and I drag myself out of bed, biting my lip as a burning sensation lights up my core.

Nathan and I had sex. At least we used to when we were back in Florida, but he never pushed me to my limits like Zane.

And he only used his fingers.

I once again imagine his cock buried deep inside me, and the burn turns to longing as my legs clench. There's no doubt that my body wants him; I just have to let my heart run wild. I have to stop thinking about what's done, or what could have been, and focus on how I feel. Because if I do, I bet I'll come to realize I never stopped loving him.

"Leave her alone, Cade," Jenna calls out, drawing my attention while I frown. *Is she talking about me?*

Wrapping my robe around my shoulders, I open my door and find Cade staring back at me, his arms folded over his chest, a glare marring his features.

"What's that look for?" I roll my eyes, crossing my arms to match his stance.

"You know what it's for."

"I really don't."

"Where's Zane?"

A laugh escapes me but I stifle it when he groans. "Oh, stop. I'm an adult now, Cade. You can drop the overbearing big brother act."

"It's not an act."

"Sadly, I know that."

"Well then, you must also know that I'm not going to stop caring about you. I know Zane was here when we got home. Did he spend the night in your room?"

I consider his question for a beat. My answer could go either way, and I want to make sure I give the response that's going to piss him off the most. "He did, but he's not here now."

"What do you mean he's not here? What time did he leave?"

"I don't know. I was sleeping."

"You were *sleeping*? Did that fucker sneak out?"

"I wouldn't put it that way."

"Why couldn't he wait until you woke up?"

For someone that constantly complained about missing his best friend and told me I should have talked to him when he was in Jacksonville after the hospital, he's sure quick to change his mind. And now I'm the one that's pissed off.

"It's a Monday, Cade. Don't football teams practice or work out on Mondays?"

"Most do, yes. But most also expect their players to travel home with the team after the Sunday game, and that didn't seem to bother him. He could have stayed."

"Aww. Do you miss him?" Jenna teases and he redirects his glare. "Is that what this is about?"

I burst out laughing while Cade huffs in annoyance. "No. This is about Blair."

"And I'm *fine*. I don't know why you're getting so worked up about this. I thought you wanted Zane and me to talk. I thought you wanted him back in our lives?"

"I *did*. I *do*. But that was before he slept in your room and snuck out ahead of sunrise."

"You're being ridiculous." I walk back into my room and Jenna follows, slamming the door in Cade's face when he tries to come in.

"I'm calling Dad," he yells out from the other side of the threshold, but I ignore him. We both know he'd never talk to Dad about this stuff. Mom maybe, but Dad, no. I have way more on him than he has on me.

"So." Jenna lifts herself onto the desk in my borrowed room and crosses her ankles, swinging her legs in what appears to be giddy anticipation. "Did you two work things out?"

"We had a good talk, yes." I school my features, trying hard not to give anything away.

"Talk?"

"Yep."

"Was he talking while his dick was inside you?"

"Jenna!" My cheeks heat, giving the impression that I'm guilty even though that delicious appendage was nowhere near my pussy. Okay, it was close, but it wasn't inside me and that difference is important.

"Sorry." Jenna bites back her smile. "I just want the best for my girl."

"And having sex with Zane shortly after breaking up with Nathan is what's best for me?"

"Hell, yes! Did that not happen? I could have sworn I heard groaning." She purses her lips and turns away, lost in thought. "Maybe it was Cade?"

"Ew, don't make me picture that."

"It must have been him if it wasn't Zane."

"It was Zane, dammit." I cover my face with my hands and groan as she celebrates.

"I knew it. Was it good?"

Peering through my fingers, I cringe, preempting her reaction. "We didn't have sex."

"What?" She does a double take, her jaw dropping to the floor.

"God, you're dramatic sometimes." I laugh before sucking in a breath to tell her the truth. "He... ahhh..."

"Ate your pussy?"

"Jesus, no."

"Jesus, no? Please tell me he at least fucked you with his fingers and the groaning wasn't just a reaction to a hot make-out session."

"Ugh. If you must know, there were hands and fingers involved. With both of us getting a happy ending."

"Yes! I want details."

"No."

"Why?" Her face scrunches. She's so confused it makes me giggle. "*I* give *you* details."

"Do I ask for them?"

"No." She frowns. "Not usually. Why is that?" Her head tilts, and she stares at me with intrigue.

"Because not everyone likes to talk about that stuff."

"That stuff being life? Talking about sex shouldn't be any different than talking about the weather."

"Maybe not, but it is."

"I don't want to hear about your sex life, Little B," Cade calls out before a loud thump echoes through the room, and I imagine him banging his head against the wall.

"Go away, Cade."

"This apartment isn't that big; please remember that."

Cade's complaint grows distant as he walks away, and when the front door slams, Jenna and I burst out laughing.

"In all seriousness, was he good to you?" she asks, her expression turning almost motherly.

"He was. That's always been consistent with Zane. I've never had to question that."

"But he left without telling you? Did he leave you a note?"

"No, but honestly, I don't mind. He shouldn't have even been here. He was supposed to fly home with his team last night. I'm sure I'll hear from him later."

"Good, because as much as I like him, I need you to remember why you broke up with Nathan. Communication is key."

I internally cringe. *What am I doing?* "Zane and I aren't a couple, Jenna."

"Not yet." She bounces her eyebrows and I roll my eyes.

We can't be a couple. I just split up from my long-term boyfriend. That would be crazy...

Right?

I'm halfway through breakfast when Cade comes back, his face red, sweat pooling on his forehead.

"Jesus, where did you go? The sauna?"

"I went for a run."

"In jeans?" My eyes widen at the thought and he scoffs.

"It's what I was wearing. I needed to clear my head, and I couldn't risk seeing you again before I did."

"Do we need to talk about the birds and bees? When a woman hits maturity, she needs certain things and—"

"Fuck. Stop." He covers his ears. "I'm not in denial about you having sex, Blair. Although I wish you'd have waited until you were thirty like I asked you to all those years ago. I'm *worried* because you just broke up with your boyfriend, and I'm not sure you're thinking clearly."

"Are you referring to the boyfriend you hated? Because I would have thought you'd be over the moon about me ending things and quickly moving on."

"I didn't *hate* him."

With my arms folded over my chest, I lean back in my chair and stare at him unmoving. There's no way I can dignify that bullshit with a response. Not unless my response is my knee in his balls.

"Okay. Okay." He holds his arms up in surrender. "I hated him. But I tried really hard to be civil."

"When?"

"At Christmas and birthdays."

"You refused to speak to him. You avoided him like the plague."

"That was me being civil, Blair. If I had my way, we would have spent all of those events with my fist pounding his face. There are some things you don't—"

I groan, jamming my palms into my eye sockets, hoping he'll stop. We've had this argument so many times, I honestly don't know why I brought it up again.

"That part of my life is over, so it's time to move on. But—"

"Good. You de—"

"*But*," I interrupt Cade when he interrupts me. "He was your pass. Your only pass. If you ever treat another one of my boyfriends the way you treated him, I will cut you off completely. You said you hated the distance between us when I started dating Nathan. Well, that will be nothing compared to the distance you feel when I refuse to speak to you again."

Cade blinks a few times before he frowns. "Boyfriends? Multiple?"

"Are you serious right now?" I huff out an incredulous laugh as Jenna joins us in the kitchen.

"You're digging a pretty big hole there, Stevens," she says, patting Cade on the back. "I think you should just agree and zip those pretty lips of yours."

"My lips aren't pretty."

"Not the point."

I groan again and quickly shove a spoonful of oatmeal in my mouth so I don't say anything I'll regret. Cade's always been protective, but he's never usually this obnoxious.

"Just be careful with Zane. Please. He's not the same guy he was before he left. Before the accident. I *do* want the two of you to sort your shit out, but jumping into bed with him is something else entirely."

"I didn't—"

"He left without saying goodbye, Blair. He's—"

My phone buzzes on the counter, drawing our eyes, and when it's Zane's name lighting up my screen, Jenna snorts while a giddy warmth takes over me.

"What were you saying, Cade?" I arch a brow, biting back my grin.

"You make it sound like I wanted him to be an asshole. I'm glad he texted. The Zane I once knew never would have ghosted any of us. But we don't know him anymore. I just want you to be careful."

"Awww." Jenna fawns while I smile in appreciation.

"I will. I promise. There's no me and Zane. Like you said, I just ended a relationship."

"Get back on a horse, I say." Jenna bounces her eyebrows as Cade rushes to give his opinion.

"Take your time." He shoots Jenna another glare. "You're young. There's nothing wrong with being single for a while."

"I know. Thanks for looking out for me, Cade. But next time, remember I'm capable of making my own decisions. And if I fuck up, it's on me."

"Okay." His face contorts uncomfortably. "Okay."

"Good. I'm glad we got that sorted." Jenna heads over to the fridge, grabbing the orange juice and pouring herself a glass. "Cade, can I get your help in my bedroom? There's a spider that needs removing."

Cade rolls his eyes but jumps up from his chair. "Lead the way." He motions toward the hallway.

I frown as Jenna walks past. She's not scared of spiders; we had that conversation when we found a nasty looking thing on her balcony last week.

Seeing my confusion, she squeezes my arm and winks before pointing to my phone. "You're now free to enjoy your oatmeal in peace." She mimes texting with her hand as her wide eyes bore into mine.

"Thanks, Jenna. I will."

The second they're gone, I reach for my phone, opening Zane's message as fast as I can.

> ZANE: Morning beautiful. You looked too peaceful to wake but now I'm regretting it. Why the fuck do you live so far away?

A laugh bursts out of me and I cover my mouth to stifle the noise.
I shouldn't want him, but God, he makes it impossibly hard not to.
He always has.

CHAPTER THIRTY-SIX

ZANE

I text Blair "good morning" in the Uber on my way to the stadium, and don't pocket my phone until I get out, waiting for a reply. I'm running late for our weight session, but it's hard to be bothered by that with the taste of Blair's lips still at the forefront of my mind.

My phone buzzes as I enter the locker room, and I smile like a sap before I've even read her reply.

"Fitzpatrick!" Coach Pierce's booming voice pulls me to a stop midstep, my hand hovering in midair. Fuck. I internally groan. I was sure the locker room would be empty by now, but of course it's not. "Is your watch broken?" he asks, his voice gruff.

I don't actually wear a watch, but something tells me that now is not the best time to mention that fact. "It's recovery." I shrug, making it worse. Like my response is set to cockiness autopilot. "I'll make up the time at the end of the day."

"That's not how this works. We do recovery as a team."

"I missed twenty minutes; I'm sure they've survived without me. Unlike the game yesterday." I mumble the last bit and immediately regret it.

"Excuse me?"

"I said, unlike the game yesterday, Coach." *And fuck, he is fuming.*

"I heard you the first time, but I'm here to tell you...the *team* won. It's not an individual sport."

The disappointment on his face has me flinching and my shoulders drop. "Just tell me the fine and I'll pay it."

"God, you're a—" He stops abruptly, glancing at something over my shoulder, *something* or *someone* behind me. I don't dare look; I've already dug myself a big enough grave. But at least I'm here. I'd much rather be with Blair—there's still so much to talk about.

Coach Pierce growls under his breath before shaking his head. "Get dressed and catch up with your teammates. You know, the guys you're *supposed* to care about."

What? I balk. Guilt gone. He did *not* just say that. "Are you suggesting I don't care? What about Reed? Did I *not* care when I came to his rescue? Was that me *not* caring when I tackled Landon to the ground, suffering a stab wound to my side?"

"If you truly cared about Reed"—he lowers his voice as he takes a step closer—"you wouldn't be fucking around right now, risking your spot on the team, while he's too injured to be here. He'd do anything to take your place and you're wasting it."

"You say that as if it's *my* fault he can't play." *Jesus.* Why the hell can't I keep my mouth shut?

"No, I'm—"

"Pierce," our new GM, Wes, calls out from behind me. "I need a word with Zane."

Huh? I spin around, my eyes wide while Wes's gaze remains on Coach.

"Take him, but he needs to make up time for the weight session he missed, or I might not be able to play him."

"Come with me," Wes says, his attention shifting my way as he ignores Pierce's threat. I want to ask why, but with the no bullshit look in his eyes, I follow without question.

This can't be good.

We're both silent as Wes leads me to his office, his stride confident, his unidentifiable expression never once wavering. I can't tell if he's pissed off or genuinely doesn't care.

When we reach the door, he nods, gesturing for me to walk inside before closing the door behind us. And the second we're alone, his expression morphs into a grin. "So...Zane." He pats the table as he sits down, his gaze light and a little unnerving. "I'm not sure you're aware, but Dylan spoke to my wife about a job for a friend of yours, and now she won't stop talking about it."

"The fuck?" *This is about Blair?* Wes frowns at my response and I rush to apologize. "Sorry." I grimace. "I clearly forgot who I was talking to."

Wes chuckles before leaning back in his chair. "From what I've heard about you, I doubt you're sorry at all."

"You're right. I'm not sorry about that; I just didn't want to fuck things up for Blair."

"That's nice of you, but I can assure you, Lucy wouldn't let that happen. She said, and I quote, 'I don't even know her but I got the impression she was sad and I'm worried. I think she needs this new start.'"

"Wow."

"Yep, and if you knew Lucy, you'd understand that she's not going to let up until she knows your friend is okay. Actually no, more than that, she'd want to know that she's good. Great even." He huffs, but a small smile pulls at his lips and I'd say he loves that about her. "What I need from *you* is reassurance that your friend is in fact *great*, and that you'll talk to her about the job."

"Trust me, I want her to take the job. But Lucy's right; she's going through a lot at the moment and trying to find herself again. I promise I'll talk to her. And I'll let her know that Lucy cares. She'll be happy to know there's more people that do."

"Thanks."

"You're welcome." I stare awkwardly, not really knowing what to say next with this being the only conversation we've ever had. "You know, I always thought our first interaction would involve you yelling at me about something."

Wes frowns. "Why? Do I have that reputation?"

"No, not at all. *I* do."

"Right." Wes laughs. "I do recall that I'm supposed to be telling you to make up your weight session or you'll be sitting out during the next game."

"'*Might*' be sitting out. I'm pretty sure he said '*might*.'"

"Right again. Well, since you heard him and you know what's at stake, you better do as he asked."

"I will." I nod, jumping up as Wes picks up his phone, our conversation seemingly over.

With an incredulous laugh under my breath, I head to the door, only turning back at the last second. "Please tell your wife I said thank you. It means a lot to me."

"I will," he repeats my words back to me, hitting me with a smile before he resumes his work. And I've got to say, I did *not* see this conversation coming. But I'm kind of glad that it did.

Our weight room is clearing out when I arrive for my recovery session, and I'm met with a sea of sweaty teammates as I make my way inside. After talking to Coach Pierce and Wes, I'm now so late the guys are moving onto their cooldowns, and yet, Luke and Reed are still hovering near the bench press.

"Shouldn't you be heading across the hall?" I point to Luke. "You'll miss out on all the good treadmills. And you." I turn to Reed. "Shouldn't you be at home?"

Reed grins while Luke rolls his eyes. "They've got me on light workouts now," Reed tells me. "And I saw you coming, so we thought we'd keep you company."

Great.

"How did it go with your *friend*?" Luke asks, his lips pulled into a smirk as he raises a brow.

"Which friend?" Reed's quick to ask, until realization hits him. "The one that needed a job."

"That's the one. And it was good." I try to keep my expression schooled but I must do something because Luke fakes a gasp.

"I knew it! You like her."

"Fuck off."

"That response doesn't change my mind."

"It's none of your goddamn business."

"He's right, Luke," Reed finally cuts in. "He'll tell us he's in love with his friend when he's good and ready."

The fuck. Thanks, Reed.

I throw my towel at Reed's face and he laughs out loud. "I'm kidding. But even if you do have a thing for her, what does it matter? *We* can't exactly talk."

"He's not wrong."

"Okay. Are you done with your little gossip session? I'd like to start my workout before I get cut from the next game."

"I could keep going," Luke begins but Reed follows my lead, throwing my towel at *his* face.

"How can we help?"

"I don't need your help. It's just a recovery session. I'll be fine."

"Okay. We'll be cooling down," Reed tells me as he turns away, grabbing his towel and looking back over his shoulder. "Don't forget we're watching tapes in thirty minutes."

Fuck. There goes my workout. "I'll be there."

The locker room is quiet again when I finally finish my session *after* the tape analysis with the team.

What should have been a few hours turned into most of the day, and I'm desperate to check my messages again.

Grabbing my phone, I find several notifications. One from Blair, the rest from the group chat. And it's not their messages that have me grinning.

> BLAIR: I actually think I live close now, considering I used to be in Florida

She's not wrong, but she's still not here.

> ZANE: It's not San Francisco

> BLAIR: And they said you were bad at geography

> ZANE: Who said that? I'm good at everything

I wait a minute for her next response but when it doesn't come right away, I reluctantly read the group chat messages.

> DYLAN: Zane, Lucy is bugging me. Please for the love of God, help!

I snort before reading the rest.

> LUKE: What did I miss?

> DYLAN: Nothing that concerns you

> LUKE: Everything concerns me

EASTON: I thought that was Reed

REED: Ouch, man

LUKE: No fighting. We all care. That's why we
have this group chat

The damn group chat. I'm ninety-nine percent sure Easton added me as payback. This is torture sometimes. And now the stupid thing is named after me. I don't need a support group.

ZANE: I'm very tempted to block this chat. If
that's possible?

EASTON: Why didn't I think of that?

LUKE: You're never leaving. Either of you

ZANE: Yeah, yeah

ZANE: Dylan, I'm on it. Thank you again

DYLAN: No worries. And thank YOU

LUKE: Tell me what I'm missing, dammit!

I roll my eyes even though no one can see me then exit out of my messages, but before I put my phone away it vibrates in my hand. I groan until I check the screen and my heart jolts. The damn organ is already way too invested for my liking. I need to slow the fuck down.

Tomorrow.

For now, I read Blair's latest message, knowing I'm going to reply straight away, because what can I say... I'm obsessed.

BLAIR: You're definitely good at something. In
fact, I'm sore from how good you are

> ZANE: Dammit, B. How the hell am I supposed to concentrate now that I'm thinking about making you come? When can we do it again?

I smile but my heart flickers uncomfortably in my chest. This has to be a dream. Tomorrow I'm going to wake up and realize I imagined it all. Or worse, I'm going to discover she doesn't feel the same way I do.

> BLAIR: I'm not sure that's a good idea. I need time to think

Fuck. There it is. My stomach knots until I remember that deep down, she's still the same Blair. I know her better than anyone ever has, including her asshole ex. And she knows me.

If I was a nice guy, I'd probably agree with her. They just broke up and she's trying to figure her life out. But, I'm not a nice guy. Blair's joked about that herself. I'm selfish, and now that she's back in my orbit, I'm not letting her go. Not again.

> ZANE: On the contrary… It's a great idea and you know it

You better be ready, B. I'm coming for you.

CHAPTER THIRTY-SEVEN

BLAIR

I read Zane's latest message and let out a strangled laugh before pocketing my phone. I wish he was wrong but he's not. I'd love nothing more than to have him touching me again, but that's exactly why I shouldn't.

If he'd stayed, I have no doubt I would have taken things further, but he left and unfortunately that gave me time to think.

It turns out thinking is dangerous, especially when it comes to Zane. I don't *want* to want him like I do, because that's a ticket to heartache, and I don't think I have the strength to go through that again.

We've been here before, and while I'm certain it'd be different this time around, we'd still have to hide it initially. I just ended a four-year relationship. With another football player. The last thing Zane needs is more media attention when he's been through so much.

And Nathan doesn't deserve that. We may have ended things between us, but I'm not a bitch. Just because I don't feel the same anymore, doesn't mean I want to force him into the spotlight for all the wrong reasons. He's only starting to find his footing here.

Speaking of footing, I'm yet to find my own. Entering into a scandal is not the best way to start.

Giving myself a moment to formulate a convincing argument for Zane —one that he'll actually listen to—I watch a movie with Jenna, while Cade catches up with a college buddy that moved here last year.

I only make it halfway through the steamy rom-com when my frustrations take over. "Ugh. Why are these movies never realistic?" *Why can't I have a love like that?*

"Because real life sucks. For most people. I'm actually enjoying mine." Jenna smirks to herself, and I've got to admit her bubbly nature is infectious.

"Who's got you smiling like that?"

"Two people, actually."

"Oh, yeah?"

"One you're not going to love."

"That's where you're wrong. Unlike my darling brother, I don't care what he does with his personal life, unless of course, he screws you over."

"You knew?" She frowns.

"I guessed." It became obvious when it took forty minutes to kill the spider that Jenna was lying about. And the faint groans didn't help their cause.

"Well, it's only casual. He can't screw me over. No feelings, no pain."

"Works in theory."

"It hasn't failed me yet."

"I hope it never does. Who's number two?"

"Just a friend."

I raise an eyebrow before realizing what I'm doing and schooling my features. "I'm being serious." Jenna laughs. "I don't juggle. Yes, I only do casual, but never two people at once, unless it's two people *at* once."

"I don't follow?"

She bites back her smile before squeezing my arm. "What I wouldn't give to be as innocent as you are."

"I'm not... Ohhh. A threesome?"

"Exactly."

"Have you had many of those?" I ask until a thought hits me and I panic. "Oh, God." I raise a hand between us. "Please don't tell me if one of them was with my brother. I don't mind knowing he's having sex, but I don't need that kind of detail."

Jenna barks out a laugh. "I've had four but none of them with your brother."

"Thank God, because this time, I think I want details."

"Really?" I nod and she beams with happiness. "Oh, Blair, you just made my night."

An hour later, Jenna jumps up to grab a drink after regaling me with stories of her adventurous sex life, making it even harder not to think about Zane and his magical fingers. I'm not sure I could handle pleasing two people at once, but God, it sounds thrilling, and I'm not ashamed to admit that with the way she's described it—in great detail—I was wriggling in my seat, struggling not to text Zane, wishing I could summon him to come and finish me off. But it's not that simple.

As though I conjured him with my thoughts, my phone buzzes on the couch beside me, and reality comes knocking.

> ZANE: Don't overthink it, B. I don't plan on ever hurting you again

My heart jolts but it's not *my* pain I'm worried about. What if I realize I'm not ready, and he's the one that gets hurt? *On top of our relationship being dissected by the media.* We need to take this seriously. *I* need to take this seriously.

> BLAIR: I want you. I do. But I shouldn't. And that's a lot to work through

> ZANE: Too late

> BLAIR: I know. I'm sorry. I shouldn't have let this morning happen considering my feelings. You're just really hard to resist. And a big part of me wanted it

> ZANE: Good to know. 😉 But that's not what I meant

> BLAIR: What did you mean?

Someone knocks on the front door and my gaze darts in that direction. "Nooo. He wouldn't."

"He would," Jenna laughs from behind me, and I spin to face her. "I just buzzed him up."

"What?"

"Zane. He texted to say he was out front."

"Jesus." I bury my face in my hands and groan.

"Nope, not Jesus. *Zane*. And I'd say he's more of a god."

"I see he sucked you in, just like he always does."

"I'm not going to lie; that man has charisma, but I let him in for *you*."

"Ugh." My shoulders drop while my heart skips a beat.

"Do you want me to send him away?" She takes a step toward the door, but I don't let her get far, rushing to stop her.

"No. I want him here. But I don't *want* to want him here. Not yet."

"If it had been a month since you ended things with Nathan, would you feel differently?"

"Probably. It wouldn't be as big of a story and—"

"Then it's been a month." Jenna shrugs, like it's that simple. "Have fun." She skips past and opens the door for Zane. "Sorry about that. We just had a little existential crisis to overcome, but we're good. I'll leave you two alone." She continues out the door, and when Zane steps into my line of sight, my entire world shifts.

Having him here fills me with a familiar warmth that sets my soul on fire. He's changed so much—he's taller and his muscles now fill out his shirt with the ridges of his abs visible through the tight material. Just a glimpse conjures memories of the deep V that guides a path toward the dusting of light hair across his—

What am I doing?

It's like I'm a teenager again, getting swept up in Zane's world, pushing the consequences of my feelings out of my mind.

We hurt each other once; we can do it again.

No... hurt is not a strong enough word. He destroyed me once, and from our talk last night, I destroyed him all the same.

I need to be mindful of that. We both do.

Zane closes the door while I'm lost in my head, but as he turns my way, I pull myself out of it.

"Hi," he says softly, his usually cocky grin replaced with a smile that exudes genuine comfort, his soulful eyes meeting mine. My breath hitches. *How are my feelings so present after all these years?* I thought I was stronger than this. I thought I'd be able to think straight, but he touches me once, and I'm thrown back to my late teens and the giddy feelings he gave me.

I wish I'd never told him I wanted to wait back then. At least now I wouldn't be craving it, wondering what it would be like to have him inside me.

The thought brings me back to last night, and my body sizzles before I smile.

"Thank God." Zane walks closer, kicking off his shoes before lifting his hand to my cheek, running his thumb along my lip. "I was almost certain you'd tell me to fuck off."

"I should." I step back, out of his grasp.

"I know."

"I deserve time to think. I told you I needed that and you ignored me."

"I did."

"Now you're invading my personal space, intruding on my sanctuary without so much as a text message for notice."

"B, I'm not even going to pretend that I'm sorry. I couldn't walk away if I tried. Anything else?"

"Yeah." I step back again, dropping my hands to my side as heat courses through me. My next words leave my mouth before I've had time to think them through, but I don't regret them. I can't. "If you don't kiss me right now, I'm going to riot."

The briefest of grins lights Zane's face before he schools his features and nods. "That I can do. Always."

I barely get time to take in a breath before he's covered the distance between us, his hands cupping my face, his inquisitive gaze boring into mine, as though still not convinced this is real.

But it is, and I've never wanted anything more.

Grabbing his shirt, I curl my fingers into the soft fabric and pull him impossibly close, angling my face until our eyes lock once more.

Zane quietly groans, and the sound of it travels from his lips to my chest, filling me with desire.

"Zane," I whisper on a breath, my skin heating as a blush undoubtedly coats my cheeks.

"I always loved this about you, B." He pulls back, gently stroking my cheek, confirming my suspicion. "I never had to guess how you felt."

"I didn't think you ever had to question it?"

"Not then, no. But now..." he trails off and a moment of doubt creeps into my mind until his hand glides into my hair, and his lips descend on mine, wiping my doubts away.

"We should have had more of these," he whispers. "We should have had a lifetime."

His lips brush mine, gently at first until he increases the pressure, his hand tugging on my braid, tilting my head to deepen the kiss.

I moan longingly, because while he's kissing me now, it'll never make up for all that we missed.

My grip on his shirt tightens along with his hold on my hair, and when he tugs again, I gasp. A shiver runs through me as he sweeps his tongue into my mouth, and when he groans in relief, I get it. I feel the same.

We begin softly, slow and explorative until the energy shifts along with our fervor, morphing into a mix of desperation and need. Zane sucks on my lip, while my hands roam his body. He groans; I gasp. He squeezes my breast, and I buck against him, the new sensation and force of his kiss sending me stumbling backward.

Zane puts his hand out, softening my fall seconds before I hit the wall, his body crowding me in.

"Falling for me, Little B?" he whispers against my lips, his curling into a smile.

"Never," I lie, my voice breathy, when what I should really be saying is...*I never stopped.*

CHAPTER THIRTY-EIGHT

ZANE

Blair's soft lips electrify me as my body throbs with desire, but when she bucks against me for the fifth time, I reluctantly pull away, my breaths ragged.

"We have to stop."

"What?" She stares up at me, her eyes wide as her lids flutter.

"I heard what you said earlier. Well, texted. Either way, you wanted time, and I'm going to give it to you."

"But you're here?" She bites back a smirk, and it takes everything in my power not to replace her teeth with mine.

"I'm here because I want to be. But I'm still going to respect your wishes."

"What if I've changed my mind?"

"Prove it."

Blair wraps her arms around my neck and pulls me closer, pressing her lips to my mouth.

She tastes delectable today, like my favorite flavor of ice cream—strawberry; I think it's her gloss and it's fucking intoxicating—but instead of sucking her lips to savor it, I do the opposite and pull away again.

"For my sake, I am going to regret this for the rest of my life, but for yours... that's not the proof I need."

"What?" Blair frowns, confused. "Do you want me to strip or drop to my knees and—"

"Fuck." I cup her mouth so she'll stop filling me with visuals, when this is already hard enough. I'm not used to doing the right thing, and it fucking sucks. "I want to see the list, B."

"The list?"

"Come on, you know what I'm talking about. I want your pros and cons list. If you were worried, and now you're not, then it means you worked through your concerns and—"

Blair's lips part as she takes in a sharp breath, momentarily distracting me. She's so beautiful when she gets all flustered like this. I almost forgot that I had this effect on her.

"My lists?"

"Oh, B. We've had this conversation before. I remember everything about you. So... where's the list?"

"I don't have one. And I'm confused because I don't remember specifically telling you about my lists."

"You didn't have to. I saw it with my own eyes. Several times."

"When?" She squints, challenging me.

"When you were deciding which college to attend—ours or NYU. After an extensive pros and cons list which I remember took days, you opted to follow me and Cade."

"I wasn't following you. It had a great English program and..." She trails off when I smirk. "You're an ass. You knew that too, didn't you?"

"Of course. I'm the one that told you about the fellowship they offered." Tears prick Blair's eyes and my stomach sinks. "Fuck, I'm sorry."

"No." She shakes her head frantically. "Don't be sorry. I'd forgotten how good you were to me. For me. Actually no, I didn't forget. I pushed it from my mind."

"B. You—"

"What's number two?" She changes the subject, wiping her eyes as she smiles.

I pause, running through a quick pros and cons list of my own, deciding how to proceed. I should encourage her to talk about her feelings, but at the same time, she let me move on when I couldn't say my sister's name, so she deserves the same respect.

"When you were deciding whether or not to hook up with me."

Heat creeps up Blair's neck, dusting her cheeks in a beautiful pink glow, and I know I've got her. "Please tell me you didn't see that list."

I raise a brow, teasing, but quickly shake my head. "I didn't. But God, I wish I had. I've always been curious as to how close it was between the yeses and nos."

"The yes won by a point." She stares at me deadpan and I burst out laughing.

"Sounds right. So... Do you believe me now, that I know how big of a deal this is?"

"Yes."

"Good. Want to write a list together?"

"What?" She giggles and the sound makes my heart thrash against my ribs. Fuck, I crave her. But right now, she feels like sin, and while I'm ready to get burned, I don't think she's ready for the fire. To prove my point, her gaze narrows in intrigue. She's considering my offer.

"You want to write a pros and cons list together? To determine what exactly?"

"Whether or not you're ready to move on with me."

"Are you?" she counters, her expression stoic as she challenges me. And fuck if it doesn't make my chest tighten.

"Am I what?" I ask, though I think I know the answer. She wants to know if I am ready to move on from our past.

"Are you ready to start over?"

It's a valid question, and until she voiced it, I was certain I knew the answer. But it's more complicated than that. "Maybe the list can be for both of us."

Blair smiles, the brightness of it warming me. "I think that sounds perfect." She grabs my hand, dragging me down the hall toward her bedroom. "I have pens and highlighters in here."

"Highlighters?" *Fuck, what did I get myself into?* "Can't we just write it in the notes app on my phone?"

Blair stops in her tracks and spins to glare at me. "I thought you knew me, Zane. Does that sound like something I would do?"

"No, but I was kind of hoping we'd take a little bit of you and add a little bit of me. I like to keep things simple."

"Hmmm." She purses her lips and I smile when it appears she's actually considering my request, until... "Nope. We need highlighters."

"You're lucky I love you, Little B. Because—"

"What?" Her face pales, making me chuckle.

"It's a figure of speech, Blair. You'll know when I say it for real. Trust me."

🏈 🏈 🏈

An hour later we're still writing the damn list when Jenna comes home. "I'm back. I'm here. I'm in the house. Please acknowledge that you heard me so I know you're going to keep the sex noises down. I don't want to be tempted to join you."

I raise an eyebrow, and Blair buries her face in her hands, groaning when Jenna calls out again.

"Hello."

"Yes, we heard you, Jenna. Rest assured; we're not having sex."

"Finished or on the way?"

Blair's face reddens and I hide my smile behind my hand.

"Neither," she calls back, sitting tall. "You can open the door if you'd like. We're both fully clothed and not even touching each other."

I fake a pout because I'm annoyed at both those truths, and when Jenna walks in, she frowns in solidarity.

"I'm not sure if I'm more shocked or disappointed. How blue are those balls, Zane?"

"It's not—" Blair begins to speak but Jenna cuts her off.

"I'm kidding. You two have a lot of shit to work through, and just because I use sex to solve my problems doesn't mean others do. Nor should they. Especially you two. So..." She walks over and perches on the edge of the bed, smiling. "What are you doing, then?"

"It doesn't matter," Blair says, at the same time I admit...

"We're writing a pros and cons list."

"Oh, B is famous for that. I've heard stories."

"You what?"

"Cade told me. He said you never do anything without weighing the pros and cons, which is why he's so worried. He thinks you've gone rogue. He'll be happy to know that's not the case."

"I don't plan on telling him."

Jenna laughs out loud. "Even better. I like your brother, but God, is he a little over-the-top sometimes. As long as you're happy. What does it matter how you work things out?"

Blair frowns for a beat before it morphs into a grin. "Thanks, Jenna."

"Anytime. But I'm not into lists so I'm going to have a bath. Let me know if you decide to get dinner. I want in."

She doesn't wait for either of us to respond, walking away, and Blair laughs when she's gone.

"Where were we?" She holds up the list, running over what we've got. "Pros... We like each other, we're good for each other, Cade knows this time, Blair's more herself around Zane..." I tune out because I know the list, and while it's great and color coded, it's missing one vital point...

"I have never and will never want anyone else in this lifetime. The sooner we acknowledge that, the better."

Blair's gaze darts to mine and she gapes, a sheen of tears coating her eyes.

My expression softens. "Come on, you knew that."

"To a degree, yes, but this feels more absolute." She turns away and draws in a breath, swiftly wiping her eyes before facing me again.

"How so?"

"Because I'm about to add it to our list and these things are like law to me." I chuckle lightly, and she finally smiles.

"Never felt that way with the fucker?"

"And there's another con... Zane won't shut up about Blair's ex-boyfriend. His jealousy knows no bounds."

"Jealousy?"

"Admit it."

"It's less jealousy and more blind rage. You know you can do better than that." *And he deserves to be miserable for all the shitty things he's done.*

"And you're better?"

"Than him? Yes. Absolutely. I know you better than anyone, B. Probably better than Cade."

"Con... we know each other too well."

"That's a con?" I balk.

"It can be. There's a lot to be said about that initial love bubble when you're getting to know each other."

"You don't think we could have a love bubble? You seemed pretty giddy at the prospect of getting to know my piercing."

Blair's cheeks heat again and I don't bother hiding my triumphant grin.

"Fair point, but I'm leaving it on the list."

"Agree to disagree then."

"Deal."

We run through a few more cons until Blair mentions our living arrangements, something I'm happy she brought up.

"Con... You live in San Francisco, and I live in LA."

"You're not staying here, are you?"

"I haven't decided yet. But if I leave, I could go anywhere... Florida, New York. Hell, I could move to London."

"By that logic, you could move to San Francisco. Right?"

Blair's shoulders drop and she releases a sigh. "I honestly don't know, I—"

"Come and stay with me for a week. See if you like it. I have to go back tomorrow night, but I want you to come with me."

"What?" Her voice rises as she stiffens. "That's crazy." She blinks frantically, clearly worried.

And that's the exact reason I want her to come, to prove to her that I'm not going anywhere.

"Why is it crazy?"

"Because we only just reconnected."

"B, I've been obsessed with you for *years*, and most of those were spent apart. I don't think my feelings are changing any time soon."

"That's not the point. We still haven't finished the list. What if the cons win?"

"They won't."

"How can you be so sure?"

"Confidence."

Blair stares at me with narrowed eyes, and it only makes me want her more. I've always loved the way she challenges me. Most girls I hook up with would bark like a dog if I asked them to. I know this because I may have tested the theory once or twice. I'm an asshole, I know.

"Is this your way of extending our time together, so that I have time to think, while you're there if and when I'm ready to fuck you?"

I wince at her words but answer her easily. "B... I thought you knew me better than that. If it was just about the sex, I'd leave you here and fly back to meet you the second you wanted me. But I want you *with* me. All the time. Every damn second."

"Zane—"

"In fact, to prove my point, I'm not going to touch you at all for the rest of today or tomorrow. You're not even getting a kiss."

Blair rolls her eyes, but she can't hide the smile gracing her lips. "What are we going to do then?"

"I'm taking you out."

"Oh, yeah?"

"Yeah."

"How well do you know Los Angeles?"

"I know four places. The stadium, the national forest where I met you a few weeks back, Bo-Bo's restaurant, and here. Oh, and my hotel." I wink and her laughter fills the air.

"The hotel would be pointless if you're not going to touch me. But I've heard great things about Bo-Bo's."

"I'm not going to lie—it's like an orgasm for your mouth. You will not be disappointed."

"Then it looks like you're taking me to dinner."

"And a hike, tomorrow?"

Blair hesitates, her pinched expression making my insides knot. *Did I say the wrong thing?* I'm about to suggest another idea when she smiles softly.

"A hike sounds good. There's a couple of places I've been meaning to try out."

"Perfect." I smile back at her, still sensing she's holding something back.

No matter how good things feel, we still have a lot to work through, and I'm ready to put in the effort.

Chapter Thirty-Nine

BLAIR

How is it that I still feel the same lightness and strength when Zane's here as I do hiking alone? This was always something I did by myself. For myself. Even after meeting Jenna and knowing she loves hiking, we never go together. It's my solace. My sacred space.

But when Zane asked me, a spark electrified me, and for some reason, I wanted to say yes. I wanted to share the experience with him.

And it turns out...I feel great. The breeze floating through the trees still invigorates me, and the dirt under my feet is still just as grounding. Everything's the same. As though he's not even here.

But he is.

Now I've got that goddamn tingling giddiness you experience when you're first getting to know someone. Because this is new for us.

Zane was right. We can't put that on the con list.

"So..." I hesitate, my face pinched in annoyance. I hate getting lists wrong. "I owe you an apology."

"Wow, you look positively sick about it." He chuckles and I grin.

"Shut up." I lightly shove him. "It's possible that we may not know each other as well as I thought we did."

Zane's brows pucker, until they shoot up to his hair line, and he smirks. "You want to take our knowledge of one another *off* the cons list?"

"I do."

"Why? What don't I know?"

I take a deep breath, letting the cool air slowly fill my lungs before breathing out with a sigh. "I started hiking after you left. Dad suggested it for when I wanted to clear my head because I hated the workout torture."

"His workouts were always brutal."

"Exactly. So, when he suggested hiking, I jumped at the idea, and it only took a few minutes out in the fresh air for me to realize I found my place. From then on, it became my sanctuary. The scenery could change. The sounds. The smells. None of it had to be the same. But if I was out here, alone, I was healing. It worked better than any of the psych's suggestions."

Zane smiles but something about his expression appears troubled. I'm even more convinced when he rakes a shaky hand through his already messed hair. "I thought I knew everything."

"I found hiking after you left. How could you possibly have known about it?"

"Because I know *you*. There were signs. You hesitated when I suggested a hike yesterday. I thought it was because you were weighing up whether or not to spend more time with me. But it wasn't that at all. This is your thing and I'm invading it."

"Actually, you're not. I never once invited Nathan or Jenna, or Dad for that matter. But when you mentioned it, I wanted you to come. And nothing has changed. If anything, I feel more alive. More confident and strong. Because you bring that out in me. You've been bringing the old Blair back bit by bit ever since you walked back into my life. And I liked her."

My cheeks heat at the admission, but I smile through it because Zane's the one person I have always been myself around, and that hasn't changed.

"I happen to like her too." His warm smile sends a spark down my spine, but when he bounces his eyebrows, I laugh.

"Thank you. I'm not sure I've said that."

"You haven't. But you can make it up to me."

"How so?"

"Come with me to San Francisco." His eyes sparkle as his lips part in a goofy happiness that he never usually projects. I've seen it before and it always sucks me in. When my bad boy shows his good.

"I'll come with you," I finally agree. "But I have to be back in a week. I promised Jenna I'd go to an advanced screening of her latest series."

"Deal. I can work with a week."

"You can what?"

"A week gives me plenty of time to court you."

His lips purse as his face contorts, and I can't stop the snort that bursts out of me. "That didn't feel right, did it?"

"Fuck, no." He shivers. "But you get what I mean."

"You don't need to win me over, Zane. I know who you are and I know you're not going to purposely hurt me. That's not what I'm worried about."

"What are you worried about?"

"That it will happen regardless, without either of us meaning it."

My chest grows tight as Zane releases a sigh. The last thing I want to do is hurt him. But—

"You're right. We have to work harder, be honest with each other, and promise we'll never run. I think being here now has proven that doesn't work. It'll waste more time when we inevitably end up back together again. It's fate, baby."

"Baby?"

"Too much?" He smirks.

"Definitely. But I like the thinking. When do we leave?"

"How about now?" Zane eyes are alight with mischief before he throws me over his shoulder, jogging toward our car.

"Stop," I squeal between giggles. "I'm too heavy."

"You're what?" Zane freezes momentarily. "I bench press more than your weight. You just want me to put you down, but it's not happening until we get to the car. We have a flight to book."

I laugh at his craziness and let my body go limp, accepting my fate.

"God, I wish everyone else saw this side of you."

"No can do, Little B. This is for you and you alone. Always has been."

We pull up at a beautiful apartment building with a marble archway and pillars so grand they make my jaw drops as a shiver runs through me. I've been a ball of nerves since we got off the plane, and I can't quite pinpoint what it is that has me so worried. Seven years ago, I would have given anything to spend a week with Zane, but just like back then, we have to hide our relationship—even if we're only friends—so maybe that's it. Or maybe I'm worried that even if I try to love it here, I still won't find my place in this world.

Yes, I have issues and constantly put too much pressure on myself, but I need a purpose or I'm going to go insane. Vacationing with Zane is not going to help with that. Though it will be nice.

Taking a deep breath, I squeeze my leg and smile to myself. It's going to be good for us. "I've got to be honest, Fitzpatrick," I say with my eyes on his building, finding my inner strength. "This doesn't feel like you."

"You mean you don't think of me as a pretentious millionaire with rich taste."

"Nope. I always pictured you in a beach house."

"Well, you're in luck. Here's another one of those 'we don't know each other as well as we think we do' moments."

"Really?"

"Nope. It's a rental close to the stadium that has a doorman and great gym. I chose it because it was the first one I saw, and I was already sick of looking."

I nod, biting back a smart-ass response. That decision-making process is exactly what I'd expect from Zane. I was always the planner. He was always the one to make decisions on the fly. Unless it came to making our relationship public. That was well thought out and nothing was ever going to change his mind.

"I'd love to find a beach house one day," he adds, and I laugh. "But for now, welcome to my home sweet home. Your home for the week."

"How many bedrooms do you have?" I ask as a doorman opens my door.

Zane jumps out on his own and jogs to the trunk, grabbing my bags. Plural. Because rather than unpack and repack the suitcases I'm living out of, I just brought the two that housed my winter clothes, a couple of nice dresses, and my workout gear. Much to Zane's pleasure, since that meant we could leave sooner.

"I have two bedrooms," he tells me, waving me off when I try to grab one of my bags. "Before you say anything, the second is reserved for those I share a platonic relationship with. I'm afraid since we've kissed, that rules you out."

"How many other non-platonic relationships have you had in your room?"

"Lucky for me, none."

"Lucky for you?"

"Yep. Because I have a feeling that if I'd had anyone else in my bed, there's no way you'd be considering sleeping there right now."

"You're half right."

"Only half?" He pauses before we've reached the huge glass doors.

"Yes. I'm not considering it. I've made up my mind."

"And?"

"Since you're not going to touch me until I'm ready, it's a yes. I'll sleep in your room."

A groan rumbles from the back of Zane's throat, and his hands clench around the handles of my suitcases, the movement causing the veins in his arms to bulge beneath the ink of his tattoos. God, it's sexy.

I gulp, my gaze traveling from his wrist to the cuff of his rolled-up sleeve.

"B—" Zane warns, snapping me out of my trance.

"What?"

"You can't expect me not to touch you, then stare at me like I'm your next meal." His voice may be low, but I don't miss the way it strains as he speaks.

I open my mouth to sass him, but nothing comes out. I don't want to rush things, but at the same time, he's hard to resist. Clearing my throat, I shift my gaze, but before I get the chance to move on from the desire consuming me, we're interrupted.

"Mr. Fitzpatrick, it's nice to have you home." A beautiful blonde with a headset and a peppy bounce in her step holds open the door for us, her appraising gaze shifting my way. "Would you like me to arrange help with your bags?" She smiles, directing her question back to Zane.

"No, thank you, Kate. I've got this. But I'd love to have my car ready in an hour if that's okay."

"Of course. I'll buzz you when it's here."

Zane nods, holding his arm out and gesturing for me to walk through the threshold. "Ladies first. The elevator is straight ahead."

"Thank you."

I smile as I pass Kate, but her fake grin barely reaches her eyes until her gaze moves behind me. To Zane.

"If you need anything else, you've got my number." She speaks louder than necessary, and I hold back from rolling my eyes.

Zane doesn't say anything, and it takes everything in my power not to look back to check his response. But instead, I pick up speed, reaching the elevator a few seconds ahead of him. It's only when my jaw aches that I realize I've been clenching my teeth. *Dammit.*

Forcing a smile, I turn to look at Zane, and the second he sees me, his lips pull into a triumphant grin.

"Is that jealousy?"

"What? No. Do I have a reason to be jealous?"

"That depends. Would it bother you if one of our building concierges had a crush on me that I never reciprocated?"

"No."

"Then you're fine."

My face scrunches of its own accord and I groan out loud. "She's really beautiful, Zane."

"She's not you." He's so quick to respond that it momentarily stuns me. If it was anyone else, I'd assume that was a line, a well-practiced move to get the girl. Hell, if Nathan had said it, I'd probably cringe. Yet, I know with absolute certainty that's not the case with Zane. He means it. He's never been one to mince his words.

Having said that, at some point we have to discuss his reputation as a ladies' man, and there's no time like the present.

The elevator arrives, so I wait until we're inside before I hit him in the jugular. Metaphorically speaking, of course. "How many women have you slept with?

"What?" Zane chokes and I have to admit, it brings me joy. I actually don't mind that he slept around while we were apart. I may have only had one boyfriend, but I wasn't exactly celibate myself. And reconnecting with Zane was never on my radar.

But I am curious. I've seen the articles. I've got a fair idea.

"I... Ah..."

"Since when do you get tongue-tied?"

"I don't." He grips the back of his neck. "I'm just not sure what the right answer is here."

"The truth. Always."

"Well in that case, I never kept count, but it was a lot. Right up until you walked back into my life."

"And then?"

"None."

He's mentioned that before but still I inhale sharply, the force of that one word knocking the breath out of me. I shouldn't be surprised. Nothing Zane does should ever surprise me, but he continuously does.

"When are you going to believe that I never stopped loving you?"

My heart jolts, and I freeze as Zane squeezes my arm, his gaze boring into mine, his words and emotion chipping away at my walls.

"Zane? You—"

The door opens on Zane's floor, halting my response, and I'm thankful since I have no idea what the hell I was going to say.

I knew his feelings were strong. Back then. I knew how he felt about me, but he never once said the words. He even threw me off when he jokingly said it yesterday.

The only person that ever heard those words come out of his mouth was Sierra, so I imagine "love" has even more meaning for him now.

"You know what?" He grabs my hand when we're in the hallway, running his thumb over my skin. "How about we pretend I never said that. When you're ready to believe it, I'll say it again."

My heart pounds in my chest as his beautiful eyes stare deep into my soul. "I don't want you to hold it back."

"Honestly, B, it shocked me too. I know I feel it, it just..." He trails off but I don't need him to say it. I know exactly what he means.

"It's forgotten, but..." I bite my lip, as emotion wells in my chest. "Thank you."

"Yeah, yeah. Come on." He spins one of my suitcases around so he can hold them both with one hand and wraps the other around my shoulders. "If you thought the entry was nice, wait until you see my apartment."

CHAPTER FORTY

BLAIR

After our little "love" mishap, things between Zane and me settled into a nice rhythm, and I have to admit, it's likely because I finally stopped questioning everything he said. The feelings are there—I probably shouldn't be feeling this strongly so close to ending another relationship, but that's another issue—we just need time to work out how this can possibly work. If we can truly be together without constantly being taken back to that day. The day that changed it all.

The following evening, Zane walks in after practice, and a loud thud tells me he dumped his bag in the entry. "Honey, I'm home," he announces, his voice lifting in a light chuckle. "For the record, that didn't feel right either. It felt like something my teammate Luke would say."

His voice gets louder as he makes his way down the long hall, and I laugh, picturing his face pinched in disgust.

He wasn't kidding when he said his apartment was impressive. The condo I shared with Nathan was big, but it always felt cold and stiff. Which probably had something to do with the furniture I hated so much. This place is double that size and it still warms me like a home, from the bright pictures on the wall in the entry that welcome you inside, to the high ceilings and pendant drop lights. The sunken living area has not one, but two plush leather couches, that wrap around you like a cloud when you sink back into them.

His marble kitchen is big enough for a small restaurant, but everything about it screams homey comfort—untidy letters and notes on the end of the counter, random coffee mugs lined up next to the machine. It's designer for sure, but it's also not.

And don't get me started on the bedrooms. Both the bedrooms in our home back in Jacksonville could fit into Zane's master. It even has a goddamn hot tub boasting a view of San Francisco with one-way glass—I asked—and a walk-in closet that would impress a New York socialite.

When I mentioned that to Zane, he told me he could test that theory with Easton's girlfriend, only that it was more trouble than it's worth. He then proceeded to tell me about his dickish mistake of sleeping with Easton's ex. Except he didn't call it a "mistake" because he claims he didn't know at the time. In his mind the mistake was made in the way he handled it after.

And according to him, because he can admit that, he's growing.

I wait for Zane to reach me before responding to his "honey, I'm home" comment, only the second he comes into view, words fail me. His hair is still wet from his post practice shower, and he's wearing a fitted black Henley that accentuates the size of his arms. He runs a hand through his hair when our eyes meet, and the movement has his top lifting, and my gaze falls to the strip of his ripped stomach followed by the sneak peek of his V. I've seen him shirtless before; I saw it last night in bed. But I've always been attracted to athletes, and right now, he's showing me the goods.

"You're doing it again." He groans and I laugh at being busted.

"Don't come home looking like sex on legs, and I wouldn't stare. Did you even bother to towel off your hair, or will I find drips of water down your back if I look."

Zane smirks before spinning to show me, and sure enough, the neck of his top is wet. "I didn't have time. I had places to be, people to see."

"Oh, yeah?"

"Yeah. By the way, I like hearing the word 'home' come out of your mouth."

I try to fight it but my eyes roll of their own accord.

"There's the sass I remember. How was your day?"

"Great. *Mostly.*"

"Mostly?"

"Yep. I spent a big part of the day researching Heartwood University and writing my lists, while the rest of the time was spent with my finger hovering over the call button."

Zane's face lights up, but he's quick to school his features. "It's a big decision. I think it's good that you're taking the time to weigh your options." He nods and I burst out laughing.

"Please tell me how you really feel?"

"Are you sure?" His excited smile reappears.

"I'm sure." I nod, keeping my own expression as emotionless as possible.

"Good. Well, location aside, if this job was in Jacksonville or even LA, you'd be jumping at the chance to work for a football team. It's a match made in heaven. For both you and the team. The way you know the game means you'll see things before others see it. I have no doubt that you'd already be aware of a player's injury before he walked into your room. And while yes, your job would mostly consist of checkups and assisting the doctor, I think you'd be a huge asset to any team."

My chest tightens at his reasoning but he's only half right. "If this job was in Jacksonville, or LA, I'd be just as conflicted. A year ago, I would have jumped at the role, but now, I'm trying to decide where I want to be and I'm not sure where that is. But I don't think it's Florida."

"Cade is going to hate that."

"Yep, but that goes on the pros list." I smirk and Zane throws his head back with a laugh.

"What about San Francisco?"

"You mean Heartwood?"

"Nope. I mean San Francisco. If you choose to live in Heartwood, I'll support it. But I'm not going to pretend I love the idea. It's a long way from the stadium, and that would mean earlier mornings for me, and—"

I throw a pillow at his face as a laugh bursts out of me. "I knew you wouldn't be able to have this talk without making it about you."

"About us, you mean? I'm making it about *us*."

"If you say so."

"I do. That aside, I'm here to help. Do you want to run through the list together?"

"Maybe. But not today. I need a break from it. I need time to think. Can I let you know?" My stomach rumbles and I cough to hide it. Truth be told, I haven't stopped thinking about it since he left this morning, and I forgot to eat.

"Have you eaten?" Zane questions me, proving once again that he knows me, or that he reads minds.

"I haven't eaten recently, if that's what you mean."

"Come on." He walks closer and grabs my hand, interlacing our fingers. "I'm taking you out."

"Wait." I pull back panicked, but he doesn't release me. "I can't go out dressed like this. I'm in yoga pants and an oversized tee."

"So?"

"So?" I balk, my heart racing as I wave my hands at my casual attire.

Zane frowns before his tongue juts out to swipe across his lip. "Mmm. You're right. You definitely need to change. That damn outfit is doing crazy things to my insides. The way your tee falls from your shoulder makes me want to suck your neck, and... Has anyone ever told you that you have a great ass?"

He's messing around, but my breath hitches and I struggle to take in air, a memory of Nathan asking me to change assaulting my mind. *How did I let that happen?* For *four* years.

"B?" Zane takes a step toward me, his expression morphing to one of concern. "Are you okay?"

"Yes, sorry. You've mentioned my ass before." I wave off his worry. "Only it was much perkier back then."

"Where did you go just now?"

"I was just thinking. All good, I promise."

Zane's brows crease until I laugh, squeezing his arm. "I'm going to change. What should I wear?"

"Wear whatever you want. You always look amazing."

My heart jolts but I don't let myself react externally. This is new. The compliments. The lack of control. I'm still not sure I'm ready for any of this, but I want to try.

With a quick nod so he doesn't hear the emotion caught in my throat, I walk away, stripping the tee over my head the second I'm in the spare room. While I may be *sleeping* next to Zane, I opted to keep my things separate so I could ensure some level of privacy, like getting dressed without being watched.

"Actually, wear something frumpy," Zane calls out and I snort. "That way, you won't have to worry about me ogling your body." He groans before continuing on, mumbling his words. "And I won't have to worry about anyone else doing the same."

A buzz runs through me, and I smile to myself while my reality saddens me. I knew I was broken from the events of my past, but I didn't realize how much I'd let it affect me. The old me never would have let someone else control what I wore and yet, for years, I accepted it from Nathan. And never once questioned him.

With a weight pulling me down, I dress in a conservative sweater and a skirt. Not frumpy, but also not revealing. "How's this?" I say softly, walking back into the hallway to find Zane's face in his phone.

"Hang on." His fingers bounce around the screen for a few more seconds before he lifts his gaze, and the smile he bestows melts away my nerves, sending my pulse rocketing. "Beautiful as always, B. How would you like to come to our practice on Friday?" His question throws me off guard and I pause, my heart jumping.

"Really?"

"Yep. I just got the okay."

"Uh. I don't know." I want to. I'd love to go, but that seems like a girlfriend thing to do, and it's too soon to open that can of worms. In public. All it would take is one person sneaking a photo of me, and Nathan seeing—

"It's a closed session, if that helps with your decision. No media."

"Oh." *It does.* "Okay. Thanks. I'd love to see you in action. But are you sure?"

My question makes me jolt and I'm once again thrown by the person I've become. But like always, Zane instantly puts me at ease.

"Fuck, yeah, I'm sure. I'd love nothing more than to have you there."

CHAPTER FORTY-ONE

BLAIR

Zane's still asleep when I wake the next morning, and I bite back a groan as I wriggle out of his hold. No matter how far away I am when we first go to sleep, at some point during the night, we end up like this—wrapped around each other, legs tangled, making it difficult to determine where I end and he begins.

Yesterday, he was the one to extract himself from me after his alarm went off, and though it woke me, I was still in a half dreamlike state and couldn't move to help him. Instead, I let him lift me gently and reposition me on my side of the bed, his palms warming my skin, his deep breaths making me melt.

This morning, it's my turn. But unlike me, Zane makes it known that my movements have woken him.

"Don't go," he whines. "My alarm hasn't gone off yet."

I allow him to pull me back into his rock-hard chest, and hold my breath, knowing his delicious scent is about to attack me. Other than these little moments in bed—when both of us pretend the rest of the world, along with all of our problems, no longer exist—Zane kept his word about not touching me. Even though it kills him, he's respecting my wishes and I'm grateful for that.

"Mmm." He buries his face in my neck and groans, his raspy voice rumbling in my ear, sending a shiver down my spine. "You smell good."

I smile at our similar thinking but before I can respond, a light buzzing permeates the air before Zane's alarm blares. I like that he has a little pre-alarm alarm. It makes me less jumpy when I hear it.

"Dammit." He groans again, this time out of annoyance. "I quit."

"No, you don't. You love football. And I love football players."

"Ugh, don't remind me. Is *that* why you—"

"Don't even finish that question, Fitzpatrick." I roll over and glare his way. "Especially not when I'm wrapped up in your arms. Do you want me to freak out and decide this is all a mistake?" I'm joking, but the mention of Nathan does him no favors.

Zane clears his throat before rolling me onto my back and reaching over to silence his alarm. "Good morning, beautiful. When did you wake up?"

I laugh at his attempt to restart the day, but a little part of me swoons.

"Your alarm woke me just now." I play along, smiling up at him as he hovers above me, careful not to touch me, now that we're out of our overnight bubble.

"Did you sleep well?" he asks, always putting his concern for me ahead of everything else.

"I did. You?"

"Never better. I had this dream about a curly-haired goddess sharing my bed, and the feel of her tucked in beside me seemed to have a drugging effect. The good kind. The kind that gives you a peaceful night's sleep."

He chuckles to himself, but there's a moment of sadness to it before he hides it away.

"How often do you have trouble sleeping?" I lift to my elbows and Zane sits back on his heels, putting some space between us.

"Most nights," he rasps, clearing his throat before continuing on. "It's been that way since..." He trails off and I wish more than anything that I knew how to comfort him. The problem is, I suffer the same fate.

It doesn't escape me that I had the best sleep in *years* last night too.

"Have you spoken to anyone about it, about..." I trail off myself, stopping short of mentioning Sierra's name. He's opening up, and I don't want him to shut down again.

"I have and they've prescribed a million things, but I don't want to put anything in my body that doesn't come from the team doctors, and while I'm at peak performance, they have no reason to question me."

"But are you...playing at peak performance? Maybe the extra sleep would take you to the next level." I grimace because I hate talking to him like I know what's best, but I also want him to have what's best.

Zane smiles, lifting his hand toward my cheek, and my breath hitches as a heated energy fills the room. With a pounding heart, I anticipate his affectionate touch, but before he's made contact, his alarm goes off again, and he curses out loud.

"Fuck. Sorry."

"That's okay. You have to go. I know that."

"I do, but God, I don't want to."

"I'll be here when you get back," I offer and his eyes light up.

"Thank you. Sometimes I think this is all a dream and you're going to disappear out of my life again." He smiles, squeezing my arm as he gets up, as though making sure I truly exist. Turning away, I swear he mumbles something about not being able to suffer another great loss, and a weight settles on my heart. It's not hard to figure out what he means. We're both mourning so much, but I sometimes forget Zane lost a hell of a lot more than I did. Sierra wasn't just his sister. They were best friends, a team, and that's not something you can easily get over.

Zane disappears through the closet, and a few seconds later the shower turns on.

While I wait for him to get ready, I lie back down, pulling the sheet tightly around me, snuggling into his side of the bed. I breathe in his scent, my mind drifting to a life that could have been, a life I've never let myself entertain. But with Zane in the next room, it's closer than ever.

I will never get over what happened to Sierra, or my part in it, but I can't help wondering... Could I truly be happy again?

I'm not sure how much time passes before I feel movement beside me and Zane kisses my head, his whispered goodbye floating into my subconscious. I smile and stretch, ready to force myself up, but the next thing I know, I'm startled awake, my nineties ringtone snapping me to attention.

"Hello?" I answer groggily. I must have fallen back to sleep.

"Blair, it's Ron. Fitzpatrick." I sit up, my body jumping off the bed.

"Hi, Ron." Despite the fact that I've known him all my life, Ron announces his full name every time he calls. I used to find it amusing, but today, the mention of Zane's last name makes my skin prickle. "How are you?"

"Not great. I'm guessing the news has died down in LA because you haven't checked in for a while. Here, it's still very present, and Fiona's terrified they're going to release her name. That Sierra's going to be thrust into the headlines."

My stomach knots but I rush to reassure him. "She was underage at the time and was never charged. Zane was never charged either. They have no reason to mention her name. If anything, we should be worried about him."

"Zane?"

"Yes."

"I don't want to talk about him. Do you know how long it's been since he called us? Years, Blair. For all our sanity, it's best if we try not to think about him. We're lucky we've got each other."

Gulping back a lump in my throat, I nod as tears coat my eyes, guilt consuming me. The Zane he describes doesn't come close to the Zane I know, and I'm struggling to marry them both in my mind.

"Have you tried calling *him*?" I ask, and instantly regret not talking to Zane about this. I got caught up in the moment and let my feelings take over. But this situation is important.

"I told you; I don't want to talk about him."

"Then what do you want?" I raise my voice and wince. "Sorry, I just woke up. I'm not thinking clearly."

"Sorry. I forgot you're in Los Angeles now. It's early there."

My guilt thickens, eating away at me. If he'd said California then I would have been fine. I'm still in California, but I'm not in LA. I'm in San Francisco, with the son he seems to despise.

"It's okay. How can I help?"

"I think Fiona would just love to see your face. To talk about Sierra with her friend. To have a moment of light in her otherwise gray world."

Oh. Shit. "I'd love that," I say through a forced grin, thankful he can't see me. "We could do a video call?"

"You're not coming here? It's your dad's birthday next week and—"

"I'm not sure yet."

"I understand. Well, we'd love to have you over. But if not, a video call would be great."

"I'll let you know. Please send my love to Fiona."

"I will."

He hangs up and I fall back onto the pillows, groaning. I've always ended these calls emotionally drained, but it usually comes with built-up anger toward Zane. Now that I'm spending time with him, I can't help but question if I'm seeing the full picture. I can't imagine *this* Zane abandoning his parents like that. It was okay to believe that when I didn't know the man he'd become, but now...my guilt shifts from his parents to him, and an uncomfortable feeling settles in my chest. All this time, I made assumptions without getting his side of the story. It's time I found out.

After finally dragging myself out of bed, I strip my pajamas off and step under the cosmic waterfall shower, letting the hot water run over me, washing away the tension caused by Zane's dad. But no sooner have my muscles relaxed than a new life issue springs to mind, one I can't put off any longer.

The job at Heartwood U.

As reluctant as I am to admit it, the job is like a dream come true. And now that Nathan and I have split up, there's really no reason for me to hold myself back from any opportunity that presents itself. I came to that conclusion when my pros list heavily outweighed the cons. And yet, I haven't made the call. Because that one blaring con is the one thing that's stopping me.

What if it doesn't work out with Zane?

Ending things with Zane last time almost destroyed me. But as much as it pained me to watch him leave, it was easier to believe I could move on when he wasn't in my face.

Heartwood and San Francisco are an hour apart. Lucy is the sister of Zane's teammate. If things end badly between us, that constant reminder would always be there. And if I'm honest with myself, I'm worried I won't survive it.

I stand under the jets for longer than I should, and it's not until my skin starts to prune that I finally switch off the tap.

If Zane and I do make a go of it, and it doesn't work out, I'd be shattered. But if it does work out, having a job that I love would be incredibly fulfilling.

Not to mention, it's part time, so I'd get a chance to consider writing again.

My heart jolts at the thought. I haven't allowed myself to dream like that since before the accident. *Is it possible to have it all?*

My mouth quirks into a smile of its own accord as a fresh ball of energy works its way into my chest.

Fucking Zane. I laugh to myself. How dare he have me believing again.

I towel off quickly and throw on my workout gear, grabbing my phone before I change my mind.

Then without wasting another second, I call Lucy, my breath caught in my throat as I wait for her to answer.

CHAPTER FORTY-TWO

BLAIR

The smell of freshly cut grass fills the crisp morning air, and a giddiness runs through me. For years, I imagined watching Zane practice in the pros, and I'm here. A little unbelievably so.

Folding my arms over the fence surrounding the state-of-the-art facility, I lean in, rapt with attention.

Zane's receiver coach calls him to line up for their Red Zone game plan, and I watch, my feet bouncing in excitement, as he gets into position alongside one of his teammates.

I've been to open practices before and loved every second, but this is something else. It's more intimate. More real. The players aren't here for anyone's enjoyment; they're here for themselves, and it's obvious from the contrasting energy surrounding them.

Don't get me wrong—they're all forces on the field. Determined. Powerful. Ready. But when the whistle blows and they have even a second to relax, it's glorious to watch their personalities shine through.

After only forty-five minutes of practice, I can tell you that Bennett is as cocky as they get and lives to make people laugh, while Wilder is a broody type—he didn't even acknowledge Bennett when he called his name. Despite obviously hearing him.

I may not know them at all, but it's nice to see them act how I imagine they'd be in the locker room when the pressure is off.

That is, until I get to Zane. He's different on the field then he is with me. He's more serious. More cocky. And a hell of a lot more broody. He's like a mix of the other two guys. And I've got to admit, it's sexy as hell.

There's something about the way his presence demands attention that makes me want to—

"Blair?" A gruff voice calls my name and I spin around in a panic, my cheeks heating at being caught perving on Zane. "Sorry." He smiles. "I didn't mean to startle you. I'm Wes."

"Wes." *Oh, God.* Wes Johnson, ex-NFL player and Storm's general manager, just caught me checking out his team. "Hi. It's nice to meet you." I shake the hand he holds out for me and pray he doesn't register how hot and flustered I am. It's not exactly hot outside.

"Zane tells me you're a league expert."

The heat in my cheeks turns to a burn and I have no doubt I'm blushing. Fucking Zane. Not only is that not true, but I'm fan-girling a little here, and this man is ridiculously sexy.

"I wouldn't say I'm an expert but I love the game." I stand confidently, trying to appear calmer than I am.

"Okay. What do you think of all the talk surrounding Myers next year?" Wes challenges, raising an eyebrow with a smile, and I instantly relax. This I can talk about. But he's letting me off easy.

"Myers was amazing last year. His reach is unlike any others. And despite his age, he's killing it. If Kelly retires like the rumors are suggesting, it's critical to have a replacement. He'd be a great fit." A laugh escapes me because I'm sure he knows if the rumors are true.

"You don't think our second QB could step up?"

I cringe. *Dammit.* Why did I have to run my mouth? "From what I've seen, he's a phenomenal player, but he was protecting his left leg in the preseason game last year and then again in the game against Seattle a couple of weeks back, when Thomas hurt his shoulder in the second half. Thank God Thomas is okay, by the way. No one wants to end their career like that." I cringe again, suddenly remembering that Wes's career ended after a knee injury during a championship game. It was awful and the wrong thing to say just now.

"Sorry."

"You're fine. I've accepted my past."

"Good to know. Anyway, what I'm trying to say is that Lawrence, your second, was still favoring his right leg in practice just now. Meaning it hasn't improved over the past year."

Wes's lips thin before he chuckles, smiling in admiration. "Wow. I'm impressed. If I didn't think Lucy would divorce me, I'd try and poach you for our medical team."

"Lucy?" I frown. "Lucy's your wife?"

"She is. Zane didn't tell you?"

"No. But he only mentions the job if I specifically talk to him about it. I think he's trying to respect my wishes. I asked him to let me decide for myself."

"Ahh...wise of him then."

"Definitely." I laugh out loud. "But I'm excited to be meeting Lucy tomorrow."

It's Wes's turn to cringe this time as his eyes flash to something behind me. "The thing about Lucy is that she's not very patient when she's got an idea, and she's not one to sit around and wait for something to happen."

Tension fills me. I'm supposed to be making the drive to Heartwood University tomorrow to meet the team and chat about the job. Zane's even letting me borrow his car. But something tells me those plans are about to change.

My pulse spikes as I fight not to turn around. "She's behind me, isn't she?"

"She sure is."

As if perfectly timed, I hear fast footsteps approaching and a stunning woman appears by our side, her blue eyes sparkling with glee as she pulls me into a hug. "Oh my god, Blair. It's so nice to finally meet you."

"Lucy, hi." I smile through my unease. "I wasn't expecting to run into you today."

"I know, sorry. When Wes said you were coming to practice on my day off, I couldn't stay away. I promise, no shop talk. I just wanted to meet you. And I've been meaning to come and see a practice."

"I'll leave you ladies to it." Wes nods before pressing a kiss to Lucy's brow and waving to me. "Come by when you're done," he whispers to Lucy, and she smiles before turning to give me her full attention.

"So, don't tell Wes I said this, but are you sure you and Zane are just friends? That man is gorgeous."

I bite back a grin as we walk closer to the fence, and it takes me less than a second to find Zane. He's not the biggest guy on the team, but he's tall and his tattoos stand out from a mile away.

When I glance back to Lucy, I find her grinning my way and I let out a laugh. "We're friends. Who knows what the future might bring, but we have some history to work through."

"Ahh, damn baggage. If we didn't have it, we'd be boring, but God, some of it weighs you down. Want to know a secret?"

"Always."

"Wes has taken a liking to Zane. He said he can see through his cockiness. He mentioned D'Angelo feels the same."

Pride consumes me and I can't stop my beaming smile. "I always hoped people would see him the way I do, but he's good at putting on a front."

"Aren't we all?"

"I'm not. At least not when people bother to look." I physically jolt at the words leaving my mouth, and rush to retract them. "Don't mind me. Wes used to work at Heartwood U, right? Did you meet there?"

Clearly, I have some baggage with Nathan that I also need to address. Particularly, how it took me so long to realize that he didn't always see me or see the way I was hurting. Then again, I didn't see myself either. And maybe that's why I loved him. Because he wasn't constantly bringing up my pain like everyone else was.

Lucy frowns at my abrupt change of subject, but after a beat, she lets it slide.

"Actually, we met when I decided to kiss a stranger on the beach to piss off my ex. That stranger being the one and only Wes Johnson. The rest of it is a long story."

"Luckily we've still got an hour to go." I shrug and Lucy bursts out laughing.

"If you insist." She playfully rolls her eyes, but I can tell she loves sharing this story.

When practice ends, Lucy keeps me company while I wait for Zane to finish in the locker room, and while she promised no shop talk, I can't help but bring it up. She's made me feel so incredibly comfortable that I no longer mind the fact that it was technically an ambush.

"Have you found a doctor for the team yet?" I ask, eliciting another bright smile to her face.

"We have, and you're going to love her. Shaylee. She'll be there tomorrow. She doesn't have much knowledge of football though, so you might have to teach her a thing or two." She pauses. "If you take the job, that is."

Her confidence makes it sound like I'm meant to be on the team, and in turn, makes me love the idea more and more, the longer I'm in her presence. But it's still not a done deal. Not yet.

"I'm glad you've found someone. But didn't she have any nurses to recommend?"

"She had plenty. We'll look into those *only* if you turn us down. No pressure, of course. We just all agree that having a passionate employee is always better for the team."

"You're not worried I'll be *too* passionate, if you know what I mean?"

I bite my lip and an over-the-top laugh escapes her. "I'll admit that thought definitely crossed my mind, and the mind of Shaylee, but I'm no longer worried."

"Why?" My brows crease in confusion.

"Because I saw the way you were watching Zane, and I doubt you'll be single for long."

"Oh."

"Sorry." She laughs. "I have a habit of putting my nose in where it doesn't belong. I just love seeing people happy. And from what Wes tells me, that man's been through a lot. I think you have too."

"I have. And you're right about Zane. But it's not that simple. Our hurt is connected and…" I trail off, not wanting to bring down the mood.

"A relationship doesn't necessarily help with the healing," Lucy finishes for me, summarizing my fears in one little statement.

"Exactly. But we're working on it." The truth passes through my lips without thought, and an overwhelming strength takes over me. I want to work on it. Even if we have to hide it again, I want a relationship.

My heart races at the internal revelation, and I have to fight not to outwardly react.

I loved Nathan, but it turns out, I never stopped loving Zane. And like he said, it's inevitable. We're inevitable. It's time I stopped denying us the joy we could be living.

"Something just happened?" Lucy squints, her expression puzzled.

"I think I just had one of those aha moments."

"Ooh, I love those."

Anxiety swirls inside me but this time it's a good tension, a healthier dose, if that's even a thing. And when Zane walks out of the locker room, his penetrating gaze instantly finding mine, it sets me on fire, confirming I'm making the right choice.

His lips pull into a smile as his long stride brings him closer, and I can't wait to have him in my arms.

"Your ride has arrived, so I'm going to head off." Lucy's voice gets my attention and I break the spell Zane has me under, glancing her way. "I'll still see you tomorrow though, right?"

"I'll be there," I say confidently, a resolute feeling settling into my chest. "I can't wait."

"Us either. See you then."

Zane stops a few feet in front of us and Lucy gives him a nod. "Zane," she says, making him frown before he hides his confusion.

"Hi." He waves and Lucy laughs before walking away.

"Who was that?"

"I'm surprised you don't know, since her husband knows all about me." His confusion doesn't waver until I tell him her name.

"Oh, shit. I had no idea she was going to be here." He panics and I drop the teasing act, putting his mind at ease.

"I know. Wes told her I was coming, and she couldn't stay away."

"How did that go?" Zane scratches the back of his head, doing nothing to hide his concern.

"It was good. No, it was great. She's lovely and while we didn't talk much about the role, I still feel positive about it."

"Oh, yeah?" His expression brightens.

"Yeah. I'm glad she surprised me." A warmth fills me as I stare into Zane's piercing eyes, my hesitation washing away. Lucy's presence helped me more than she knows.

"Good." Zane smiles, unaware of my change of heart. "Are you ready to get out of here? I was thinking we could go somewhere fancy tonight."

"Fancy?" My eyes widen.

"Yes. I can be fancy, despite this rough exterior." He rubs a hand over his stubble and I laugh.

"I never said you couldn't. But I was hoping we'd stay in."

Zane jokingly raises an eyebrow, and this time our thoughts are on par.

I think I'm ready for more, and I can't wait to tell him.

Chapter Forty-Three

ZANE

Something feels different on our drive home, almost as if there's a fresh energy hovering in the air, and I've got to admit, it brings me hope.

If Lucy's visit today helped seal the deal with Blair, I'll forever be grateful for her and Wes. They may not know it, but securing a job is the first step toward Blair finding herself again, and God, she deserves the break.

"If you didn't talk about the job, what did you and Lucy talk about?" I ask, curiosity getting the better of me.

Out of the corner of my eye, I note Blair's lips curling into a grin before she giggles softly. "You?"

"Me?" I point to myself, feigning shock. "She knows who I am?"

"Nope. She had no idea until I told her." I throw a suspicious gaze at Blair and she fakes a sympathetic frown. "Does that break your heart?"

I will never get tired of her playful side. Ever. And I love playing along. "It does." I pout. "I thought everyone knew me."

We pull up in front of my building, and I switch off the ignition, jumping out of the car before Blair's had a chance to respond, running around to open her door.

There's a spark in her eyes. A radiance about her. Just the hint of her gleeful smile lights up the room, and I haven't seen her this free since she was a teenager.

I watch her quietly as we head up to my apartment, her expression giddy as she fills me in on her chat with Lucy and the way Wes challenged her football knowledge.

She turns to face me when we reach my door, her breathtaking smile so illuminating that my heart clenches.

What the fuck am I going to do if this doesn't work out?

What if Blair has all this time to think, then decides her life would be better off without me?

My ears ring as I unlock the door, and when Blair steps through, her brows furrow as she studies my face. "What happened?"

"What?"

"You were all smirks and happiness and now it's gone."

My shoulders drop as I blow out a breath. I promised honesty and I at least owe her that. I'm refusing to acknowledge how much more I owe her, how much I stole from her and my sister, with one stupid decision.

"I'm terrified I'm going to lose you again. Because if I'm being honest, you deserve better." I turn away to shut the door, slowly taking off my shoes before facing her again. Anything to delay the pitied look I have no doubt will be marring her features.

She says seeing me again has been hard, and I'm sure she thinks I'm not struggling like she is, but I am. I've just been living in denial. Only the more time I spend with her, the more it comes to the surface.

I don't deserve a second chance. One day she's going to wake up and realize that.

The air's thick when I finally glance her way, but instead of finding her sympathetic expression, she's mad.

Hand on her hips, brows raised high on her forehead, her lips are thinned. "No. You don't get to do that. You're the confident one. You're the one that's steadfast in our relationship. I deserve what I *want*. And what I want is *you*."

"What?" I inhale sharply, my heart now pounding heavily in my chest.

Blair's stance relaxes as she watches me, and after a beat, she lets out a breathy laugh. "I want you, Zane. We have a lot to work through but—"

I don't let her finish before I'm locking my arms around her waist and lifting her into the air, spinning her around.

"What would the guys say if they saw you like this?" She giggles.

"I don't care what they think about me. But I'd happily take a swing at any of them, if they made you feel anything other than amazing."

Blair grabs my face when I drop her to her feet, her expression soft and caring. "After all these years, you still surprise me with your tenderness."

"Bad boys can't feel?"

"You've never been a bad boy."

I raise an eyebrow, my lips quirking into a mischievous grin. "I haven't?"

"Nope", she states firmly but her eyes darken with desire. "Nothing you do will convince me otherwise."

"Is that a challenge?" I step back and bite my lip, loving when the movement draws her gaze. She mimics me without realizing, trapping her glossed flesh between her teeth.

The things I've done in the past could easily prove her wrong, but this isn't about that right now. The last thing I want to do is bring down the mood. I have a better idea.

"Bring it." Blair waves me closer with a come-hither motion, and I maintain a straight face, taking a step toward her.

"You. Are. On."

"I'm ready," she says confidently until I grab her under her knees and race down the hall, ignoring her squeals as I go.

I lower her beside the bed, stopping her when she tries to sit down. "Don't move."

"What?"

"I said, don't move."

Her lips part in a gasp, and the sound of it heightens the invisible tension in the room. What I'm about to do will be as hard on her as it is on me, but I've made my bed and now I'm going to lie in it.

With my heart still pounding, I step closer, curling my hands under the hem of her sweater and tee before lifting them both over her head and tossing them across the room.

I reach for her jeans next, unbuttoning the fly, slowly lowering the zipper without ever touching her skin.

Need sizzles between us, and since we're both quiet, I hear her gulp, hear the slight hitch of her breath as her chest rises.

When her jeans are over her ass, I bend to my knees, my face lining up with her black lace panties, the see-through material showing just enough to make my cock ache.

I lick my lips, desperate for a taste of her. But I can wait. I want her begging for my tongue, pining for the touch of my fingers. I want to hear her say it. Again.

Blair squirms under my intense gaze, and she's intoxicating. I feel like the addict getting my fill without actually taking a hit.

Sitting back on my heels, I bite down on my lip, stopping myself from groaning, and stare at her beneath hooded eyes, ignoring the pull low in my stomach, the ache of my cock hardening to unbearable levels.

Blair trembles, and when I finally glance up at her, she's staring back at me, her lips parted, a flush to her cheeks that has me growling in the back of my throat.

Craving the feel of her soft skin, I finally reach for her panties, my knuckles grazing her flesh as I work to pull them down.

Her legs clench with need and my eyes close as I fight my restraint. She's so close I could poke my tongue out and lick her, but in the end, it's going to be worth it.

Standing up, I walk behind her, flicking off her bra with two fingers, smiling when she gasps. I'm not proud of the fact that I've mastered that skill, but in this instance it's helpful.

Goose bumps coat Blair's skin and I itch to touch, but I need her a little more primed and a lot more pissed off if I want to prove my point.

Without giving her an explanation, I turn and climb onto the bed, lying down before lifting to my elbows once I'm settled.

"What are you doing?" She frowns as she spins, her gaze dropping to her very naked body while I remain fully clothed.

"I'm getting comfortable."

"What the fuck, Zane? If this is part of your plan, it's not working. This is Zane the *ass*, not Zane the *bad boy*."

I bite back my smile as my dick pulses in my sweats. I like her feistiness. Always have.

"Oh, B. You have no idea. I'm here because I want you to ride my face."

"What?" Her lips part in a silent gasp and I let my smirk free. "I want you to crawl up here and ride my face."

"No."

"No?"

"Zane, that's crazy. What if I hurt you?"

I stifle a groan and fight the urge to ask if that means she's never ridden anyone before. I almost grin triumphantly, but I'm smarter than that. "You won't hurt me. You can trust me on that."

"Why? Because you've done this a million times?"

"Do you really want me to answer that?"

"Yes. No. *God.*"

"I've never used my mouth on anyone other than *you.*"

Her breath hitches. "Bullshit."

"Honest to God truth."

"Why?"

"It felt too intimate and I wasn't there for that."

Blair nods, pretending to be unaffected, but I don't miss the way her throat bobs.

Letting her process those feelings, I give her a second, watching her eyes flutter before patting the bed. "Are you coming?"

She snaps out of her shock to hit me with a wicked grin. "I guess that depends on how good you are."

"Is that another challenge?"

"Maybe?" She bites her lip, and instead of waiting for her to crawl, I dive forward and drag her on top of me, her squeal making my balls tighten. I expect her to argue, but when I let her go, she sits up, straddling my waist, and I'm fucking awestruck by how incredible she is.

As I wrap my hands around her hips, she sucks in her stomach, making me groan at the idea of her not liking any part of herself. She is and will always be the most beautiful woman I have ever laid eyes on, and I won't let her think otherwise.

"You're a goddamn knockout, B. Exactly as you are." I stare at her pointedly, making sure my words sink in, and she nods as she shivers, silently willing me to keep going.

Doing as asked, I glide my hands up her sides, dipping in the curve of her waist before molding my palms around her breasts. Her breath hitches again and she lifts off of me, her entire body shaking.

Her nipples pucker under my touch, and I make a note to suck them later, wondering if I could get her off just with that alone.

As I roll my thumbs over the buds, I let my gaze drop to her bare pussy, and I struggle to focus, picturing her rocking against my face, her glistening core soaking my mouth.

Blair jolts forward and gasps, turning to look behind her. "You're so hard."

"Of course I am. I have a fucking goddess sitting naked on top of me, her pussy primed and ready to be eaten."

"Zane."

"Please, B. This mouth is desperate for your clit."

"God, you're full of it." She tries to scold me but her voice comes out breathy.

"Just get your ass up here."

"My ass?"

"Hey, if that's your thing, I'm not opp—"

"Okay. Stop." A beautiful pink hue travels along her neck before she stands and shifts up the bed, settling herself on top of me, her knees on either side of my head.

The sight silences me, my throat dry as I thirst for her arousal on my tongue. "Fuuck. You're glistening. One would think you like the buildup."

"Zane?" she cries out, her head falling back, angling her pussy closer to my mouth.

"Yes, B?"

"Please."

"Please, what?"

"I need you to touch me. Lick me. Anything. I'm so goddamn ready, I'm gonna make myself come if you don't start soon."

"It's cute that you think I'd let you. But—" She groans, cutting me off, her legs clenching around my head. "But,"—I pry her legs open—"you just had to ask."

Her gaze shoots to mine as I pull her down, spreading her lips and flattening my tongue against her core. She buckles as she cries out, her taste so delicious it's my own personal ecstasy. And her sounds...fuck, she's so sweet. *Innocent.*

Mine.

She has no idea how dangerous she is, no idea that she's always had a hold on me, and with the way I'm feeling now, I'd give everything up to be with her.

I lick a path toward her clit, and she clenches again, her knees shaking as she lets out an audible moan, trying to lift herself up.

"B," I warn, speaking against her pussy.

"I'm trying. But it's too good and I'm going to lose control."

"So *lose* control."

"What if I h—"

"Did that fucker ever pleasure you?" I interrupt her, getting a little pissed off, wondering why she keeps questioning her body and weight. If this is his fault, I want to erase him from her memory. And mine.

"Do you really want me to answer that?" She throws my question back at me, and I stupidly say yes. I have never been a jealous guy, but I will always regret not taking all her firsts. Not making sure she knew her worth, knew how beautiful she was *every single day*.

Though I will admit there's a certain level of satisfaction knowing I have this one. Seems only fair since she's taking one of mine.

Blair sighs before giving me her answer. "He did. But not like this."

That's what I thought. I smirk, internally gloating, until Blair's moans bring me back to her.

Spreading her again, I lap up her arousal before pushing the tip of my tongue inside her, my thumb massaging her clit.

She jolts, her body spasming as she shakes her head. "Oh, God. I'm so close. *Zane.*"

I push my thumb inside her this time, circling her clit with my tongue while she constricts around me, crying out as she finally takes control.

She grabs my hair and rocks her hips, rolling her pussy against my mouth, using me, taking what she needs as I pleasure her, replacing my thumb with two fingers at first and then three, getting her ready in case she wants to take this further.

Her body stiffens before she screams out my name and collapses against the headboard, her pussy convulsing as I continue my ministrations, slowing my moves until she's begging me to stop.

"God. Please. Jesus." She speaks between breaths, lifting to her knees, her sated gaze staring down at me.

My heart squeezes at the sight of her and when she smiles, I'm absolutely done for. More so than I was before.

Blair's breathing slows and a second later she smirks. "Okay. You win. That *was* badass." She shakes, her smile turning into a laugh. "But I'm only giving you half a point. It was still more ass than bad boy."

A chuckle rumbles out of me and I grab her waist, squeezing her flushed skin. "Noted. But I won either way. Now get over here and come lie down." I pat the bed next to me. "I want to fucking hold you."

CHAPTER FORTY-FOUR

ZANE

Blair shivers as I run the tips of my fingers up and down her back, watching the sheen of goose bumps coat her beautiful, flushed skin. I pause and she trembles.

"Don't stop," she murmurs softly, and even though it's practically a whisper, it's impossible to miss the pleading nature of her tone.

As if she has to beg.

She clearly has no idea I'd do anything for her.

"I want more." She shifts slightly, looking up into my eyes. "I'm ready."

My heart jolts, hoping she means what I think she means, but I don't let myself get too excited. Since I just gave her a mind-blowing orgasm—her words, not mine—it's possible she's referring to sex.

"More?" I ask hesitantly, brushing a wild curl away from her eyes, my skin heating when my knuckles brush across her cheek.

"*Everything.*" The word leaves her lips on a sigh, and it penetrates my heart.

"Everything?" I want her to spell it out for me.

"I want it all. I want *you*. We're going to have to keep things quiet for a while and away from the media, for all our sakes. But I want to make this work. I want to make *us* work."

"So, this isn't about sex?"

"No." She giggles. "But I want that too."

"You know things have changed since we were younger. I no longer think we have to be official before sleeping together."

"So, you don't want to be a couple?" She pouts but she knows me better than that.

"I have never wanted anything more."

"Good. Because I want us to be connected in every way possible. I need it." She pauses and huffs out a laugh. "That was easier than I thought it would be."

"Did you think I was going to say no? Or make it difficult for you?"

"No. I thought I'd struggle to get the words out, but I should have known that wouldn't be the case. Not with you."

She has no fucking idea how intoxicating she is. "I'm glad I make you feel comfortable, and I'm happy that part was easy..." I trail off for dramatic effect. "Because the next part is not going to be as smooth sailing."

"Hiding our relationship?"

"Nope. You taking my cock for the first time."

Blair sucks in a breath, and her body tenses against me.

"Are you ready for that?" I lift off the bed and strip out of my tee, giving Blair a moment to ogle my chest before curling my fingers into the waistband of my sweats, smiling when her gaze follows.

She bites her lip, and my cock pulses as I let it spring free.

Blair shifts uncomfortably before she moves closer, and I almost come at the hunger in her eyes. "Have you ever gone bare?" she asks and I choke, my control wavering.

"I haven't," I rasp, my voice failing me.

"Do you want to?"

Fuck. What kind of a question is that? "I do." I try to keep my cool, but when Blair bursts out laughing, I know I've failed. "I really fucking do." I chuckle, shaking my head.

"Good. I'm on the pill and Nathan and I..." She trails off when I frown. I'm holding my dick in my hand; I don't want to be thinking about him. But this conversation needs to be had. "I had a checkup recently, just in case. But we didn't go without. He wasn't ready for kids. Nor was I."

"But you're on the pill?"

"He wanted to be sure."

"Dickhead."

Blair laughs again before her expression turns serious. "I want this with you."

Jesus Christ. "I want that too." Whether I can handle it, though, remains to be seen. I'm already close to blowing my load from the thought alone.

Taking a deep but subtle breath, I get my shit together and step out of my pants and briefs, reaching for the lube in my top drawer. I don't think we'll need it moving forward, but for Blair's first time with a pierced man, I'm not taking any chances.

I don't have to look to know she's watching my every move. I can feel it. And as I slowly squeeze the gel into my hands, liberally coating my length, her breath hitches.

Desire flickers in her gaze as I glance up at her, and instead of the cockiness I'd usually feel, emotion swells in my chest.

"Are you sure you're ready?" I ask, my voice gravelly with need, precum pebbling on my tip.

"Yes," she whispers, her voice breathy. "I'm not a virgin, Zane."

Her response brings me out of my stupor and I bite back a smile. "In this case you are. Trust me. You have never experienced what I'm about to do to you."

I climb onto the bed, holding back a groan when her legs fall open.

Her gaze follows me, and when I line up with her entrance, she inhales sharply, her body rising off the bed when I haven't even touched her.

"I promise I'll be gentle."

"I'm not worried about *you*. It's been a while and—" My interest piques and Blair huffs out a laugh. "You'll be pleased to know Nathan and I hadn't had sex since before I saw you in the hospital."

That makes me so fucking happy, and I'd love to point out how that one little fact holds a hell of a lot of meaning, but I'm not going to purposely ruin the moment. I can gloat when we're done.

"B, you're ready. You can take me. We'll ease into it."

Her eyes widen, most likely because I didn't take the opportunity to make a comment about her ex, but she nods, her gaze dropping to my hand wrapped around my cock, her eyes locked on my piercing.

"Will it hurt?" Her throat bobs.

"It might at first, but I promise, I'll make it feel good."

"Okay."

"Ready?"

She nods again and I slowly push inside her, just the tip at first, gritting my teeth as my body jolts with a new kind of pleasure. It's so intense that I'm not sure I'll ever be able to go back, and I really hope I don't have to.

I wait a beat before pushing in farther, her pussy squeezing me as she cries out. "Oh, shit. I can feel it."

"Take a deep breath," I grate, trying to appear more in control than I am. "I've got you. It's just a moment of pain before an explosion of pleasure."

"God, you're full of it sometimes."

I chuckle as Blair slams her eyes shut, and when I sink deeper, her pussy seizes me with a vise-like grip, cutting my laughter off. "Jesus, you're so tight. I'm starting to question if that fucker ever serviced your needs."

"Are you kidding me right now? Why do you always bring him up?"

"That's the last time. Because I'm about to make you forget he existed. This pussy should have been worshipped. You're about to learn how incredible sex can be."

I push in another inch and she cries out again, her eyes filling with tears while I fight not to come before we've even moved. A few seconds pass before our eyes lock and Blair smiles, her expression full of want.

She holds her breath before nodding her head, trying to convince one of us that she's good. "You can move."

I bite back a laugh. It's great she thinks she's the reason I'm pausing, but as much as I wanted to take my time *for her*, this moment is all for *me*.

"I will," I grate, my teeth clenched so tight my jaw aches. "I just need a second."

My balls are so fucking full that I'm at serious risk of ending this early. Why the fuck would I agree to go bare for our first time together?

Blair giggles and the sound of it shoots a spark straight to my cock, making me shudder.

"Oh. God." Her laughter cuts off as her mouth falls open. "That... Jesus. Your piercing." She lets out a wanton moan and quivers. "Do that again."

"I didn't do anything. That was all you."

"Then *move*."

"Fuck. Okay." I'm like a goddamn teenager again. And fuck, I wish we'd done this when we were teenagers. Then maybe I wouldn't be so worked up after years of foreplay.

Taking another deep breath, I lean forward, bracing my hands on the bed beside her head, my arms locked with tension. Blair shifts her gaze, her breath hitching as she stares at my muscles bulging beneath my tats.

I groan and rock into her, making her gasp as I finally fill her to the hilt. "Yes. Oh Jesus."

"Fuck, you feel so good wrapped around me. You were made for me, Blair. I knew it back then and I'm finally getting to prove it to you."

"God. Yes. I know. But I need you to move."

"On it." I let out a restrained chuckle and slam my lips to hers, pumping into her, groaning and grunting against her mouth, my balls tingling with every pulse.

Blair mewls and gasps, meeting my fervor, her movements impatient, rushed. She grabs my back, her nails digging into me as she changes position, planting her feet to the mattress, angling her hips to free up her movement.

I sit back, grabbing her hips to pull her into me, and she screams out, the new angle giving me the exact reaction I expected as my piercing rubs against her wall.

"Fuck, Zane. That... Oh God." She thrashes against me, her breathing ragged, her face flushed as her eyes slam shut.

"You take me so well, B. So fucking well. I could do this all night, but it feels too good."

"I'm close."

"Tell me what you need."

Rather than using her words, she lowers her hand between her legs and rolls her finger over her clit, her body flying off the bed when I lift her ass higher, slamming into her as I flick her hand away.

"I've got this."

Leaning back, I pull out slightly and rub my thumb through her arousal, spreading it over her pussy and clit before rocking back into her and pressing down on her bud.

She cries out again, my name on her lips, her body jolting in ecstasy. "More. Please."

"Anything for you." I'm so close myself that it takes all of my strength to hold on, but I'd never deny her.

Rolling my thumb over her clit, I pump into her, moving faster as I increase the pressure. I'm just about to beg her to let go when her body convulses and she squeezes me so tightly that my cock explodes without warning, my cum shooting into her as she screams out my name.

"Zane. Yes. Oh. Jesus."

The shock of my release has my body shaking, but I keep moving until she begs me to stop, her breathing shallow, gasping for air.

"You are a fucking goddess, B." I fall forward, bracing my hands beside her head, my arms shaking as I still inside her. "That was…"

"Incredible?" Blair finishes for me when I trail off, the word full of awe.

"Incredible," I agree, groaning as I pull out of her, falling in a heap beside her. "I'll help clean you up in a second. I just need a moment."

With my last shred of energy, I curl my arm around her waist and pull her into me, burying my face in her neck. Her scent's familiar as I breathe her in, giving me one little clue that this is real.

She giggles, her body shaking against me, and I can't help but smile.

I've finally got my girl back, and this time, I'm never letting go.

Chapter Forty-Five

BLAIR

My muscles tighten with nerves as I'm buzzed through the glass doors at Heartwood University's athletic center.

Despite meeting Lucy yesterday and being sure of my decision to work here, I can't help thinking back to all my previous interviews. I'd been sure of myself with those too, and yet—

"Blair, you made it." Lucy rushes toward me, her warm smile working to ease my mind.

"I made it." I smile back, working hard to hide my nerves.

"How was the drive? It's not bad, right? You could easily live here or there, or somewhere in between."

"I could. If I get the job."

"*When* you get the job. Let's think positively. But...if for some reason you and Shaylee don't click, then I'm ninety-nine percent sure Wes would snap you up. He already asked me if we're sure we really need someone. As if I'd been lying this whole time."

Lucy and Wes could very well be joking around, but a comfort settles in my chest, like they've got my back and maybe things are finally turning around.

"Thanks, Lucy."

"For what?"

"Everything." I let out a soft exhale and her smile brightens.

"You're welcome." She spins on her heel. "Are you ready for a tour?"

"I am. I can't wait."

"Great. Shaylee will be ready for you at eleven, so we can take our time.

You're going to love it here." I nod as the nerves flare up again. *God, I hope this is it.*

We spend an hour touring the facilities, and just like with the Storm stadium, I'm completely in awe. The D1 college I attended in Florida was great, but I never got to experience it like this. It's hard not to get caught up in the high intensity energy filling the space just from the sights and sounds alone.

Players pass with their bags casually thrown over their shoulders, while men and women in suits ignore us as they walk, their fast-paced conversations adding to the buzz.

Everything is perfect, and exactly what I hoped it would be.

When we get to the medical suites, I pause, breathing in the citrus-scented cleaning products and fresh white linen. It's a far cry from a busy hospital ward, and I have no doubt I'm going to love the change.

If I get the job.

I need to keep that in mind, reel in my fantasies. Because that's what this is—a dream. Just like Zane said it would be.

My phone buzzes in my pocket, and while it makes me jump, I otherwise ignore it. It'll either be my mom or Zane, the only two people that know I have a job interview today.

I usually tell Dad everything, but in this instance, I wanted to surprise him if I got the gig, and Mom happily agreed. Though admittedly she expects the location to put a slight damper on the surprise. Dad always hoped that if Nathan and I broke up, I'd move back to Jacksonville, and he's been waiting for me to announce my homecoming since I told them the news.

Mom doesn't mind though. She's strict, but she's always been supportive of my dreams, wherever they may take me.

After showing me her room, Lucy knocks on the door labeled medical office, and a throat clears on the other side of the threshold, moments before Shaylee calls me in. "I'm decent," she sings, and I immediately like her.

Lucy opens the door and we're greeted by a smiling Shaylee. "Sorry, I was going to open up for you, but I lied. I was *not* decent; I had a piece of parsley stuck in my tooth. All good now. Come on in. Blair, it's lovely to meet you." She holds out her hand for me to shake. "I've heard so much about you."

The cliched *all good things* rests on the tip of my tongue, but I bite it back, shaking her hand with a warm smile of my own. "Thank you, I'm happy to be here."

Dressed in a patterned, yellow knee-length dress and a long cobalt-blue blazer, Shaylee gives off a vintage vibe. One that's laid-back and caring, while her neat desk, ordered color-coded shelves, and pristine white coat hanging off a wrought iron rack tell me she's organized, knows what she wants, and gets things done. *That* or she's incredibly good at faking it until you make it.

Lucy and I follow Shaylee inside and she gestures for us to take a seat, the chairs arranged around her desk rather than in a them versus me situation, easing my tension just that little bit more.

We chat about the unseasonable weather before we're joined by Heartwood's new general manager, Graham, a giant of a man with a shaved head and round glasses that he has to keep pushing up his nose. All three of them make me feel incredibly comfortable. There's a warmth in the air, and it almost borders on familiarity, yet I've never met any of them, except Lucy, but that was only yesterday.

I want to say it feels like they're my people with the way they light up when they talk about the team. Even Shaylee. Lucy claimed she knew nothing about football, but there's a pride in her voice when she talks about the players, and I know with absolute certainty that I've found my place.

I just have to hope they feel the same.

No. Not hope. I spent the better part of my life as the optimist among my friends and family, but it took one spring break to take it all away. Now I want it back. I'm reclaiming my superpower. I've continued to be optimistic when it comes to the people around me, but whenever I think of myself, a darkness creeps in.

And that ends today.

I will get this job.

I have this job already.

I'm perfect for the role and they know it.

We just have to make it official.

"And that's it. Do you have any questions before we wrap up?" Shaylee grins and my heart seizes. I always hate this part. But in this case, I have one.

"If you're concerned about my lack of experience in California, is there an extra course I can do, or a certificate to ease your mind?"

In Florida, I only had one interview before I got a job straight out of college, and within a year, I was promoted. But here...I can't even elicit a smile most of the time, this interview aside.

Graham starts shaking his head as Shaylee responds. "That's not an issue. I came from Washington State myself, and our second nurse, who'll be working the days that you're rostered off, came from Colorado."

"Not to mention, I'm from Boston," Graham announces. "We don't tend to look at where you're from when we hire. It's all about finding the right person for the role."

I hold back a sigh. "Great. I love that."

"Great. Well, Lucy and Graham have to head back to their official duties, but I'd love to continue our chat if you don't have to run off. Just a little getting-to-know-you time."

"Of course." My voice lifts and even I can hear the nerves lacing my tone.

Shaylee laughs, her expression so full of glee that her smile reaches the faint wrinkles beside her eyes. "Don't worry, I just want to know your favorite TV shows, whether or not you like rom-com movies, and what music you like playing while you work."

"Oh." My sigh finally releases. "That I can do. But if you don't like rom-coms, I'm going to have to cut this short."

Lucy snorts and even Graham chuckles, while Shaylee stares at me deadpan. I'm worried I've said the wrong thing until she bursts out laughing. "Doesn't everyone?"

A giddiness fills me and I laugh along with her.

Yep. I've definitely found my place.

It's another thirty minutes until I finish with Shaylee, and I hold my breath as I press through the door to exit, stifling my excitement until I get to Zane's car.

Emotion overwhelms me and I fight back the tears.

They offered me the job. I have a job.

My breath wavers as I slam the driver's door shut, squealing under my breath. "Oh my God. Oh my God." I did it. My pulse dances beneath my skin, and my heart races from the adrenaline coursing through me.

Not only do I have a job, but it's a dream come true. Cade is going to cream his pants over this. And Dad... Hell, he'll probably want to move to San Francisco so he can be a part of my journey.

I'm following in my dad's and grandfather's footsteps. I may not be a player, but I'm part of a team. And that means everything to me.

I did it. I really fucking did it.

An electrifying buzz fills the air as I reach for my phone, desperate to call Zane, to share in my joy, a laugh bubbling out of me when I find ten missed calls. I can already picture the proud smile adorning his face and hear the love in his words.

I dial his number, and even though I'm certain he's supposed to be at practice, he answers on the first ring.

"Thank God." He sighs in relief. "I was starting to worry."

"Starting? Or having a full-blown panic attack?"

"Well, since I'm risking a fine by answering this call, it's safe to say the latter."

"You're on the field?"

"Yep. I'm hiding behind Reed. These guys are very much team Blane."

Last week, hearing Reed's name would have triggered memories of seeing Zane in the hospital, making me spiral until my mind cascaded into the darkness of Sierra's death. But since reconnecting with Zane, it's impossible to think that way. I'm okay. Zane's okay. And so is Reed. All I can see is light.

I smile to myself until his words register. "Team what?" A laugh bursts out of me.

"Blane. Blair and Zane."

"Wow. Just wow."

A deep laugh rumbles in the background before Zane tells them to shush. "So, how did it go?"

"Before I tell you... Where were you hiding your phone?"

"You're killing me here." He groans, the strain in his voice heating my skin.

"I'm not going to answer until you tell me."

"Fine." He groans again. "Reed had it in his waistband. He's technically not allowed to practice yet, but he attends to keep up with the plays."

I stifle a snort. "I thought you didn't have many friends on the team?" I joke.

"Yeah, well, they're growing on me. But enough of that. I showed you mine; you show me yours."

"I got the job!" I yell it so loudly that Reed must hear because the two of them start cheering before it abruptly cuts off.

"Ahh, fuck. I've got to go. I'll call you back in thirty minutes. But I'm so proud of you and— I know." His voice trails off, the softness replaced by a curt tone. "I'm hanging up. Jesus." I hear a rustling before he sighs. "I'm in trouble. But you're amazing, B, and I can't wait to hear all about it. Drive safe, yeah?"

"Of course. I'm sorry. I didn't mean—"

"It was all worth it. I'll call you back soon."

He hangs up and I sink back into my seat, dropping the phone into my lap. My stomach flutters, and a content smile spreads across my face.

I'm ready for the next era. I'm ready to move on.

Chapter Forty-Six

BLAIR

It doesn't escape me that I'm more excited about game day today than I have been since I used to watch Zane and my brother play.

I loved attending games with Nathan, but this feels different. My guess is that it has something to do with the fact that I was dreaming of this day growing up. Actually, dreaming isn't the right word. I was *expecting* it.

Before our fight on Zane's birthday, I was convinced we were in it for the long haul. It was just a matter of time. And even *after* our fight, I was certain we just needed to get over that little hurdle. That once we were both at college together, everything would work out.

Zane made me believe that.

And if the accident hadn't happened, I truly think that would have come true.

Now I'm here, potentially beginning the life I always imagined, and it's making me giddy, filling me with a lightness I haven't felt in years.

"I really wish I'd gotten you a jersey." Zane groans from behind me, flicking my braid as he wanders past.

"I told you; we need to be subtle for now. And me having a Storm jersey with 'property of Fitzpatrick' written on the back is not at all subtle."

Zane chuckles. "I would love to put 'property of' on your back, but jerseys don't really work that way."

My eyes widen. *Did I just say that? Jesus.* "I know that." I roll my eyes and laugh to cover the uncomfortable feeling settling in my chest. Is that what I felt like wearing Nathan's jersey? That he owned me?

Turning back to the mirror, I tuck my sweater into my jeans, then brush a loose curl behind my ear.

Zane steps up behind me, resting his chin on my shoulder as he wraps his arms around my waist, humming. "Mmmm, I am going to play the fuck out of this game." He inhales as though breathing me in. "Nothing beats knowing you're there in the crowd, cheering me on. I still remember the buzz I got in high school. Thinking about you watching me, and not being able to tell anyone. There was always something forbidden about it."

"I'd say hooking up with your rival's ex-girlfriend, a week after she broke up with him, is extremely forbidden."

"Very true." He squeezes my waist, making me jump. "I'm a lucky man."

"Don't ever forget it."

"Trust me, that's not going to happen. But I've got to go. You have everything you need, right?"

"I do. Honestly, I would have been fine with a ticket in the nosebleed section." I spin in his arms and bounce my eyebrows, making him chuckle again.

"You know, sometimes you make it hard to believe you are a football genius."

"I like to keep people guessing. Now go, before you're late." A feeling of déjà vu hits me as Zane kisses my nose and turns to walk away, but I can't tell if it's familiar because I've done this with Nathan, or I've done this with Zane in another life. The life we were meant to have.

I'm on a high until Dad and Cade call for our usual game day chat, and I have to lie to Dad. Not because I don't want him to know about Zane, or that I think he'll be disappointed, but I want to talk to him about it in person, when I know exactly how my life's about to change. We're close, and he always takes on my worries like they're his own. I can't put him through that just yet.

The afternoon flies by and I think I'm in control, but the second I step onto the elevator for my journey to the suites, my confidence wavers. *Dammit, Zane.*

Why the hell would I agree to watch the game with the wives and girlfriends? I know he means well and doesn't want me to be alone, but I don't know these women. What if they're awful, or bitchy? Or worse, what if they're boring and spend more time talking about themselves than they do watching the game?

My stomach lurches when the chime signals that I've reached my destination, and I almost press the button for the ground floor. Maybe I'd be better off watching the TV near the food stands, then—

"Blair?" A smiling redhead greets me as the doors open, and I startle at the sight of her. "Oops, sorry. I probably should have waited until you actually stepped out."

"No, that's okay. I was in my own world. I'm Blair." *Shit.* She knows that.

"I'm Keeley." She smiles, brushing her hair behind her ear before stepping back to give me space. "I think we met in the hospital."

"The hospital?"

"Yeah. I was there when Zane and Reed were—"

"Oh, yes." Now that she mentions it, she does look familiar. "It's lovely to officially meet you."

"And you. Zane asked me to help you get settled. I work for the team so I can't stay, but Lucy Johnson mentioned she was coming, and said to let you know she'd be here by the time the game begins. Do you know her?"

"I do. I've just accepted a job at Heartwood University."

"What? No way! That's amazing. Lucy's great. I met her a while ago through Dylan, but I've really gotten to know her since Wes started late last season. She tries to come to most games. Not that you have any reason to be coming to most games." She pretends to zip her lips and I laugh.

"Zane filled you in then?"

"A little. He said it was better if you kept things quiet for the time being."

"That's right."

"I can promise you, the ladies here are all wonderful and understand the need to be discreet. As do I."

"Thank you. I can't wait." My voice comes out shaky, and when Keeley laughs, my cheeks heat.

"And... I promise, you're going to have fun. If you loved Lucy, you'll love the rest of them. They're the most genuine humans I've met. As are the guys."

My shoulders drop and I relax, her genuine smile filling me with warmth. She could be lying, setting me up for heartbreak, but she has no reason to do that, and it's not the first time I've heard that about them.

Zane said the same. Though admittedly, he also said he barely knows them.

"Well, there's no time like the present. I'm ready."

Keeley's eyes light up. "There's the spirit. You've got this."

"Thanks. I hope so."

She leads the way to a glass door, and I study the women on the other side of the panels, taking them in before they undoubtedly do the same. They're all sunshine and rainbows, laughing and smiling at each other, but that doesn't mean anything. I've met girls like that before and they were not what they seem.

Keeley opens the slider, and as though they planned it, the four ladies in front of us fall silent until one of them gasps.

And it's freaking *Hayley Jackman*, Hollywood's IT girl of the moment. How the hell did I forget that she'd be here?

"Blair?" She rushes forward. "Oh my God. It is *you*." Hayley pulls me into a hug and I internally wince for not mentally preparing myself for this moment. I knew she was dating Reed, both from the hospital and from Jenna reminding me, yet here I am, my chest tight with awe and my belly full of nerves.

Jenna and I watched her movie—after I got over Jenna's disloyalty of talking about me behind my back—and Hayley was incredible. "Reed mentioned that you were his nurse." She pulls back to look at me again. "I forgot about it until just now. I kept thinking of you as Jenna's friend." As she laughs, she brushes her long, blonde hair away from her face and bounces on her toes, her genuine excitement impossible to miss.

"Jenna is going to kill me for not inviting her today. She thinks the world of you."

"The feeling is mutual. She matches my energy, and there weren't many others that did on set."

"I heard. I'm glad you had each other."

"And I'm glad we figured out our connection to you and Zane." She bites back a smile but I get what she's saying. She had a hand in me being here today. In a roundabout way.

"So am I."

A throat clears behind Hayley and she laughs. "Okay, okay. Sorry." She reaches for my hand and drags me closer. "Let me introduce you to the girls." She spins to face the others, but before she can speak, Keeley taps my shoulder.

"You're in good hands, but if you need me, I can stay." The kindness in her eyes has me instantly smiling.

"No, I'm okay. You have work to do."

"Okay. I'll be back at halftime to check in."

"Thank you." She waves to the group then disappears, and when I turn back around, I have four gorgeous faces staring my way, happiness lighting their features.

"This is Amelia, Paige, and Lainey," Hayley says, pointing to the three women I haven't met. "And over on the other side of the room are Jessica, Kylie, and Bree. They're lovely." She forces a smile, leaning in close. "But they have their own little clique, so we don't talk to them that often."

"Noted." I nod, my eyes briefly flashing to the other women who are currently ignoring my presence. "It's lovely to meet you all."

"Likewise." The woman Hayley said was Amelia steps forward, bouncing a beautiful little girl on her left hip. "I'm Amelia, Luke Bennett's wife, and this is our daughter, Juliet." Juliet smiles, burying her face in her mother's shoulder, and I can't help but laugh.

Of the four women, Amelia's the most casually dressed, wearing a Storm jersey and boyfriend jeans. She doesn't stand out as much as the others, but there's a spark in her eyes that makes me want to get to know her.

The next woman to step forward has to be a model. She's tall with perfect features, her brown hair pulled sleekly off her face to highlight her sharp cheekbones and flawless complexion—and come to think of it, she looks familiar. "I'm Easton's girlfriend, Paige," she announces, her warm smile making her a little more approachable as she pulls me into a hug. Paige. Paige. Wait. Paige D'Angelo. I've seen her in magazines. I can't believe I never made that connection when Zane was talking about the team's owner.

"Fiancée," Hayley says from behind me, interrupting my thoughts. "She's Easton's *fiancée.*"

Paige giggles, brushing her off. "It's still fairly new."

"It's been months."

"Okay." Paige raises her hands in the air, winking at Hayley. It's easy to see they have a close friendship. And with the way Amelia and Lainey laugh, I'd say they're all pretty tight.

I wait for my stomach to knot, realizing I've walked into some kind of sisterhood of the football playing partners, but that's not what happens. Instead of making me uncomfortable, it has the opposite effect, and a weight lifts. This is what I thought being a football wife would be like. This is what I was craving with both of Nathan's teams. This friendship, comradery.

God, I hope they actually watch the game.

I get properly introduced to Lainey next, Thomas Kelly's wife, and marvel at her stunning teal hair.

"I usually keep it pink or purple," she tells me. "But Thomas has been begging me to match the team colors for *years,* and since this is his last season, I finally obliged."

I laugh as the girls fall into easy conversation, with me nodding along. But when cheers ring out in the stadium below us, my attention shifts.

My heart jolts as I contemplate breaking away from the group, but the panic doesn't get a chance to set in when Hayley squeals, rushing over to the windows. "It's go time. Here's to another win."

Without a discussion, they all spin around and beeline for the glass, their priorities changing the second the men hit the field, while the other three women continue to talk over near the drinks.

While it's exactly what I wanted, it takes a second for it to all sink in, and my eyes water. *Is this real?* Please don't let it be too good to be true. Because right now, it feels like some kind of good karma, and I'm not sure I deserve it.

As promised, Lucy joins us at the start of play, and just like me, she and the rest of the girls are hooked on the game. We spend the entire time yelling at refs, cheering on the men, joking about the high levels of testosterone. Even Paige, who claims to have no clue about football, calls out when she thinks the Storm has been wronged.

I may have watched with my chest tightening to uncomfortable levels, but my heart was full, and I don't think I've ever met a group of people more welcoming. It's almost hard to believe.

The final whistle blows with the Storm winning by six points, and we celebrate in the suite until it's time to head down to meet the guys.

Hayley links her arm through mine as we walk, her smile exuding comfort, and it feels like I've known her for years.

"How would you like us to play it down there?" she asks, turning to give me her full attention. "Did you and Zane talk about it?"

"We did. I'm actually heading back to his place now, instead of waiting for him. It's easier that way." Hayley pouts and I can't help but laugh. "It's okay. I'm used to it. We had to hide our relationship once before. When we were younger."

"But you're adults now."

"I know, but I just broke up with my boyfriend and—"

"You don't have to justify it to me. I get it. I'm just bummed I don't get to hang out with you. Actually—" She pulls me to a stop, spinning abruptly. "What do you say we have a welcoming party for Blair this week?" she asks the others, and I panic.

"Oh. Uh...that would be lovely but I have to go back to LA." And I'm not sure that Zane's ready for that. He filled me in on the tension he caused with his teammates, and I'd say it's still a work in progress.

"Damn. Next time then. When will you be back?"

Despite having an answer, the question stills me. I don't think it's quite hit me that I'm moving here, somewhere, to work at Heartwood U. "I'll be back soon. I'm starting work with Lucy next month."

"Amazing. Let Jenna know we're throwing you a party when you're here. It will be great to spend time with you both."

"I will, thanks. She'll love that."

"Good."

I turn to walk away but Hayley calls out, stopping me before I get too far. "And Blair... Welcome to the team."

My heart jolts but I smile through it, another small weight lifting.

Because while for the longest time I've felt like I'm lost, I finally feel like I'm home.

CHAPTER FORTY-SEVEN

ZANE

Blair and I fall back onto the bed after another mind-blowing session of sex, and I sink into the mattress, a satisfied smirk gracing my lips. Blair has come into her own over the past week, and her confidence is growing in all aspects of her life.

Including the bedroom.

"Fuuck." A contented sigh falls from my lips, and I smile when Blair curls herself into my chest.

"I...can't...speak." She gasps between words, her breathing ragged, her voice strained. "That angle. My God. You know how to use that thing."

I chuckle to myself, squeezing her tightly. "That's the trick. So many douchebags get pierced thinking it's going to improve their sex life, but you have to know what you're doing *before* you get it done, or it's useless. Or worse, you'll hurt your partner."

"Mmm," Blair moans but there's an edge to it. "I'm not sure how to take that. Do you know what you're doing from practicing often?" she asks, biting back a delicious grin.

"Oh, B, I was a god *before* we started dating back in high school. I would have blown your mind."

She giggles and I'm about to roll her onto her back for round two when my phone buzzes. Not once but for a solid ten seconds. Message after message streaming through.

I groan, covering my face with my hands. "Remember that group chat I mentioned?" I ask Blair without looking her way.

"Yes!" She shifts and I imagine her excited gaze boring into mine.

"That'll be them."

"Aren't you going to read it?"

"Nope. But feel free to do the honors."

She falls silent and I peek between my fingers, finding her lost in thought.

"What's going on?" I lift to my elbows, trying to keep my gaze off her naked chest, and it's not an easy feat.

"I'm trying to decide what will be more entertaining. Me reading them to you, or forcing you to read them aloud?"

"Both suck because I have no doubt that either will have you laughing at my expense."

"Ooh. I'm going to read them."

She climbs over me, still naked, and my cock twitches. I am more than ready to go again, but I doubt that's an option anymore with Blair well and truly distracted.

"Are you ready?" she asks cheerily.

"No."

"Too bad."

> LUKE: Zane, you're going to have to marry Blair. Amelia loves her, and she was very excited to talk about the game when we got home. She was quoting stats!

> REED: Hayley loved her too. Twenty-four hours later and she's still talking about her

> EASTON: Same with Paige. Look at you doing something right

Blair reads Easton's message with no intonation, but I can still hear the sarcasm in his tone.

> DYLAN: Summer's reading these messages and wants to meet her. Lucy was talking about her today and now Summer's feeling left out

> DYLAN: And she just whacked me with a pillow

I smile when Blair snorts, her eyes alight with a happiness she should never go without.

> REED: Hayley's organizing a welcome party for when she moves here

> DYLAN: You made Summer's day

> LUKE: Zane... where are you?

> LUKE: Ooh he's seen the messages

Dammit, fuck. "Can I switch that off so they don't know when I've read something? Or in this case, you've read something."

"I have no idea, but I love this. And it's titled Zane's support group? What does that mean?"

Dammit again. I groan, grabbing Blair's pillow to shove it over my head, hoping she'll move on without me having to answer. But no such luck.

The pillow disappears and Blair stares down at me, her breasts jiggling as she waves the phone in my face. Her nakedness distracts me, and I lazily reach between her legs, my wanton gaze roaming her body. God, she's—

"Ouch."

My hand aches from where Blair slapped it away, her no bullshit expression making me shudder. "I need answers."

"*Fine,*" I huff. "Apparently this group chat started when Luke needed help after finding out Amelia was pregnant with his baby. They were enemies at the time. Reed started it."

"That makes sense considering you said Reed was the caring one of the group."

"He is. A little *too* caring sometimes. But anyway, it started with Luke and then Easton needed help dealing with his crazy ex—"

"The one you slept with."

"Yep. That one. And the group became his. Then Reed needed it to get over a crush on his best friend...or something, I don't know. It was before he had Hayley, and— *god-fucking-dammit,* I shouldn't know all this. It's gossip, like we're living in a fucking daytime soap."

"So, why is it your chat now?" Blair ignores my outburst, her brows pinched in intrigue, and I can't *not* answer her.

"They thought I needed help after the incident with Reed and Hayley. I think they felt sorry for me." I cringe, hating the thought.

"You don't think they were thankful, and genuinely wanted to be your friend?"

"Reed, yes. Maybe even Luke. But it was Easton that added me to the group. I half wonder if it's payback."

Blair giggles before covering her face with her hands. "Sorry, it's actually not at all funny. But when it comes to that, I'm team Easton. You were a dick."

"*I didn't know.*" I feel like a broken record saying that over and over.

"True, but you could have at least apologized after you found out."

"I was young and bitter."

"Wasn't it last season?"

"Two seasons ago. And I didn't have *you*."

I stare at her pointedly, my gaze boring into hers, hoping she sees through my humor. She's changed me. My life is better with her in it. *I'm* better with her in my life. I probably *would* have apologized for being a dick if Blair had been around. Not that I ever would have slept with someone else to begin with.

Blair smiles at the intensity of my gaze, and I wink until a flicker of something else mars her features.

"What was that?"

"What was what?"

"The sadness that crossed your face."

"Oh." Her eyes widen as though she hadn't meant for me to see it. "It was nothing."

"What's going on?"

"Nothing. Just thinking about my life before you came back into it."

Fuck. "More specifically, me sleeping around? B, if I could have spent that whole time only fucking you, I would have, but I—"

"No, it's not that."

"Thank fuck." Air rushes from my lungs as I run a hand down my face. "Though you have every right to hate me for that, I should have known you'd come back. I should have—"

"What? Stayed celibate? Let's not forget I didn't wait around for you. I don't fault you for that and never will."

"Likewise. Though I do wish I'd been your first. I was an idiot back then." I laugh, expecting Blair to do the same, but her face drops before she schools her features.

"We can't change the past, but we can make the future better." She gets up and grabs my T-shirt from the floor, pulling it over her head, and the energy shifts as though someone sucked the happiness right out of it.

"B, what's going on?"

"Nothing." She smiles, but it may as well be invisible since I see right through it, a thought coming to mind.

"Why does Cade think I was your first?"

Blair inhales sharply, and it's not the response I was expecting, making me regret asking the question. I assumed it was going to lighten the mood. But her expression is anything but light.

Holding my breath, I wait for her to answer. And when her eyes flash to mine, a sheen of water making them glassy, I feel sick.

"Don't worry," I rush out, standing to pull her into a hug. "It's none of my business and—"

"No, it's not that. I didn't realize he'd mentioned it to you."

"He did. He was pissed I hadn't told him." I huff out an incredulous laugh and Blair recovers for a beat, rolling her eyes.

"God, he's nosy sometimes."

"Sometimes?" I raise a brow, and she lets out a small laugh of her own, her somber mood lifting momentarily.

"Okay, all the time. That's part of the reason I told him you were my first. But it's not that big a deal. I'm going to take a shower."

"Wait." I reach forward and grab the hem of her tee—*my* tee—letting go when she flinches. "B, what's—"

"You know how you can't say Sierra's name?" She spins my way, and despite there being no venom in her voice, I rear back again like she slapped me. "You know how it burns to even try whispering it aloud?"

"Yes." I choke on my simple reply. *I can't even think it.*

"Well, this is like that." Her voice trails off as she turns away, and my body goes numb. *What am I missing?*

"B—"

"I can't."

"But."

"*Please*, Zane." She glances back, her red swollen eyes completely gutting me. But I can't let it go. Not now. Something is wrong, and I can't let her walk away when she's hurting. For the first time, it hits me how she feels when I refuse to talk about my sister.

My thumping heart lodges in my throat as I sit back on the bed, sinking my head into my hands.

If I expect her to talk...

I take in a breath, my lungs failing to let in any air. Images of the accident play on repeat in my mind, but I try to focus, try to see through the pain.

"I fucking miss her, B," I finally say, my voice barely above a whisper.

Blair's movements still, and when I glance up, I find her frozen in place, her hand clasped around the handle of the bathroom door.

"I can't say or *think* her name because it's torture to me. Just hearing you say it is like a dagger to my chest. Every day, I have to remember that it's *my* fault. That I killed my sister, that I left you when you blamed yourself. That I took the life of an innocent stranger because she happened to be driving along the same road when my drunken ass wasn't paying attention. It doesn't matter that I wasn't driving. I fucked up. Every day I think about that accident, but I *survive* it. Because keeping her name off my lips makes it a little less real."

Blair turns to face me, tears rolling down her face. "I—"

"Wait. Please. I'm almost done."

She nods and I continue, my throat hoarse with each word grating me from the inside. "S—" I pause, swallowing back my emotions as tears threaten to fall. I can do this. For Blair. "*Sierra* deserved better than the life I gave her. *You* deserve better. But since you're here, saying you'll take me back, I'm going to do everything in my power to do right by you. Even if neither of us like it. And if that means saying her name, so that you'll share your burden...I'll say it. I *said* it. But please don't make me say it again."

I smile as the first tear falls from my eye and Blair rushes forward, throwing herself into my arms.

After a moment of shock, I fold her into me, holding her tightly as more tears threaten to escape.

"I'm so sorry for everything you've been through," she whispers as she gets up and repositions herself beside me, her face downcast, her gaze locked on her hands as she plays with the hem of my tee. "I'm sorry that after all this time, I'm still holding back. I just don't want *you* hurting anymore. *I* don't want to hurt anymore."

I lift her face to mine and brush a curl behind her ear, staring into her eyes. "You don't have to tell me. You don't ever *have* to do anything when it comes to me. But I want to help. Let me share whatever it is you're holding on to."

"What if it breaks you?"

"Me?"

"Yes." Her voice is so soft and delicate that my heart shatters without her having to say what it is.

"I'm here, B. If you want to say it, I'm here."

There's a moment of quiet between us and Blair glances away, fresh tears falling as she shakes her head, making me nervous. "I'm so sorry, Zane. So fucking sorry."

"You have no reason—"

"I lied to Cade because it was better than him knowing the truth." She pulls away from me, wrapping her arms around herself.

"What's the truth?" I ask, despite the dread lurking in my chest.

"My first time was with Nathan."

A sigh escapes me. *Thank fuck.* Nathan was my first thought. And while I hate the guy, I'd already resigned myself to the fact that they were fucking, though it's good to know they stopped after we reconnected. "Cade's overprotective, but I don't think he would have questioned you for that—"

"I didn't say when."

When?

I stiffen beside her. "What does that mean?" The confusion of what she's about to say has my voice rasping, but I need to know. Why would sleeping with Nathan cause her so much grief. Unless...

"I didn't mean for it to happen." Blair cuts into my thoughts, her panic-stricken expression devastating me.

"What happened?" A thought comes to mind and my stomach sinks. Did he hurt her? *No.* She wouldn't have stayed with him if he did.

Blair shakes her head as though unable to say the words, and realization hits me. "Did you sleep with him while we were together?"

She shakes her head again but then nods, more tears flooding her eyes. "After our fight at that party, after the kiss, I left to go to Nathan's. And I got drunk."

Fuck. It was that night? A pain shoots through me, and I want to stop her. I want to do anything I can to make the pain go away, but I *need* to hear this.

"Nathan kept me company for the first hour, but someone broke his mom's favorite vase and he had to take care of that." *Typical, always focused on himself.* "He asked his friend to look after me, and we had another drink together while we were waiting for Nathan to come back."

My muscles tense, as a memory washes over me. "How much did you drink there, B?"

"I didn't think it was that much, but I'd already been drinking before I got there."

Bile rises in my throat and my fists clench beside me, my thoughts going back to Nathan's fucking parties and the rumors surrounding them. "Did Nathan hurt you?"

"No. Of course not." Blair's quick to reassure me, presumably noticing my glare. Only it's anything but reassuring. "*But* if I'd been sober, it never would have happened. I don't even remember how I got there. I was dancing with his friend, and then I was in bed with Nathan. Someone walked in on us and it momentarily sobered me up. But it was after we'd... ah...it was enough to make me bleed."

My stomach sinks as my entire body numbs. "Fuck. *Fuck.*" I tug at my hair, my heart pounding so hard I can hear it in my ears. "This is my fault," I whisper. "I knew it. *I knew.*" The words feel heavy as they leave my lips, full of the weight I've been carrying by hiding that asshole's past but never confronting him about it.

"I'm sorry. It—"

"This is not your fault." I cut her off, pulling her into my arms as anger wells up inside of me. "You were *drunk*, Blair. Who was the friend? That gave you the drink? That fucker took—"

"I don't remember who it was. But—"

"No fucking *buts*," I yell, moving away from her, and immediately regret it when she flinches. "I'm sorry." I flex my hands, trying to stop myself from clenching while rage vibrates through my body. "What I mean to say is that you were under the influence, and Nathan took advantage of you. Even if you think you might have consented."

"You don't know that. He—"

"You don't know either." With my teeth clenched, I do all that I can not to raise my voice, but it's a struggle. Blair's not to blame for this. She doesn't deserve any of my wrath, but someone does. Cade and I suspected Nathan and his friends of drugging girls. No, we *knew* it. Deep down, we did. And yet we never said a word.

But would he do that to Blair?

Blair sighs and her gaze shifts to just above my shoulder, refusing to meet my eye. "He's self-centered but he's not a bad guy, Zane. I wanted to be there with him that night. I just didn't want to go that far."

My shoulders drop and I fall back against the wall, running a hand though my hair. I did this to her. Like everything else. My silence broke her. And she has no idea.

"After that night, I pushed it from my mind and told everyone who asked that you were my first. I even tried to convince myself." She smiles, but I can't bring myself to smile back.

"I'm sorry for making you relive it again, but Blair, he hurt you. You were dru—drunk. You—"

"He'd been flirting with me from the moment I arrived, and I liked it, Zane. We were both drunk. It happens."

"It doesn't just happen, you—"

"I didn't tell you this because I thought he hurt me; I told you because I thought I hurt *you*."

"B, if he cared about you at all, he never—"

"That's not what's important here, Zane."

"It's pretty fucking important from where I'm standing."

"Zane—"

"I don't understand how you—"

"Zane, stop!" Blair's voice rises and I freeze. *Jesus.* She's breaking and I'm letting my anger take over.

"I'm sorry."

"Are you?" She stands up and takes a step farther away from me, her body shaking. "Do you want to know why I broke up with Nathan? Do you?" She points at my chest and I stiffen.

"Why?"

"Because he *never* listened. Now you're doing the same thing. I haven't spoken about this to anyone. Ever. And I'm telling *you*. So, sit the fuck down and listen to me."

I blink a few times before dropping to the edge of the bed, shuffling closer to Blair. When our eyes lock, I almost smile, only I know better than that, and this isn't the moment. But God, I love her. I never fucking stopped.

"You have my full attention," I rasp and mean it. "You've always had it."

"I know. Thank you."

"Please go on."

"What I was trying to say is that I will always regret what happened that night, all of it. But not for the reasons you're thinking. Nathan and I talked about what happened. He apologized. I forgave him. But I never forgave myself. That's why I blame myself for the accident. Because I slept with someone else, and I called you to pick up the pieces. I'm sorry I never told you that before. But mostly, I'm sorry it happened. You should have been my first. And in my dreams, when I'm happy and the world's a different place, you were. But in reality, I messed up and I don't know how I'll ever get over it."

Chapter Forty-Eight

ZANE

After convincing Blair that she didn't do anything wrong, she finally falls asleep in my arms, her tears coating my chest. While I fight hard not to break down.

I can't sleep, my stomach twisted in knots. Nausea goddamn consumes me. Everything aches as I spiral into darkness. I knew my actions that night —and in the lead-up—fucked up her life. I'd been aware of that from the moment I walked away. But I had no idea of the extent of her pain, the depths of her torment.

When I'm still awake at three a.m., I get up and pace the hallway, careful not to wake her but itching to do something.

Assault or not, what happened to Blair shouldn't have happened. She never should have been at the party, but more than that, she shouldn't have to walk around with that pain in her heart, that guilt weighing her down. It was bad enough that she thought the crash was her fault.

But having to carry this? When she doesn't even know...

My stomach heaves and I fall into the wall before sliding to the floor, sinking my head into my hands.

I shouldn't have left. I should have stayed to protect her. I should have been there to make her happier.

Always.

I glance down at the address on my screen, silently thanking Jenna for once again helping me out.

After spending my morning at the stadium and hiding my feelings from Blair, I then watched her walk through the gates toward her plane, and rushed over to the information desk, booking my own flight.

I should have confronted Nathan well before now. But I'm finally righting that wrong.

Taking a deep breath, I look up at the complex in front of me and my nostrils flare.

This place doesn't even suit Blair. There's no greenery. No warmth. Sure, the stems of the brightly colored flowers are green, but there's no grass, no trees. Even before I discovered Blair's love of hiking, I knew she'd live somewhere surrounded by nature. Not plants and flowers that look like they've been imported from other countries but native trees full of birds and wildlife.

I'm surprised she agreed to start a new life here.

But what do I know? I'm just the guy she had a fling with in high school. Nathan was supposed to be the real deal.

With a fresh anger coursing through me, I stride toward the condo at the back, a scowl forming as I go. And by the time I reach his door, I'm ready to break something. None of this even matters. It's all superficial. What matters is the fact that this fucker hurt Blair, and he deserves to feel even an ounce of the pain she feels. He deserves to face the truth. That someone knows the man he truly is.

"Morgan!" I call out when I reach his front door, pounding my fist on the faded wood paneling. "It's Tuesday so I know you don't have practice."

At least, that's what Blair mentioned once when she was comparing our schedules. He could very well be out, but it's nine a.m. so I doubt it. Unless he never came home.

When he doesn't respond, I knock again, louder this time until I hear faint movement inside. The clunking gets louder before Nathan throws open the door, his glare matching my own.

"What the fuck do you want?"

"Excuse me?"

"I'm not in the mood for niceties. Did you think hiding Blair in the Storm suite would stop the world from seeing her? One of my teammates texted me. His friend was taking a photo of that Hollywood actress. And look who's beside her." He shows me the photo of Hayley and Blair. "At a

Storm game. Barely more than a week after we broke up. It's fucking embarrassing. So much for the breakup not being about you. That cheating—"

"Say another word, and as God is my fucking witness, I will end you. I don't need much more of an excuse."

"How many would that be then? Three? Or are there other deaths we don't know about?" He smirks as his words slice me in half, but I smile through the pain.

"This isn't about me, asshole. This is about you and Blair. More specifically, the fact that you fucked up her life. She deserved better than a piece of shit like you."

"So, you're the one that put that idea in her head."

"Nope. If she said that to you, it's all her. But I'm fucking proud of her for figuring it out."

"Then I'll repeat, what the fuck do you want?"

"I think you should invite me in. Trust me. You don't want anyone to overhear what I'm about to say. Or your response."

"What are you talking about?"

"Let. Me. In."

"Jesus. Okay. You're not a fucking vampire. If you're that desperate, have at it." Nathan steps aside and my skin burns as I walk past him. It's definitely not me that's the vampire. He's the one that sucks the life out of anyone he comes into contact with.

He points me in the direction of the living room, and I actually laugh when I see the furnishings. "I bet Blair *loved* that couch," I say sarcastically, and Nathan's eyes widen.

"She probably told you."

"She didn't have to. I know her."

"Fuck off. Say what you have to say so I can enjoy the rest of my day off. Your jealous rage must be important since you flew all this way to see me."

"You're going to wish that's why I was here. Because what I have to say has nothing to do with jealousy."

Nathan's expression twists but it doesn't bring me the satisfaction it should. "Get to the point," he seethes and my knuckles ache from how tightly I'm clenching my fists, using all the restraint I have to hold back from knocking him out, before I have answers.

A little part of me knows I might be wrong, and I'm holding on to that knowledge with a tight grasp, but my grip is slipping. "Remember that fucked-up game you played in high school? The one that could send you to prison?"

Nathan's eyes widen but he's quick to school his features. "I don't know what you're talking about."

"You don't? Well, let me remind you." I step closer, edging him back. "It involved the date rape drug and a handful of unsuspecting girls. Girls who just wanted to feel popular for once in their lives. Ring a bell?"

Nathan's face pales but he stands a little taller, likely preparing himself to brush off whatever he thinks I'm about to say.

"I bet you thought no one knew," I continue, studying his reaction. "I bet you thought you'd managed to get away with that fucked-up part of your life. Just because no one reported you. You were wrong."

"*You're* wrong. Like I said, I don't know what you're talking about." He shrugs and that little gesture pushes me over the edge. I move closer still and he shuffles back again, bumping into the wall behind him.

"Are you really going to deny it, fucker?"

"I don't—"

"Cut the bullshit. It's just you and me here. Man up for once; admit you did something wrong."

"You're delusional. Whatever proof you think you have—"

"My proof is Blair."

"What?" Nathan recoils, his expression morphing to one of shock, and I have to admit his response appears genuine.

"You did it to Blair."

"Why the fuck would I do it to Blair?" The conviction in his voice has me pausing momentarily. *Is it possible he didn't know?*

"The night of the accident. She told me she didn't want to sleep with you, and yet, for some reason she did."

"What?" Nathan's stunned for a beat until he blinks a few times and complete devastation flashes across his face. "I didn't... I'd never... fuck."

"Fuck, alright. Did you tell any of your teammates that you wanted her?"

"Yes, but—"

"Someone fucking drugged her, Nathan. And *you* took advantage of it." There's no way she drank enough to consider losing her virginity at a fucking party, not in that short space of time. That's not Blair. "Admit it. You know she'd never have slept with you that night if she'd been of sound mind. You're not that blind."

"No." He shakes his head, and if I thought he was pale before, it's nothing compared to now.

"Bullshit."

"I love her."

"It doesn't make it right. Whether you drugged her or not, you were part of the game. You did this. It's why she left. Why she called me. Why Sierra was driving that night." Sierra's name rolls easily off my tongue and it shocks me. But I don't show it.

"No," Nathan repeats. "No."

"Yes! Blair trusted you. She came to your house because of *your* invitation. And you left her alone."

"No. No." Nathan's denial comes back in full force, but this time he at least has the decency not to hide his emotions. He looks like he's going to vomit.

"No, what, Nathan? No, you didn't do it? Or no, you can't believe that you took advantage of the girl you claim to love?"

Bile rises in my throat. They'd been playing that stupid game for years. Plying girls with alcohol, then slipping them something to push them over the edge. Most of the girls accepted what happened. One of them even joked about it with Cade once. That's how we first found out. But when we'd asked around, we got a similar response. They all laughed it off. Blamed themselves.

But we fucking suspected it and did *nothing*.

My throat burns as I turn away, needing a second so I don't fall apart.

If I'd told the police what I thought—told *anyone*—Blair would never have been attacked.

Fuck, if Cade finds out, he'll never forgive himself. Nor should I. We stayed quiet because it was easier than drawing attention to ourselves. No one would have believed us anyway. We had no proof.

Fuuuck.

My head spins but I refuse to let Nathan see it. I refuse to spiral. Not again.

"Tell me, asshole. *Now.*" I turn back to face him, my muscles tense, my venomous gaze locked on his.

"I didn't know."

"Didn't know *what?*"

"That Blair had been drugged. She was on a no-go list. It was too dangerous. If she told you or Cade, you would have destroyed us all."

Are you fucking kidding me? "She should have been on the no-go list because she's not a toy for your fucking pleasure. *Not* to save your own ass. And while we're on the topic, there shouldn't have been a list to begin with because it shouldn't have been fucking happening."

My muscles ache from how tightly they're wound and my head throbs. *I let it happen.*

I came here wanting to confront Nathan, to hurt him, but I'm just as bad as he is.

"Blair lost a piece of her soul that night. Because of you. Because of your games. You deserve to rot in hell. You deserve for me to call Cade so we can both beat the shit out of you. You deserve for me to tell Blair *everything*. But instead, I'm going to let you stew over this. Then I expect you to tell her yourself. Do the right thing, or I'll take it to the media."

I'm lying because I'd never do that to Blair, but if Nathan cares about anything, it's his career and reputation.

He backs away, his body trembling as he covers his face with his hands. "I didn't know. I didn't—"

"It doesn't matter. Maybe this will teach you to think about someone other than yourself. You've got twenty-four hours to tell her. I hope you spend that time drowning in shame."

My face curls in disgust, and I make sure he sees it when I walk past, but the second I turn away, the disgust turns to anger. Everything comes back to that little fucker. It's been like that for years. And now—

"I loved her, you know. I still love her. I'd never do anything to purposely hurt her. Not like you did."

And my rage boils over.

My fists lock, and without thinking through the consequences, I spin around, covering the distance between us in two quick strides, rearing back my hand. "This is for Blair."

My knuckles burn when they connect with his jaw, but I couldn't give a fuck right now. This has been a long time coming.

"And this is for inviting her to one of your fucked-up parties." My fist meets his face again, and I plan to go for round three until he begs me to stop.

"I'll call her." He sniffs, wiping his sleeve across his lip, staring down at the blood. "Just stop."

"You're lucky I'm not the asshole they say I am. And you're lucky I believe you when you say you didn't know. But if you don't tell her, I won't hesitate to fuck you up."

I'm shaking as I turn around. My knuckles sting and my fist throbs, bruising already starting to appear, but it's my chest that aches the most. All our pain could have been avoided. *All of it.* And as much as I'd love to blame Nathan, it all comes back to me.

The front door slams against the wall as I storm outside, my chest tight, my lungs burning.

I struggle to take in air, and I'm dizzy as I walk down the steps.

My phone rings, but it takes me a second to register the sound. "Yeah," I answer without checking the screen, grabbing the wall for support.

"Zane Fitzpatrick?"

"Yes."

"This is Sergeant Lennon from the Jacksonville Sheriff's Office."

Fuck. My ears ring as the world around me fades.

"How can I help?" I respond nonchalantly while inside my stomach is churning.

"Circumstances have changed and we need you to come in for some additional questions."

"Can I do it over the phone or—"

"We'll see you here tomorrow. District One in Jacksonville."

My head screams no, but I have no fucking idea what I respond or if I even bother to speak before hanging up. I can't even remember how I got back to my rental. But the second I'm inside, my body crumbles and I struggle to fight back tears.

And while I'm aware of how fucked I might be, all I can think about is Blair.

One more thing that is going to crush her.

CHAPTER FORTY-NINE

ZANE

AGE NINETEEN

My phone rings and I stare down at the screen before raising it to my ear. "Blair?"

"Zane?" The phone crackles and her voice breaks. "Zane. Can you hear me?"

"I can. What's going on?" There's loud music but it's impossible to miss the terror in her voice.

"I messed up. I'm at Nathan's party. I shouldn't have come. Why did I leave?"

"Nathan's?" Fuck. My heart races. Panic takes over me. He wouldn't— Focus, Zane. "Blair, are you okay?"

"No." Her voice wavers and my chest burns.

"Where are you?"

"Still at Nathan's." A door slams. The music softens and her sobs fill my ears. "I'm at Nathan's but I'm out front now."

"Stay there. I'm coming. Don't go back inside." I scan the room for anyone sober, and my eyes land on Sierra. She hates driving my truck, but for Blair, she'll do it.

"Are you alone? Is there anyone there you know? Anyone that can wait with you."

"No."

"That's okay." I try to remain calm, waving to get Sierra's attention. "Stay out front. I think you're only ten minutes from us."

"I didn't mean it. I wouldn't have done it. I—"

"Are you hurt?" I hate cutting her off, but I need to know. "Did anyone hurt you?"

"I don't know."

My body heats as my throat constricts. "What—" I croak before clearing my throat. "What do you mean you don't know? What happened?"

"Please hurry up."

"I'm on my way. I promise. Can you stay on the phone?"

"No. I've got a low battery. I need to save it."

"Blair—"

"I'm going to walk toward you."

"Blair, no!" Sierra's gaze snaps to mine.

"It'll be faster."

"Blair, please just stay there."

"I'll be fine."

"Blai—" Her phone goes dead just as Sierra and I reach my truck, and I swear the blood drains from my body. "Fuck."

She has to be okay. She has to.

"Hurry up, Sierra." I'm jittery as we drive toward Nathan's. I've driven this road a million times before, and yet at this moment, I can't recognize a single tree. I have no idea how far away we are.

"I'm going the speed limit, Zane," Sierra's quick to snap back. "What do you want me to do, break the law?"

"Yes! If it will get us there faster. You didn't hear her on the call. Something's wrong and Nathan—" I stop short of admitting my suspicions. I could be wrong. I hope I'm wrong. "She was angry at me when she left but she still called me. We have to find her."

"I'm not speeding just because you pissed Blair off. We're ten minutes away."

"Ten minutes?" Fuck. I thought we were closer than that. Her annoyed gaze briefly snaps to mine but I don't care.

"Please. Hurry. This is bigger than you think and—"

"Zane, stop. You're drunk and panicking. You need to calm down."

"I. Am. Calm. And I love you but I swear to God if you don't speed the fuck up..."

"I'm pulling over." She puts her indicator on and gives me a shove. "You're not thinking clearly. I promise I'll protect her but I'm not letting her see you like this. You're a mess."

"No. Keep going. There's no time. I'm not getting out."

"Zane."

"No, Sierra. Stop." I grab the steering wheel and push it away from me, spinning my truck back onto the road. "Just—"

"Zane!" Sierra's scream fills the air, tires screech, light flashes, and then...

Chapter Fifty

BLAIR

CURRENT DAY

My phone vibrates and my heart jumps, but when I see that it's Mom, my hope fades. I texted Zane when I landed yesterday and he still hasn't responded. At the time, I assumed he'd just fallen asleep, since we'd had a long night, but at almost twenty-four hours and three texts later, I'm worried.

"Was that him?" Cade asks, his nagging tone pissing me off.

"Again, *why* are you still here?"

Cade shrugs like it's no big deal. "I told you. I needed a mental health break. I'm here on vacation."

Ugh. No matter how many times he says it, it's still annoying. I arrived back at Jenna's and found brother dearest still crashing on her couch. I would have sent him packing if I didn't feel bad for not really supporting him through his breakup.

"I'm sorry. I'm just a little stressed. That was Mom. Happy?"

"She misses you. You should come home. I know the job in San Francisco sounds amazing—"

"And right up my alley."

"And right up your alley," he reluctantly agrees. "But I still don't like it. You'll be alone in another state. You'll be starting life from scratch."

"I accepted the job, Cade. You know that. I'm going home next week to tell Dad in person. Plus, I wouldn't be alone. Zane lives in San Francisco."

"You're alone right now, so I'm worried."

"So am I. But *I'm* worried about *him*."

"Why?" His tone turns accusatory and it pisses me off even more.

"Because this isn't like him, Cade. He's not the type to just disappear."

"Are you kidding me? Did you hear what you just said? He disappeared for years, B."

"Because I asked him to." My loud tone draws Jenna's attention and she peers around the corner, her expression sympathetic. Like me, she's worried. But unlike me, she thinks Cade's just looking out for me.

Cade sighs, his shoulders dropping as he sinks back into the wall behind him. "You don't even know him anymore." He runs a hand down his face. "I shouldn't have let him come back here."

"Let him? It's not your choice if I see him or not."

"I know, but he told us what he was going to do and we laughed, thinking he was joking." As if to prove his point, he laughs incredulously. "I'm such an idiot."

"What do you mean?" My brows furrow, my tilting gaze locked on his.

"He said he was going to *fuck* you and *ghost* you, and he did, didn't he? You slept together, right?"

My lips part and I stare at Cade deadpan, replaying his words over in my mind just as Jenna cuts in. "He *was* joking, Cade. Don't be a dick."

"It may have seemed that way. But he did it. Tell me I'm wrong?"

"You're wrong," Jenna and I both say at the same time, to which he scoffs.

"Everything's good then? And you're moving to San Francisco to be with him?"

"No, Cade. I'm moving for my dream job." *And to be with him.*

"I thought your dream job was to be a *writer*," he accuses and I freeze. He hasn't mentioned me being a writer for years and suddenly he's bringing it up.

"After all this time, you still don't want me with Zane. I thought it was because you didn't want to lose a friend? You're not even friends anymore."

"*I* didn't think you were 'with Zane.'"

"Well, I am." I sigh, my body sagging in defeat. I'm never going to make him understand. And whether I'm with Zane or not is beside the point. "It shouldn't matter what I do with my life, Cade. You should want me to be happy, no matter what I choose."

"I—"

"You've never done that. You weren't happy when I changed my major to nursing. You weren't happy I was with Nathan. And you're not happy *now*. I can't win."

"You don't know Nathan as well as—" I shoot him a death stare and he stops talking for a beat. We're not having this argument again. That's not the point.

"You're wrong." He changes direction, clenching his fist, clearly upset. "If I believed you were truly happy with any *one* of those life choices, I'd be shouting it from the rooftops. If you were happy, I'd be so ecstatic, you'd think it was sickening. But Blair, you haven't been truly happy since the day Sierra died. Actually, no. You haven't been happy since Zane's nineteenth birthday, and I'm only now realizing why."

My breath hitches, and my chest grows tight. Cade turns away and I'm grateful for the reprieve. I don't want him to see my tears. Because he's right. Only, it took me until last week to see it.

Cade curses under his breath while I frantically wipe my eyes. And when he glances back at me, his expression distraught, my heart breaks.

"It's always been him, hasn't it?" he asks, shaking his head. "It's my fault you kept it a secret."

God, the fault game is getting old. "It's no one's fault anymore, Cade. It happened. For now, I just want your support with whatever choice I make."

"If you're not choosing Zane, will you consider coming home?"

"No. Not for any longer than a vacation."

"Please."

"No. You know me, Cade. I'm going to be a nurse for the Heartwood University Lions. For a D1 college football team." My heart swells with joy and I shake my head in disbelief. "Don't you see—" I pause when Cade starts smiling, a genuine warmth surrounding him.

"There it is."

"There what is?"

"Your happiness. That look right there. That's what's been missing since you were seventeen."

He steps forward and reaches for my hands, bending down so he can look me in the eye. "Does Zane make you *this* happy?"

"He does." I nod.

"Well, okay." He releases my hands and pulls me into a hug, his tight brotherly hold almost suffocating me, like it always used to.

"But,"—he steps back, his expression turning serious again—"if he doesn't have the best fucking excuse for ignoring your texts, I'm going to have to hurt him."

"If that happens, you can get in line." I smile innocently, and Cade laughs.

"Bit by bit she's all coming back. God, help us. I love you, but I'm not sure I'm ready for the full force of the old B to return."

"Then it sucks to be you. Because she's already on her way."

I wasn't lying when I said Zane gave me the strength to walk away from Nathan, and even if he never calls, even if Cade's right, *which he's not*, and that Zane's ghosted me—*he hasn't*—no one can take that away. Because deep down, I know Zane cares for me. I know he still sees me as the girl I once was, the woman with dreams who knew she deserved the world. The woman who's starting to reappear.

More than that, he sees the woman I am now and he loves them both.

Which is why I'm worried.

But if I'm wrong, and he's just taking his sweet-ass time to get back to me, then you better believe that I'm hunting him down.

And he can thank himself for that. After all, it's his fault I'm finally standing my ground. Finally seeing my worth.

The silence on the mountain has me on edge and when a stick snaps beneath my foot, I startle, almost dropping my phone as my heart races, but at least I've still got service.

Taking a deep breath, I let the air fill my lungs and walk a little farther, never letting myself go too far in case he's unable to call.

I'm being ridiculous. I know that. But I needed to get out of Jenna's apartment and away from their sympathetic gazes. I needed a moment to think. But I also want to be available if Zane tries to call or finally messages me.

For all I know, Cade could be right. Zane could be running away again after I told him I slept with Nathan the night of Sierra's accident. But something tells me that's not what's going on. Something deep within my soul. The part of me that's always been Zane's, even when I wasn't.

I reach another peak on my hike and check my phone again. One bar. If I go much farther, I'm likely to lose it and I can't risk that.

What if he needs me? Or worse, what if something happened to him?

When he'd kissed me goodbye at the airport, I could tell something was off, but he assured me that everything was okay, and I have no reason not to trust him. He's never shown me otherwise. Something must be wrong and—

My phone rings, cutting me off mid-thought and I fumble to answer. My heart races but when I see that it's my old Jacksonville work friend Kayla, I sigh.

"Hey Kayla. How are you?" I try to keep my voice light but I'm struggling.

"Blair. Thank God." Kayla's frantic voice filters through the phone before she sucks in a breath.

"Are you running?"

"No. Well, yes. I ran to find my phone. Remember that famous patient we had, the one involved in that knife fight?"

"Yes?" I whisper, a new fear working its way into my chest.

"He died, Blair."

Her words echo through my head and I pray I heard wrong. "What?"

"He died," she repeats, and a stabbing pain shoots through me. "It's not common knowledge yet, but I remember you asking me and Ruth to take over looking after him, along with his teammate, because you had history there. I thought you might want to know."

"Oh, God." My head feels light as the blood drains from my face. I never gave Kayla much to go on back then, but I could tell by her sympathetic expression that she understood. And God, am I grateful.

"You knew them, didn't you?"

"Only the teammate and this is going to break him."

"I'm sorry."

"Thank you for letting me know."

We chat for another minute or so but I'm numb, going through the motions, and when she hangs up, I immediately dial Jenna, though I have no idea what to say.

"Hey, you."

"Jenna." My voice wavers as I fight back tears on my way down the mountain, desperate to get home. "He died." My stomach churns as nausea takes over me, and I can't stop myself from shaking. Sucking in a breath, I try to get air in my lungs, but nothing I do seems to work.

"Who died?"

"Blair?" Cade's voice filters through the phone. "Blair. What's going on? You're freaking me out."

"The guy in the coma. The guy Zane hurt. His teammate. He *died*."

"Motherfucker," Cade curses under his breath.

"What?" Jenna's panicked voice hits me. "Tell me."

I want to explain, but Zane's grief-stricken face shadows my mind and all I can do is mutter his name, listening while Cade fills her in.

This is going to kill him. No wonder he hasn't called.

Images of Sierra's lifeless body flash through my mind before morphing into Zane and the vision of his devastated expression when he discovered her death.

My breath shakes as I shatter.

This'll push him over the edge.

I have to find him.

CHAPTER FIFTY-ONE

ZANE

I'm numb as I walk through the airport, the smiling faces all a blur, a ringing in my ears that I haven't been able to shake since I left Nathan's condo.

The adrenaline from our fight has well and truly worn off, and now I'm empty, unsure what I'm supposed to do or where I'm supposed to be.

Someone knocks into me and my heart stops as I struggle to take in air.

I'm not sure how much time passes but I somehow make it to a cab, and it's not until we're speeding down the highway, my window down, the fresh air filling my lungs, that my head finally clears enough to replay the conversation I had with the officer.

"Circumstances have changed."

Circumstances. Have. Changed.

I don't want to believe it but that can only mean one thing. Right?

He died.

After all this time, Landon *fucking* died. That piece of shit is about to ruin more lives and he'll never even know it.

I stopped him to save my friends and destroyed myself in the process.

A loud cough drags me from my thoughts, and I glance up to see my driver staring at me through the rearview mirror.

"We're almost there. Anywhere specific you want me to drop you?"

I'm heading to my hometown. My parents live there, my old friends, yet I have nowhere to go.

"The extended-stay hotel downtown," I tell him, turning back to the window.

"That's a dump."

"I know. But that's where I want to be dropped." I half laugh at the reality I've found myself in. My life's a mess; it makes sense to stay in a dump. Plus, it's where I'm least likely to be seen. If I'm right, and the news goes public, I'm going to be hounded, and I need time to think before I make a statement.

I need to say something that will keep Blair and... my sister out of the news.

My phone buzzes with another text from Cade, but just like the one before, I don't even open it. It's not hard to guess it'll be some kind of big brother threat.

If I knew he'd show up here and beat the shit out of me, I'd welcome it. I deserve it. But I'm not stupid. He'd send Blair, and right now, she needs to stay the hell away from me.

For her sake and mine.

CHAPTER FIFTY-TWO

BLAIR

My bag gets caught in the door as I'm rushing outside to meet Cade, and my phone rings as I fight it, my panic rising with each tug.

"Goddammit. I hate you." I drop the bag and reach for my phone, pulling it out of my pocket in time to catch that it's Zane's mom, not Zane, and she couldn't have called at a worse time.

I glance up at Cade, my eyes pleading with him to help as I consider my options, but he's no use. Sometimes he needs people to spell things out for him.

My phone stops ringing, but before I can sigh in relief, she calls back, and as much as I want to reject it, I can't. *Maybe she's heard from him.* I'll try anything right now.

"Fiona, hi."

"Have you heard the news?" she rushes out, her voice equally as panicked as mine, and my fears deepen.

"What news?" I play dumb since Kayla mentioned it wasn't common knowledge yet.

"That kid that Zane beat up *died* this morning." Her voice is somber but holds an edge I don't like.

"Yes, I heard, but I didn't know it had hit the media. I'm on my way to see Zane. He must be—"

"What? You're seeing Zane?"

"Yes. I'm on my way to the airport. I promise, I'll make sure he's okay."

"I thought the two of you weren't speaking anymore. I didn't know you knew where he lived."

"What? Ah... we hadn't spoken until recently. But now we are. It's complicated but I promise to explain it soon." I don't know why I'm talking as though Ron didn't imply Zane was dead to him last week, but I refuse to believe she feels the same until I hear it from her mouth.

"I'm shocked." *And there it is.* "That's really disappointing. After everything he's done."

My fists clench but I take a deep breath as Jenna opens the door, releasing my bag from its shackles.

I mouth "thank you" and stalk toward Cade's car. "What is it that you *think* he's done?" I ask, throwing the back door open and shoving my bag inside. Cade opens his mouth to argue but when I glare his way, he thinks better of it.

"Zane's the reason we're constantly being hounded by reporters. And now this other kid's dead, it's going to be ten times worse."

"Are they back?" I ask somewhat distractedly as I settle in the front seat, positioning the phone between my shoulder and ear as I try to buckle my seat belt. But just like the bag, it fucking jams.

Come on. You...stupid...belt.

"Not yet," Fiona's voice rings in my ear. "But they will be. It should have been him."

I jolt and the seat belt snaps back into position as I let go, a deafening ringing in my ears. Surely I heard wrong. "Did you just say it should have been Zane?"

"I did. And I'll say it again. He forced her to get in his truck. She hated driving that thing and he knew that. But he didn't care. He was too busy trying to get God knows where."

"What?" My heart slams in my chest as tears prick my eyes. "He never told you where he was going?"

"He might have, but it didn't matter. I've been holding this anger in for too long. Ron told me not to voice my thoughts because people would judge me. But he's gone too far. And to sink his claws into *you*. He's poisoning your beautiful soul and you don't even realize. Just like he did with Sierra. Did you know she was drinking that night? They found traces of alcohol in her system. Her reputation is tarnished because of him. We will never forgive him for that. Don't go to him, Blair. He doesn't deserve it."

"I've gotta go."

"Blair, no. Listen to me, I—"

"No, you listen. Zane was coming to *me*. He asked Sierra to help for *me*. Because I was distraught and needed him."

"What?"

"If Zane hadn't picked up his phone, I would have called Sierra next. Either way she'd have been in that truck. I was drunk. I was crying and I needed help. Zane loved Sierra. He *loved* her. And he loved you. You told me you needed me because he ran. But did you really expect him to stay when you felt that way about him? If something happens to him, it's on you." I move to hang up, but stop myself. I have more to say. "And for the record, I gave Sierra the alcohol. *Me*. So if you're going to blame anyone—"

The phone's ripped from my hand and I spin to see Cade ending the call. "What the fuck, Cade?"

"You are not taking the blame for that, Blair. Not to them. Not to anyone. You hear me? Sierra wasn't drunk. I'd been speaking to her less than ten minutes before Zane asked to help and she was completely sober. She'd even offered to drive *my* car home."

"That doesn't change the fact that—"

"No." He throws a hand up between us. "No. Have you been blaming yourself this whole time?"

I sit tall. I'm not having this conversation again. "Yes."

"Jesus, Blair." Cade slams his eyes shut and when he opens them again, they are watering. "The accident was not your fault."

"You sound just like Zane."

"Good. I'm glad he agrees with me. It means I don't have to kick his ass."

"He blames himself."

"Of course he does." Cade shakes his head, his voice exasperated.

"Now his teammate is dead, so..."

"God, this is fucked up."

"Yep." I nod.

"I'm coming with you."

My eyes widen and it's my turn to shake my head. "You don't have a ticket."

"I'll buy one. It's probably time I went home to face reality anyway. I can leave from San Francisco."

"What about your clothes—"

"I'll buy new ones if I have to, but I've got plenty at home."

"Thank you. But I want to do this alone. Zane doesn't need an ambush. He needs support. I'll be okay. I promise. But maybe you should head home. In case Ron and Fiona decide to talk to Mom and Dad."

"Shit. Do you think they will?"

"If they think I'm being a disobedient child, yes."

"That won't shock them." Cade bounces his eyebrows and I laugh.

"I have no doubt that Mom and Dad will side with me. But they might need one of us there to explain the situation. I never told them how much Zane's parents relied on me."

"God, you're annoying sometimes. If you'd just let others share the load, you wouldn't be carrying so much that it's weighing you down."

"Again, that's kind of what Zane said."

"Seems like he knows you." Cade smiles and I allow myself the hint of a grin before the dread returns.

"He does, and I know him too. Which is why I'm certain he's not in a good place. Come on. Let's get moving. I've got a plane to catch."

With my stride confident, I head for the concierge's desk and internally curse when it's the same blonde who was here last week. The one that practically eye fucked Zane from the moment he stepped out of the car.

She's smiling as she talks on the phone, but when she sees me, it fades. "I've got to go. I'll call you back." She hangs up and fakes a grin. "Can I help you?"

"Yes, I'm here with Zane Fitzpatrick but he's not answering his phone. Can you buzz me up?"

There's a brief moment of awkward silence as she stares my way, until she bursts out laughing. "Do you know how many times I've heard that? Look, I'm sorry he fucked you and never called. But if I let every scorned woman up to either knee him in the balls or beg for a second go, he'd never have peace. And I'd be fired."

My stomach rolls and for the briefest second, I let her get to me until I force the doubt back down.

"Are you finished?" I fold my arms over my chest, thinning my lips so I don't say anything more. And she fucking laughs.

"Yep. I'm done. Have a nice day."

"I'm not leaving. You saw me here, with my bags, when I first arrived last week. Then again three days later. Do you think that sounds like a one-night stand?"

"Three-night stand then. It's the same deal."

"Call him."

"You said he's not answering."

"Then how about you go up and knock on his door, or let me do it. It's important."

"Fine. I'll call him."

She picks up her phone just as mine rings with Nathan's name flashing across the screen, taunting me. Nathan. Nathan. Nathan. Not Zane. Zane. Zane.

I don't have time for this. "Nathan?"

"You answered. How are you?" His voice wavers but I don't have time to question it.

"I'm fine. But now's not a good time. Can I call you back?"

I'm not even sure why I answered, but it was better than staring at the blonde's smug face while her call rang out.

"Please, Blair, I just need a second. It's important."

"No answer." Blondie smirks and my nose flares as I glance down at her badge. Kate. Fucking Kate.

"Try him again," I demand, convinced she probably faked the last one.

"I'm sorry but Mr. Fitzpatrick isn't here."

"You don't know that or you would have told me when I first walked in. Try him a—"

"He's not there," Nathan blurts with some urgency, momentarily stunning me.

"What?"

"He stopped by our place earlier today."

I walk away from Kate, not bothering to apologize for the fact I was wrong, and push through the glass door, walking down the road toward the park Zane showed me last week.

"Why?" I question, my chest tight. "Why would he visit you?" And why didn't he tell me?

"He, ahh... wanted to talk to me about what happened the night of the accident and said I should talk to you about it."

My heart jolts as my legs stop moving. "What? He told you to talk to me?"

"'Told' is putting it nicely. He threatened me."

"Why?"

"Because...ah...I. I promise I didn't know."

"Didn't know what?"

"I'm sorry for everything I did to you, and everything I didn't do." He pauses and I gape. I think that's the first time I've heard him actually apologize to me, and that's a sad reality. "Blair, I may hate the fucker, but Zane's right; you deserved better. You deserved the chance to move on properly, and I helped you bury your feelings under a rug." He groans and I picture him running his hand down his face. "In my defense, I thought that's what you wanted. You were happy that Zane was gone because it meant you didn't have to confront your grief all the time. You wouldn't have the accident thrown in your face on a daily basis. But I can see now that it was the wrong thing to do."

"Nathan—"

"I'm not finished."

I stifle a groan. This is Nathan to a T. He's talking about wishing he'd been better during our relationship while making it all about himself, just like he's always done.

"You don't have to apologize, Nathan. You're free. Be the man you've always wanted to be. Just tell me what's going on with Zane."

"I will, but... fuck, this is hard."

"My God. *What*?"

"I think you were drugged the night of the accident as part of a game we used to play. A game *my friends* used to play. I never actually participated but you could say I was the host."

I rear back like he slapped me. "What the fuck?"

"You were supposed to be off-limits. I promise, if I'd known they'd given you something, I never would have... you know."

I blink a few times, confused with what I'm hearing, but not hurting the way I'd expect on hearing that news.

"I was drugged?"

"Yes."

"And Zane knew you used to do that?"

"He guessed."

"And Cade?"

"I don't know. But I'd say he guessed too."

"Was it a bet or something?"

"No. I didn't know they'd done it. I just told them I thought you were hot and... fuck. I joked about wanting to—"

"Stop." I cringe. "I get it. Thanks for telling me."

"You're thanking me?"

I pause for a second, checking in with my emotions, and while it's strange...I'm okay. It actually explains a lot. "Yep. At least I know."

"You're not angry?"

I'm fucking livid. With Cade. If he had suspicions, he should have fucking told me. But when it comes to Nathan... "I'm disappointed." With him and myself. "But I can't change the past. I need to focus on the present. And right now, I need to find Zane." My chest tightens but Nathan sighs, finally giving me what I need.

"I heard him on the phone with someone. He mumbled something about going home. To Jacksonville."

"Shit. That's not good. What time was that?"

"I don't know. Around ten, maybe?"

"Jesus Christ. It's been hours."

"I'm sorry, Blair."

"Stop fucking apologizing." He says it once and now he can't stop. "I couldn't care less about me right now. Zane's the only one I'm worried about."

My body tenses. If he's in Jacksonville... God. He just found out about his teammate. He's alone. And most likely spiraling.

I take in a shaky breath, struggling to fill my lungs.

He needs me. "I've got to go."

CHAPTER FIFTY-THREE

ZANE

The shadows move across the off-white wall of my cheap hotel room as I sit staring. Unable to move. Watching as night morphs into day. Darkness into light.

After ordering shitty room service last night, I tried to sleep. But every time I close my eyes, the image of Sie— Fuck, why can't I say her name again? The image of my sister fills my mind, making me nauseous. It's not even a memory. She's blaming me for her death, telling me that if I'd died instead, it would have prevented all this from happening. But I'm not too far gone that I'd believe that notion. She'd never say that.

Even if her ghost was haunting me, those words would never leave her mouth. She'd never even think it.

She might blame me for her death, but she'd never suggest I should have taken her place. She was inherently good. That wasn't in her nature.

She didn't deserve to die.

Hell, Landon fucked up. He attacked Reed and Hayley and *he* didn't deserve to die.

But neither do I.

I don't think...

My alarm goes off, signaling my impending date with the Jacksonville Sheriff's office, but I still can't bring myself to move.

My blood feels like lead, weighing me down as it races through my body.

I want it all to go away. I need it to go away. I can't do this to them again. I can't bring them all down because of my goddamn fuckups.

My phone rings on the bed beside me, and though I only manage to move my head an inch, I can still see the screen and Reed's name flashing to get my attention. He's not the first teammate to call since I texted to tell them I wouldn't be at practice, but he's the only one likely to know why.

He probably got the same call I did. Only, I'll bet his interview can be done over the phone or with his local police, while I'm stuck reopening old wounds.

I'm still staring at my phone when it stops ringing and the notifications hit me like a dagger.

Blair—twelve missed calls.

Cade—six missed calls.

Unknown number—three missed calls.

And that's only in the last few hours.

There've been many more but they disappear as the new notifications bury them. I remember who they were though... Luke, D'Angelo, Wes.

Not to mention the barrage of text messages and voice mails.

I know I'm fucking up even more by not answering my phone. Especially with Blair. But I can't bring myself to face her. I can't bear to hear her shattered voice when it's still so loud from the last time I did something that broke her heart.

I stare at the wall in front of me, the uncomfortable hospital bed making my ass numb. The doctor is talking to me but I tune him out the second he says, "You're lucky to be alive." Who the fuck says that to a survivor of a car accident when the other two people are dead? I'm well aware that I'm lucky. But I don't need him to remind me of that little detail and all the guilt that comes with it.

He pats my shoulder and I flinch, his rushed apology barely registering in my ears.

When he's done, I nod, thanking him for God knows what as my gaze follows him out the door.

And that's when my world ends.

Blair's standing on the threshold. Her hair a mess, her eyes bloodshot, her face marred with black tears.

She doesn't speak. But I guess neither do I. I can't. I don't know what to say. Not anymore.

A murky darkness fills the space between us, and she takes a step forward, ripping my chest open as I struggle to breathe. I can't face her. But I also can't handle the thought of sending her away.

She pauses for a beat, shaking her head and stepping back, her shoulders dropping as someone calls her away.

"B," I finally croak out as she turns to leave.

She pauses and her pained expression splits me in two. "I can't," she whispers, her voice breaking. "It hurts too much."

...

Sitting up, I Inhale a ragged breath and bang my head against the hotel wall as my memory assaults me. But it's not the worst of it. And when that worst comes to mind, I force myself to move, running to the bathroom as I dry retch.

...

Sierra. Sierra. Wake up. Come on. Come on. You have to wake up. Don't you dare die on me. Sierra!

...

My stomach heaves as I fall to the cold tiles, tears in my eyes, my heart lodged in my throat.

I need you, S. And God, I need Blair.

I'm not sure how the fuck I got myself here, but after my breakdown in the hotel, my alarm went off again and I somehow managed to clean myself up, getting my ass to the station. Right on time.

Two officers greet me. The first one introduces himself as Holt. He's an older man with a porn star mustache and light red hair shaved at the sides, his expression cocky. The second, a younger woman with smiling eyes and dark, slicked-back hair, introduces herself as Officer Nelson, her tone much more professional.

They escort me through the halls until we reach a dark room, and when the lights switch on, I'm not sure if it's my vision or an interrogation technique, but it doesn't get much brighter.

Officer Nelson gestures for me to sit, and I've barely lowered my ass when I'm hit with the words I was dreading.

"Mr. McKenna was pronounced dead yesterday morning. We've asked you here today to give your official statement over the incident that occurred on..." Mustache man, Holt, continues his rant but I zone out, trying to replay the events of that night, with my mind overflowing with all the fucked-up things I've done in my life. *What if I'm wrong?* What if my memory of that night is based on lies, conjured to protect myself. A way of ensuring I wouldn't break down if it ever came to this.

Not that it helps if that's true.

I want to believe it was self-defense, I do, but he fucking died. I slammed his head into the pavement so goddamn hard that he *died*. Even if it was self-defense, it's still my fault. I still killed another human. Making my number three.

"Mr. Fitzpatrick?"

"Sorry, yes." I snap out of my head, my stomach rolling with nausea.

"Can you state your full name for the record, please?"

"Yes, it's Zane William Fitzpatrick."

"Thank you."

"Can you please confirm that you don't wish to have a lawyer present?"

Fuck. "Am I under arrest?"

"Should you be?" Holt questions me while Officer Nelson shakes her head beside him.

"No. You're not. We're just making sure we have all the information now that the circumstances have changed."

Circumstances have changed. That makes it sound so much less permanent than it is. *He fucking died.*

"At this stage, this is just routine," she adds.

"Unless you have more information to tell us."

What? My eyes bounce between them as my head aches. Are they fucking good cop, bad copping me?

"Please state for the record—"

"I don't wish to have a lawyer present." I repeat their words back and my heart clenches. *Did I just make the biggest mistake of my life?*

"Thank you. Now, as we said, Mr. McKenna was pronounced dead yesterday after three months on life support. You're here to fill us in on everything you remember from that night. Even the details you think are irrelevant. We'll also be speaking to the other parties involved as well as hotel security who were rostered on that night."

I nod, unsure what to say, and Officer Nelson smiles. "Take your time."

"I don't need to take my time. I've been thinking about this nonstop for months. The details haunt me. But I can't think of anything else that I haven't already said."

"Then just repeat what you told the police back in August."

"Okay." Releasing a slow breath, I recall everything that happened that night—from our preseason game, to seeing Reed and Hayley outside the hotel, and passing Landon on my way to the bar. "He was acting strange. Talking to himself. He didn't even notice I was there. But at the time, I didn't think anything of it. I barely knew him. Maybe he was going over the game. Maybe it was something he always did. We all have our postgame rituals. When I heard Hayley scream, Landon was the furthest from my mind. But I ran. I knew something was wrong and I ran. I reached Reed and Hayley, just as Reed was pushing her out of harm's way, toward me. And that's when I saw him stab Reed somewhere in the chest. At least, I thought it was his chest at the time."

"Sorry, by him, you mean..."

"Landon. Mr. McKenna. He stabbed Reed once and pulled back to go again. That's when I tackled him."

The next few seconds are the ones I'm questioning, wondering if my mind's playing tricks on me. Not that I tell them that. I tell the officers that Landon stabbed me, and he must have because I have the scar to prove it, but I also tell them I feared for my life when I slammed his head into the pavement.

Yet *I* was pinning *him* down. I was bigger than him, stronger than him. Is it possible that I fell on the knife and my anger caused me to do more? How the fuck will I ever know that?

"Anything else?" Holt asks, his expression suspicious.

"No. Well, yes. When he stopped moving, I heard Hayley crying and realized that Reed was unconscious. I ran over to help her. She was kind of hysterical."

"But you didn't think to help Landon?"

"Honestly, I didn't even look at his face. I assumed he stopped moving because he'd given up the fight. Believe it or not, an asshole that had just stabbed my friend wasn't high on my priority list."

"Your friend?"

"Yes." The word comes out shaky because it's not exactly the truth, but he's a teammate so close enough.

"Would you say you were friends because you were teammates, or was it more than that?"

"Yes, because we *are* teammates." Reed may not be playing right now, but he's still very much a part of our team. He won't leave.

"How would you say your relationship was with Mr. McKenna then? Since he was also a teammate."

"He was a rookie."

"And so were you not too long ago."

"I was. But I didn't get the chance to get to know him."

"Right. Did you have any issues with him?" He glances down at his notes. "I understand he was on track to be a starter soon. Was there any concern that he'd take over your spotlight?"

"Are you fucking kidding me? We don't...didn't even play the same position. And if he was on track to be a starter, as you say, I didn't know. There are hundreds of guys waiting for their shot, but the only people who discuss that are the coaches and maybe the GM. We don't all sit around as a team drinking tea and chatting about the upcoming roster. *I had no idea.* That thought had never crossed my mind. Let's not forget the big issue with Landon, that you haven't mentioned today... He was stalking Hayley...and Reed. He chose to attack them. This wasn't premeditated by me."

"But it's opportunistic."

"The fuck?" I pound my fists on the table, and mustache Holt leans back in his chair, smirking.

"It seems you've got an anger issue, Mr. Fitzpatrick."

"No. I've got an issue with being accused of something I didn't do."

"We're not accusing you," Officer Nelson says, subtly glancing toward her partner. "We're just trying to get all the facts. Can you remember anything else?"

"No. That's it."

"Thank you." She smiles but I'm too pissed off to smile back. "We just have a few more questions about Landon's behavior in the lead-up to that game and then you're free to leave."

"For now," the douchebag adds.

"I told you, I barely knew him. I can't even remember seeing him before the game."

"We'd still like to ask you. Just in case."

I sigh, giving in, and I spend the next thirty minutes locked in that stuffy blue room before they finally release me.

When I walk outside, my eyes water in the bright sunlight as though it's been hours since I saw it. Honestly, it feels that way.

And it's not even over.

God only knows how long this nightmare will go on.

But what's worse is that I'm stuck here until tomorrow, just in case they have any follow-up questions, and I don't know what the fuck I'm going to do.

Chapter Fifty-Four

BLAIR

It takes me fifteen hours to get to Jacksonville, and I spend every second of those hours with my heart lodged in my throat and a tingling in my chest.

After my Uber driver decided to take the scenic route to the airport, my late-night flight was delayed because a passenger left their carry-on bag in the fucking McDonald's eating area and the airline decided to wait for them because their bags were already loaded. Then to add to that joy, we had to wait in line for a gate when we finally landed two hours later than scheduled.

I'm a mess. Not just mentally for all the fucked-up thoughts running through my mind, but physically too. My hair's falling out of my braid, I have mascara caked under my eyes from my thoughtless rubbing, and I threw on a T-shirt that I thought was clean only to find it's not, and now it's ninety degrees so I have to take off my sweater revealing the hot chocolate stain on my boob.

So yeah, I'm a hot mess, minus the hot.

Thank God the car rental ran smoothly because if I'd been forced to take an Uber or cab to get around, I would have lost my mind.

Why the hell won't he answer his goddamn phone?

The familiar sights of my hometown come into view, but instead of the comfort I expect it to bring, my anxiety increases. *What if he's not here? What if Nathan was wrong?*

As I stress, I search the obvious places that Zane might go, like the bar in the city where he said his team went to celebrate when they were here—which is of course closed. I check Halo's pub where he used to hang out with my brother, and one of two expensive hotels he told me he was going to stay at when he turned pro. I try the police station—but don't go in—and the park between our houses. I even drive past Cade's, not that Zane's ever been there, but I figured if he knew where it was and knew Cade wasn't going to be there, he might use it as a place to hide away.

I'm running out of ideas when my family home comes into view. I don't stop, but the urge to call in reinforcements is strong, and before I've thought it through, I'm dialing my dad.

"Hey, Princess, how are you? Are you finally going to tell me what's going on? Your mom won't even give me a—"

"Dad..." I sniff back the tears threatening to fall. *Where the hell is he?* "Something's happened. Zane's missing. He's here somewhere in Jacksonville but I've been driving around for an hour and I have no idea where he could be."

"You're here?"

"Yes. And so's Zane. But he's in a bad place. His teammate died. The one who was in a coma."

"Fuck. I mean, *dammit*. Sorry, love."

I smile at his outburst. My dad never curses around me unless he's watching football. And even then, he apologizes at the beginning of the game, covering himself in case anything untoward flies out of his mouth.

"I think this moment calls for cursing. You're forgiven."

"When did he find out?"

"I don't know. He won't answer my calls or texts. It's been two days. Kayla called me from the hospital to tell me the news. But I was already worried. I know something's wrong. I feel it in my gut. I *know* him."

Mom and Dad knew Zane and I were close, but we never once had a conversation about it. I'm sure they had an idea that we were more than just friends—at least after Zane left, and I completely fell apart—but it always went unspoken. Even now it feels strange speaking this aloud.

"He wouldn't disappear on me unless something was wrong, Dad. Not again. Trust me."

"I believe you. Hang on."

There's a rustling sound before I hear muffled voices and then silence. "I'm back."

"What were you doing?"

"Kissing your mom."

"Why?"

"Because I always kiss her goodbye and I'm leaving to help you find Zane. Have you tried the beaches? Or what about the place the two of you had your first kiss? Locations with happy memories. If he's in a dark place, he might seek solace in that."

"What?"

"Come on, Princess. Your mom and I are old but we're not stupid. We also have eyes. I'm pretty sure Zane's only truly loved two people in his life. Sure, he loved his mom and dad like anyone does. But he loved two others with that I'd-walk-through-fire kind of love. Sierra and *you*. Since it's not something he feels often, he was never good at hiding it."

"Oh, God." My face heats but I don't think it's from the embarrassment I'm feeling over my dad knowing my secret. I'm burning up because of the fire igniting in my chest, the flames threatening to destroy me from the inside. "I have to find him, Dad."

"We will."

"I've tried the beaches, but you could try— Wait." I slam on my brakes, my eyes wide as I focus on the broken figure hunched over on the front porch. "I found him." Relief fills my lungs and I take a few deep breaths, trying to calm myself. "He's here."

"Where are you?"

"His childhood home. I've got to go, Dad. I love you."

"Wait, Blair."

"I'll call you soon."

After pulling up to the curb, I rush out of my rental and through the front gate of Zane's run-down family home, only slowing when I'm a few yards in front of him. My heart breaks as I watch him.

If I didn't know him like the back of my hand, I would have driven past. He's a shadow of his former self, shattered and weak.

Actually, he's the man I remember from the hospital when Sierra died. The ghost. And I'm terrified I'm going to lose him again.

"Zane." My voice cracks when his name escapes my lips, and while it's barely above a whisper, his head snaps up, his distraught expression worse than I feared.

"Oh, Zane." I race forward, falling to my knees in front of him, wrapping him in my arms, desperate to keep him safe. "I'm here. You're okay."

"Blair?"

"Yeah, it's—"

A throat clears loudly and my gaze lifts to the gate at the same time Zane's does, both of us freezing. "Dad?" Zane whispers, while I suck in a breath, my eyes locked on the menacing gaze staring back at us.

"Ron, what are you doing?" I jump up and run ahead, stopping him from getting to Zane. The last thing he needs is someone else making him feel bad. "I think you—"

"How dare you come back here?" Ron yells over my head. "To our home. *Her* home."

He tries to move around me, but I step in his path, continuing to block him. "I'm not—"

"Let him through," Zane calls out, his voice low in resignation. "Let him say what he needs to say."

"No." I stand my ground. "I let self-loathing consume us both once. I refuse to do it again."

Zane doesn't speak, and I glance back to see him stand up and walk forward, his usually confident stride severely lacking.

"It's okay, B. I promise."

When he's close enough, he grabs my hand and drags me backward, positioning me behind him, as if I'm the one that needs protecting.

"I'm not trying to cause trouble. I was just walking around and ended up here," Zane tells his dad, his voice stripped of emotion.

"So, you thought you'd what? Just sit and reminisce about the past? Get the fuck off my property."

"Ron!" I scold, trying to move around Zane, but he holds me in place.

"No, *Blair*," Ron says my name like it's poison. "This house holds all our dear memories of Sierra. It already contains enough of his darkness; we don't need anymore."

"If it's so dear to you, why are you letting it decay like this?" Zane finally raises his voice, waving his hand at the devastation surrounding us, a little of his fight coming back. "Why aren't you protecting her memory?"

"Don't you dare talk to me about Sierra. You're the reason she's dead. And instead of manning up and taking responsibility, you ran."

"You wanted me to leave!" His sudden outburst startles me, but the gasp out of my mouth comes from his words.

"What?" I grab his hand. "But—"

"No buts, Blair. They both wished it had been me. They hated having to look at me, knowing what I'd done."

"You didn't *do* anything."

Zane glances over his shoulder, the hint of a sad smile gracing his lips. "You know that's not true."

"This is wrong." I turn back to Ron and try to step around Zane, but as if he's a linebacker all of a sudden, he continues to block me. "Ron, you should be helping each other heal. You should—"

"You disgust me," Ron spits, his venom aimed my way. "I thought you loved Sierra. I thought—"

"Don't you dare speak to her like that." Zane steps closer, invading his dad's personal space. "You have a problem with me, fine. But you leave Blair out of it."

Zane doesn't touch his dad, but he's so close, it's intimidating.

"Get out of my face," Ron snaps, his voice unwavering.

"No. Not until you walk away."

"I should have known." Ron shoves Zane backward, but he stands tall, his hand out behind him, still holding me back. "Come on," Ron taunts. "You like to fight. So hit me."

Zane sighs and his body sags. "I'm not hitting you, Dad."

"Why not? You don't give a shit about family. Hit me."

"Ron."

"Are you a pussy all of a sudden? Is it because you killed that kid? Your teammate?"

"Ron. Stop," I scream, pushing between them. "This is—"

"No." Ron shoves me aside, and I momentarily lose my footing, making it appear much worse than it is. And when Zane stiffens, I panic.

"Zane—"

"How dare you fucking touch her." He grabs Ron by the shirt, his fingers curling in the material.

"I'm okay, Zane. I promise."

"Yeah, Zane. She's okay. Unlike your sister."

I don't have time to blink before Zane's slamming his fist into Ron's face. Hard. His lip busts open, the blood smearing across his cheek. Zane rears back to hit him again but I jump up.

"Zane, no!" I scream so loud that it hurts my ears, but it's pointless. Zane connects a second time, and this time, Ron fights back, curling his hands around Zane's throat, his fingers so tight that he struggles for air.

"Ron, Zane. Stop it!" I scream again as they stumble toward the overgrown lawn, but I may as well be mute. Neither of them listens. Or perhaps they're too far gone to hear me. "Please."

"Ron, stop!" My dad's booming voice slices through the air, seconds before his door slams and he runs toward us.

To my surprise, Ron releases Zane, stumbling backward, his back knocking the tree swing behind him.

I watch the swing drift through the air before my eyes dart back to Zane, noticing his fists clench at his sides, his expression murderous. Running forward, I wrap my arms around his waist, tucking my head under his neck. "You don't have to do this. Please. Let me help you."

His stiff body softens, and I feel the moment a little of the tension leaves him before his muscles relax. "Jesus, B. I'm so fucking sorry."

"It's okay. That wasn't your fault. None of it's your fault. It's okay."

Dad and Ron are quiet and when I glance over, they're talking in hushed tones. Dad must say something he doesn't like, because Ron shoves him backward, walking away.

I'm about to ask what happened when sirens blare through the silence, and I lose my breath. Zane stiffens beside me, and I slam my eyes closed, blocking out the red and blue lights, praying I imagined them.

But when I finally look up, my heart shatters into a million pieces, Zane's expression making me buckle.

How could they do this to him?

Chapter Fifty-Five

BLAIR

I pace the function room of the diner across from the police station, my anger growing with each heavy-footed step. *What the hell are they doing?* It's been hours and no one will tell me what's going on. All I know is that he's being questioned and that they have the right to hold him overnight.

My body aches from how tightly I'm wound, and it pisses me off that I can't do anything to help him.

His own fucking father.

As if Zane doesn't have enough to worry about, now he's facing an assault charge.

I'm not sure how much time passes while I drive myself insane, but when Ron walks out of the station, looking smug, it takes everything in my power not to get myself thrown in jail with Zane.

I open the door of the diner as Fiona follows behind him, and when our eyes lock, she at least has the decency to show remorse. But it's too little too late.

Stepping forward, I'm ready to give them a piece of my mind when someone grabs my hand, and I spin to find Dad hovering behind me.

"Leave it," he warns, his voice low so only I can hear him, waiting until they're in their car before he says anything else.

"Your mom's on her way. She finally got in touch with our lawyer friend who suggested a criminal attorney from Orlando."

"Orlando? Do you think he needs an attorney?"

"I don't know. I hope not. But I'm not taking any chances."

"Have you spoken to him?"

"I have. He's calling the station to get more information. I'm waiting to hear back. But I promise, we'll do everything we can to help Zane."

My world stills for a beat before my chest expands and I leap forward, letting Dad engulf me in his arms, allowing myself to break. "I'm sorry you got dragged into this, Dad." I sniff through the tears. "But God, I'm glad you're here."

"There's nowhere else I'd be, Princess. I wish I could do more."

My phone buzzes at the same time Dad's rings, and he excuses himself apologetically, stepping away. I consider ignoring my message, but if it's Cade, he'll just keep bugging me.

> UNKNOWN ADDED YOU TO THE GROUP "GIRLS GONE WILD."

What the hell?

> UNKNOWN: Hey Blair, this is Hayley. Hayley Jackman. I hope you don't mind that I got your number from Jenna. We just wanted to check in on you and Zane

> UNKNOWN: Hi Blair, it's Paige. Dad's been trying to call Zane, but he's not answering

> UNKNOWN: Amelia's on the chat too, as well as Lainey and Summer who you haven't met, but she's Lucy's sister-in-law so I'm sure you'll meet soon

> UNKNOWN: Hi Blair. This is Amelia

> UNKNOWN: Hi. It's nice to meet you. Sort of.

I add in everyone's contact information, assuming the last number is Lainey's since she's the only one not to text, then I take a deep breath and fill them in on what's going on.

> BLAIR: Hi everyone. And nice to meet you, Summer. Thanks for reaching out. It's been a hell of a few days. I'm not sure how much Jenna's told you, but Zane's not in a good place. He was arrested a couple of hours ago and I'm still waiting to hear what the hell is going on

I press send and physically deflate, my body sinking as I blow out a breath. It's possible I should have kept that information to myself, but I get the feeling they all care and want to be Zane's friend, even if he's reluctant.

My phone rings as I'm lifting it to check, and when I see that it's Hayley, I grimace. I must have worried her.

"Hello?"

"Zane was arrested? Because of Landon? Because of us?" Her questions hit me like rapid fire and guilt takes over me.

"No. Shit. He got in a fight with his dad. It's a long story. But I'm sure the stuff with Landon doesn't help his case. Like this arrest doesn't help with that case either. I don't know what's happening and I'm going insane."

"Oh, Blair. I'm so sorry."

"You have nothing to be sorry about." I smile at the sincerity in her voice. I never really made close girlfriends after Sierra, and now I have Jenna and maybe the wives.

"God," Hayley huffs under her breath. "He doesn't deserve this and neither do you."

"We'll be okay, but I appreciate you all thinking of us. I just wish I had better news to share."

"What can we do?" Her voice lifts suddenly as though she's shifted into action mode.

"Short of making this all go away, I don't know."

"Okay. We're on our way."

"What?" A laugh bursts out of me.

"Sorry I made that sound like a spur-of-the-moment decision, but Reed and I were already planning to fly there, and he just handed me a note to say D'Angelo's organizing a jet. I showed Reed your text before I called, and he took off running. Now I know why."

"You don't have to do that."

"We know. But we're doing it. I'm not sure how long it will take, but we'll hopefully be there early tomorrow morning."

A sigh escapes me as my heart fills with gratitude. "Thank you. He may never admit it, but I'm sure Zane will appreciate the support. He needs it."

"Are *you* okay?" Hayley questions, throwing me a curve ball. I hadn't exactly stopped to ask myself that. "I know you're worried about Zane, but we're not just coming for him. You're one of us now."

"A girl gone wild?"

"Whoops." Hayley giggles. "We forgot to change the name. That's left over from a girls' night we had a few weeks back. I assure you it was very tame. The group name was used ironically."

"Shame." I bite back a smile until reality hits, and it falls from my face. Now is not the time for jokes.

"We are going to be great friends. No doubt."

My chest warms and I have a feeling she's right. I already feel comfortable around her. "Thank you, Hayley."

"You're wel— *Okay*." She calls out to someone that isn't me before saying my name again. "I have to go. Daddy D came through with the goods."

"Daddy who?"

"Never mind." She giggles again. "We're on our way, okay? If you need us before we arrive, please call me. I'll have my phone with me at all times."

"Thank you. See you soon."

She hangs up and it finally hits me who she meant—Paige's dad... Daddy D—something tells me the group name wasn't ironic at all.

"Good news?" Dad asks when I turn his way, and my face falls.

"Shit. No. I'm sorry. I shouldn't be smiling while all this is going on."

"Why? I'm pretty sure Zane's in there wishing he could make you happy."

"I'm sure he's not."

"Princess. From what I've heard, the man lives to make you happy."

"What?" I snort, despite knowing that's potentially true. It's just weird talking to my dad about it. "Who told you that?"

"He did. While you were being questioned by the police."

"Bullshit. There was no time for a heartfelt conversation."

"It wasn't a conversation. He said 'I'm sorry for dragging Blair into my mess. *Again*. It may not look like it but I promise I live to make her happier.'" Dad curses under his breath. "Damn. Sorry, I was wrong. He said he lives to make you *happier*. Not just happy."

"Not just happy?"

"Well, I'm taking it to mean happier than anyone could be. Not happier than you are. He's always been an all or nothing kind of guy."

My stomach flutters, because that sounds exactly like something Zane would say but... "How come you never spoke this fondly of him while he was gone?"

"We did. You just didn't want to listen. I promise I had no idea about Ron and Fiona's attitude toward him. Had I known, I would have paid him a visit and told him he had a family to come home to. You're not the only one that's cared for him since he was a kid. He's always had us and Cade. And he still does. Provided he doesn't hurt my little princess."

"I'm not little or a princess. I can take care of myself."

"I know. That statement has always been true. Which is why it killed me so much to see you struggling after Zane left. It's like your determination and strength left with him. But after seeing you fight for him earlier, almost assaulting a police officer in the process, I'm thinking you got it back."

My face scrunches as I blush with embarrassment. "Not my finest moment but that guy was an ass—"

"Officer, hello." Dad speaks louder than necessary to cut off my rant. "Any news?"

I turn to find the only officer who seems to carry the sympathy gene and relax when she smiles.

But it's short-lived.

"This can't be happening. How could his parents do that? His own flesh and blood?" My pacing picks up again, but this time, it's accompanied with blind rage.

"I don't know, sweetie," Dad tries to calm me. "I could never fathom it, but I've also never lost a child."

"*A* child. Not two. They lost *one* and now they're fucking up the life of the other. I'm going over there." I spin on my heels and beeline for the door, but Dad's faster.

"As much as I admire your spirit, that's not going to help. We have a lawyer on the way, and we need to be here when he arrives. Zane's going to need our support for his hearing tomorrow. Trespassing and assault charges are not small misdemeanors. And I have a feeling that Ron has witnesses on his side, because someone had to have called the police."

"Well, Zane has *me*. I was there for it all. Ron provoked him. He pushed me. He was taunting Zane, practically begging him to hit him. Doesn't that count for anything?"

"It does, but you're also his girlfriend."

"No, I'm not. We haven't spoken in *years*, Dad. I just happened to be walking past and—"

"Don't," he scolds me, suppressing his smile. "I didn't raise my daughter to be a liar. Even if it would help immensely."

"I know." I huff out a breath. "Pity you weren't more dishonorable."

"Sorry, kid." He chuckles.

I smile until my mom pushes through the glass doors, her expression panicked, her eyes searching the space...for me. She catches my gaze and opens her arms, waiting for me to run into her hold. And like I've reverted back to the five-year-old me who just fell off her bike, I rush forward, tears in my eyes.

"Oh, Blair. I'm so sorry."

"I can't help him, Mom. There's nothing I can do."

"The best thing to do is to be there for him. All of us. It's our time to step up and be his family. He deserves to be loved."

She squeezes me tightly and pulls back, her expression sympathetic as my tears start to fall, my body shuddering from the heartache mixed with love. She's right. We're his family. It's time he found out that he has one.

CHAPTER FIFTY-SIX

ZANE

I stand as a well-dressed man enters the room, his head buried in paperwork until the door shuts behind him, then he glances up with a smile.

"How are you doing, Zane?" He walks around to my side of the table and pulls out the chair next to me, offering me his hand to shake before sitting down. "I'm Simon Rowland. Tim Stevens hired me to represent you and—"

"Mr. Stevens hired you?" *Blair's dad?* I stare at him confused as I slowly sit down.

"Yes."

"When? They told me they'd discuss representation tomorrow at the hearing."

"He called me a few hours ago. And yes, while lawyers aren't typically present at initial hearings, it can't hurt to be prepared ahead of time. Especially in these circumstances."

"You mean because I killed someone, and I'm currently being investigated?" Technically, I killed more than one but I'm not sure now's a good time to mention that.

Simon stares my way, not even flinching at my admissions. "No, that's not relevant to this case, and I strongly suggest you don't mention it unless it's brought up. I'm referring to you being a high-profile person of interest. It won't be long before you have reporters surrounding you everywhere you go."

"Right. Okay. So, what do I do?"

"First up, let's swing back to my earlier question. How are you doing?"

"Do you really need me to answer that?" I raise an eyebrow, and he laughs.

"No, I can probably guess. I'll get right to it then. You're being charged with trespassing and battery, which in the state of Florida, could earn you up to a year in jail."

"Fuck. That's-—"

"The law. But..." He pauses, and I lean forward, my entire future riding on his *but*. "In your case, both charges are bullshit. I've spoken to your girlfriend, and of course, Tim—Mr. Stevens—who have both advised me they were present at the time of the incident."

My heart jolts at his use of the term girlfriend. Only a few days ago, I wanted that more than anything. But now, look what I've dragged her into. Again.

"Blair claims that Ron only asked you to leave *once* before baiting you to fight him. If this is true, and he did that while still on his property, it will be hard for the prosecutor to make the trespassing charge stick. If he truly wanted you to leave, he wouldn't be asking you to fight him. On top of that, you grew up in that home, so it's easy to argue that you weren't aware it was trespassing at all."

"Okay, do you think that will work?"

"If the judge is a decent human."

"And the battery charge? I hit him first, but he shoved Blair aside and—"

"I know. Both Blair and Tim have filled me in on their version of the events and assured me that their police statements reflect the same. Tim also brought up the fact that your dad was choking you when he arrived, and insisted I make sure the police took it seriously. He seemed quite distressed about it. Can I see your neck? The prosecutor will argue it was self-defense on your dad's part, but it's still worth noting the effects it had on you."

Jesus. I don't even remember that happening. I can't remember much between Blair falling and the sirens blaring. Regardless, I still tug at my collar, moving it lower to give Simon a look at my neck.

"Fuck." His eyes widen. "Did you show that to the officers who questioned you?"

"Show them what?"

Rather than telling me what he's talking about, Simon makes a show of grabbing his phone and taking a photo of my throat, frowning when he turns the image my way. And I react the exact same way he did.

"Fuck." My eyes widen. I have a bright red stain across my neck, the pattern easily identifiable as hand prints. "I—" I pause. Telling him that I was so dead inside I didn't even feel it is probably not the best form of defense. "Can that help my case?"

"It certainly doesn't hurt. Going by the photos of your dad's face, this is far worse. Not that it negates his self-defense story, but with Blair's testimonial, it doesn't look good."

An image of Blair as she takes to the stand has my stomach heaving, and I fight not to beg him to keep her out of it. I hate the thought of her having to relive everything that's happened. And if I know my dad, he's going to mention my sister, so they won't have a choice.

"Do you think it will go to trial?" I ask, my chest tight with trepidation.

Simon sighs before running through the details of the initial hearing and the next steps. And while he says he's hoping for a dismissal of all charges, it does nothing to change my mood, since he doesn't really get the chance to argue the case. Not at this stage. No matter what, the prosecutor is still going to bring up that fact that barely four hours before the "alleged" assault, I was in here being questioned over the death of my teammate, after slamming his head into the fucking pavement. It's not easy to argue my innocence with those facts staring you in the face.

When it's obvious my best shot is a miracle, darkness works its way back into my head. And when Simon excuses himself to take an "urgent" call, I welcome his departure. What's the point of him hanging around? There's not much he can do right now. And he knows it.

"I'm going to do everything I can to help, Zane." He covers the speaker with his hand and smiles sympathetically. "You have to trust me."

I nod, and he moves the phone back to his ear, letting the door slam shut on his way out.

The loud bang is like a metaphor for my life, seconds away from exploding into nothing. I know I'm supposed to be thinking positively and keeping my spirits up. But maybe it would be easier on everyone else if I was gone, once and for all. Maybe then they could move on.

CHAPTER FIFTY-SEVEN

BLAIR

With every passing hour, a little bit more of my fight dies. Realistically, I know we can't do anything for Zane at one in the morning, but I can't help thinking about him stuck in that cell while his parents are at home, most likely having a peaceful night's sleep.

"His own fucking parents."

No matter how many times I say that out loud, it never gets any more believable. I will never understand how anyone could do that to someone they were supposed to love.

The light peeking through the crack in the door of my childhood bedroom dims just after two a.m., telling me my parents have finally gone to bed.

But even after being bathed in darkness, my eyes still won't close.

If they'd just let me see Zane yesterday, I would have felt better right now. The unknown is killing me. Though not as much as it's likely to be killing him.

He doesn't deserve this. Not now, with everything else that's going on. Not ever.

I don't think I've met someone more misunderstood in my life, and it's going to be the end of him. There's only so much more he can handle. If he hasn't already reached his limit.

My phone vibrates across the counter of my light green nightstand, and I rush to grab it, my heart erratic in my chest despite knowing it isn't going to be him.

Hayley's name lights up my screen, and I don't know why, but it momentarily calms me.

HAYLEY: We've landed safely

HAYLEY: Shit, I just remembered the time difference. I hope this didn't wake you

HAYLEY: I'll call you in the morning

BLAIR: I'm awake. I can't see myself sleeping at all tonight. Thank you for coming so quickly. It means a lot to both of us

HAYLEY: Of course. Want to meet us at our hotel? I'm happy to pull an all-nighter

A small smile tugs at my lips. I really hope this is the start of a lifelong friendship, because I already love Hayley. Which is why I'm not going to bring down her happiness.

BLAIR: Thank you for the offer, but I'm shit company at the moment

HAYLEY: I understand. We're here if you change your mind. Otherwise, we'll see you in the morning

BLAIR: Thank you

I'm beyond curious about who she's referring to when she says "we" but I don't ask. I'll find out in the morning. Which would come faster if I could just fall asleep.

After trying a bunch of different strategies from singing to counting sheep and then imagining my body getting heavier, I'm up before the sun, dressed and ready to go before my parents—a rarity growing up. Dad's internal alarm has been set for dawn since he was a football star, and Mom learned to live on less sleep because Cade and I always woke her up. If she gets a solid seven hours, her body won't let her sleep any longer.

I can usually sleep until my alarm goes off. Except last night. I'm not sure I slept a wink.

The cardinals singing outside grab my attention, and I watch them splash around the pond in the yard, knowing that any second now, my dad will be walking down the stairs, his footsteps heavy as he undoubtedly whistles a tune in return.

It used to piss me off. Cade too. We hated being woken by the birds, with Dad singing along. But now, I'm waiting for it, waiting for the moment I'm no longer alone.

Only this time, he's not so chirpy.

"Morning," he grates from the hallway when he finds me in the dining room. "How'd you sleep?"

"I didn't."

Dad's already sullen face drops. "You and me both, Princess. But today is going to be better. I can feel it."

I try to smile, to share in his optimism, but I'm not feeling it, and he doesn't deserve my lies. "I wish I felt the same."

"How about you go for a walk and clear your head, enjoy some peace."

As wonderful as that sounds... "I can't. Zane needs me here and I'm not abandoning him again."

"When did you abandon him?"

"When Sierra died. I told him to leave."

"He didn't have to listen. He wanted to go just as much."

"You might be right, but I still should have been there for him. I'm going to be there now."

"There's not much you can do. At least not until the hearing."

"I know." I pull at the hem of my top and let out a breath. "I'll feel more at peace knowing I'm close. Can we go back to Lucky's Diner?"

Dad smiles. "We can. Jackie said we can use their private dining room for as long as we need."

"Thank you. A few of Zane's friends and teammates are here, so I'll let them know to meet us there."

"Sounds good. It's nice to know he has a good network supporting him. Cade's arriving soon too."

"Ugh. Cade's been such a bitch about Zane and me. Can you send him back to LA?"

Dad chuckles. "He's just looking out for his little sister. You have to remember; we all saw the pain you went through when he left. It was hard on us all, but Cade didn't really handle it as well as he should have. It would break him to see you go through that again."

"That's not going to happen. I've come to realize that no matter how hard we fight it or, perhaps, how hard *I* fight it, Zane and I are meant to be. He's scared, but he's not going anywhere. I wouldn't let him if he tried."

"I believe that." Dad smiles. "When Zane puts his mind to something, he never gives up. A blessing and a curse. And you...well, you were never meant to be with Nathan. I knew that. But I'd forgotten the energy that follows you when you're truly happy. And that energy brightens when Zane's in your life. It always has."

My breath hitches, but that shouldn't come as a shock to me. He's been my person for a long time. We just had to find our way back to each other. We both needed time apart to be stronger together.

And I'm going to make sure he knows that.

It's after eight before Mom and Dad finally agree to go back to the diner, taking over their private dining room once more. I know we can't see Zane, but being closer makes it easier to breathe.

When the early morning rush slows, Dad sneaks out to grab coffee, and I'm so stuck in my head, it takes me a few minutes to realize Mom's quieter than usual.

"Are you okay?"

"Me?" Her eyes widen as she shakes her head. "I'm fine. It's you and Zane I'm worried about."

"I'm okay. But I'm not sure I can say the same about Zane."

"It's breaking my heart." She clutches her chest, her voice soft. "The hardest truth to swallow is that Ron and Fiona could do this to him. You and Cade could do just about anything, and I'd still love and protect you with all my heart."

"Even if you thought I'd killed him?"

"Even then." Her response is quick, clear, and full of conviction, and I have to agree with her, because I've been thinking the same thing.

"I can't believe I never saw it," she continues, her tone harsh as though she's scolding herself.

"I didn't see it either."

"Yes, but they were our closest friends. At least, I thought they were. You barely saw them after Sierra and Zane were gone."

I swallow a lump in my throat, my chest tight with guilt. "There's something I have to tell you."

Mom's gaze shoots to mine, and the love reflected back at me confirms she's nothing like Zane's parents and never will be.

Sucking my lips into my mouth, I fight back tears of regret. "I feel like such an idiot, Mom."

Mom rushes forward, pulling me into my arms as she whispers reassuringly without even knowing what I'm about to say. "Whatever it is, we'll get through it. Okay?"

I nod before finally telling her what's been going on. "I've actually been in touch with Ron and Fiona since Sierra died. They've been keeping in contact, hoping I'll help them feel better, I guess." My gaze drops to the floor, and I take a deep breath before glancing up and continuing on. "It tore me apart every time we spoke, but I kept quiet about it because no one else knew Sierra like I did, except Zane. They told me he stopped speaking to them after he left. They never told me they blamed him. They *lied*. All this time they made me believe he was an asshole, and it was them."

"Oh, Blair. Why didn't you tell us? We could have helped. That's a lot for you to take on. What did they expect you to do?"

"I think they expected me to heal them. Actually, I *know* that now because they were more desperate during the last few calls, and when I mentioned Zane, they got angry, making me feel like it was my fault. It took me until yesterday to realize they'd been emotionally abusing me. They—"

"They what?" Dad's raised voice booms from behind me, and I spin around so fast I get dizzy.

"Dad, I thought—"

"Repeat what you just said. I want to make sure I understand correctly."

I swallow a lump in my throat, the pain in his eyes too much to handle. But still, I do as he asked. "I think they were emotionally abusing me. But I'm not sure they realized it. They wanted me to talk through what happened over and over, to tell them stories about Sierra, to keep her spirit alive. But they made me feel guilty if I couldn't. As though I was adding to their pain."

Dad's still when I glance up at him, his hands balled into fists by his sides. "How often did they call?"

"In the early days, I met them for lunch often, but when I went away to college, they called weekly. They—"

"Weekly?" Dad's nostrils flare as he steps forward, shaking his head. "I understand their need to heal, but you were a kid. It wasn't your responsibility to heal them."

"I was almost an adult, Dad, and—"

"No, Blair. How the hell were you supposed to move forward, if they kept dragging you back? No *one* person should be someone else's life raft. Especially not someone who's sinking as deeply as they are. Jesus Christ." Dad groans, and if I wasn't already broken from seeing Zane's hopeless expression as the police dragged him away, my dad's anguish would probably shatter me. "You were a mess, Blair. For years. And they..." His voice cracks, and he trails off. "I should have known; I should have done something."

"No." I jump up from my chair, sending it skidding across the vinyl floor before running toward Dad, my heart pounding. "I never told you because I thought I was handling it, and in the beginning, I thought it would help me too. It's only recently that I let myself stop and think about the toll their calls were taking on me. More so when I realized what they'd done to Zane. He's got no one, Dad. And now this."

"He's got *us.*"

"What if that's not enough?" I sniff back fresh tears, and Dad stiffens, lifting my face so he can look in my eyes.

"It's more than enough. I'm going to fix this." His gaze burns with determination as he stands tall, his knuckles white from clenching.

"What?"

"I've got to go."

"Dad?"

He presses a kiss to my head and turns to walk away, stopping when he comes face to face with Reed Coombs. Hayley and Keeley walk in behind him, followed by an older guy I don't know but who I'm guessing is their team owner, Salvatore D'Angelo.

"Hi." Reed smiles and waves before he shakes his head. "Sorry, that was a little too cheery for the situation."

Hayley snorts and I have to admit, my lips pull into a grin.

"We'll welcome any cheer we can get." Mom steps forward. "I'm Florence, this is my husband, Tim, and I think you know Blair." She waves in my direction and Hayley bounces in anticipation.

"We do. At least Keeley and I do. Hi, Blair."

Our new arrivals introduce themselves, and my mom smiles warmly.

"Thanks for coming," Dad finally says, his mind clearly on wherever he was going. "I'll let Blair and Florence fill you in on what we know. I have somewhere to be."

"Wait." I grab Dad's hand, pulling him to a halt. "What's going on?"

"I think I know how I can help Zane."

"How?"

"I'll tell you everything when I get back." He squeezes my hand before releasing it, then beelines for the door. "Excuse me for rushing off."

"I'm coming with you." Reed stops him, his expression serious. "I'm here to help."

"Not a chance, Coombs." Mr. D'Angelo steps forward, his stare offering no room for negotiation. "You're staying out of this. You're here for support and to provide your statement to the police on another matter. You're not getting involved."

"I'll be back soon," Dad says, but only manages a step before D'Angelo taps his shoulder.

"Can I help?" He stands tall, putting his hands in the pockets of his expensive suit, his presence filling the space. He looks like the kind of guy that means business, and I want to say yes on Dad's behalf. But Dad's not so quick to jump.

He eyes Salvatore, his gaze thoughtful, before he offers a subtle nod. "Come on. You can be my witness."

My stomach drops. *Witness?* What the hell is he going to do? I turn to Mom for support but she shakes her head. "Let them go. He needs to help and he knows what he's doing."

"Do you know what he's doing?"

"No. But I trust him. And you should too."

"Okay. But I'm going to need a distraction."

"Oooh." Hayley throws her hand in the air. "I'm good at those."

Reed chuckles and even my mom laughs.

"Thanks, Hayley. What have you got?"

Hayley's suggestion for us to write character statements on Zane's behalf was great in theory, but when it came to writing it, I felt sick. If Zane's still being charged after Dad's and my statements, there's no way they're going to care about how great we think he is.

The time ticks by, way too slowly for my liking, and I'm too anxious to sit still.

It's been well over an hour, and Dad's still missing in action, doing whatever it is he needs a witness for. Cutting it close to when Zane needs us most.

"He's going to miss the hearing, Mom," I complain, picking up my pacing from where I left off yesterday.

"He's not," Keeley answers before Mom can. "Sal's been texting me. They're on their way back."

"From where exactly?"

Keeley smiles sympathetically, her shoulder lifting in a half shrug. "He didn't say."

"God. What's with the secrecy?"

"He didn't want you involved if anything went wrong," Mom answers this time, and when my gaze snaps her way, I find her phone locked tightly in her grasp.

"Has Dad been texting you?"

"Only once."

"So..." I raise my eyebrows, gesturing for her to fill me in.

"So?"

"Where was he?" For fuck's sake, does no one understand how stressful this is? In less than an hour, Zane might be ordered to face charges. "*Please*, Mom."

Noise filters in from the adjoining diner as the door opens to our private dining room and my pulse spikes. *Thank God.* I turn to ensure that it's Dad, but before I see him, Mom's frantic gasp fills the air.

"Tim!" she scolds as I suck in a breath. "What did you do?"

CHAPTER FIFTY-EIGHT

ZANE

I hear the courtroom fill behind me as I stare down at the table, the cuffs biting into my wrists, the spectacle a joke, as if I'd actually try to hurt anyone.

We all rise when the judge enters, and it's only then that I glance back to see who's watching, and my breath catches in my throat.

My eyes widen as they pass over Reed, Hayley, Keeley and D'Angelo. Emotion clogs my throat when I see Tim, Florence, and Cade. My aunt's there too, along with her second husband, neither of whom I've seen since they had a falling-out with my mom.

They're all here. For me. Smiling my way. Trying to reassure me that it's all going to be okay. When I'm not so convinced that it is.

My chest warms in gratitude, but it's Blair's forced grin that has me struggling for air. She's working hard to hide her concern, but she's never been good at faking emotion, at least not with me. She smiles wider when our eyes meet, and I force one of my own, my gaze sympathetic, hoping to convey how sorry I am. For all that I've done.

Simon lightly taps my arm, and my stomach knots as I turn back to the judge seconds before he speaks. "Please be seated."

I shiver as I sit, my body numb, his words signaling what could be the beginning of the end for me, while my concern lingers on Blair and everyone else I'm dragging down with me—her parents, my teammates.

I've brought enough controversy to the team. Yet here they are, supporting me.

Showing up like I should have been doing for them.

Since I'm first up for this session, the judge launches into it, filling me in on the charges, his course of action exactly as Simon said it would be.

I speak when I'm spoken to, nod in acknowledgment, and wait for the worst to come.

The room falls silent except for the incessant buzzing of a broken light above me. The sound irks me as I nervously bounce my leg. Someone sniffs and it's like a chain wraps around my heart, squeezing the organ until it hurts. Was that Blair? Is she crying?

The judge taps his nail on the papers in front of him, and his eyes lift to meet the room.

But instead of asking the prosecutor if she has any reason to deny my bail, like I expect him to, he skips ahead, announcing his decision.

"After considering the evidence presented to me last night *and* the new information I received as I was walking in this morning, the Court finds that there is insufficient probable cause to proceed with this case. This case is dismissed with prejudice."

My jaw drops as my heart seizes. *What the fuck just happened?* He's dismissing the case? I twist in my seat to find Blair, her expression much the same as mine, only she's crying with what I assume to be happy tears falling from her eyes.

The judge says something else, and then Simon's talking, but I can't hear anything over the ringing in my ears.

It's over.

At least, *this* issue is.

There's so much more to come.

The next thirty minutes are a blur as I'm released, and it's only when I'm standing face to face with my family and friends that I finally take in a solid breath.

"I'm sorry you wasted your time," I say almost robotically, forcing another smile, making that number ten for the day. "I bet that wasn't half as interesting as you thought it would be."

Hayley bursts out laughing and Cade chuckles, while everyone else stares at me with concern, except Blair. I'm not sure what she's doing because I can't look at her. If I do, I'm likely to shatter into a million pieces, and I need to hold my shit together. "On a serious note, I truly appreciate you all for coming and..." I trail off, my stomach tensing.

"What the hell happened to you?" My eyes lock on Blair's dad and he winces.

"Would you believe I fell down some stairs?"

"No." His busted-up face was definitely caused by a fist.

"Well, that's my story and I'm sticking to it." He smiles uncharacteristically wide and my gaze snaps to Cade's as he shrugs. *Something happened.* And I'm going to find out one way or another. They better not have gotten themselves in trouble for me.

When it's apparent that Tim isn't giving me anything else, my aunt rushes forward, pulling me into her arms. "I had no idea your parents had abandoned you. I would have reached out. I stupidly assumed she'd turned you against me."

"It's okay, Penny. It wasn't your fault. But please know that—" My breath hitches as my stomach heaves. I can do this. I've done it before. Sierra. Sierra. "*Sierra* and I always missed you," I rush out. "We should have been the ones to get in touch."

"God, no. You were kids. That responsibility was ours. We have to pick Charlie up from school"—my cousin—"but can I call you later? Maybe we can catch up for dinner or lunch before you leave?"

"I'd like that. Thanks."

They head off and then Blair's mom is the next to come forward. "I'm sorry too. But I'm sure you've got a lot to process, so I'm going to hold my grand speech until later. We'll be over at Lucky's Diner when you're ready. I think your friends want to see you." She gestures to Reed and Hayley waiting not so patiently behind her, like I've been gone for years, and they've all formed a line to see me.

"Thank you, Mrs. Stevens. I won't be long."

"Come on, call me Florence. I think we're past the Mrs. Stevens stage."

I nod, but my stomach churns. There's so much going on and I'm not sure I'm ready for any of it. Florence waves Hayley and Reed forward, and Reed smiles as he approaches, while Hayley's not so calm, throwing her arms around my neck, squeezing the life out of me.

"Choking here." I jokingly cough and she pulls back, gasping when she sees my neck.

"Bloody hell. What happened there?"

"A fight with my dad." I shrug. "Isn't that why you're here?"

"Oh, right." She bites back a smile. "That's mostly why we're here."

"Mostly?"

"We're giving our statements in person now that Landon's, you know..." she trails off and I don't hesitate to fill in the blank.

"Dead?"

"Yeah. How are you doing?"

"Ah, you know... I'm peachy."

Hayley rolls her eyes while Reed cups my arm, drawing my attention. "You're not allowed to blame yourself for his death, okay? If it hadn't played out the way it did, I would have done it myself."

"While I don't necessarily believe that, I appreciate you trying to help."

"You don't think I'd protect Hayley?" He stands taller, affronted, and Hayley laughs.

"That's not what I said. You definitely would have protected her; you just would have gone about it in a better way."

"You don't know that."

"Yeah, I do."

"Zane—"

"Thank you both for coming," I cut in. "I haven't exactly been the greatest friend, but I guess I can promise to try harder."

It's obvious Reed wants to say more, to dive deeper, but he's also the type of guy that knows what his friends need. And since I'm one of those friends, whether I want to be or not, he smiles. "We'd be grateful for you trying at all."

Hayley giggles, and I have to admit, I feel a little better knowing they're here for me. But more than that, I trust that they'll be there for Blair, if and when she needs them.

"Have you seen Keeley and D'Angelo?" I change the subject before Reed gets all mushy. "I want to thank them too."

"Ahh. I think D'Angelo had to make a call, and Keeley asked the receptionist if they had a spare office. She needs to make a statement."

"*Fuck.*" I cringe as dread fills me. I knew the media would be all over this, but didn't think it would hit so soon. "Do you know which office?"

"I'm pretty sure it was that one." Reed points toward the door I thought was a janitor's closet since it looks more weathered than the rest, and I nod my thanks.

"Are you two heading back tonight?" I ask them, despite assuming they are. Why would they stay?

"We're all heading back. I'm sure D'Angelo will tell you, but there's a spot for you and Blair. If you want it."

My eyes flit to where Blair's talking to her parents, and my chest burns.

"Last week I would have jumped at that offer—anything to get me away from this place. But now... I think I need a little more time. Even just a night. I have seven years of assholery to make up for."

"And another two years of that when you get back to San Francisco," Hayley adds, her sassy grin making me laugh as she pats me on the back.

"Hayls," Reed playfully scolds her.

"What?" She lifts her hands innocently, suppressing her laughter.

"She's right, Reed. I have to apologize to a few people back home too. Including you."

"Nah, you're in the green when it comes to us. Hayley and I will never be able to repay you for coming back to help that night."

I internally cringe. I don't want this to become a thing. "How about we call it even and never mention it again?"

"Is that what you want?"

"Yep."

"Then consider it done."

"Like it never happened," Hayley adds, and it takes me a beat to process it all.

That was easy and I almost feel like I've been let off the hook despite doing the right thing.

If only the rest of the world could forget it and move on like Reed and Hayley can.

I excuse myself to see Keeley and jump when the door flies open as I'm reaching for the handle.

Keeley gasps when we almost bump into each other, and her cheeks flush a soft shade of pink as she lowers her phone. "Zane? You nearly gave me a heart attack."

"Sorry." I cringe as her gaze darts back over her shoulder before she hastily closes the door. "I just wanted to say thanks."

"Thanks? What for?" I stare at her deadpan and she laughs. "You're such an idiot, Zane. After all this time, you still don't get it. We *all* care. We're a family. And nothing you do is going to change that."

"I bet—"

"*Nothing*," she repeats sternly, her eyes boring into mine, imploring me to understand.

I nod, my chest tight. "Thank you. I promise, I'm starting to see it."

"Good. The next few weeks are going to be trying for you and the team, but we're going to get through it. Together. One day at a time. And by the end, everyone is going to love you. More than they already do. You know people crave a redemption story."

The word "story" triggers a jolt to my heart, and my eyes once again seek out Blair. I have no idea where we go from here, but whatever happens, I need to make sure her story has a happy ending. That one day this will all be a memory and she can finally move on.

"Thanks, Keeley. If you ever need anything, I'd love to return the favor."

"Don't like being in debt, huh?"

"Definitely not."

She laughs as we join the rest of the group, and when the conversation moves to the team, I tune them out, my thoughts with Blair as she crosses the street, my chest tight with trepidation.

I'm desperate to speak to her, but at the same time, I'm terrified.

Emotion gets caught in my dry throat and it stings as I swallow, a burning question playing on my mind.

How much more pain can she endure?

How much more can any of them take?

Chapter Fifty-Nine

BLAIR

When Zane finally arrives at Lucky's, my parents don't even give him a chance to settle, insisting he'd be more comfortable at their home.

If they weren't right, I'd probably argue, but it's impossible to miss his tired eyes and crestfallen demeanor. He needs to get away from this place, and fast.

After refusing Cade's offer of a ride, I join Zane in the back seat of Dad's car, my throat dry as I fight the anxiety threatening to consume me. A strange energy sizzles between us, but despite the fact that he's clearly still struggling with guilt, I reach for his hand, holding my breath until he lets me intertwine our fingers.

He squeezes my palm, and warmth spreads through me, slowly clearing the panic that's been hovering since he said goodbye at the airport.

Only I know there's more to come.

It doesn't take long to get home, and when I finally draw my attention away from Zane, I hear Mom and Dad arguing about pie as they get out of the car. As if that's the most important question right now.

We both follow in silence, but the closer we get to the front door, the harder it is for me to breathe.

I can't let Zane go inside, because the second he does, I've lost my chance to talk to him, and I can't hold back anymore.

"What do you say, Zane? Want some apple—"

"Wait." I grab Zane's hand, cutting off my mom as I easily pull him to a stop. Even now that it's over, he's not the guy he was last week. Last week he would have tried to tug me right back.

"We'll be inside in a minute," I tell my parents, and wave when they both nod in understanding. We haven't had a moment alone since Ron arrived at Zane's childhood home, and it's time to talk.

In contrast to the loud thoughts roaming around in my head, a quiet fills the warm Florida air. But as soon as the front door clicks shut, Zane lets out a sonorous breath—one I'd think was packed with relief if I didn't know him better. He's preparing for what's to come. And I'm glad, because he needs to snap out of this funk.

"What's going on?" I grab his hand again, pulling him down onto the porch step beside me as I take a seat. "You've barely looked at me since the judge dismissed your case."

"I've looked at you. I've even smiled."

I stare at him deadpan and he smiles, albeit a little sadly. "I can't do this to you again, B. You know this isn't over. The public hasn't even caught wind of Landon's death, and while I'm likely to be cleared—"

"Likely?" My pulse spikes as my heart pounds in my chest.

"Yes." He nods. "My lawyer—your *dad's* lawyer—caught up with me just before I got to Lucky's. He said they're waiting for Hayley's and Reed's statements, but apparently, they have security footage that confirms my version of events. Short of Hayley saying I threatened Landon, they might have no option but to rule it as a freak accident."

"That's good."

"It is. If it happens. But it doesn't change the negative attention coming my way. They'll bring up *everything*. The accident. Nathan. *You*. It's better if—"

"Oh, no. You're not playing the martyr again."

"That's hardly what this is. And I didn't do that last time. It was a joint decision."

"You're right. But—"

"Wait. Before you say anything, I have to get this off my chest." He runs his hands down his face and when he's done, he refuses to look at me again. "Back then, I was broken and you begged me to walk away, so I did. This time, I'm begging you to do the same." When he glances up at me, his pleading eyes cut me like a knife, but his white knuckles give him away. He doesn't want this. "Please, Blair. I don't want to hurt you anymore."

"No," I state firmly, leaving no room for argument. "Asking you to leave back then was a mistake. I should never have done that. I knew you'd do anything for me, and I took advantage because I couldn't face you. The guilt was too strong."

"I wished you'd told me your reasons back then," he rasps, his own guilt pouring out through his tone. "I might have fought harder."

"Then fight for us *now*."

"B—"

"I won't let you blame yourself for *my* feelings anymore. I'm choosing to be here. Choosing to support you. And I'm asking you to do the same. I'm asking you to stay with me. Not physically, here, but *with me*. Together. I'm asking you to let me be there for you. And like last time, it's for selfish reasons. Because I won't survive losing you again."

"But what if I lose you?" His eyes bore into mine, his expression panicked.

"What? Why—"

"What if it all gets to be too much? What if you can't handle seeing me again? Or worse, I do something else and you have no choice?"

"That's not going to happen."

"How do you know that?"

"Because you've made me stronger. Because of you, I can handle anything. You're the reason I'm finally moving on."

"That's right. You're moving on. I refuse to drag you back down. You deserve better. You deserve an ending you read about in books. In fact, you should write that book. Write our story and give us the ending we should have had."

My heart jolts at the longing in his eyes. "We can have that ending, Zane. God, why are you being so damn stubborn?"

"Because I fucking love you, Blair. I've loved you since I was a teenager, and I can't handle the thought of hurting you again. I've hurt so many people, but hurting you would kill me. Let me do *one thing right*." His voice softens at the end, and his shoulders sag as he whispers, "What if I can't stop it?"

"Zane." His name rushes from my lips and my heart breaks for him. "That won't happen. I promise it won't." I jump up and settle in front of him, dropping to my knees between his legs.

"You can't know that."

"I can and I do. Because this time we're facing it as a team. Sharing the load. Plus, I love you too. It would be selfish on your part to make me love you from afar. It's always been *you*. Let's not waste any more time pretending we'll ever be truly happy apart."

Zane's gaze meets mine, his eyes bouncing as he considers my words.

"What if—"

"No, what-ifs. Where is the guy who wouldn't leave me alone? That wouldn't take no for an answer? Where's the guy that said, 'I have never and will never want anyone else in this life'? Where has he gone?"

"He's right here." Zane points to his chest.

"Then *prove* it."

I brace for his excuses, but he shocks me by grabbing my face with his hands and pressing his lips to mine. His movements frantic. The connection sends a spark from my mouth through my chest, and I gasp at the intensity of the feelings coursing through me.

Zane pours everything he has into the kiss while I melt, clinging to him for dear life. His lips caress mine, his tongue seeking entry, exploring at first until his hold on me tightens and his kiss turns possessive.

I've always known that I was his, but in this moment, with Zane's palms scorching my skin, his mouth controlling my heart, his words on my mind, I know that he's mine. That he'll always be mine, no matter what life brings us.

"*Zane*," I rush out, my word breathy as it escapes between kisses.

"I love you so much, B," he mumbles against my mouth, the vibrations of his words making me shiver.

I'm not sure how long we kiss, but when he finally pulls back, it feels like my world has caught fire, burning the past I've spent so long trying to outrun.

"This is it, Zane," I whisper, terrified that my words will scare him off. "Can you feel it?" I grab his hand and hold it against my chest.

"I can, and I want everything you have to give, but we still have so much to talk about. So much to work through."

My chest tightens, but I refuse to let him see my fears. He needs me to be strong and unwavering. "Get it all out in the open. After this moment, you're not allowed to second-guess us anymore. We do everything else together. Deal?"

"Deal."

"So..."

"What did your dad do? Why does he have a black eye and busted lip?"

"That's what you want to talk about?"

"One of the things, yes. Because that's the kind of destruction I leave in my wake. That's why I don't make friends, because they do shit like that and end up in trouble."

"Like what you did for Reed and Hayley?"

"What?"

"You did that. Without Reed and Hayley asking, you did 'shit like that' and look where it got you. I bet you'd do it again in a heartbeat, even knowing how it all plays out."

He pauses for a second and I can see the moment he loses his resolve. "I would."

"Exactly. My dad would do the same."

"Do what exactly?"

I huff out a laugh. Seems he's never going to move on unless he can talk about all the things he's guilty for. "He confronted your dad and baited him like your dad did to you. Told him that he was planning to ruin his life for what he did to you and me. That he's going to make sure everyone knows what kind of people they are. Etcetera, etcetera."

"Etcetera?"

"Yep. He wouldn't tell me the rest so I'm sure it involved cursing. Either way, *your* dad lost his mind, and what do you know, he tried to beat the shit out of mine. I want to say like father like son, but I'm sure now's not the time for that."

Zane snorts and it sounds more like a laugh than anything else, so I take it as progress. "Is that what got the charges dropped?"

"No, your dad boasted about it being his word against my dad's, but luckily, your boss was in Dad's car, watching it all. He jumped out and broke up the fight, and your dad withdrew his claim."

"Wait, your dad was with D'Angelo?"

"Yep. I'm pretty sure they're ride or die now." I bounce my eyebrows but he doesn't see the humor.

"B—"

"Sorry, it's not funny. But the point is Dad's plan *worked* and he'd do it again in a heartbeat. Sound familiar?"

"Then what about Nathan?"

"Nathan?" My eyes widen and I huff in frustration. "Why the hell are you bringing him up? Are we going to go through everything from the past?"

"I asked him to call you."

"He did. Can we move on now?"

"Soon, but first, what did he say?"

"He told me about their disgusting games, if that's what you're referring to?"

Zane flinches as though I've slapped him. "I'm sorry I never told you about it. I should have mentioned it back in high school. Or again when I first found out you were dating."

"Is this the last thing on your guilt list?"

"I—"

"The answer is yes, Zane."

"Okay. Yes."

"Good." I instantly relax. If that's all he's worried about then we're going to be fine. "I don't blame you for that. I'm sure you had your reasons."

"I did. But they're not good ones."

My lips pull into a smile and I let out a soft laugh. "You didn't have many good reasons for anything back in high school."

Zane smiles but it still doesn't reach his eyes. "No, most were selfish."

"Did you have proof?"

"No."

"Then not telling me was a strong move." I shrug nonchalantly and Zane frowns.

"No, it wasn't. You're important to—"

"I wouldn't have kept quiet about it, Zane. If you'd have told me, I would have confronted Nathan about it, and it would have become a big thing."

This time when Zane smiles, there's a spark to it. "That would have been fun to watch. Please tell me you tore him to pieces when he finally told you."

"Nope."

"What? You let him off the hook?"

"I let *myself* off the hook. I'm done worrying about Nathan and the selfish way he lives his life. I'm done worrying about *anything* that hurt me in the past. I'm ready to move on. I'll never forget, but I can't live my life in the shadows anymore."

"You were always so strong, and it's nice to see it all coming back."

"You're moving on too," I tell him and he raises an eyebrow, making me laugh. "I'm not kidding. It's time. Landon's death *will* be ruled an accident. I know it. Your dad's charges against you have been dropped. You've got *me*. I'm not going anywhere. You should be smiling from ear to ear."

That earns me a smirk and it lights me up inside. "I see your sass is coming back too."

"In droves."

"God, help us all."

Zane chuckles again when I lightly shove him, but he's still holding on to something, and I'm almost certain I know what it is. And it's going to be hard on both of us.

"I have an idea." I stand up, brushing myself off. "And before you say no, hear me out."

"Oh-kay."

"We're going to visit Sierra's lookout." My voice wavers slightly as Zane sucks in a breath, his body tensing. I take in a breath of my own, continuing on with a little more confidence. "We're going to her favorite spot. The one place we always knew we'd find her. Especially when you pissed her off."

"I never pissed her off."

"You most definitely did. *Regularly*."

"You're thinking of your brother."

"Him too. Sometimes Cade and Sierra acted more like siblings than the two of you did. But no matter who pissed her off, we're going."

"I can't." His shoulders drop as his demeanor darkens again.

"You can. Instead of helping you when Sierra died, I pushed you away, focusing on my own feelings of guilt. That guilt will never leave me. Just—"

"You didn't do anything wrong."

"That guilt will never leave me," I repeat, "regardless of what anyone else says. Just like yours won't. But if I know Sierra, she's rolling her eyes, looking down on us both like we're goddamn idiots for spending our lives in pain, rather than living it to the fullest. When she can't. I'm not going anywhere this time, Zane. Whatever you need, I'm here."

"Technically, I'm the one that left."

"Now is not the time to be a smart-ass."

"You're right." He reaches forward and grabs my hand, intertwining our fingers, and the simple gesture starts filling the cracks in my heart.

"If you're here for whatever I need, does that include giving me time?" He pauses, swallowing subtly before continuing on. "I'm not ready to go to the lookout. Not yet. Being back here is hard enough."

My pressure softens at the vulnerability in his eyes. "Baby steps then. How about the beach?"

Zane blows out a breath as his head falls back, his hand tightening in mine. "Okay. The beach."

"Our beach."

He flinches, his nose flaring. "You love pushing my boundaries, don't you?"

"As long as I know I won't break you."

"What if this does? Break me, I mean."

"It won't."

"How do you know that? I almost let the darkness push you away again."

"That's not possible."

"B, I—"

"No, it's not possible because I won't let you. Unless you look me in the eye and tell me you've moved on, you're stuck with me. Good times and bad."

"Are you proposing?" Zane bites his bottom lip, and despite knowing he's hiding his feelings with humor, I let him off the hook.

"Hell, no. I want *you* to propose to me one day. I want the full experience. I want to be spoiled."

"Like a princess?"

"Like a *queen*."

"*My* queen. Always." He stands up and pulls me into a hug, pressing a kiss to my hair. "Thank you. I can't promise that I'm not going to fuck this all up, but I promise to let you in."

"Good. Because I can't promise that either."

"We're going to be a fun couple, aren't we?"

"I'll be happy no matter what we are, as long as we're together."

"Good." Zane smiles, relief clear in his gaze, while trepidation still lingers. "Come on." He peps up, changing the subject, trying just like I asked. "Let's get moving before I change my mind."

Chapter Sixty

ZANE

It's late by the time Blair and I check into a new hotel. There was no way in hell I was letting her stay in the dump I'd stayed in, despite her claiming it didn't matter as long as we were together.

Yes, that works in theory, but going back to that place is reminding me of the man I was a few hours earlier, and I'm trying hard not to become him again.

Blair sighs as she sinks back into the luxury king-size bed, her wild hair breaking free from its restraint. "Thank God the day is almost over. I'm ready for tomorrow." She throws her hand over her face and groans.

I'd love to pretend today never happened, but... "Not everything about today was bad."

The last few hours were nothing short of perfect, from our quiet time on the beach together, to spending the evening with her parents and Cade, feeling a part of a family for the first time since Sierra died.

The Stevenses have always made me feel welcome, even when I was a teenager, hell-bent on fucking my life up. But tonight was different—tonight I felt their love.

"Oh my God, you're right." Blair sits up, her giddy expression confusing me. "I got to meet Reed Coombs today, and God, does he live up to his golden boy name. He's a true gentleman. A genuine soul. A beacon of happiness. A—"

"Are you done?" I deadpan, pretending I don't agree with some of what she said. The beacon of happiness was taking things too far.

"I can think of more, but I'm happy to stop." She smiles, making me wish I was a beacon for her happiness, because I will never tire of how beautiful she is when her smile reaches her eyes. I'll never stop regretting the time that we lost.

"In all seriousness, it was pretty incredible that he came, along with the others. I mean, come on, Sal hired a private jet for you."

"Sure, it was nice. But you flew from LA to San Francisco to Jacksonville in the space of twenty-four hours. I'd say that's pretty incredible."

"I had to do that. They didn't. They did it because they care about you, even when you refuse to show them the same courtesy."

She had to? I frown, confused. "What do you mean, you 'had to'? And I *care*. I just..."

"I know. You just don't show it. Those guys—the ones in your group chat and the others that have called to check in—they're not just your teammates; they're your friends. They've got your back. They deserve to know how you feel."

Dammit. My chest hollows, reminding me of the emptiness inside me. The emotions I've refused to feel. A panic sets in at the thought of letting others into my heart, but with Blair's reassurance lighting up her face, some of the darkness clears. I've been denying myself close friendships for so long that I wouldn't even know where to start but... "I promise to try." My voice comes out raspy, and the emotion behind it is not lost on Blair. Or me.

"Thank you." She squeezes my hand. "I'm sure that would mean a lot to them."

"You don't have to thank me. But if you must, you can do it by answering my first question. Why did you say you *had* to come for me?" I know she loves me, but her word choice doesn't feel right.

Blair laughs and my face muscles tighten into a scowl. "If looks could kill." She shakes her head. "I had to because if I didn't, I'd never forgive myself. How many times do I have to tell you? I'm in this. You've hooked me in and there's no going back."

My chest swells and my love is so overwhelming that I need to take a step back before it consumes me. It's been building for so long; it feels strange to finally have the girl.

"It's the piercing, isn't it?" I joke, giving myself a moment of respite.

Blair giggles, but her smile turns sympathetic. She knows exactly what I'm doing because she knows me. Still. After all this time.

I expect her to push for more and demand I face my feelings, but instead, she plays along. "I can't remember. I might need to get reacquainted with it. It's been too long."

My cock pulses in agreement. "That can be arranged. We've got this luxurious suite for the night; it would be crazy to just sleep."

"So crazy. And there's a hot tub." She raises an eyebrow, biting her lip.

"I can't help but notice you mentioned a liking toward the hot tub in my apartment too."

"Very observant. What can I say? I've always wanted to have sex in one." She shrugs like it's no big deal before jumping up off the bed and stripping her flowy black dress over her head, her ass taunting me as she walks away, wearing nothing but a thong.

My length springs to attention, pressing against the zipper of the dress pants my lawyer arranged for my court appearance. Pants I'm ninety-nine percent sure belong to Blair's dad.

Shaking that visual from my mind, I snap into action, bouncing around as I attempt to walk and strip at the same time, an urgency to my actions.

The shirt falls from my shoulders just as I step through the bathroom door, and I freeze at the sight of Blair, now completely naked in front of me.

The bathroom's mostly dark, but the light filtering in from the main room bathes her in a soft glow, highlighting the beautiful pinkish hue coating her skin. Her lips part, her raw vulnerability on full display as she stands tall, and I know she's fighting the instinct to cover herself up. *Fucking Nathan.*

She doesn't even realize how beautiful she is.

My heart races, and my chest expands as I breathe her all in, her love filling me completely.

"Fuck, you're perfect," I rasp as I step forward, crowding her until she rests back against the counter, my voice thick with emotion. "But more than that, you're *you*. My B, my love, the only woman that will ever hold my heart."

Blair gasps and her dark eyes shimmer, projecting every feeling she's trying to control.

I suck in a breath and step back, my palms flexing at my sides. I want to take my time, savor every moment with her, but that's hard to do when she's looking at me like she's ready to drop to her knees and give me the world.

A moment passes between us before she bites her lip again, eliciting a groan from the back of my throat, as my cock weeps for her.

Whether she's in tune with my body, or noticed that slight twitch, Blair lowers her gaze to my length and her throat bobs, her eyes full of want. She wets her lips, and I just about come on the spot, growling as I tug her into me.

"You can't look at me like that unless I'm inside you, B."

"And you're not allowed to growl, remember?"

"That one wasn't my fault." Slipping a hand between us, I palm her pussy, slipping a finger between her folds, growling again when I find her soaked. "Fuck, neither was that one." She's so ready for me. "I've barely touched you and I'm pretty sure I could sink three fingers inside you right off the bat."

"Oh, God." Blair melts, forcing me to support her weight as she releases a lust-filled sigh. "I don't want your fingers, Zane. Not now. I need you inside me."

Jesus, fuck. "You don't want foreplay?"

"No. Not today. Please."

I pause, the veins of my cock throbbing as I remember how it felt sinking inside her. "The hot tub?"

"Later," she rushes out, her desperate cry prompting me to lift her into my arms and position her on the counter.

She wriggles to the edge, spreading her legs, her glistening core on display. "I need you now. Please."

My balls tighten at her plea and I launch forward, lining up my tip with her entrance, my length pulsing in my hand.

I'm just as desperate as she is for a release, but the second I'm inside her, our eyes lock and I still as an electric jolt runs through me, my entire body tingling.

Blair's breath hitches and I grab her face in my hands, molding my mouth to hers, kissing the air back into her lungs, needing to feel connected to her in every way possible.

Our tongues swirl as my hands drop, and I gently stroke my thumbs across her throat, feeling her pulse quicken beneath her skin, the heat of it setting me alight.

"Zane?" she mewls between kisses, her breathing frantic, her eyes wide when I open mine.

"This is it, B. This is how it always should have been."

I rock my hips, pushing my cock farther inside her and she cries out.

"Again."

Doing as asked, I pump into her, grabbing her legs under the knees and lifting her higher, opening her up, burying myself so deep that my balls hit her ass.

We cry out in unison, my grunt matching her moan, and her walls tighten, sucking me in.

"I can feel your piercing rubbing against me, but it's different than before."

"Better?"

"Both amazing but— Oh, God."

I pivot my hips and push in again, slower this time, ensuring she feels the barbell move through her pussy, hitting her G-spot. Her body spasms, and she screams out my name, but when I try it again, she stops me.

"God, this is good but I want to feel *you*. I need it." Her eyes bounce between mine, begging me to understand, and I do. My movements slow and she matches my pace, her eyes never leaving mine, her lips parted as her breathing picks up.

My heart slams in my chest as the pleasure builds inside, and it's unlike anything I've ever felt—the mix of euphoria and love, the feeling that this moment is bigger than we are.

"You're perfect, B. You're everything I've ever wanted but never thought I deserved."

"I'm not the only one that deserves the world, Zane. This is it. You and me."

"You and me," I repeat, my body trembling as I fight to last a little while longer, never wanting this moment to end. "I love you, B."

"I love you too."

Her legs clench and her movements quicken, her body jolting as I match her speed. "I'm close. But this is too good. I— Oh, Jesus."

"I know, B." My voice shakes. "I'm with you. Come for me."

"God, Zane." She bites her lip as a scream rips from her throat, her body spasming against me, her walls squeezing me so tight that I explode into her.

I groan as my orgasm consumes me, my vision blurring, my entire body shaking from my release. "Fuck, B. There's no doubt you were made for me."

"Is that so?" She smiles through stilted breaths, and it hits me in the chest.

"Actually, no. You were made to shine. I was made to worship the ground you walk on."

Chapter Sixty-One

ZANE

I wake up to the sweet song of a bird filtering through the open window and Blair's naked body intertwined with mine. Her head rests on my chest, her legs wrapped around me, her beautiful curls tickling my chin.

I run a hand along the curve of her back, as the other strokes through her hair.

Last night was incredible. I've had sex many times before—I've even had sex with Blair. But what we did, what we shared, was beyond anything I've ever experienced.

If I was questioning my feelings—not that I ever had—last night would have been a game changer. As corny as it sounds, I felt it in my soul. Blair is my person.

Nothing could possibly ruin this moment.

My phone buzzes and I laugh incredulously. *Something's going to try.*

With my sappy loved-up smile still locked in place, I grab my phone to silence it and find a message from Keeley.

> KEELEY: Landon's death has hit the news and someone leaked that you were in lockup yesterday. We've got this. I'm not worried and neither should you be. But we're going to need to talk

And so it begins.

My stomach knots as I slip out of bed, my pulse pounding with the blood coursing through me.

I probably should be thankful that we got a night of peace—they could have been surrounding our car as we left the Stevens residence, or hounding us here at the hotel. But I wanted more time.

"What is it?" Blair's sleepy voice startles me and I'm quick to wave her off.

"It's nothing. Go back to sleep."

"*Zane*," she warns, covering herself with the sheet. "We're in this together, remember?"

My head drops as an internal war rages inside me. "How am I supposed to protect you, if you insist on knowing everything?"

Blair smiles as she stands, her steps light as she makes her way over to me, the crinkled white sheet secured tightly around her, reminding me of our night together. "I don't want you to protect me."

"Well, sometimes you don't know what you *need*, Little B." I raise an eyebrow in challenge and she raises one back, making me finally crack a grin. "Fine. I'll tell you. But I'm not agreeing to this no protection bullshit. I've been living most of my life to protect you. I can't stop now."

"Alright." She huffs adorably. "I'll allow some protection. You can step in when it comes to spiders, or wild animals stalking me like prey. I'll even let you come to my rescue if someone tries to hit on me, or I fall off my surfboard and get lost in the waves. But when it comes to words on a page, or gossip about our lives, past or present, I want to be called into play. We're better off facing that together."

I frown. "How did you know?"

"Because I may or may not have set up alerts for your name." She glances back to her phone lying on the bed. I hadn't even noticed it in her hand. "I'm here. And I'm going to need you to promise that you're going to let me help. That's the only way this works."

I swallow back my emotions as my entire future stands before me, her wide eyes staring up at me, her perfect pout making me whole.

"I promise," I say honestly. And while my stomach sinks from the idea of any of this hurting her, it's the easiest promise I'll ever have to make. Because if it comes to working as a team, or losing her completely, it's a no-brainer. "This is forever, B. And forever starts now."

🏈 🏈 🏈

We head back to San Francisco later that day, and for the next week, every time Keeley calls to chat, Blair's there, ready, her media alerts never once failing her.

She's steadfast in her promise to get through it all together, and despite the fact that I know some of the things they're saying are hard for her to read, she's never once wavered.

Even after the last headline.

Sources have confirmed that Zane's sister, Sierra, was driving the truck that killed her and another young woman on Ponte Vedra Boulevard in Jacksonville seven years ago. She was underage at the time, so her name was concealed. The same source claimed that Zane was drunk when he left the party with Sierra, and that the two of them were seen arguing shortly before driving away.

The article is mostly bullshit. We weren't arguing until we got into my truck, but that's not what hurts the most. It's that Sierra's name is being dragged through the mud when I've only just been able to start thinking it again.

"How about we go for a hike? You never know; it might work for you as well as it works for me."

Blair's been trying to cheer me up all day, and even though her attempts help ease some of the tension currently wrapped around my heart, it's too thick to be cleared completely.

"Maybe I can get into hiking during the offseason. I swear Pierce was trying to kill me in practice today, claiming he needed my muscles aching to the point that it was all I could think about."

"Did it work?" Blair giggles.

"Nope. Now I'm just thinking about everything *while* my muscles ache to the point of nausea."

"That sounds like fun. Gotta love Coach for trying. What about sex?"

I choke on thin air. "*Please.*" My voice croaks and I cough to clear it. "Please don't mention Pierce and sex in the same sentence."

"I didn't. It was two different sentences. They just followed each other. So, what do you think?"

"I think my cock has never been this soft in my life."

"That's a no then?"

"Come here." I chuckle, grabbing her around the waist to pull her down onto me. "I appreciate everything you're doing, especially when this is hard on you too, but I'm not sure I'm in the mood for anything today."

"Are you sure about that?" She bites her lip, her gaze turning innocent and doe-y. That's probably not a word, but it sums her look up completely. She's doe-eyed and she knows that makes me feral for her. Actually, who am I kidding? It doesn't take much to make me feral for her. Breathing would usually suffice. But now—

"I really can't change your mind?" Her voice is soft and sultry as she repositions herself until she's straddling my waist, rocking her hips. "I just want to make you happy."

She lets out a breathy moan, and my palms flex as they settle on her hips, my cock twitching beneath her.

Her eyes widen and while I know she felt it, she doesn't tease me. Instead, she grinds her covered pussy harder against my sweats, the material on her yoga pants so thin I can feel how hot she is, how ready.

My phone buzzes across the coffee table behind her, and she stops moving to glance back.

"Ignore it," I groan, my voice strained as all the blood travels south, gearing up for action. The message is likely to be Keeley with more bad news, or the group chat checking in on me. Neither of which are important now that Blair's succeeded in changing my mood.

I squeeze Blair's waist, bringing her attention back where it should be, but when my phone buzzes again, three more times, I lose her.

"Are you sure you're not going to check that?" she asks, clearly distracted.

"Fuck, no." I run a hand through my hair.

"It sounds important."

"You know it's not." Keeley only ever texts once, so it's got to be the group chat and they're officially cockblocking me.

I smile pleadingly, but Blair crosses her arms over her chest and stares pointedly at the phone, refusing to let me break my promise to be a better friend.

"Okay. Jesus," I grumble, lifting her off me so I can grab my phone. I play the part of a grumpy asshole right up until she smiles triumphantly, and I can't help but chuckle.

"One day I'm not going to be this whipped by you. You know that, right?"

"We'll see." Her innocent smile makes me snort while I check my messages. The truth is, I can't see that day ever coming. And I hope she knows that.

Sitting back, I read the texts aloud.

> REED: Hayley decided that since our group chat is basically a relationship starter, we need to consider making Keeley the next target

> EASTON: Absolutely not. This isn't a damn matchmaking service, it's a chat for team workouts

> LUKE: East... After all these years, are you still telling yourself that?

> EASTON LEFT THE GROUP

> LUKE ADDED EASTON TO THE GROUP

Blair laughs while I frown, confused.

> ZANE: Since I'm relatively new here. How is it a matchmaking service?

> REED: Hayley noticed the fact that whoever we name the group chat after seems to find love

> LUKE: 🐯

> EASTON: Dammit. I hate that technically she's right

> DYLAN: And that's why I've never needed the chat. Makes total sense. I'm up for helping Keeley

> EASTON: Again... No. I don't want anything to do with my sister's love life

> ZANE: I don't think she needs our help

I click send and Blair's eyes flash my way, making me realize my mistake before Easton's response does.

> EASTON: What the fuck does that mean?

Fuck. "Maybe I shouldn't have said that."

"It depends. What do you know?" Her eyes are wide but they hold a hint of mischief in the way they sparkle.

"I don't know anything. I just—"

My phone buzzes again, making me pause.

> LUKE: Ooh what do you know?

Blair laughs out loud as her phone buzzes. "Look at Luke and me on the same page. You're going to have to tell them something. And me. I want to know."

> EASTON: Zane?

What did I do? Easton's going to riot. I only just got myself off his shit list.

> REED: He probably just means that Keeley is capable of finding love on her own

> ZANE: Sure. That...

"Oh, because *that* response was believable." Blair shakes her head, not bothering to hide her giddiness over the hole I've dug myself.

I don't really know anything. It's just a feeling I have after finding her blushing at the courthouse the other day. Why the fuck would I say anything? Truth be told, I was trying to do her a solid because she's been helping me so much. I think I'm going to retire from protecting my friends; it never ends well for me.

Blair reads a message of her own and bursts out laughing.

"You're not helping," I groan and she laughs harder.

"Maybe not, but the girls are loving your group chat."

"What girls?" I ask distractedly as I watch Luke's next message come through.

"The wives and girlfriends."

"The what?" I laugh through my words, my brows rising in intrigue. "There's a girls' chat?"

"Yep."

"When did that happen?"

"I assume it's been going for a while, but I was added when you went AWOL."

I wince and Blair's smile softens as she squeezes my hand. "They're a good group of people, Zane. We're both lucky to have them."

"I'm—"

"Stop. If you're about to apologize again, I don't want to hear it."

"Okay. Jesus. You're such a ball-breaker." I smile and she laughs just as her phone buzzes for a second time.

"Oh, shit." She flashes her screen my way. "Keeley left our group chat."

"No way? Like brother, like sister."

"Apparently so."

My phone vibrates in my hand, and I can't help but open the message right away, curiosity getting the better of me.

> LUKE: You're lying, Zane

> LUKE: Oh fuck. I'm dying here. Keeley left the girls' chat

> EASTON: Good on her. Guess that means she doesn't need help. Should we shut this chat down?

> LUKE: No way. I'm now convinced she needs us. Unless Zane really does know something we don't?

> ZANE: Nope

My lips are sealed. I'm not even sure what I saw.

> LUKE: Then it's settled

> LUKE CHANGED THE GROUP NAME TO KEELEY'S SUPPORT GROUP

> EASTON LEFT THE GROUP

> REED ADDED EASTON TO THE GROUP

"Paige just added Keeley back in. Looks like it's on. We're helping her find love." Blair bounces on the couch beside me, and while it's adorable and has her tits jiggling in her fitted white tee, I can't ignore the pit forming in my stomach.

"What if she doesn't want help?" I ask the obvious question.

"No one wants help with their love life. But sometimes they need it."

"And sometimes they don't."

My gut tells me they're wrong about Keeley, but I'm staying out of this.

Blair smiles again, her expression radiant as her fingers rapidly type away at her screen, and a wave of calm rushes over me. "Are you happy, B? With me. In San Francisco?"

She glances up, and the genuine warmth exuding from her smile gives me my answer before she does. "I've never been happier. Being with you feels like I've finally found my place. And for the first time in a long time, I know who I'm meant to be."

"A WAG?" I raise an eyebrow jokingly, and she laughs.

"No. *Me*. I'm meant to be me."

My heart drums in my chest as I stare deeply into her beautiful wide eyes, finding my home staring back at me. Grabbing her phone from her hand, I toss it on the armchair out of her reach and follow it with my own, then pull her into my arms.

Our world might be chaotic, and there will be times when one or both of us wants to fall apart, or hide away until it all blows over—probably me —but Blair's right. As long as we're in this together, we can get through anything.

I'd rather spend an eternity facing my mistakes than lose her again.

I may be careless when it comes to my life, but when it comes to hers, I'm the king of fucking stability.

And she'll forever be my queen.

Epilogue One

ZANE

ONE MONTH LATER

I watch Blair as she takes in the beautiful beachside apartment, her lips parted in awe. When her eyes widen with excitement, I know I've lost her. "Are you sure you don't want to move in with me? You said you loved my apartment."

She sighs longingly. "I do love it, but I want to do this right. And to do that, I think we should start from the beginning."

"Meaning you want me to court you?" I shudder slightly, much like I did the last time I made that ridiculous suggestion.

"I'm beginning to think you *want* to court me." Blair bites back a giggle. "I'm sure my dad would love it if you asked his permission to date me."

"We're already dating. If it was up to me, we'd be more than that. Which is your fault. You and your grand 'we're in this together' speech."

It's been a month since Blair saved me from making the worst decision of my life. If she'd agreed to being better off without me, I would have walked away again, no questions asked. I'm *that* obsessed with making her happy.

But now that she's convinced me not to, I'm *all* in. I don't want to be apart anymore. Taking it slowly is a kind of torture that I'm not the slightest bit interested in.

Having Blair by my side through the aftermath of Landon's death was probably the only thing keeping me sane. No matter where I went or what I did, I was hounded with questions. Like the world was desperate to send me back to the depths of my hell.

But Blair wouldn't let that happen.

When my days were as dark as my nights, she was there, torch in hand, guiding my path. And I've never felt that kind of love, except from my sister.

And maybe Cade.

Speaking of my girlfriend's brother... We may not be the best friends we once were, but Cade's been hanging around like a bad smell, and he's growing on me again. It didn't take long to realize that if any of us are stuck in the past, it's him. He's the same guy he was back then, but if I'm honest, that's not such a bad thing. I hope he never changes. Though I am glad he's accepted my relationship with Blair. I'm not sure he would have done that back then.

Credit for my new life should also go to Keeley, D'Angelo, and Wes. And, of course, the guys from my support chat. Sorry, *Keeley's* support chat now.

They've been steadfast in ensuring I know they have my back, and I'm certain that football would have lost its appeal if they hadn't been around to help me through it all. There's nothing worse as a player than having your own fans turn against you, and for a little while there, that was my life.

But with Reed and Luke constantly singing my praises, and Easton telling the media to fuck off on my behalf, it was hard for their hatred to remain.

That and the fact that I've proven myself on the field, and showed them that I'm here for my team—*our* team—no matter what they throw at me. I'm ready to take it all the way.

Blair cringes and I can't help but smile at how lucky I am to have her by my side. Even though she doesn't want to live with me.

"We *are* in this together. Forever. But I think this'll be good for us— getting to have a proper relationship instead of rushing into things."

"You know I'd do anything for you, B. To extremes. But did your apartment have to be so far away from mine?"

"It's thirty minutes. And it's next to the beach. Somewhere you probably would have chosen if you hadn't said yes to the first apartment you viewed."

My eyes flash to the incredible view before moving to the outdoor hot tub, and I have to admit, she's right. I could see us spending a lot of time here. "Okay, let's do it. Let's get you this apartment."

"What? No. I can't afford this one." Her cheeks turn pink, her lips pulling into a sheepish grin. "I wanted to see it so I could manifest it for the future."

"What?" I frown, staring longingly at the balcony as her words take it away from me.

"I'm sure you noticed the huge difference between *this* place and the others we've seen," Blair says, drawing my gaze back to hers.

"Honestly, I thought you were messing with me when we looked at the others. I was waiting for you to tell me you were joking, that you couldn't bear for us to be apart."

"Nope." She pops the *p* and I can't help but chuckle.

"If you insist on living separately, we're getting this place. I'll be here as often as you'll allow. I should contribute."

"You're not paying for *my* apartment."

"Okay. How about this then... Blair Jasmine Stevens, I would like to hire you to write a book for me."

"You what?"

"I've said this before, and I mean it. I want you to write our story, and I want to pay you to do it."

"Goddammit." She huffs adorably. "You're not going to make this easy, are you?"

"Nope."

"Fine. You can pay for a quarter of my rent. But I still can't afford—"

"Three quarters."

"God, you're impossible. No."

"This is what people call a *negotiation*. You have to meet me somewhere. You can't just say no." A cocky smile lights up my face and Blair rolls her eyes.

"Ugh. A third then."

"Three fifths."

"Are you kidding me?"

"Nope. And I refuse to go any lower than half."

"Fine. Half."

"Thank you." Without another word, I stalk out of the bedroom, chuckling when Blair groans behind me.

"What are you doing?"

The realtor steps into view and my victorious smile widens. "We'll take it."

"*Zane.*" Blair groans again before turning to Suzanne, *her* smile apologetic. "Sorry. We'll just be a moment."

"Take your time." Suzanne waves her off, but I mime signing papers just to reassure her.

"What's going on?" I play dumb as I follow Blair outside, my brows furrowed.

"Why this apartment?" she questions me. "What does it matter?"

"Because of the hot tub."

"Your place has a hot tub."

"Oh, yeah. It does."

"Zane?" she huffs and I finally give in.

"Because it's you. B. Everything about this apartment screams Blair, and you know I want to give you the world."

"I appreciate that but—"

"Uh-uh. Just look at it." Grabbing her shoulders, I spin her around and walk her through the apartment, pointing out the little details that make this place *her* home. "Look at the ivy climbing up the exterior wall, making you feel like you're bathing in nature, while you stare out of the window, taking in the view. Now shh. Listen." I fall silent, giving Blair the chance to hear what I hear, covering her mouth when she begins to laugh. "The proximity to the beach means you can hear the waves crashing from anywhere in the apartment, reminding you of home. Of Sierra. You know she'd agree with me if she was here." Blair glances over her shoulder, her eyes wide as she looks at me, but I continue on. I'm not done yet. "Next you have the mountain view from the master bedroom. I know it's not the huge mountains you're used to in LA, but it gives the same vibe. A sneak peek of your solace. Something for you to dream about whenever I piss you off. And on top of that, you have the warmth, the quiet street, the home office. I wasn't kidding when I said you should write our story. Either way, it's perfect for you."

Blair shakes in my arms but otherwise remains silent, and I wonder if I've said the wrong thing. "B?"

She turns to look at me, her eyes glistening with unshed tears. "That may have been the corniest thing you've ever said, but thank you. For seeing me and for always putting me first, even when I think you're not paying attention."

"I'm always paying attention. *Always*. What do you say?"

With trembling lips, she nods a few times, walking backward toward the door. "We'll take it." She calls for Suzanne and spins around, throwing herself into my arms, pressing her lips to mine. Her kiss is chaste, and when she pulls back her sassy grin has me desperate to get her alone. I love it when the playful, carefree Blair comes out.

"What's that look for?" I ask, lifting her until she wraps her legs around my waist, my body heating at the thought of seeing her happy. In this home.

"I've changed my mind." She rubs her nose against mine and laughs, a new giddiness about her.

"You don't want the apartment?"

"Oh, I do, I *definitely* do. But I want it to be ours. I want you to move in with me."

"Yeah?" My chest tightens as my pulse spikes.

"Yeah. Because as much as this place is me, it's you too. And I can't imagine living here without you."

"Thank fuck." I sigh dramatically and Blair kisses me hard, most likely to shut me up. But I don't care. I've finally got the girl and we're finally starting our happily ever after.

We joke about it sometimes, but I have no doubt that if Sierra was watching over us, right now she'd be rolling her eyes, breathing a sigh of relief. She'd absolutely be thinking...*about fucking time.*

And she'd be right.

Epilogue Two

Two years later

ZANE

A warmth surrounds me as I stare out toward the ocean, Blair curled under my arm, her eyes closed as she takes in the calm.

After finally saying Sierra's name, it took me another six months to come back here. To allow myself to be happy in her favorite spot. To move on.

Now, it's a tradition. Every time we're in Jacksonville, visiting Blair's family, we make sure to come here. To take a moment to remember her. To allow ourselves to feel.

Sometimes, like now, we use the time to talk to Sierra, fill her in on the news—or gossip, in Blair's case—anything we can to keep her alive.

"Oh! Nathan got engaged to his teammate's sister. And get this... They met when she joined the team as the new nurse. The *nurse*! It was a huge deal, surrounded by a whole bunch of drama. But I'm happy for them. I'm glad he never told me that the Suns were looking for a nurse. Life turned out much better because of his ignorance. But I do hope he treats his fiancée better than he treated me."

I let out a laugh, interrupting Blair, and her eyes flash my way. "Sorry, go on."

"No, what are you laughing at?"

The curve of her brows makes me cringe. "We both know he's not treating her better. And I for one am happy he's a fuckup; it would have been much harder to get you back if he wasn't."

Blair's lips thin, but it's impossible to miss the smile threatening to break free. She knows I'm right.

Pressing a kiss to her nose, I gesture for her to continue, and she laughs until her gaze flits back to the water, her expression turning serious. My stomach drops and I focus on the wind as it tangles Blair's hair, knowing what's coming.

"Now for the bad news. Your dad was arrested for a pub brawl last month. Your mom reached out to mine for support, but when Mom mentioned talking to Zane, she ah...said some *unkind* things, and my mom hung up on her. I think she's struggling and—"

"Unkind things?" I balk, but it's not aimed at Blair. My mom's words still burn when I think about them. "She blamed Dad's drinking on me, and told *your* mom she should cut me out of your life."

"Are those things not unkind?" Blair questions, and I huff out a laugh as she continues filling Sierra in. "Anyway, as I was saying...I think she's struggling with your dad's trial coming up. He beat someone up pretty badly. We were waiting for it to come back to Zane in the media, but thankfully they seem to have moved on. It's hard for them to tear him down when he has the label of football's underdog, rising from heartbreak and seclusion to become one of the NFL's greatest."

"Fuck off." I chuckle. "That's not what they call me."

"It's not?" She furrows her brow, her expression marred in fake confusion.

"You know it's not. She knows it's not," I say to Sierra and then laugh again, grabbing Blair's face to kiss her. "If it wasn't for me, Storm wouldn't have won the Super Bowl the year all that went down, and we wouldn't be back on top again this year. Ready to win. We're going to pretend last year never happened."

"Do you know the definition of an underdog, Zane?"

"Stop," I growl and Blair's eyes spark with heat. She loves it when I do that.

"Okay. Stopping. But you're playing dirty."

"Maybe. But now that you're looking at me like that, I refuse to take it back. Hurry up and finish telling Sierra whatever you have to say." I lean forward, grabbing her hip below her tee, whispering the rest. "I want to fuck my wife before we're summoned for more Christmas festivities. I need to hear her scream."

Blair sucks in a breath and when I pull back, her bottom lip's trapped between her teeth. "I'm good."

"No, you're not. You have one more big bit of news." I raise my eyebrows, and she laughs.

"Whoops. You're right."

My phone buzzes as she begins and I mindlessly open my message, smiling when I see it's our group chat, now titled "Anti matchmaking group" based on Easton's request. With everyone being loved up and happy, we've retired the romance side of it, only occasionally using it for team workouts. It's mostly used for Luke to stay in the know, or to schedule get-togethers, like he is now.

> LUKE: New Year's Eve is locked in at the Bennett residence. 4 p.m. onward. See you all there

> REED: Hayls will be late but I'll be there with the drinks at 3:45

> EASTON: Paige says we're in, but we'll see. I might be busy

"Let me guess? The group chat?" Blair grins after telling Sierra our final bit of news.

"It sure is. Luke's confirming New Year's Eve at his place."

"Oh, like Amelia did three weeks ago?"

"Yep." I snicker under my breath. "You know Luke; he likes to feel like he's in control. Did Amelia tell you what we need to bring?"

"She was reluctant, insisting on doing it all herself. But Hayley put an end to that. We're on dessert duty."

"Dessert. That seems easy enough."

"I've already got it ordered." Blair winks and I laugh.

"Of course you do. Honestly, I'm not sure how I managed to organize my life before you walked back into it." I stare at her lovingly and she punches me in the arm, seeing through my sincerity.

"Shut up. I like being organized."

"I know. And I love it. Speaking of, what time do we have to get back to open the presents?"

"We've got an hour."

"Good. I'm not ready to share you yet." With a smirk, I type out a message to Luke, then pull Blair into my arms, pressing a kiss to her forehead. "Are you ready to tell them our news, Mrs. Fitzpatrick?"

She nods, her beautiful smile shining brighter than the sun behind her. "I am, Baby Daddy. But you know my parents are going to flip out. Especially Dad."

"Nah. I'm not worried about your dad. Or your mom. They love me and they know our reasons for not wanting a big wedding. Plus, we're giving them a wedding party when the season's over."

Despite planning a wedding, we decided to elope a few months ahead of schedule—one of Blair's few spur-of-the-moment decisions—after finding out she was pregnant while at my away game in Vegas. Since we both very much believe in fate now, it seemed fitting to have ourselves a quick Vegas wedding, my teammates and friends in tow.

"Just because they understand it doesn't mean they'll like it."

Her confidence wavers and my shoulders drop. "They already know," I admit, not wanting her to stress, grimacing when the shock I was waiting for registers in her eyes. "As you're aware, your mom and dad both call me to check in. Often. Like I'm their third child."

Blair's surprise softens, making way for her tender warmth. "Technically you are. You're their son by marriage."

"That's true. Maybe that's why I did what I did."

"What did you do?" Her gaze narrows as her face contorts into an accusatory scowl. I'd be worried if I couldn't see the hint of intrigue in the depths of her eyes.

"Your mom asked me if she could help with the wedding planning, telling me how proud she was at how far the two of us had come. And I couldn't keep the secret anymore. I couldn't stand the thought of her being angry at me. Of course, she told your dad right away, and there were congratulations and welcomes to the family. And *tears*—the good kind, I think. But I didn't mention the baby." I cringe, my expression pinched as Blair stares at me deadpan.

I'm just about to apologize when she bursts out laughing, an adorable snort making her pause. "Sorry." She covers her mouth with her hand, still giggling. "You are so freaking cute sometimes."

"I'm not cute."

"Yeah, you are. No amount of tattoos or brooding glares will ever convince me otherwise. But that's why I love you. Because you're different around those you care about. More true."

"You make me sound soft."

"Oh, Zane." She curls her arms around my neck, her dark eyes staring into my soul. "There is nothing soft about you."

She winks and I chuckle, my heart jolting along with my cock.

"An hour you say?" I raise an eyebrow, my lips pulled into a smirk. "Come on. I know exactly how to pass that time."

Life is good, and with a kid on the way, it's about to get better.

BLAIR

I'm lost in my work when the door to my home office creaks open and Zane tiptoes in, gently placing a mug of steamy hot liquid in front of me. He squints in the low light. "Are you sure this lamp is good for your eyes?" he asks, pressing a kiss to my head.

I pause my typing, smiling up at him. "It's perfect. But thank you for checking on me. And for the tea."

"It's hot chocolate."

"What?" I swivel in my chair, reaching for his hand as I lean over to smell the drink, moaning as the rich chocolate aroma permeates my senses. "Oh my God. You're like an angel sent from heaven. Thank you." I press my lips to his fingers, then pull his face to mine, giving him a chaste kiss. "I love you."

"I love you too. How's the session going?"

"Four thousand words and counting." My smile widens as a proud warmth takes over me. I've finally found my groove, seamlessly juggling life between being an author and a nurse. Just in time for it to all go up in beautiful flames when our baby comes along.

I can't wait.

"Do you need a break? Maybe some inspiration?" Zane bounces his eyebrows and laughs. When I gave in and finally agreed to write our story, I told him I was planning an emotional romance. Zane being Zane decided to flick through a few of the emotional romances on our shelves, and his exact words were, *"Holy hell, is this what you're writing?"*

I wasn't, but despite telling him that, he's taken it upon himself to try and change my mind, offering suggestions, asking if he can help.

"I could tie you up or..." He snaps his fingers as though an idea came to mind. "You could tie me up. Fuck, that would be hot."

I laugh again, playfully shoving him away. "You know what? You already gave me inspiration. So, thank you. I'm ready to keep going."

"The tying up thing?"

"No." I bite back a smirk. "Bringing me a hot chocolate."

"Oh. So it's a *sweet* story? Only loosely based on our life?" He laughs, shaking his head. "Just kidding. I can be sweet. What about I draw you a bath with candles and soft music? I could blindfold you and help you get in. Wash your body. Set you on fire with my featherlight touch."

My lips part as that visual sinks in. "That sounds kind of perfect."

"Yes! I'll go start the bath."

He moves to leave but I grab his hand again, pulling him back to me. "Actually, can we do that tomorrow night? Tonight, I'm writing about it. I can vividly picture the scene playing out."

Zane's face drops and it takes all of my power to school my expression. Especially when he glances down at the semi bulge in his sweats, stifling a groan.

Forcing a smile, he lifts his gaze and stands. "Anything for you, B. Tomorrow it is."

With a quick thank you and a nod, I shift my attention back to my computer and smile as he walks away. But he's only halfway out the door when I give in, barking out a laugh. "Run the bath, jackass. I've got the epilogue to finish, but it'll be impossible to concentrate after *that* visual. You better worship me, Fitzpatrick. I deserve it."

"Always, Little B. Always." His panty-melting smile lights me up and my heart pounds in my chest. I will never take for granted how lucky we are to have found our way back to each other, but I will take advantage. Every chance I get, I remind myself, letting myself bask in his love.

Zane often says I deserve the world, and that may be so, but I'm more than happy to share it with him.

Epilogue (Blair's novel)
   Claire
   The plunging water mimics the sound of rain as it echoes through the apartment, and a calming shiver runs through me. Curling my hands around my forest-green mug, I breathe in the delicious smell before taking a sip of my hot chocolate, the warm liquid adding to my peace.
   The last two years may have been full of ups and down, but Zack's love and promise to protect us has never once wavered. And neither has mine.
   We're a team. In it for the long haul.
   And nothing is ever going to change that.

Thank you for reading Zane and Blair's story. Are you ready for the final book in the series... Fierce Storm - Keeley and Sal's story is now live. Keep reading for a sneak peek.

If you want more of Blair, Hayley and Jenna... you can read Jenna's story in Mistletoe Mail, set after the events of this book.

ALSO BY KATHERINE JAY

COMING SOON

Beckett's book (details TBA)

Callum's book (details TBA)

SAN FRANCISCO END GAME SERIES

Beautiful Storm (Luke and Amelia)

Delicate Storm (Easton and Paige)

Reckless Storm (Reed and Hayley)

Careless Storm (Zane and Blair)

Fierce Storm (Salvatore and Keeley)

HOLIDAY ROMANCE

Mistletoe Mail (Mason and Jenna)

SYMPHONY OF SOUND DUET

The Sound Of Silence (Jesse and Willow)

The Sound Of Forever (Jesse and Willow)

HEARTSTRINGS SERIES

When Nothing Else Matters (Summer and Dylan)

Still Here Without You (Joel and Delilah)

It Had To Be Us (Logan and Dani)

Truly Madly Deeply Mine (Wes and Lucy)

A Sky Full Of Stars (Thomas and Lainey)

Ain't No Sunshine (Nate and Cory) – novella

ALL KATHERINE'S BOOKS ARE AVAILABLE ON AMAZON AND
KINDLE UNLIMITED

SNEAK PEEK OF FIERCE STORM

SALVATORE

D'Angelo. D'Angelo. Where is fucking D'Angelo?

I can't remember another time when I heard my surname said so much. Even as a CEO. Dad, yes. Salvatore, yes. Even Sal. But Mr. D'Angelo and *sir*? I'm not my fucking father. Sure, I have a dusting of salt in my previously pepper hair, but that doesn't warrant the grandeur. Most of the salt came from the stress surrounding my divorce. I'm only fifty and I've been graying for years.

Why does it feel like my new role as team owner for the San Francisco Storm is going to speed up the process?

My mind runs rampant with the million things I have to get done, and I internally groan.

Book a meeting with the coaching staff.

Organize dinner with the board.

Meet the players.

Check in on Paige.

Paige.

Fuck. I can't let work take over again. I only just got her back. She left her mother and moved here to be with me. It's a big deal.

It's all a big deal. *Everything.* Not one thing on my goddamn mind is small and God, my head hurts.

I hold my breath as I stride through the halls of Lightning Stadium, breathing a sigh of relief when I make it to my office without anyone stopping me. The door clicks shut behind me, and I jolt. Even that's too loud for the hammering pain pulsing through my head.

What am I doing?

"Fuck. Fuuck!" I toss my phone across the room, but it lands softly on the couch, giving me no satisfaction. I wanted to see it shatter. Better the phone than my confident composure, because God knows, that's wavering.

After kicking off my shoes, I lie back on the couch like it's a psychiatrist's office and cover my face with my hands.

Five minutes. That's all I need. Five minutes, and I'll be Mr. D'Angelo again. San Francisco Storm's team owner. Business titan. New York billionaire. I just need a moment to be Sal. Father. Son. The man that built his empire from the ground up while still remembering where he came from.

I only manage a few deep breaths before knuckles softly rap against my door. *And there goes that.* With a huff under my breath, I stretch my toes and reluctantly sit up, pulling on my shoes before standing. *I've been found.*

"Yes?" I call out, keeping my tone as even as possible.

"Sorry to interrupt," Tabitha, my new assistant, speaks quietly through the closed door, and it's nearly impossible to hear her. "Keeley's needed for a media call."

Did she say Keeley? "What?"

"Keeley's—"

"You can come in, Tabitha. I'm not naked in here."

The door opens and my assistant pops her head in, her messy brown hair escaping from her ponytail, as though she's been frantically rushing around, her flushed cheeks suggesting the same. She smiles shyly and fuck my life. This isn't going to work if she feels the need to tiptoe around me all the time. "Thank you. What were you saying?"

"Oh. Ah..." She frowns, her eyes darting around the room. "I thought Keeley was in here."

"Who's Keeley?" I tilt my head to the side, lips pursed as I follow her gaze. Other than me, my office is empty.

I was advised to bring my own assistant, but no, I left her in New York to keep an eye on my new general manager, while I gallivanted to the other side of America to follow a childhood dream. *Just because one has enough money to buy a football franchise doesn't mean they should.*

Tabitha rubs her forehead in confusion, which in turn confuses me. "Keeley's our media liaison. You haven't met her?"

"Tabitha, I've met a hell of a lot of people today, but I'm ninety-nine percent sure I would remember that name."

"Okay. Well, she's great. You'll love her. Now I have to try and track her down because I said she was here. Do you need anything before I do that?"

"Why would you— Never mind. No. I'm good. Thank you."

"Good."

Tabitha turns to leave, and my pounding head makes me stop her. "Actually, can I have fifteen minutes to myself? Uninterrupted."

"Yes, of course. I'm sorry." Tabitha's pink cheeks darken, and I internally curse myself.

"You don't have to be sorry, Tabitha. You're doing your job."

"Thank you, sir."

"Please don't call me sir."

"Okay, sir."

For fuck's sake. I force a smile and wave her away before I fall back onto the couch, my fingers immediately moving to rub my throbbing temples. This is a goddamn shit show. Financial issues, management power struggles, a fucking TV show. It's a mess. And I'm the idiot who volunteered to pick up the pieces. Actually, I didn't volunteer; I paid a shit ton of money to do it. All because of a fucking dream.

"Fuuck." This day needs to end and it's only eleven thirty.

"Can I help?"

"Jesus Christ." I stiffen at the honeyed voice coming from above my head, dropping my hands to reveal a beautiful woman with thick auburn hair cascading down her shoulders. She stares down at me, her expression confident as she pops her hip. *Where the hell did she come from?*

I push up from the couch, preparing to greet her, thankful that I'd left my shoes on this time. As I stand, my gaze sweeps along her fitted navy suit, following the line of her dress pants until it stops at her pointed-toe stiletto heel. The kind that tells me she means business.

Though, the fact that she's standing in my office *unannounced* should have given that away.

When I'm at full height, she straightens, standing taller, but still has to lift her gaze to meet mine, and her striking blue eyes catch my attention.

"Can I help *you*?" I counter, my lips curling into a forced grin. "I'm Salvatore, and you are..."

"Keeley. *Sir.*"

"Keeley?" She winks and my brows raise so fast, I guarantee it looks comical. "Right. So you *were* in my office?" As the question leaves my mouth, it occurs to me that she could have just walked in, until I remember the way she said "sir." *She was here.* But where?

"I was," she confirms, and while her confidence never wavers, the hint of guilt flashes in her eyes.

"I just told my assistant you weren't."

"I heard." She cringes adorably before a smile lights up her face, telling me she doesn't actually care about my mistake. "You also asked for fifteen minutes of uninterrupted alone time." Her smile widens as she stares at me pointedly, and when I understand her meaning, I actually laugh. My first since I got here. *What a fucking day.*

Fierce Storm is available on Amazon and Kindle Unlimited.

RECKLESS STORM
A fake dating sports romance

Reed Coombs has it all — Super Bowl rings, adoring fans, and a golden boy reputation. But beneath the glamour lies a decade-long unrequited crush he's desperate to move on from. Enter Hayley Jackman: a fierce Hollywood starlet who needs her wild reputation tamed for a coveted role. Their solution? A fake relationship that gives them both exactly what they need.

Or so they think.

What starts as a playful ruse quickly becomes something neither of them bargained for, and suddenly their feelings are anything but fake.

Seems simple enough.

But what happens if falling in love turns out to be the least of their worries?

FIERCE STORM
A forbidden, age gap sports romance

He's her boss, her brother's future father-in-law and her best friends dad. She's twenty years younger than him and the one woman he can't get out of his head.

What happens when they give in to temptation?

Find out when the final Storm book releases in June 2026

ABOUT THE AUTHOR

Katherine writes angsty and emotional, character-driven romance full of banter, steam and the kind of love that's always worth fighting for.

When she's not lost in a fictional world (writing or reading), she's travelling, falling down a binge-worthy television rabbit hole, or letting the perfect song absolutely wreck her.

Katherine lives in Australia with her husband and two boys, which means she's constantly outnumbered, but wouldn't have it any other way.

For more information, visit
https://www.katherinejayauthor.com

If you want to stay up to date with all things Katherine Jay, come and join her Facebook Reader Group – The Angsty Lovers Playlist — for fun, exclusive content and sneak peeks. Or sign up to her newsletter via her website.

Are you following Katherine on social media? If not, you can find her on Instagram, Facebook and TikTok.